MERMIN™

BOOK ONE: OUT OF WATER

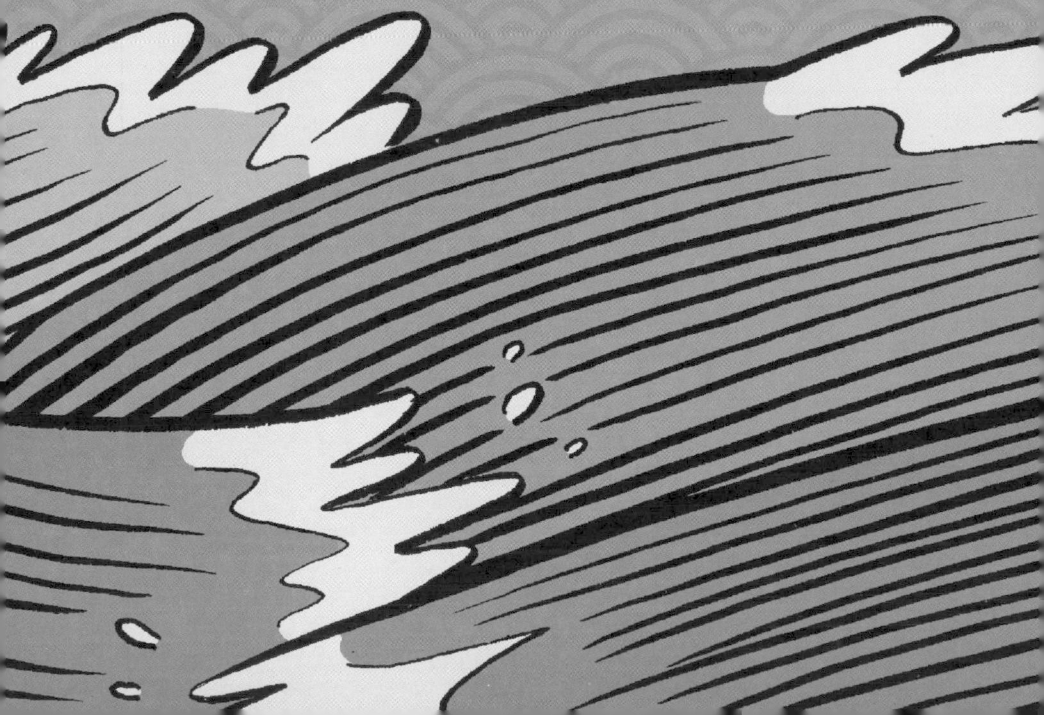

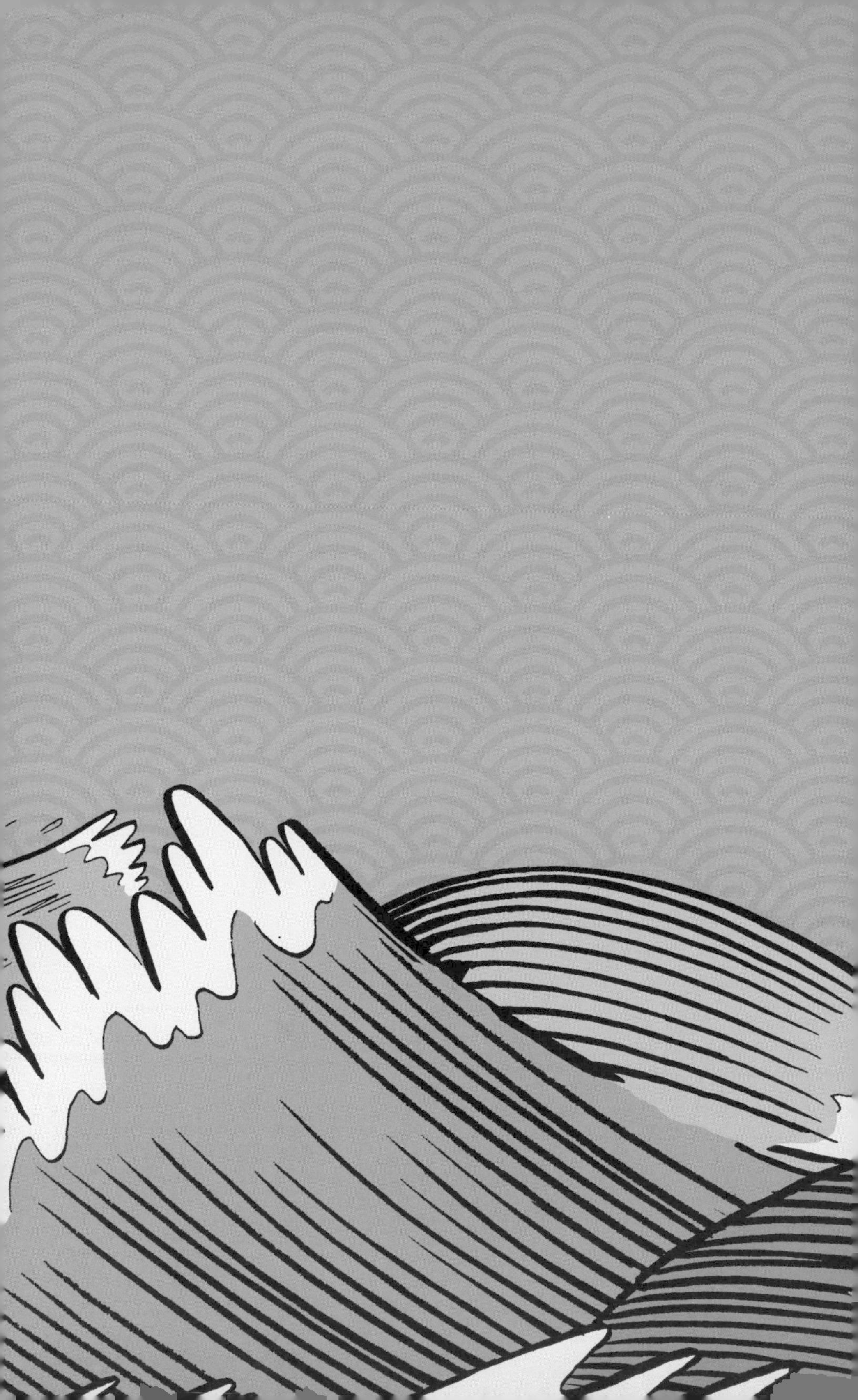

MERMIN™

BOOK ONE: OUT OF WATER

Written and illustrated by
Joey Weiser

Edited by
Jill Beaton

Designed by
Keith Wood

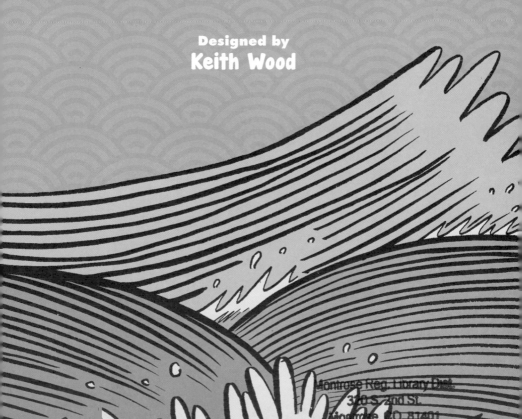

Oni Press, Inc.

publisher, **Joe Nozemack**
editor in chief, **James Lucas Jones**
director of sales, **Cheyenne Allott**
marketing coordinator, **Amber O'Neill**
publicity coordinator, **Rachel Reed**
director of design & production, **Troy Look**
graphic designer, **Hilary Thompson**
digital art technician, **Jared Jones**
managing editor, **Ari Yarwood**
senior editor, **Charlie Chu**
editor, **Robin Herrera**
editorial assistant, **Bess Pallares**
director of logistics, **Brad Rooks**
office assitant, **Jung Lee**

onipress.com
facebook.com/onipress
twitter.com/onipress
onipress.tumblr.com
instagram.com/onipress
tragic-planet.com

First Edition: May 2016
ISBN: 978-1-62010-309-8

Mermin: Out of Water, May 2016. Published by Oni Press, Inc. 1305 SE Martin Luther King Jr. Blvd., Suite A, Portland, OR 97214.

Printed in China.

Library of Congress Control Number: 2012953664

1 2 3 4 5 6 7 8 9 10

CHAPTER ONE

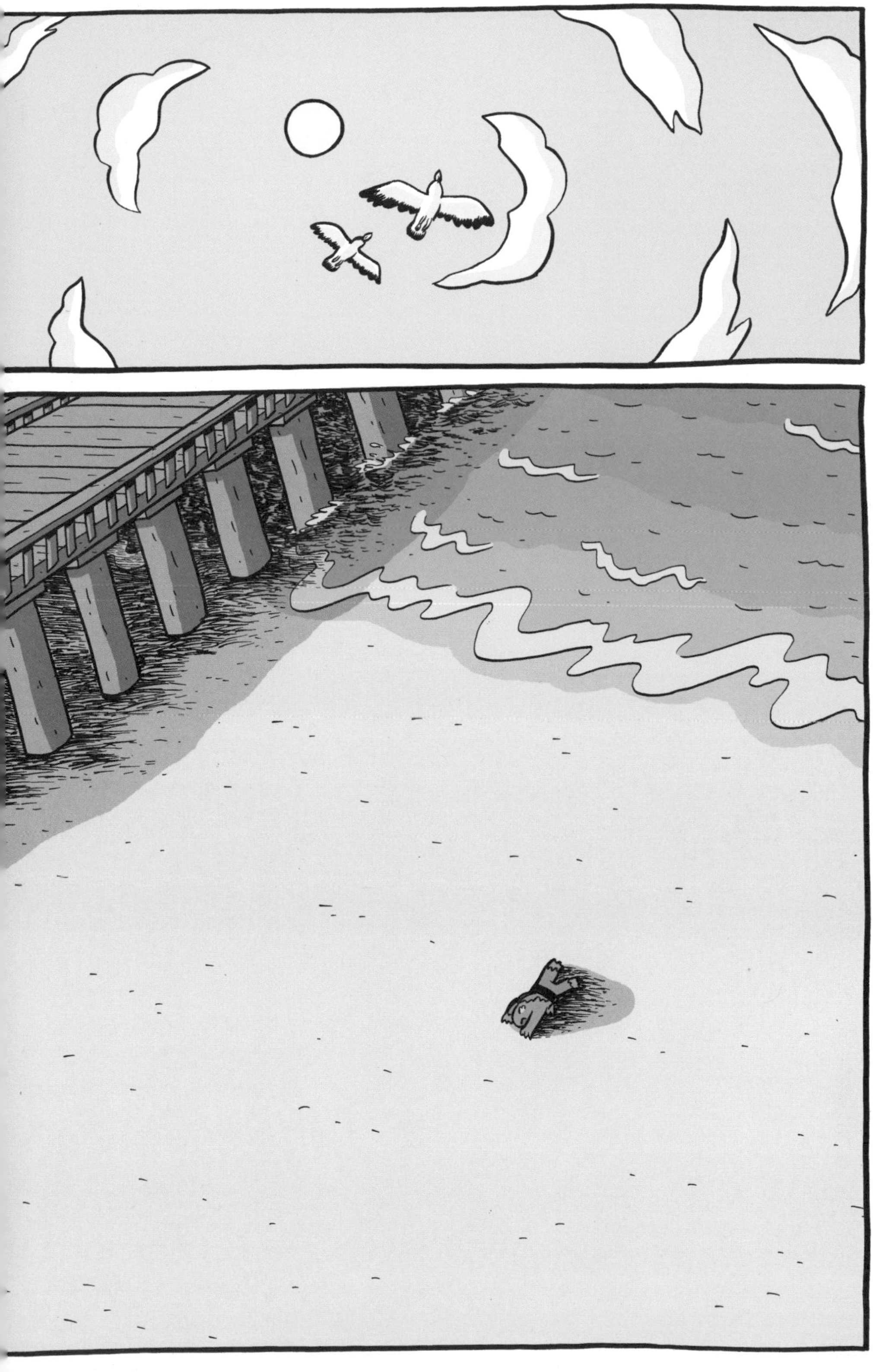

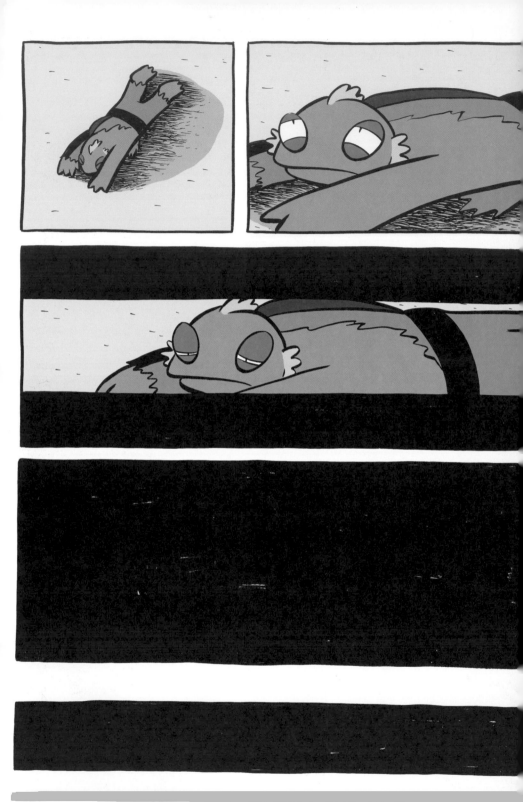

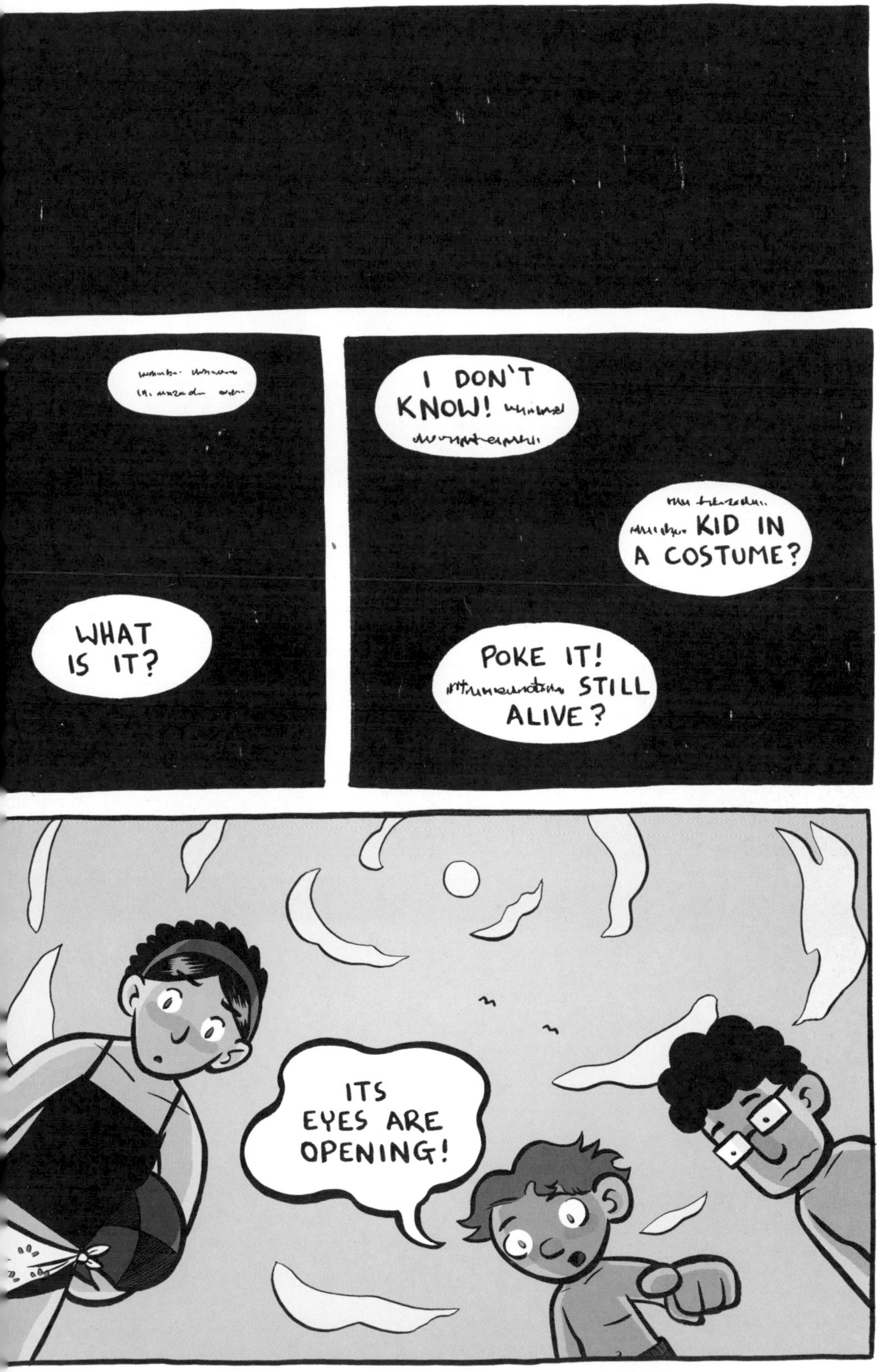
WHAT IS IT?
I DON'T KNOW!
KID IN A COSTUME?
POKE IT! STILL ALIVE?
ITS EYES ARE OPENING!

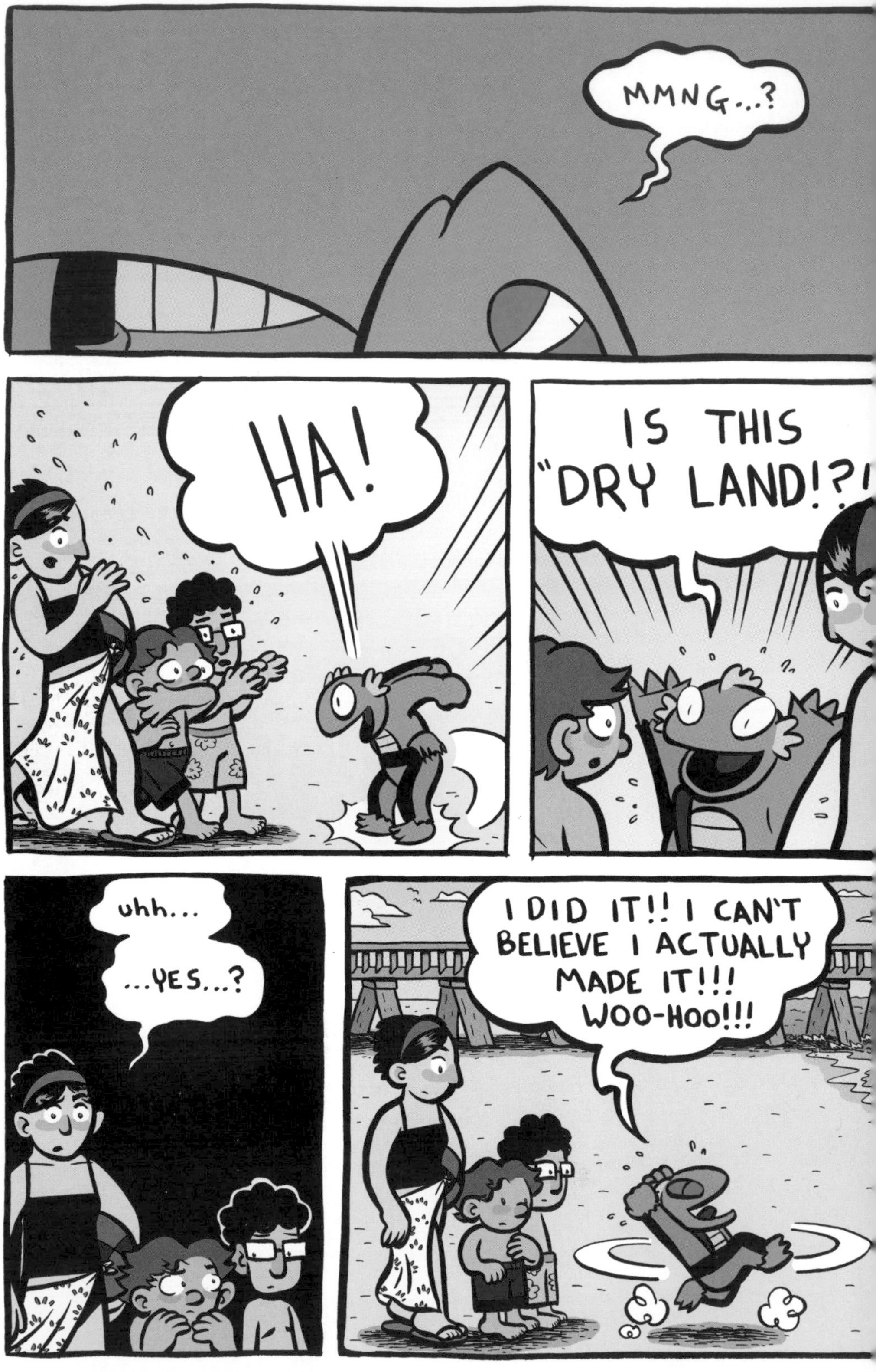
MMNG...?
HA!
IS THIS "DRY LAND!?!
uhh...
...YES...?
I DID IT!! I CAN'T BELIEVE I ACTUALLY MADE IT!!! WOO-HOO!!!

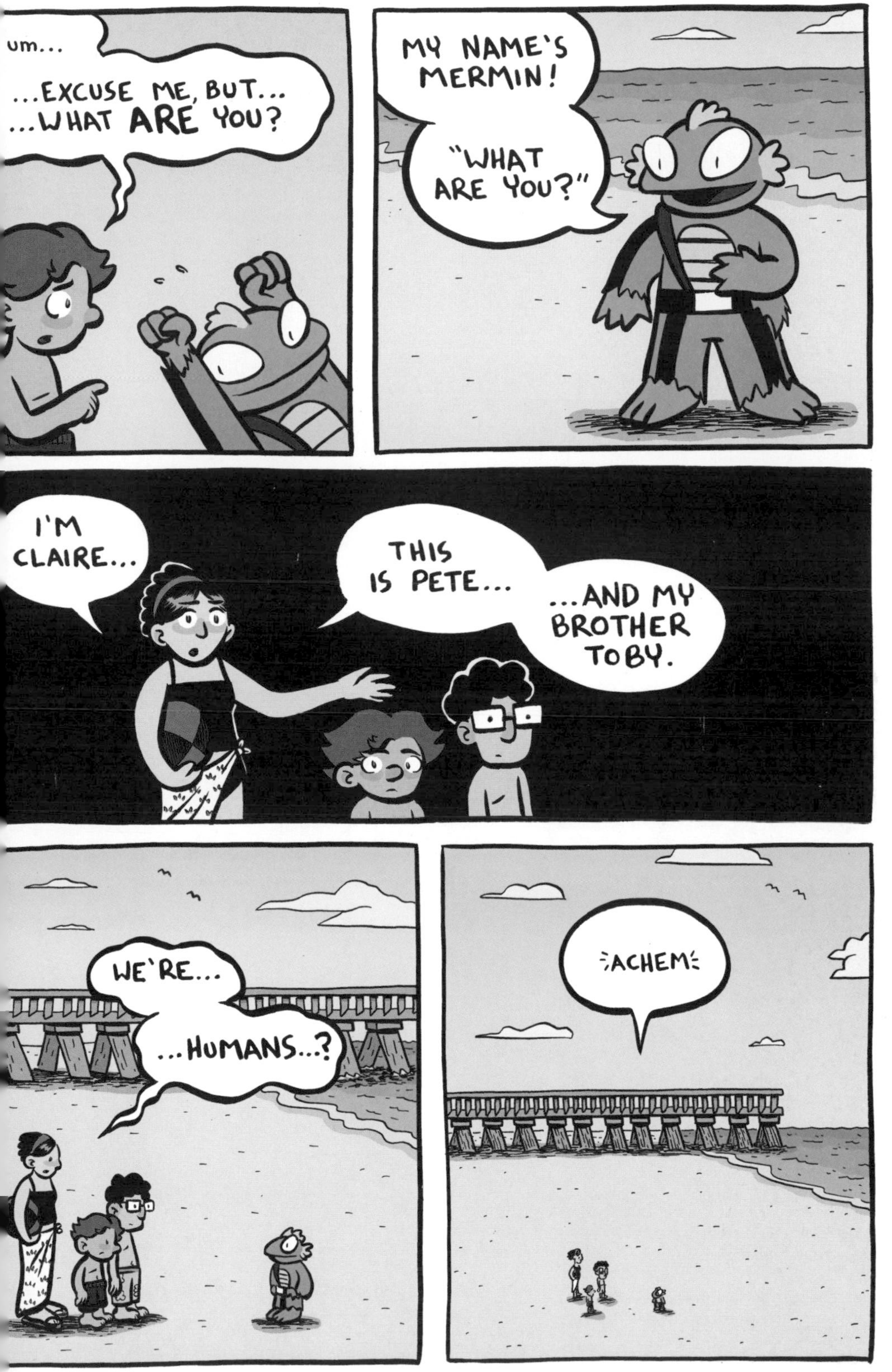
um...
...EXCUSE ME, BUT...
...WHAT ARE YOU?
MY NAME'S MERMIN!
"WHAT ARE YOU?"
I'M CLAIRE...
THIS IS PETE...
...AND MY BROTHER TOBY.
WE'RE...
...HUMANS...?
ACHEM

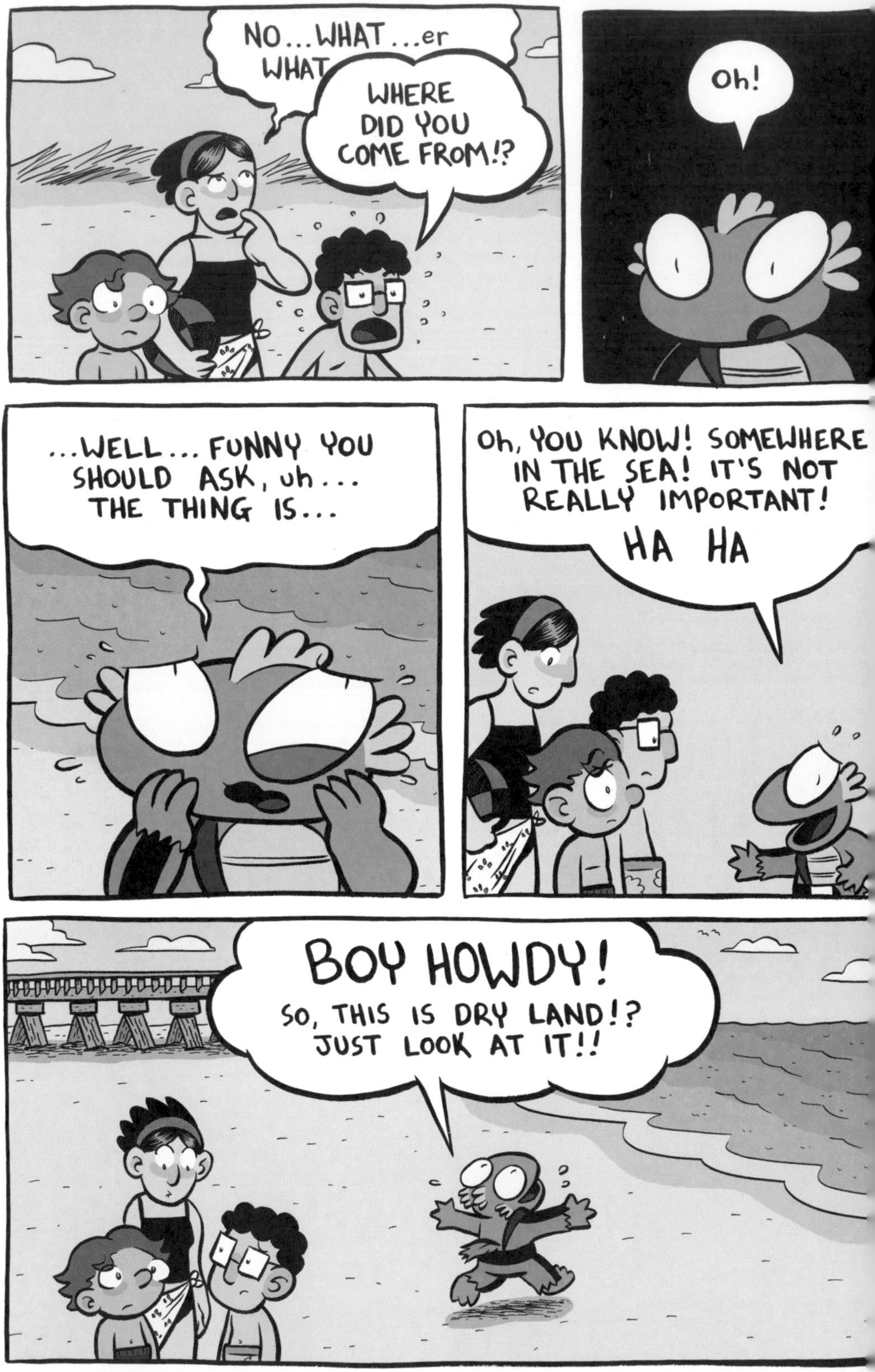
NO...WHAT...er WHAT
WHERE DID YOU COME FROM!?
Oh!
...WELL... FUNNY YOU SHOULD ASK, uh... THE THING IS...
Oh, YOU KNOW! SOMEWHERE IN THE SEA! IT'S NOT REALLY IMPORTANT!
HA HA
BOY HOWDY!
SO, THIS IS DRY LAND!? JUST LOOK AT IT!!

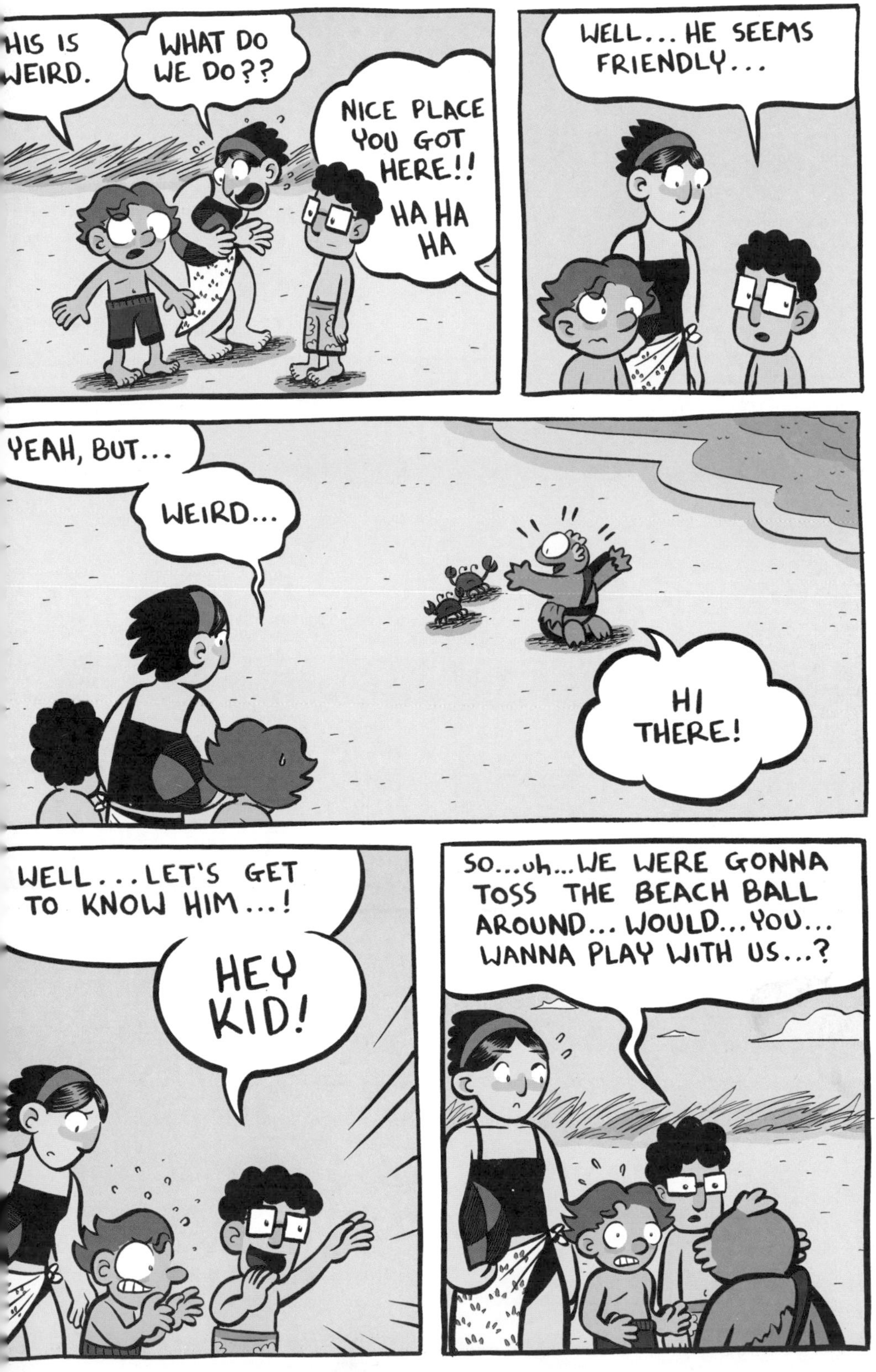
HIS IS WEIRD.
WHAT DO WE DO??
NICE PLACE YOU GOT HERE!!
HA HA HA
WELL... HE SEEMS FRIENDLY...
YEAH, BUT...
WEIRD...
HI THERE!
WELL...LET'S GET TO KNOW HIM...!
HEY KID!
SO...uh...WE WERE GONNA TOSS THE BEACH BALL AROUND... WOULD...YOU... WANNA PLAY WITH US...?

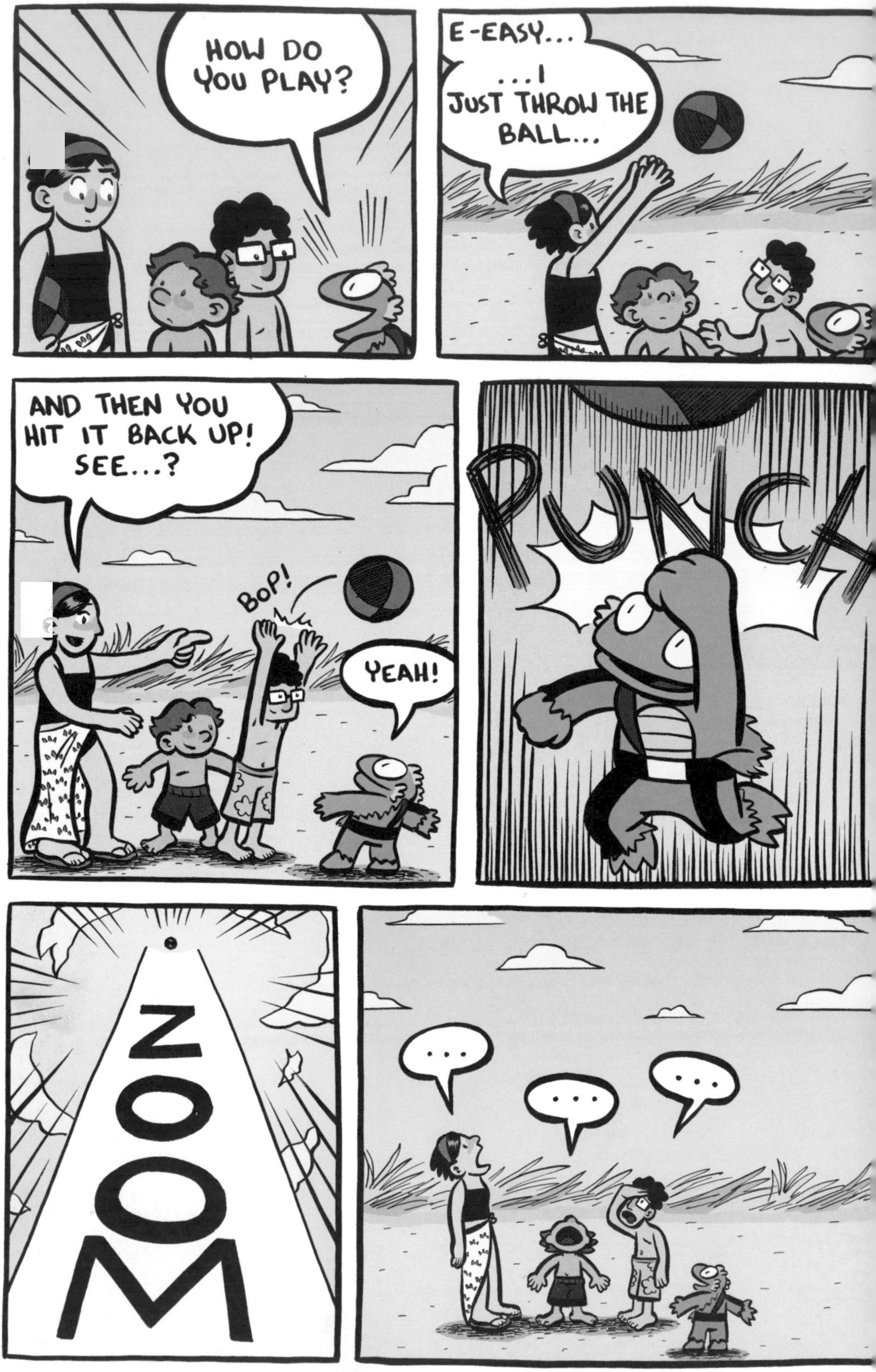
HOW DO YOU PLAY?
E-EASY...
...I JUST THROW THE BALL...
AND THEN YOU HIT IT BACK UP! SEE...?
BOP!
YEAH!
PUNCH
ZOOM
...
...
...

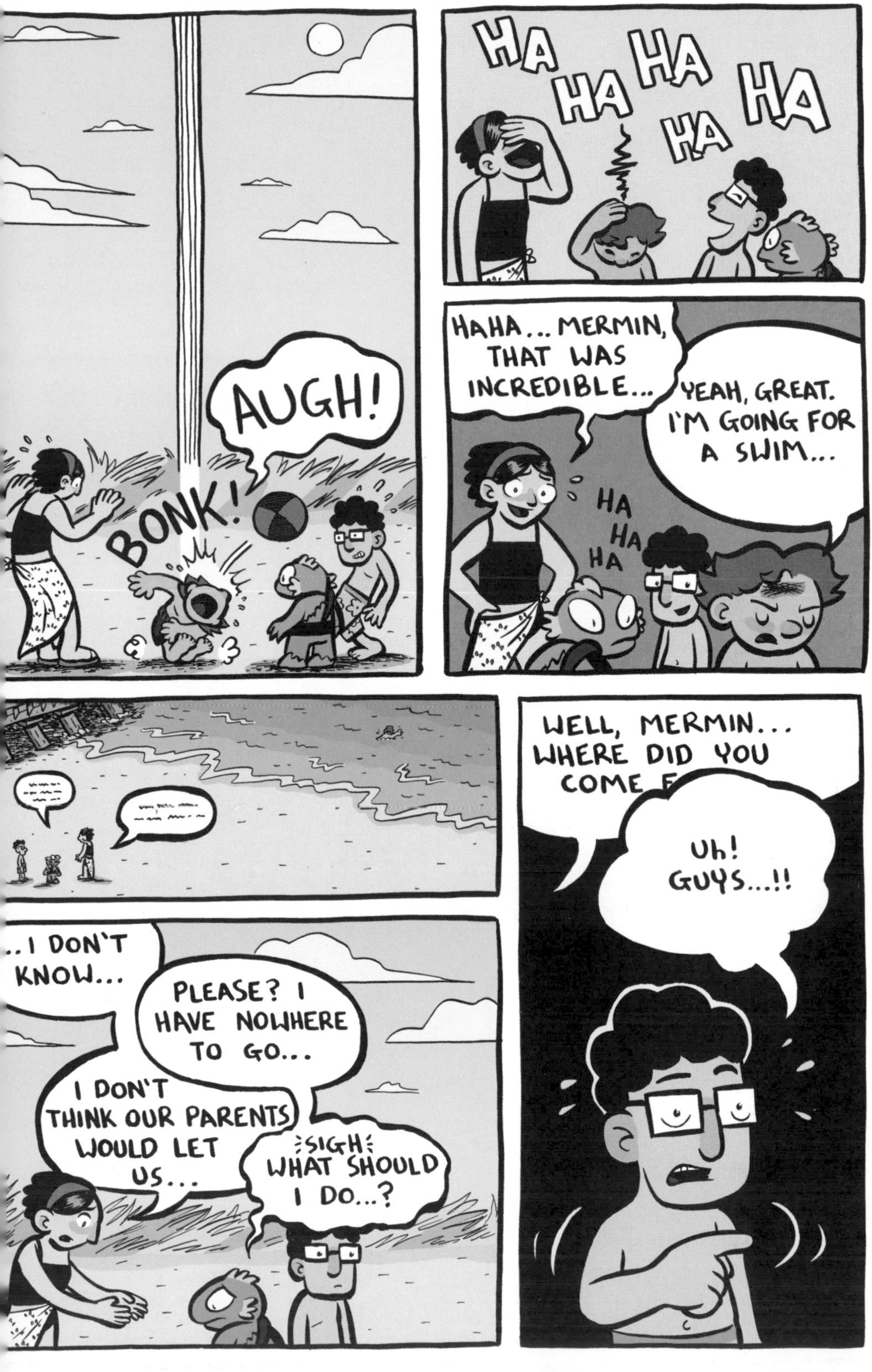
AUGH!
BONK!
HA HA HA HA HA HA
HAHA... MERMIN, THAT WAS INCREDIBLE...
YEAH, GREAT. I'M GOING FOR A SWIM...
HA HA HA
WELL, MERMIN... WHERE DID YOU COME F
Uh! GUYS...!!
..I DON'T KNOW...
PLEASE? I HAVE NOWHERE TO GO...
I DON'T THINK OUR PARENTS WOULD LET US...
SIGH WHAT SHOULD I DO...?

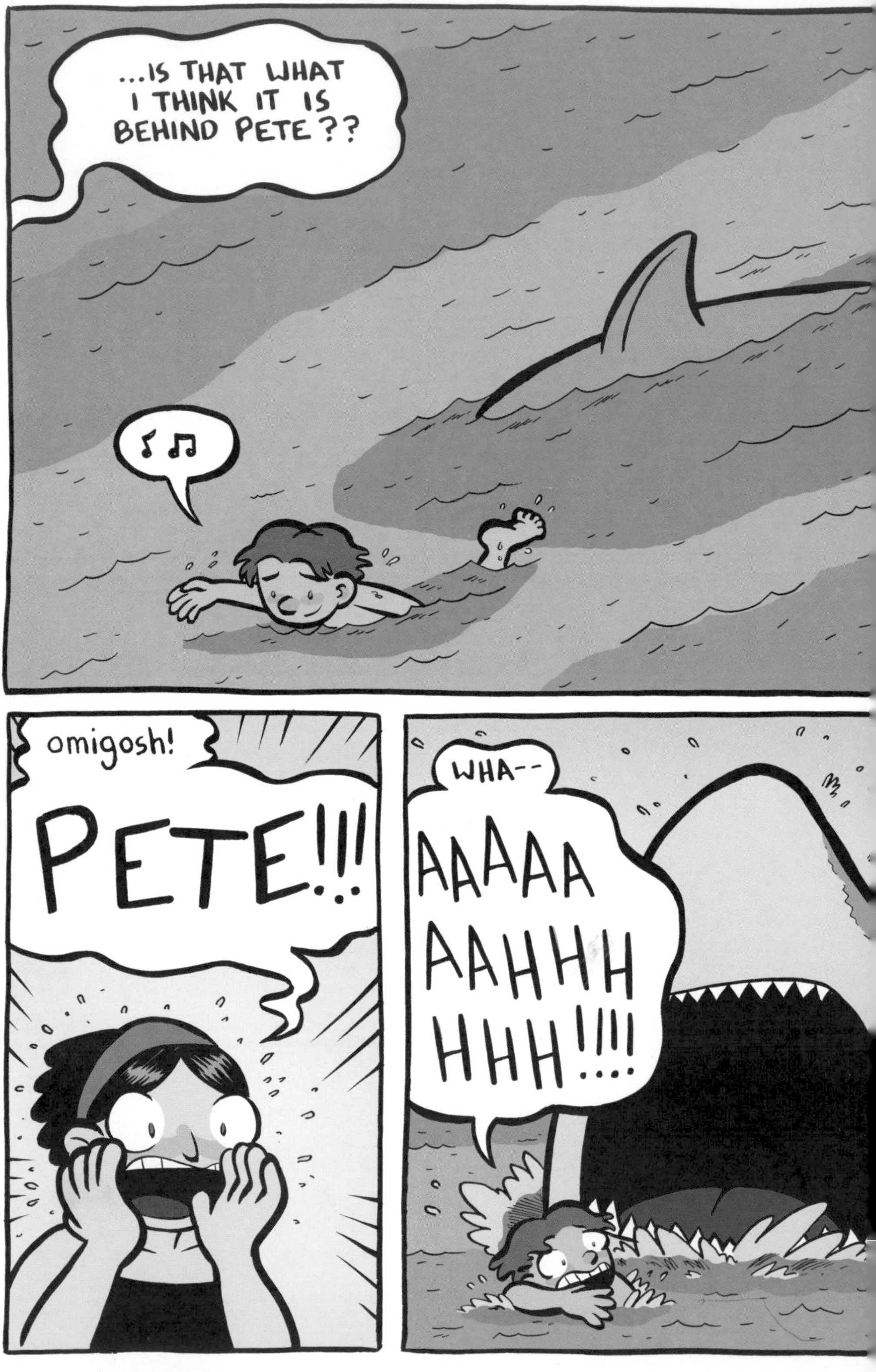
...IS THAT WHAT I THINK IT IS BEHIND PETE??
♪ ♫
omigosh!
PETE!!!
WHA--
AAAAAAHHHHHH!!!!

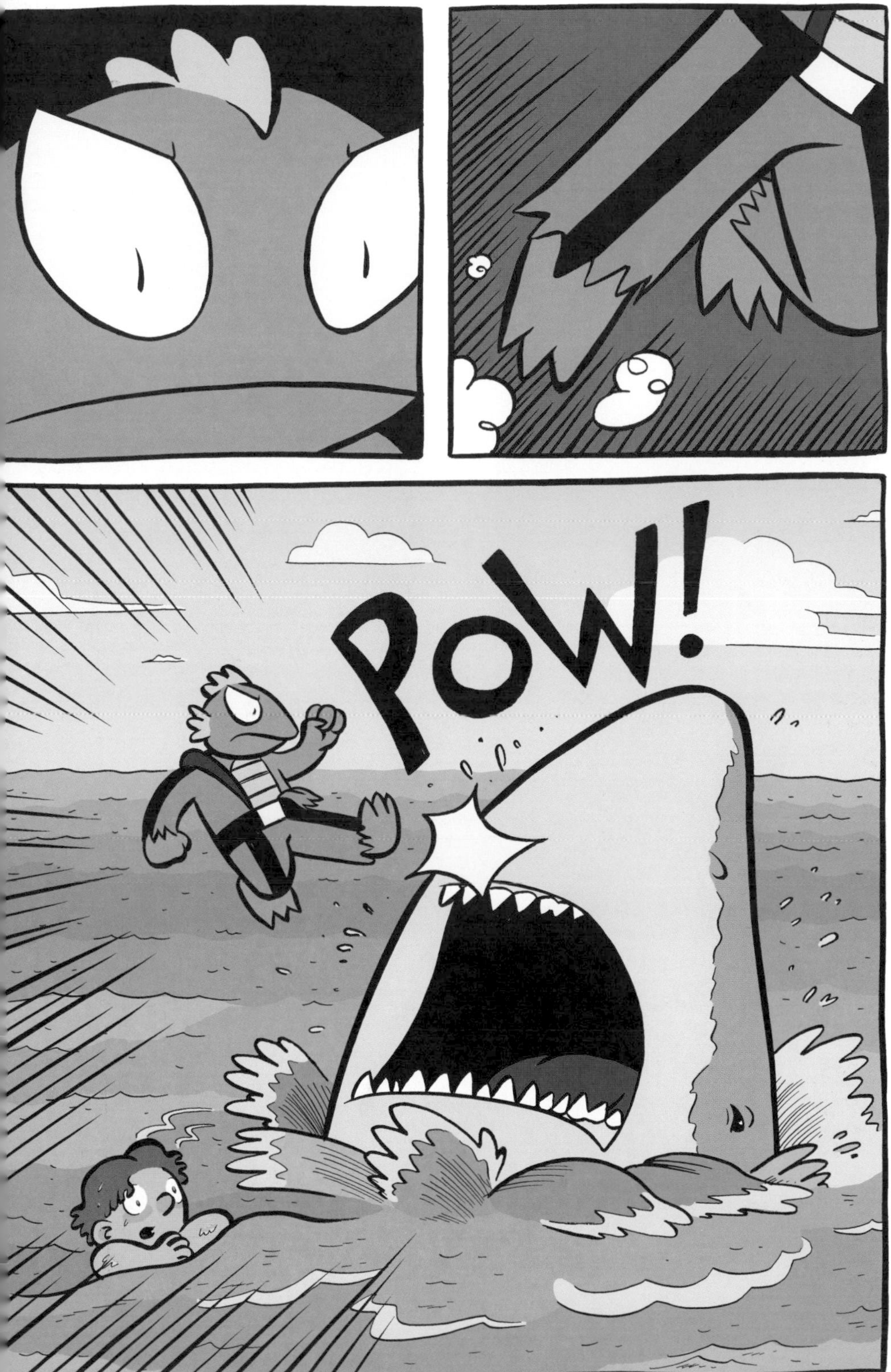
POW!

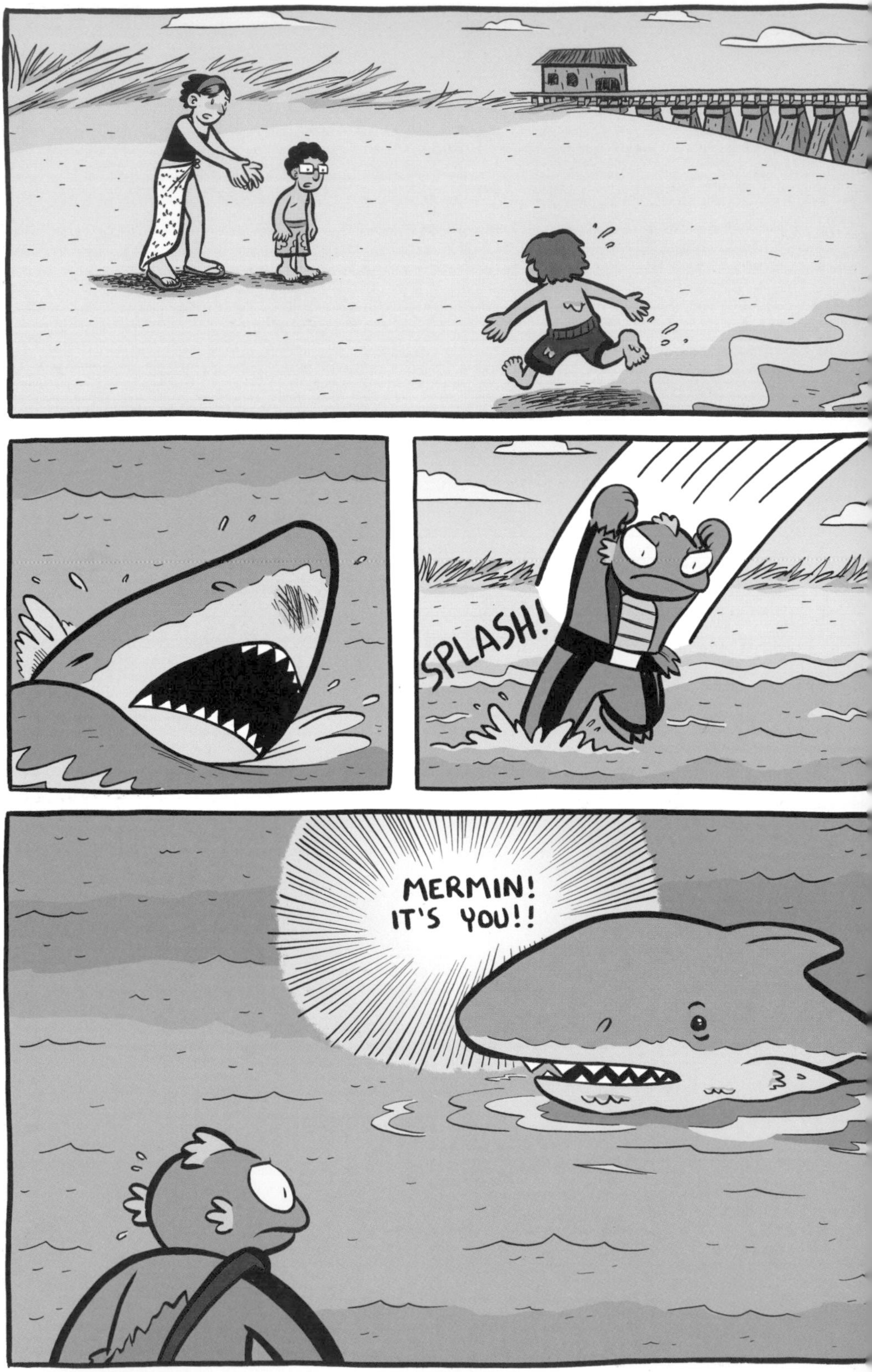
SPLASH!
MERMIN! IT'S YOU!!

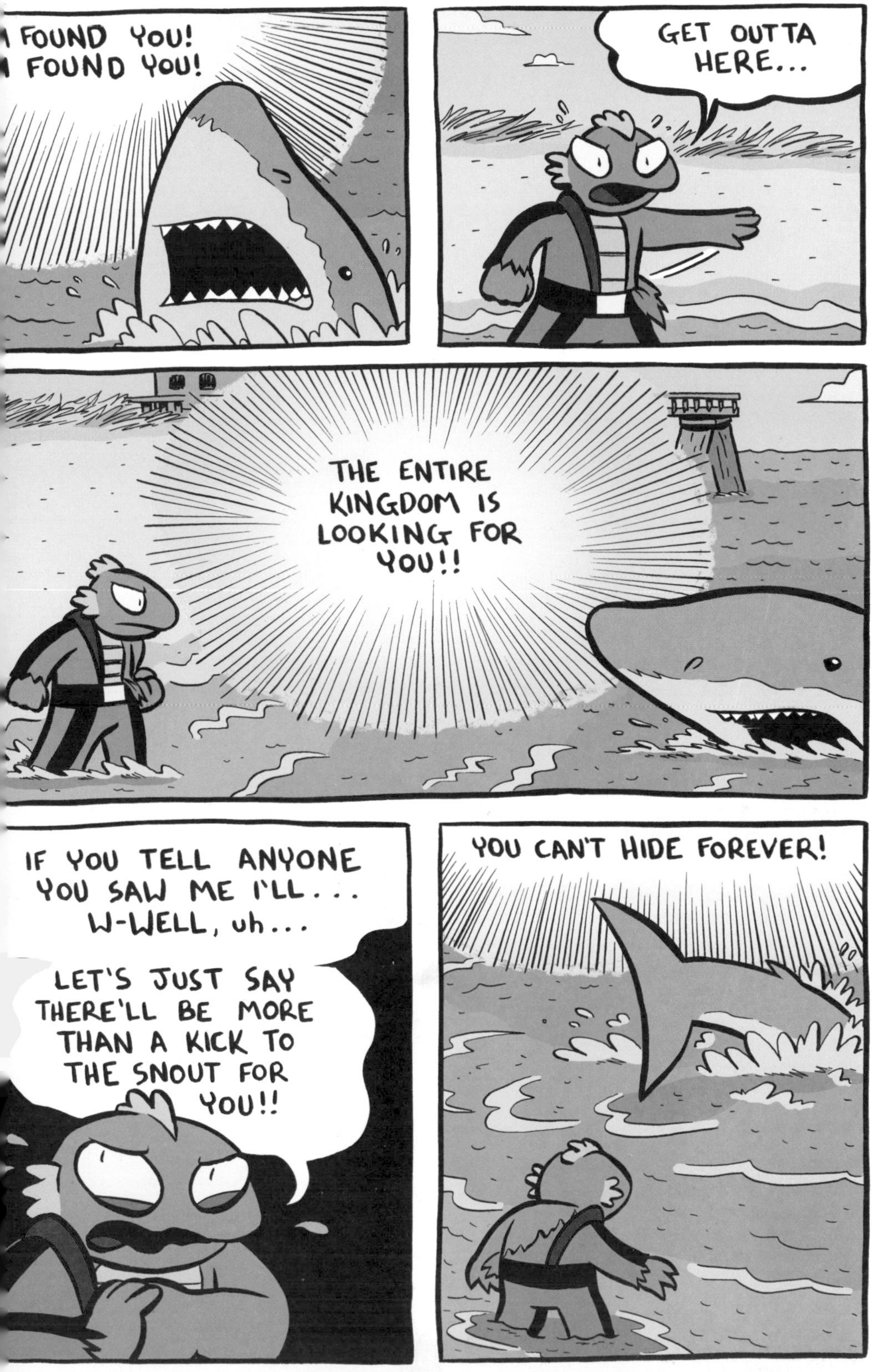
I FOUND YOU! I FOUND YOU!
GET OUTTA HERE...
THE ENTIRE KINGDOM IS LOOKING FOR YOU!!
IF YOU TELL ANYONE YOU SAW ME I'LL... W-WELL, uh...
LET'S JUST SAY THERE'LL BE MORE THAN A KICK TO THE SNOUT FOR YOU!!
YOU CAN'T HIDE FOREVER!

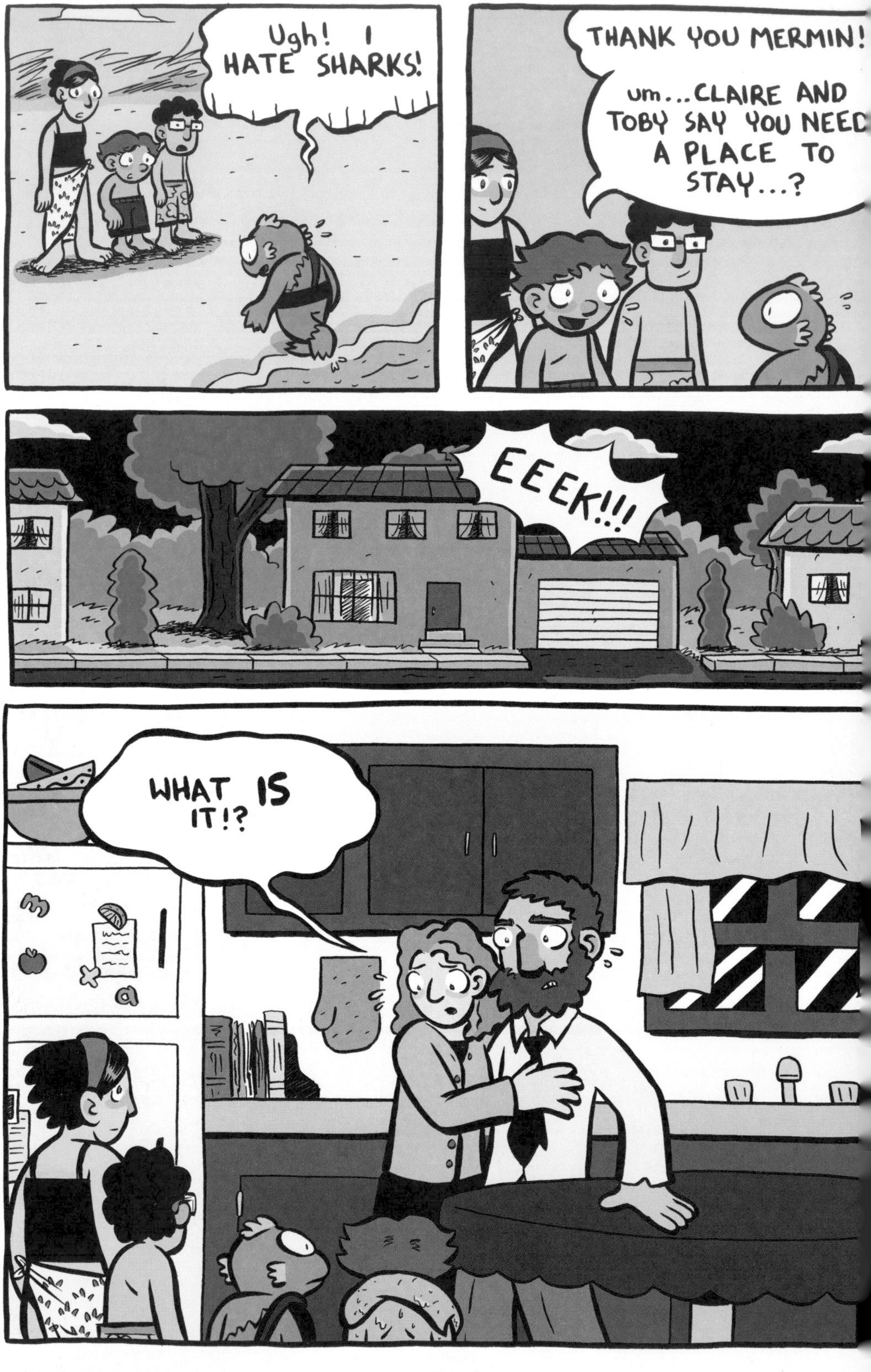
Ugh! I HATE SHARKS!
THANK YOU MERMIN!
um...CLAIRE AND TOBY SAY YOU NEED A PLACE TO STAY...?
EEEK!!!
WHAT IS IT!?

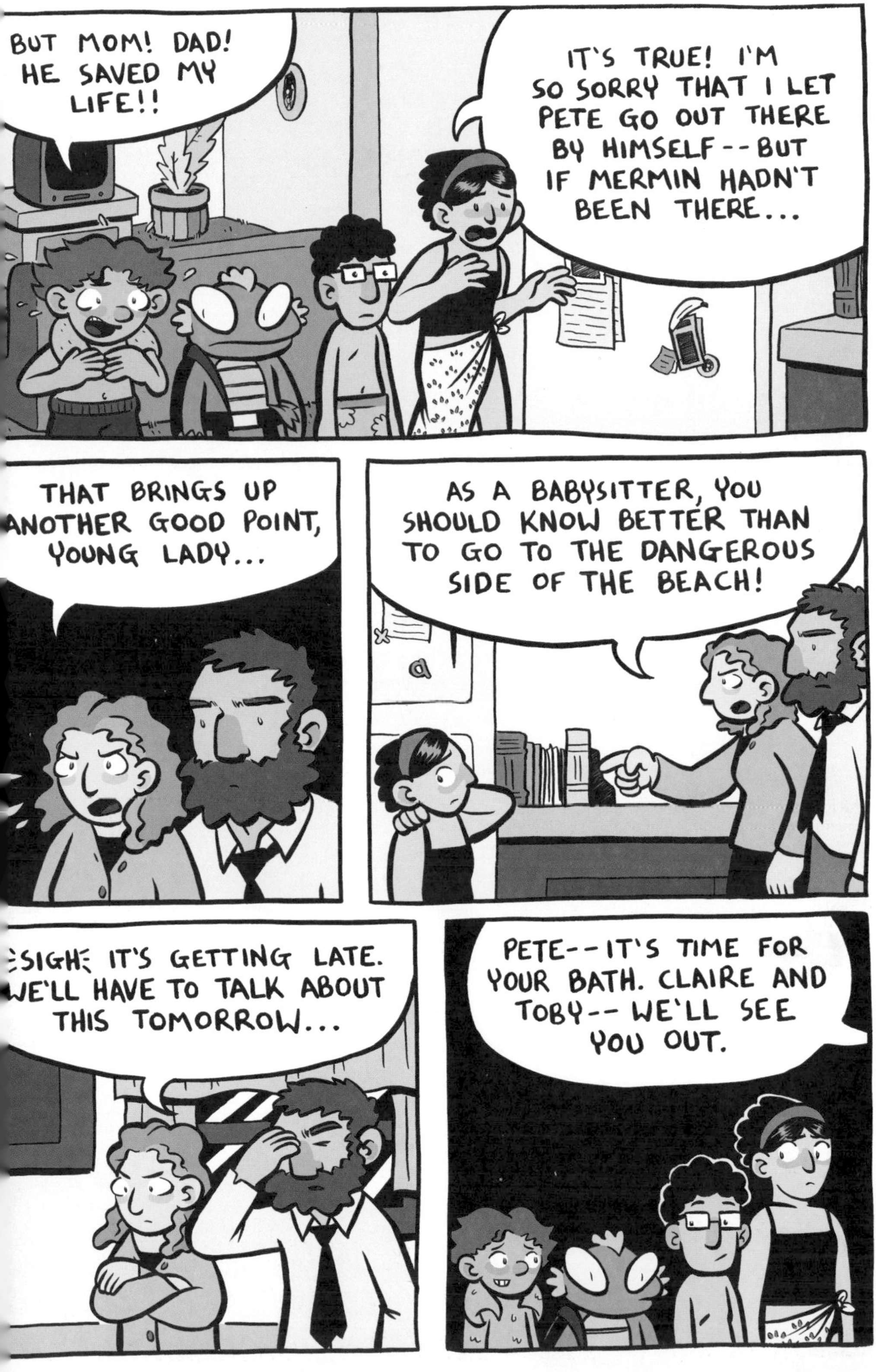
BUT MOM! DAD! HE SAVED MY LIFE!!
IT'S TRUE! I'M SO SORRY THAT I LET PETE GO OUT THERE BY HIMSELF--BUT IF MERMIN HADN'T BEEN THERE...
THAT BRINGS UP ANOTHER GOOD POINT, YOUNG LADY...
AS A BABYSITTER, YOU SHOULD KNOW BETTER THAN TO GO TO THE DANGEROUS SIDE OF THE BEACH!
SIGH IT'S GETTING LATE. WE'LL HAVE TO TALK ABOUT THIS TOMORROW...
PETE--IT'S TIME FOR YOUR BATH. CLAIRE AND TOBY-- WE'LL SEE YOU OUT.

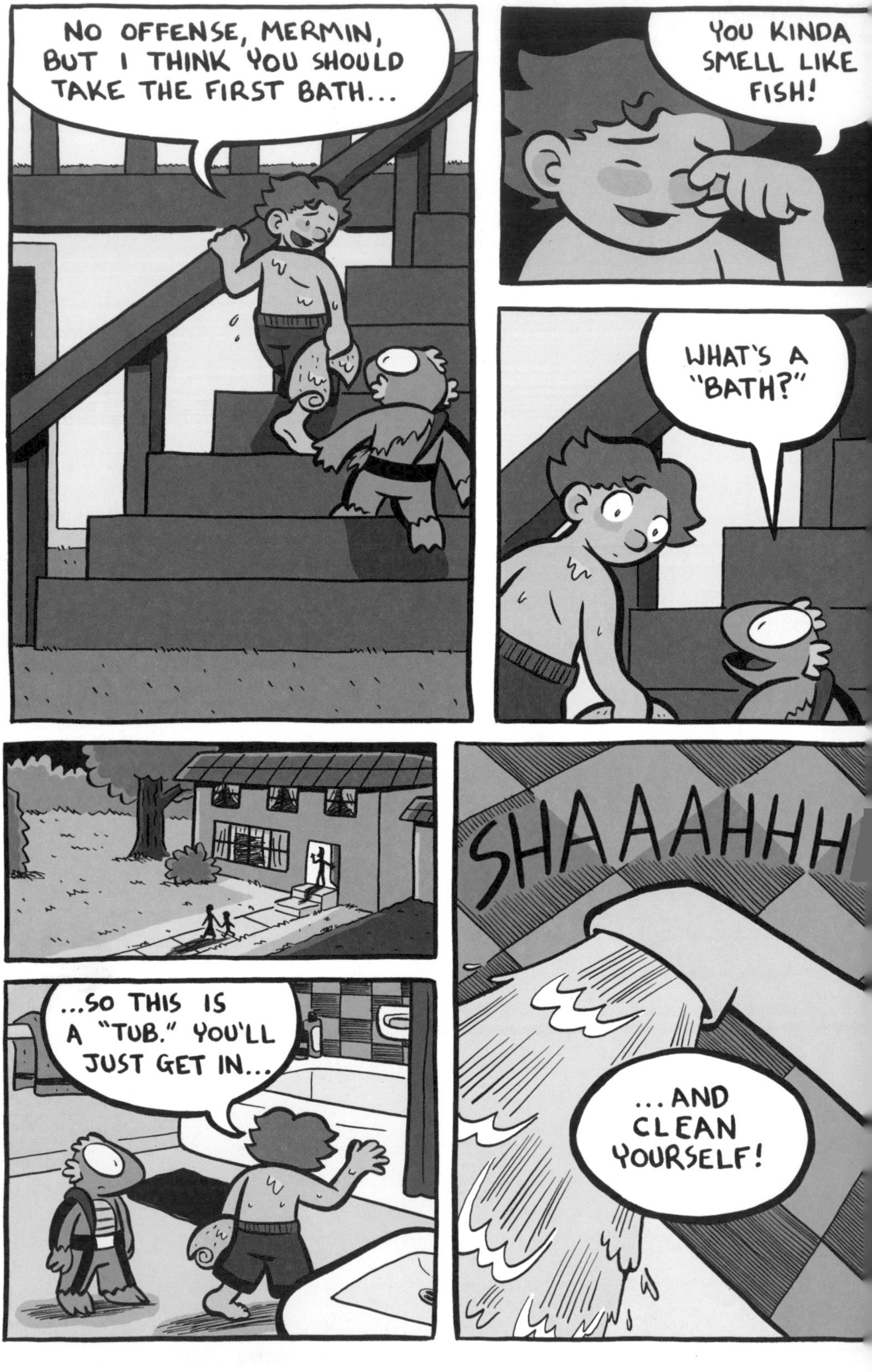
NO OFFENSE, MERMIN, BUT I THINK YOU SHOULD TAKE THE FIRST BATH...
YOU KINDA SMELL LIKE FISH!
WHAT'S A "BATH?"
...SO THIS IS A "TUB." YOU'LL JUST GET IN...
SHAAAHHH
...AND CLEAN YOURSELF!

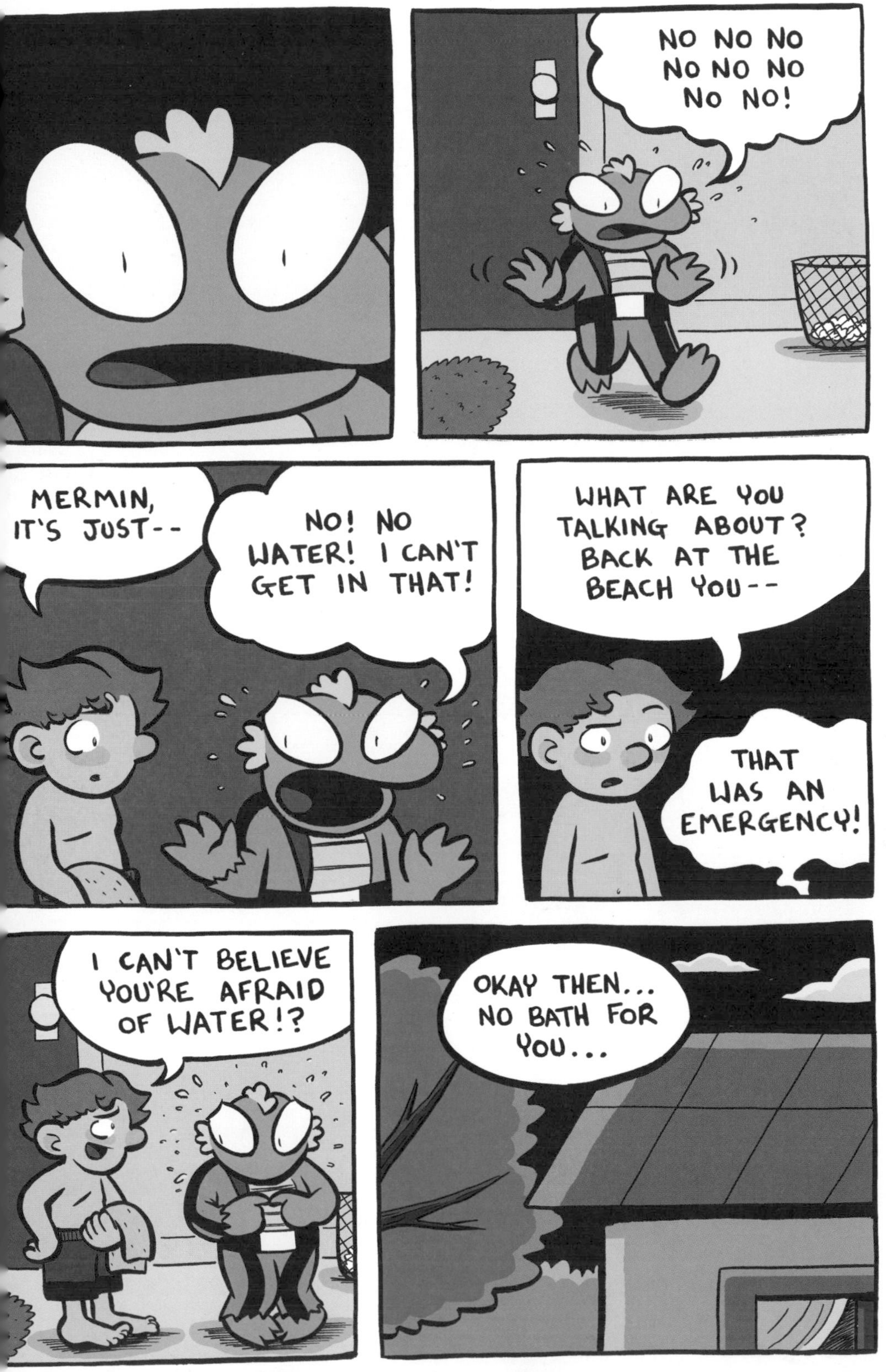
NO NO NO
NO NO NO
NO NO!
MERMIN, IT'S JUST--
NO! NO WATER! I CAN'T GET IN THAT!
WHAT ARE YOU TALKING ABOUT? BACK AT THE BEACH YOU--
THAT WAS AN EMERGENCY!
I CAN'T BELIEVE YOU'RE AFRAID OF WATER!?
OKAY THEN... NO BATH FOR YOU...

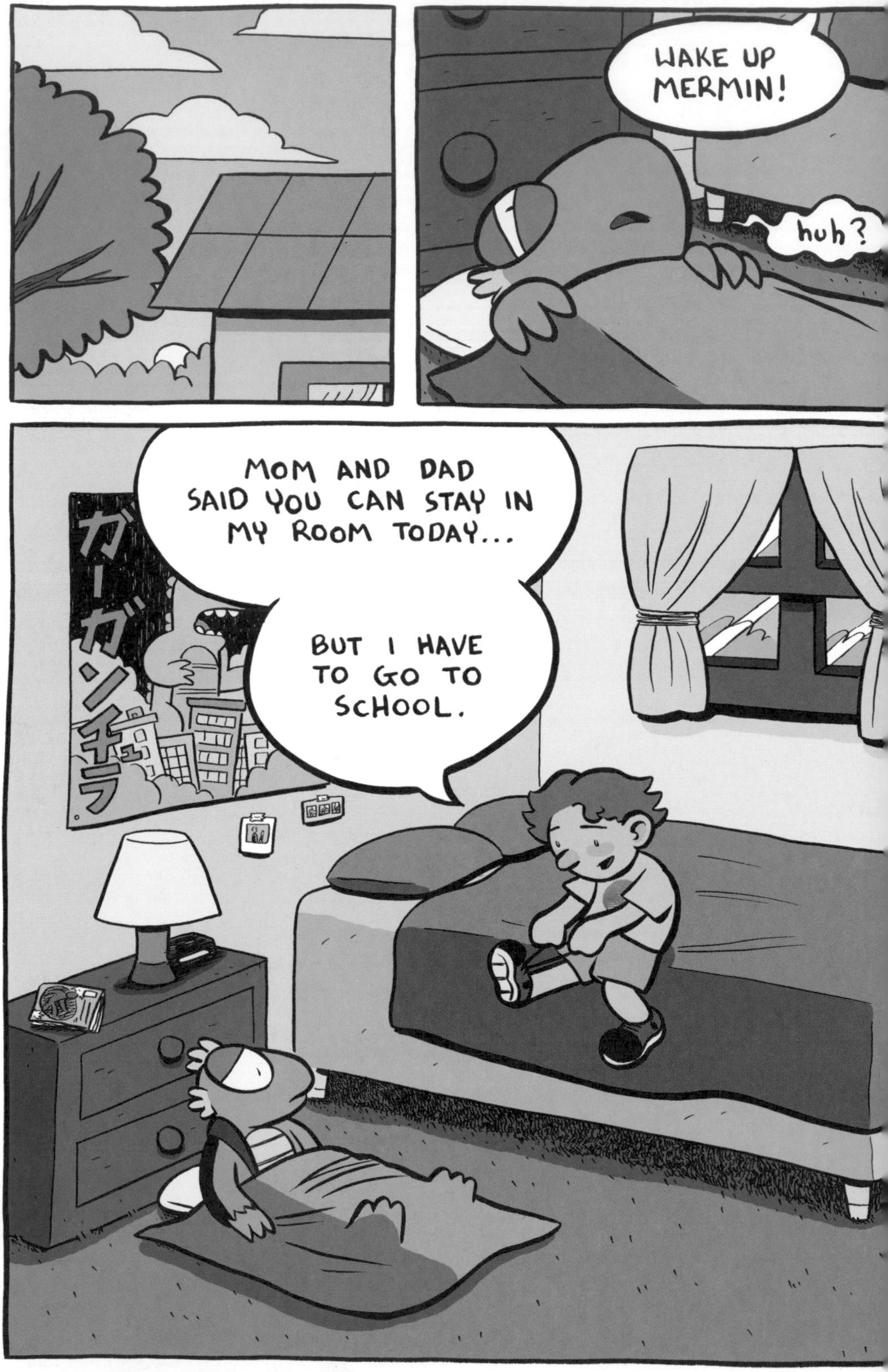
WAKE UP MERMIN!
huh?
ガーガンチュラ
MOM AND DAD SAID YOU CAN STAY IN MY ROOM TODAY...
BUT I HAVE TO GO TO SCHOOL.

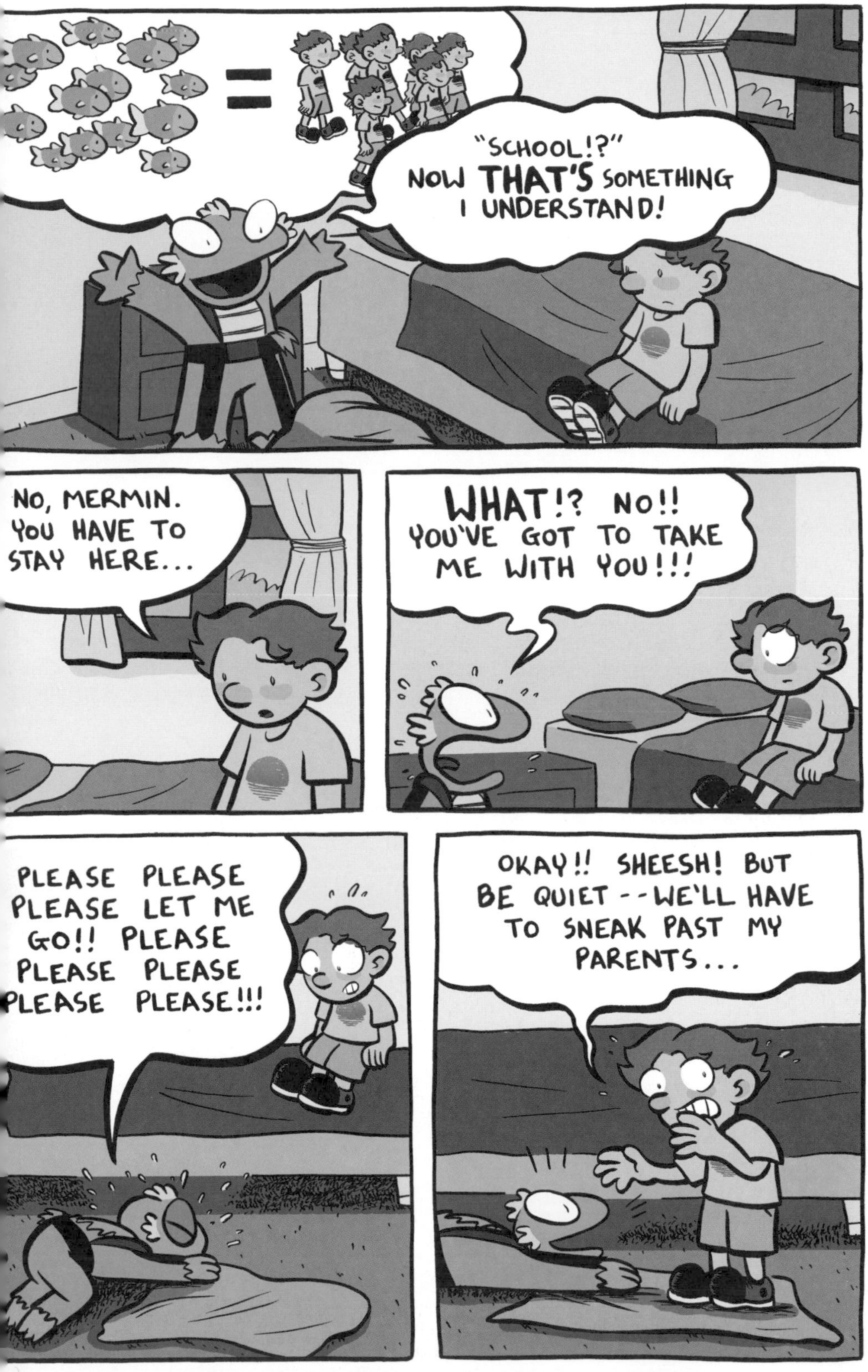
"SCHOOL!?"
NOW THAT'S SOMETHING I UNDERSTAND!
NO, MERMIN. YOU HAVE TO STAY HERE...
WHAT!? NO!! YOU'VE GOT TO TAKE ME WITH YOU!!!
PLEASE PLEASE PLEASE LET ME GO!! PLEASE PLEASE PLEASE PLEASE PLEASE!!!
OKAY!! SHEESH! BUT BE QUIET--WE'LL HAVE TO SNEAK PAST MY PARENTS...

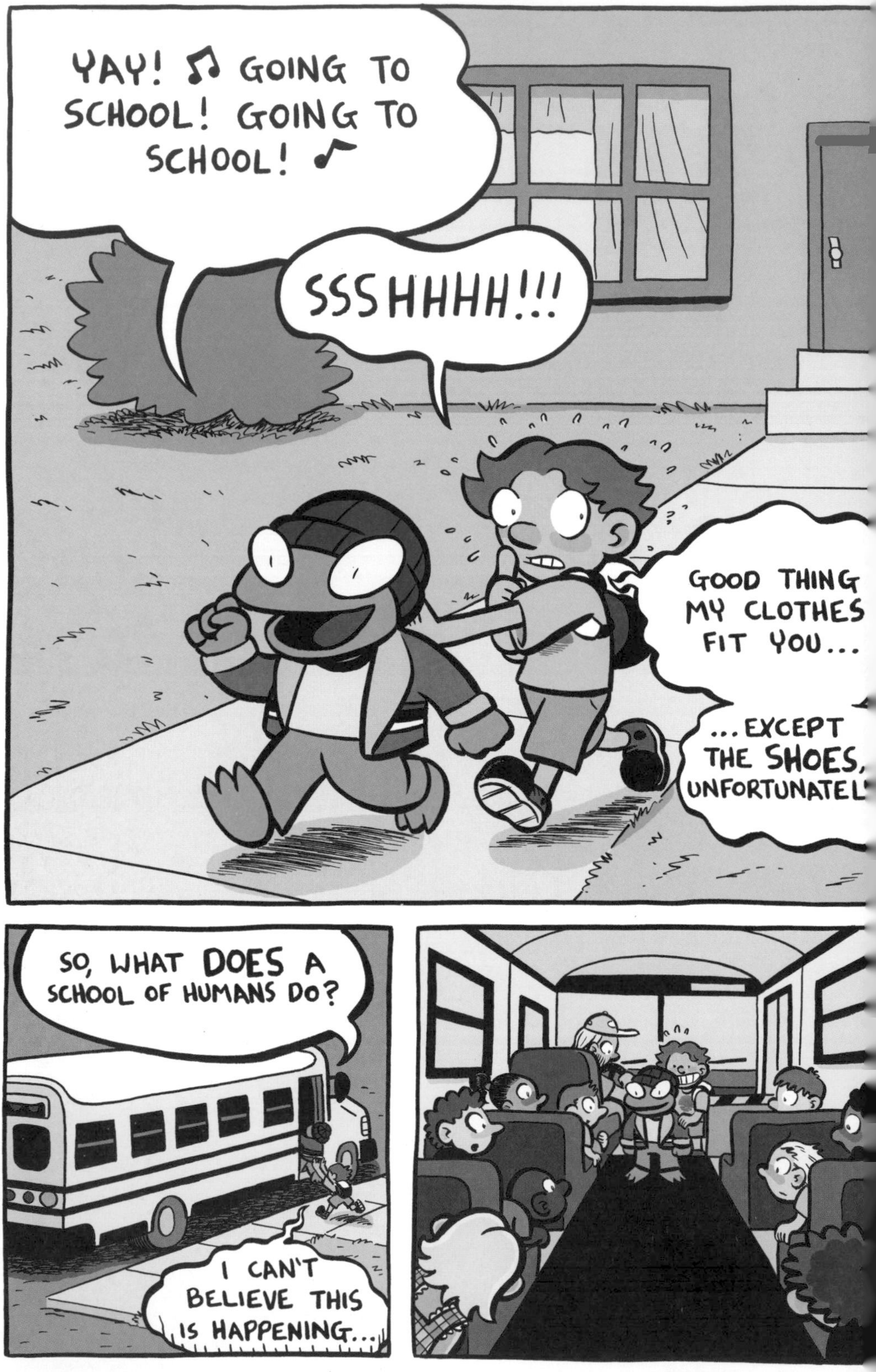
YAY! GOING TO SCHOOL! GOING TO SCHOOL!
SSSHHHH!!!
GOOD THING MY CLOTHES FIT YOU...
...EXCEPT THE SHOES, UNFORTUNATEL
SO, WHAT DOES A SCHOOL OF HUMANS DO?
I CAN'T BELIEVE THIS IS HAPPENING...

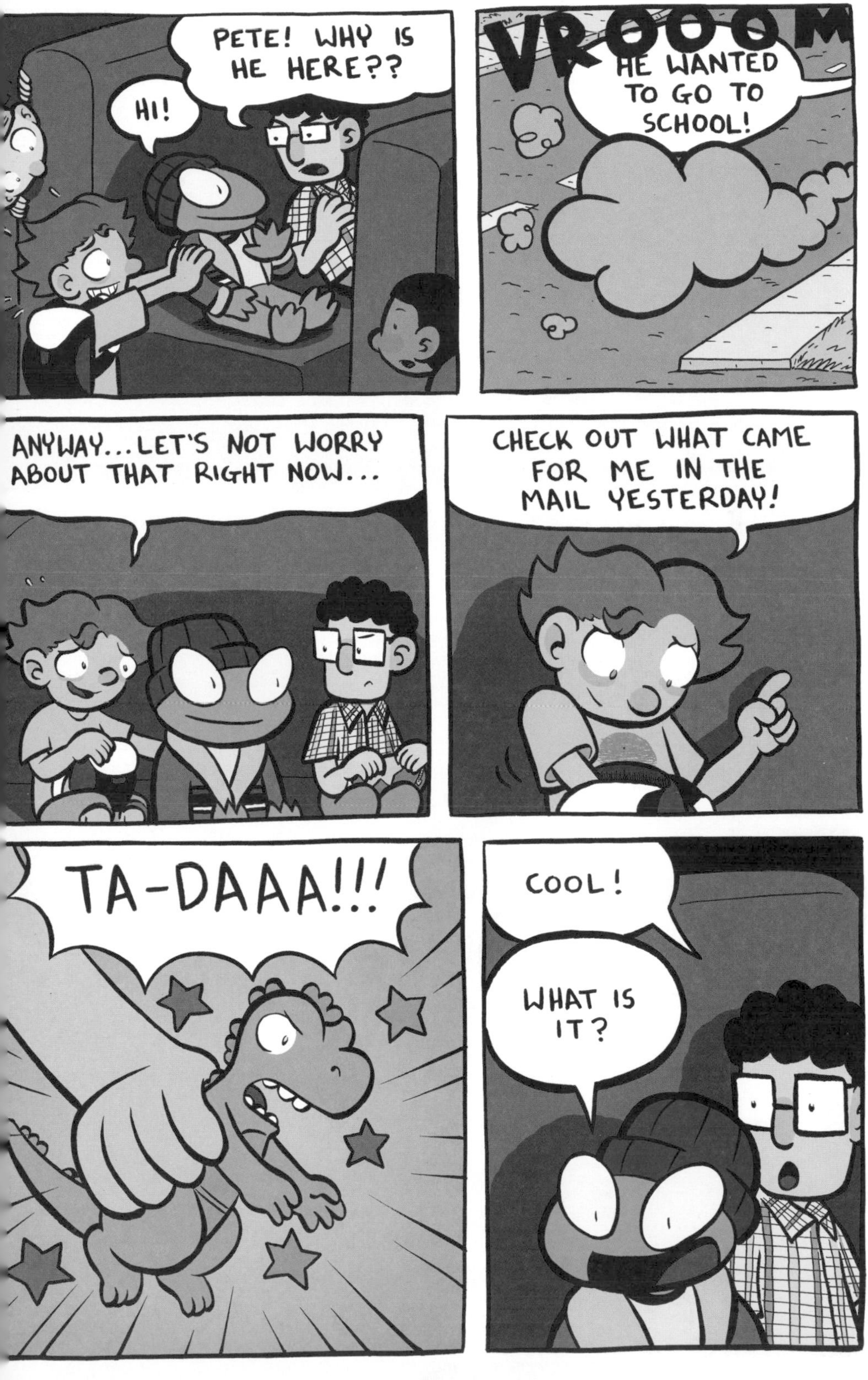
PETE! WHY IS HE HERE??
HI!
VROOOOM
HE WANTED TO GO TO SCHOOL!
ANYWAY... LET'S NOT WORRY ABOUT THAT RIGHT NOW...
CHECK OUT WHAT CAME FOR ME IN THE MAIL YESTERDAY!
TA-DAAA!!!
COOL!
WHAT IS IT?

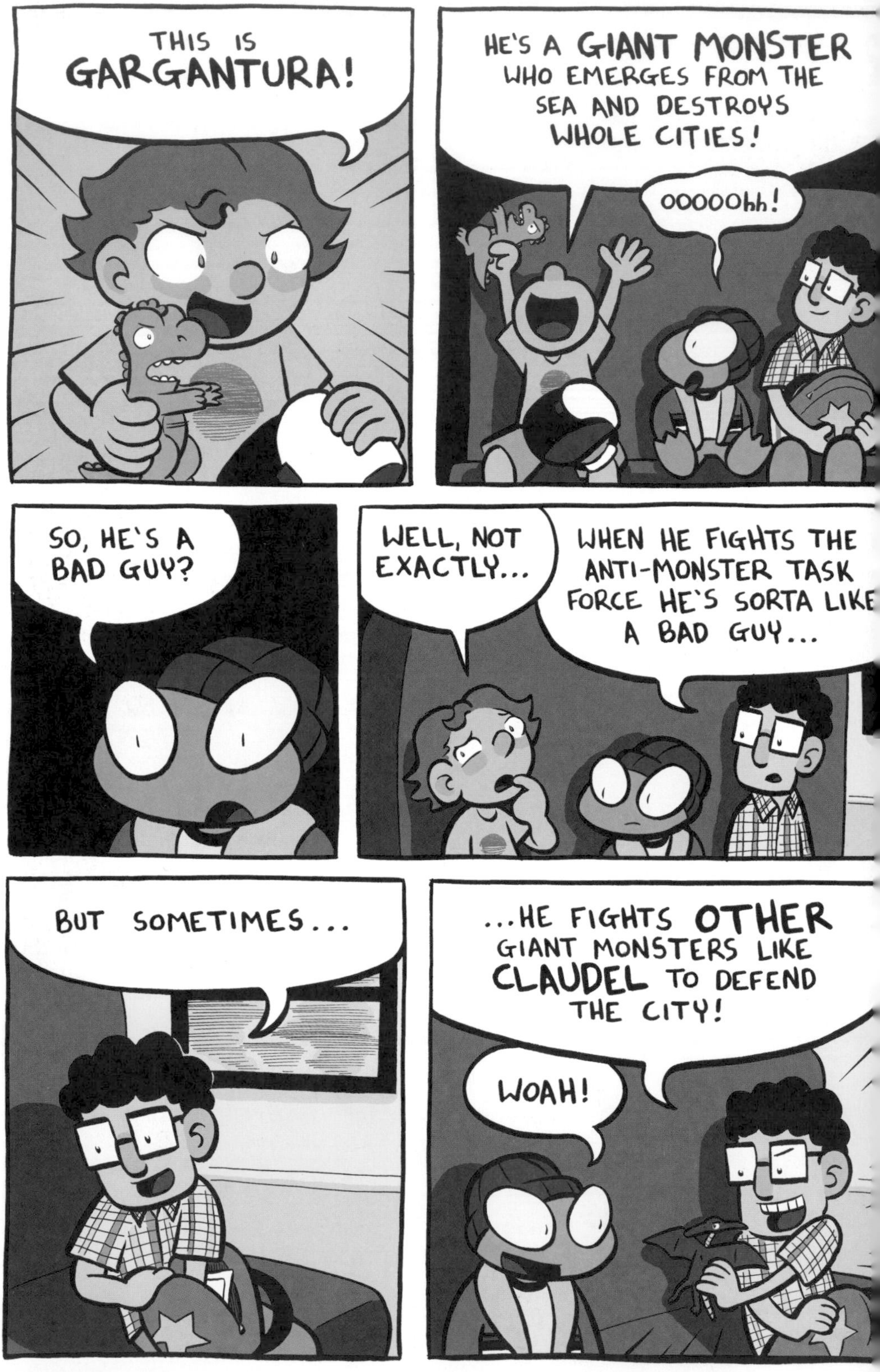
THIS IS GARGANTURA!
HE'S A GIANT MONSTER WHO EMERGES FROM THE SEA AND DESTROYS WHOLE CITIES!
OOOOOhh!
SO, HE'S A BAD GUY?
WELL, NOT EXACTLY...
WHEN HE FIGHTS THE ANTI-MONSTER TASK FORCE HE'S SORTA LIKE A BAD GUY...
BUT SOMETIMES...
...HE FIGHTS OTHER GIANT MONSTERS LIKE CLAUDEL TO DEFEND THE CITY!
WOAH!

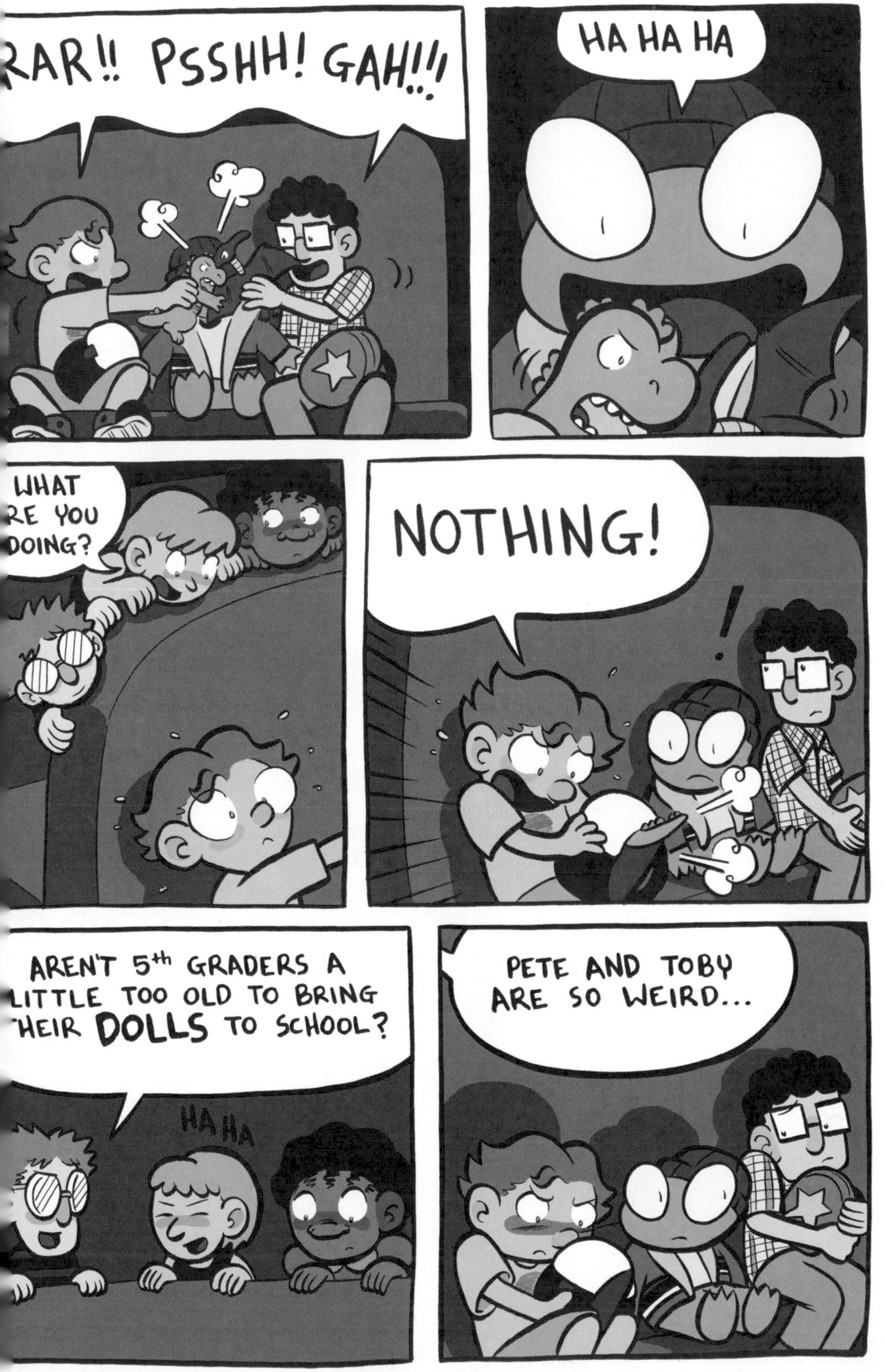
RAR!! PSSHH! GAH!!!
HA HA HA
WHAT RE YOU DOING?
NOTHING!
!
AREN'T 5th GRADERS A LITTLE TOO OLD TO BRING THEIR DOLLS TO SCHOOL?
HA HA
PETE AND TOBY ARE SO WEIRD...

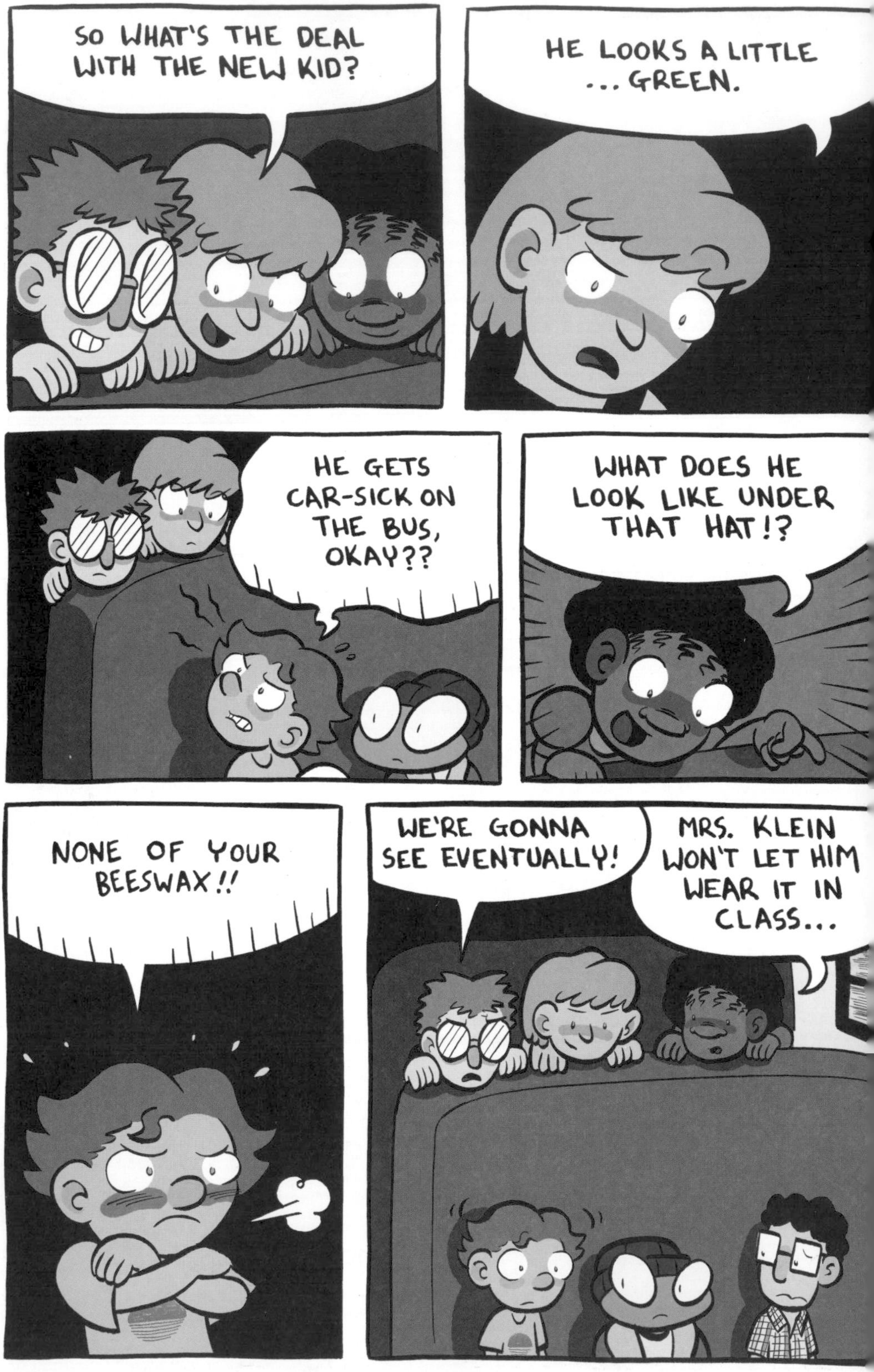
SO WHAT'S THE DEAL WITH THE NEW KID?
HE LOOKS A LITTLE ... GREEN.
HE GETS CAR-SICK ON THE BUS, OKAY??
WHAT DOES HE LOOK LIKE UNDER THAT HAT!?
NONE OF YOUR BEESWAX!!
WE'RE GONNA SEE EVENTUALLY!
MRS. KLEIN WON'T LET HIM WEAR IT IN CLASS...

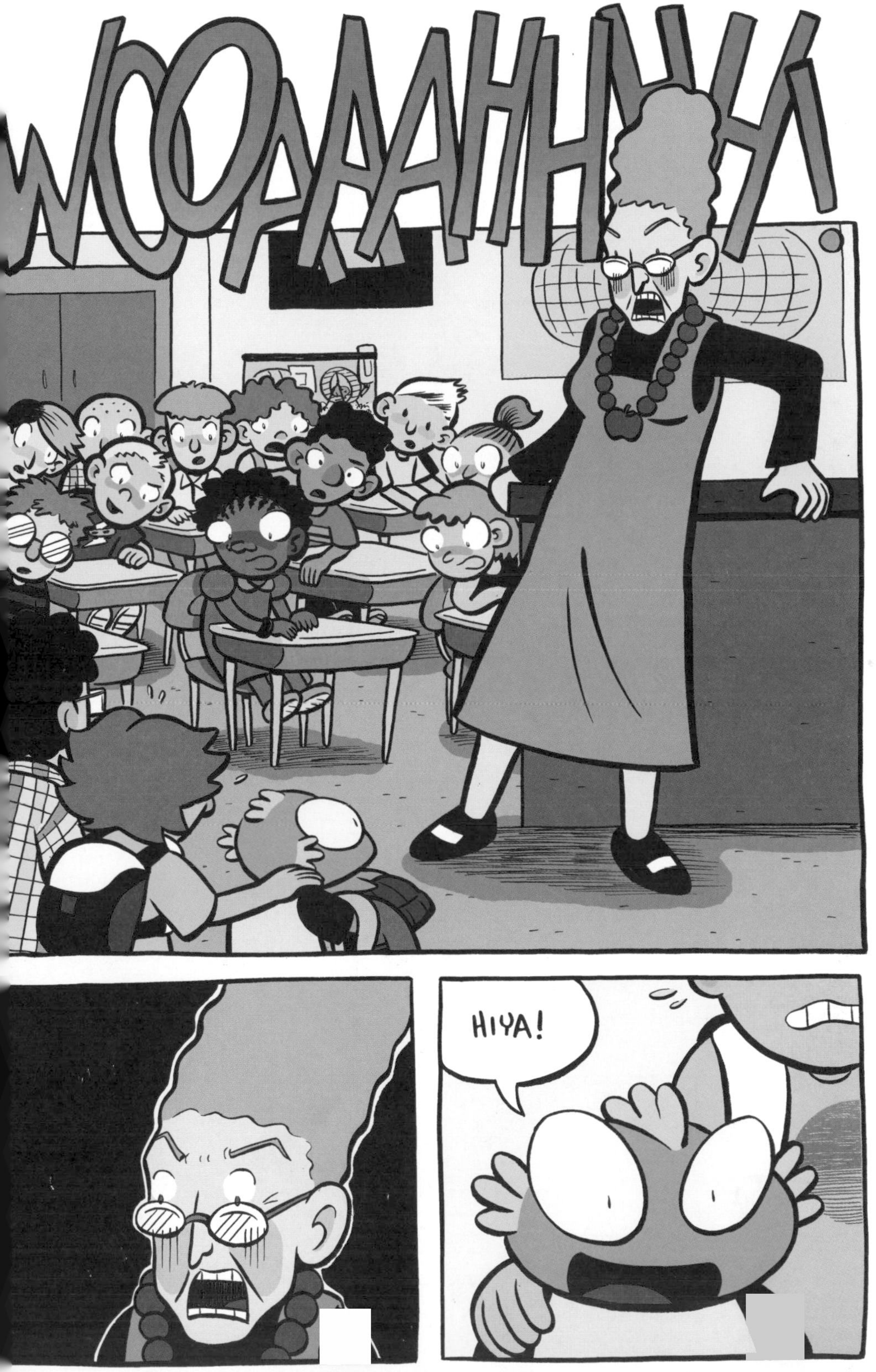
WOOAAAHHHYAH!
HIYA!

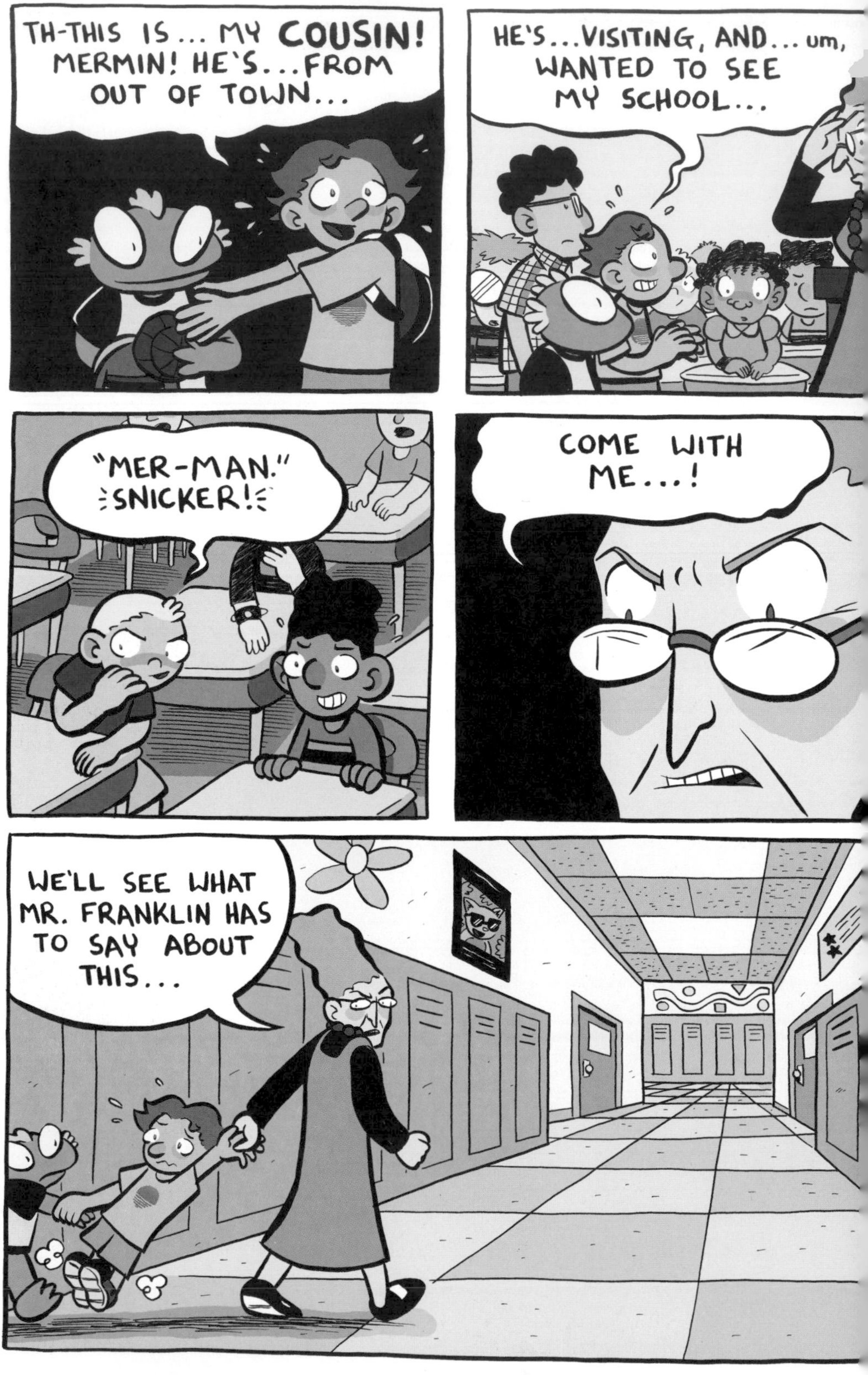
TH-THIS IS... MY COUSIN! MERMIN! HE'S...FROM OUT OF TOWN...
HE'S...VISITING, AND...um, WANTED TO SEE MY SCHOOL...
"MER-MAN." SNICKER!
COME WITH ME...!
WE'LL SEE WHAT MR. FRANKLIN HAS TO SAY ABOUT THIS...

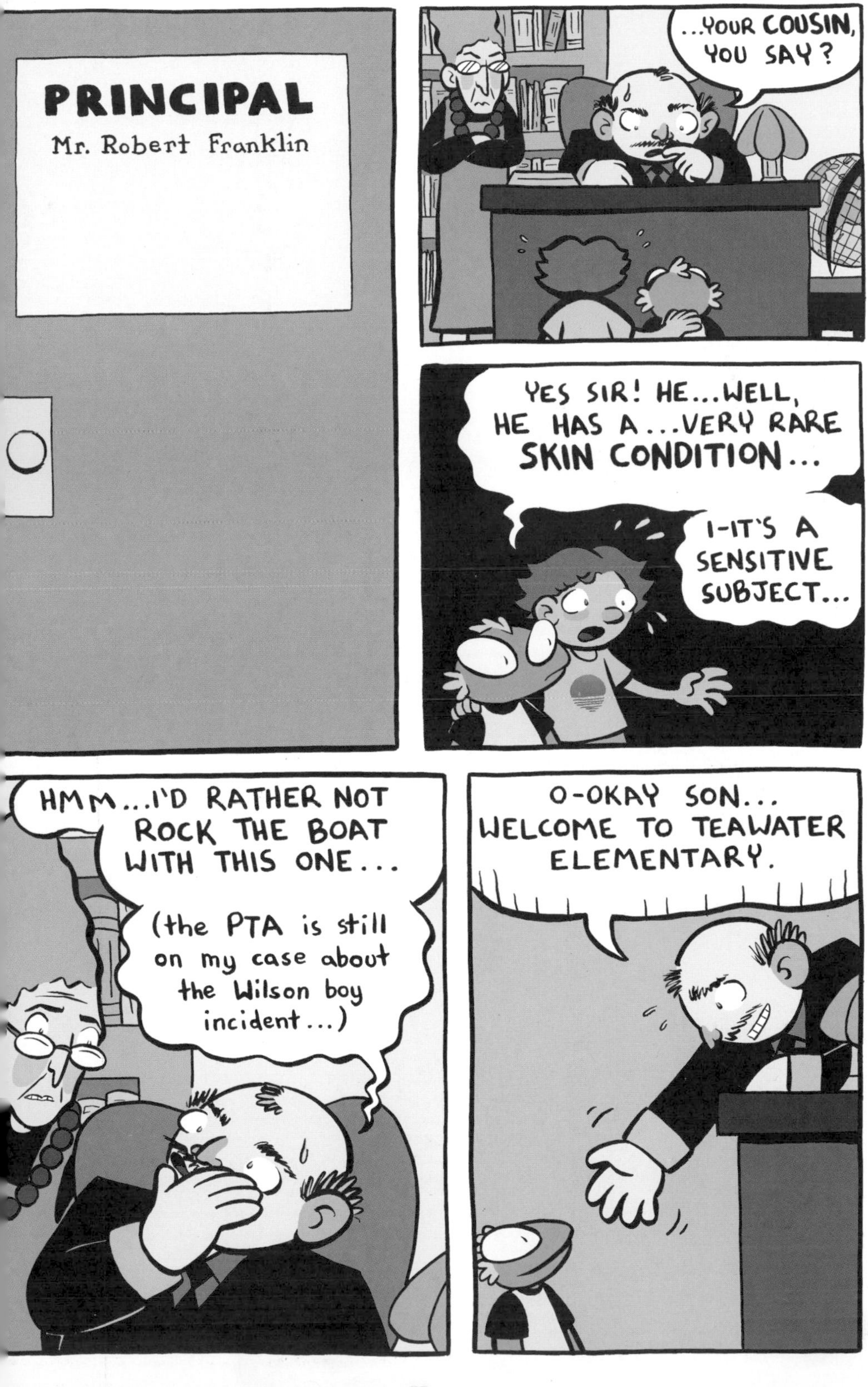
PRINCIPAL
Mr. Robert Franklin
...YOUR COUSIN, YOU SAY?
YES SIR! HE...WELL, HE HAS A...VERY RARE SKIN CONDITION...
I-IT'S A SENSITIVE SUBJECT...
HMM...I'D RATHER NOT ROCK THE BOAT WITH THIS ONE...
(the PTA is still on my case about the Wilson boy incident...)
O-OKAY SON... WELCOME TO TEAWATER ELEMENTARY.

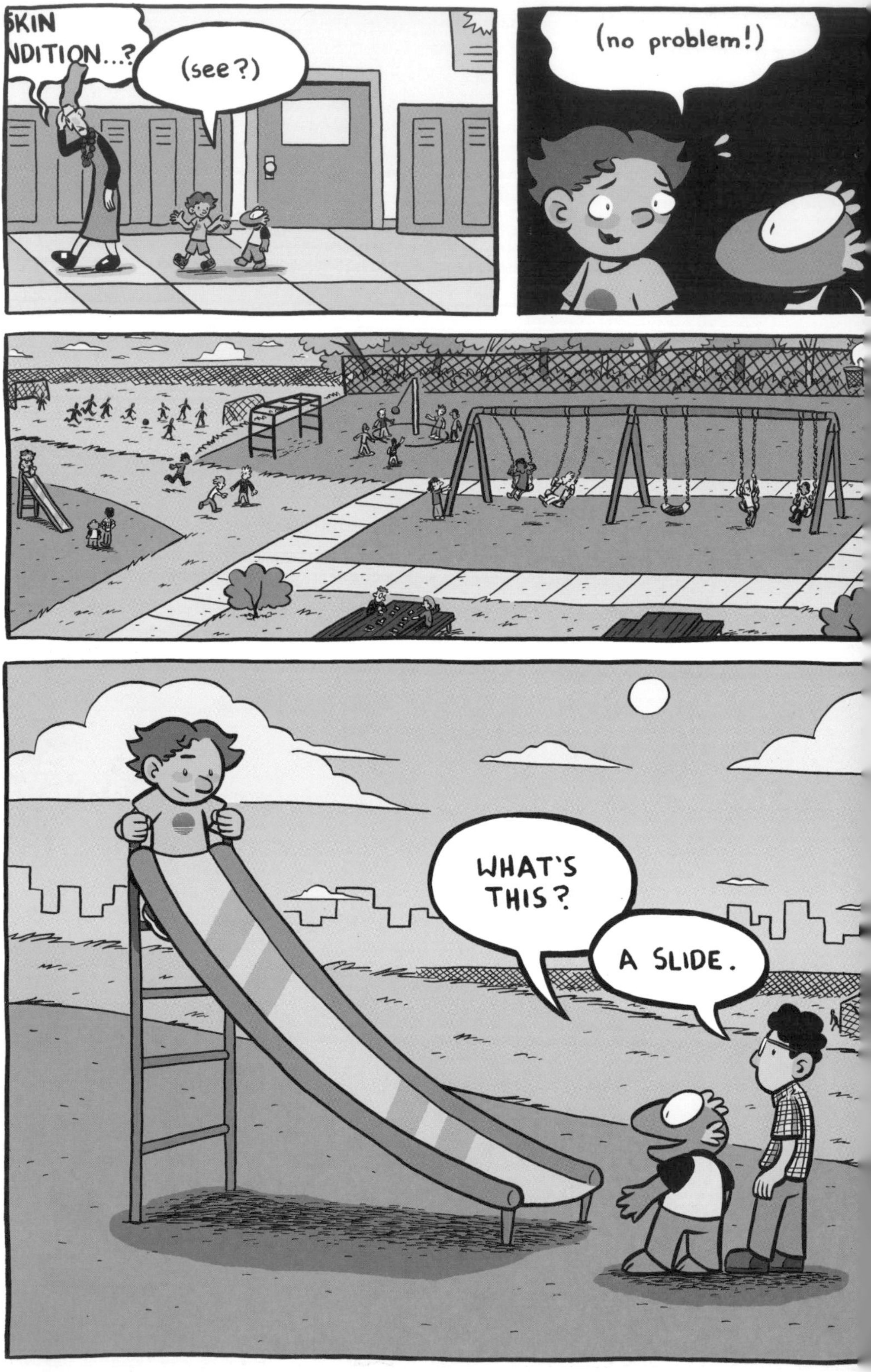
(see?)
(no problem!)
WHAT'S THIS?
A SLIDE.

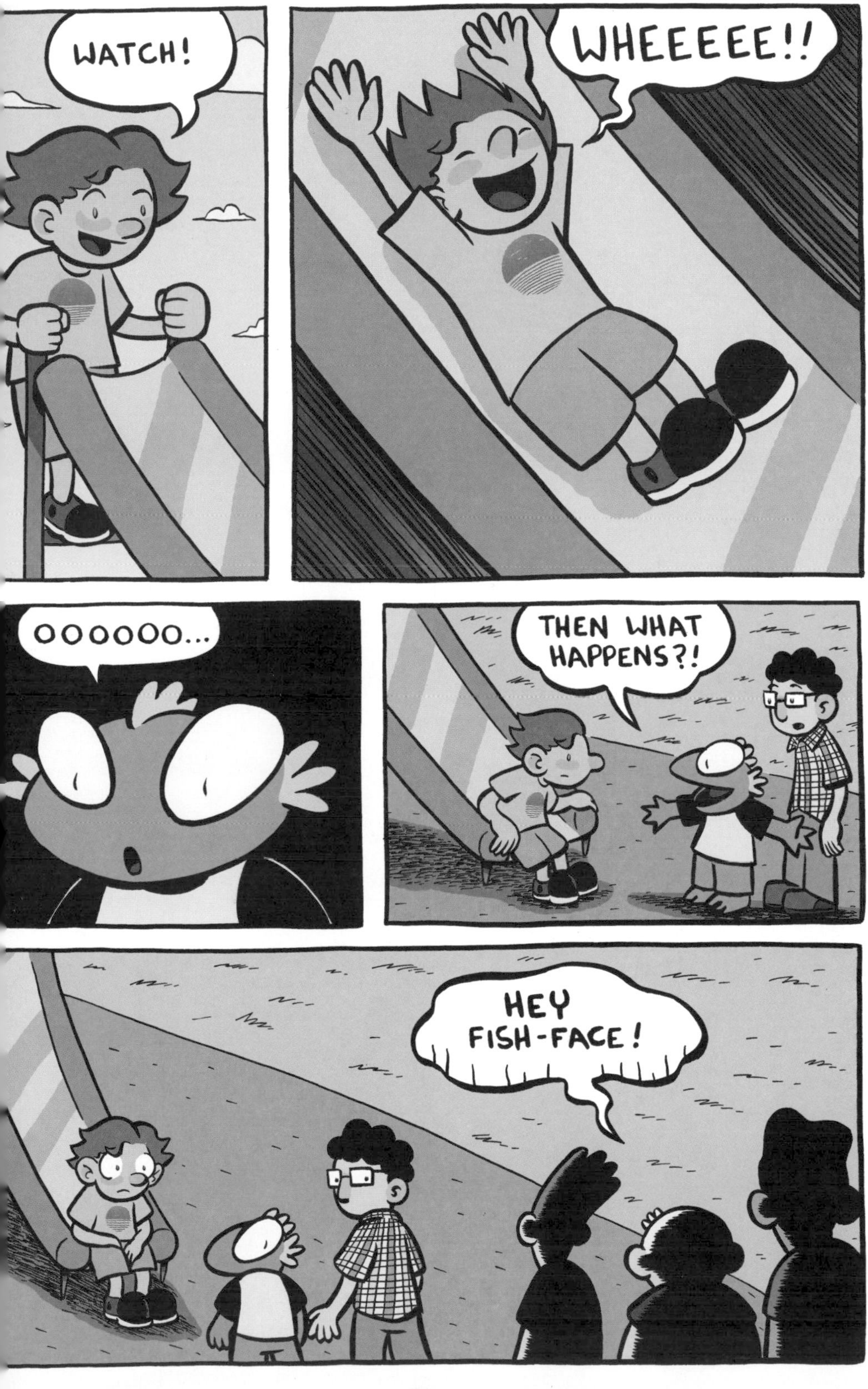
WATCH!
WHEEEEE!!
OOOOOO...
THEN WHAT HAPPENS?!
HEY FISH-FACE!

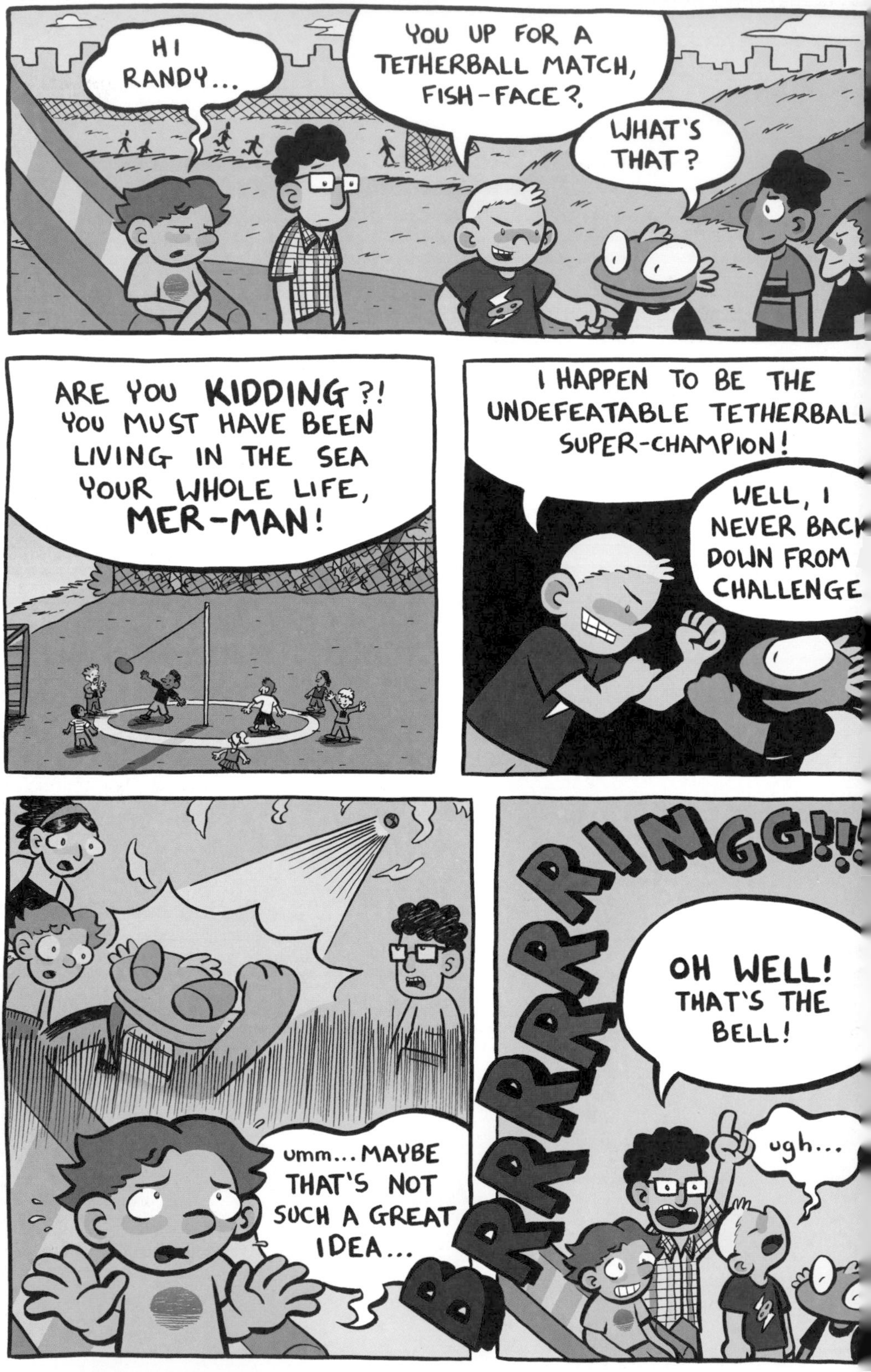
HI RANDY...
YOU UP FOR A TETHERBALL MATCH, FISH-FACE?
WHAT'S THAT?
ARE YOU KIDDING?! YOU MUST HAVE BEEN LIVING IN THE SEA YOUR WHOLE LIFE, MER-MAN!
I HAPPEN TO BE THE UNDEFEATABLE TETHERBALL SUPER-CHAMPION!
WELL, I NEVER BACK DOWN FROM CHALLENGE
umm... MAYBE THAT'S NOT SUCH A GREAT IDEA...
BRRRRRINGG!!!
OH WELL! THAT'S THE BELL!
ugh...

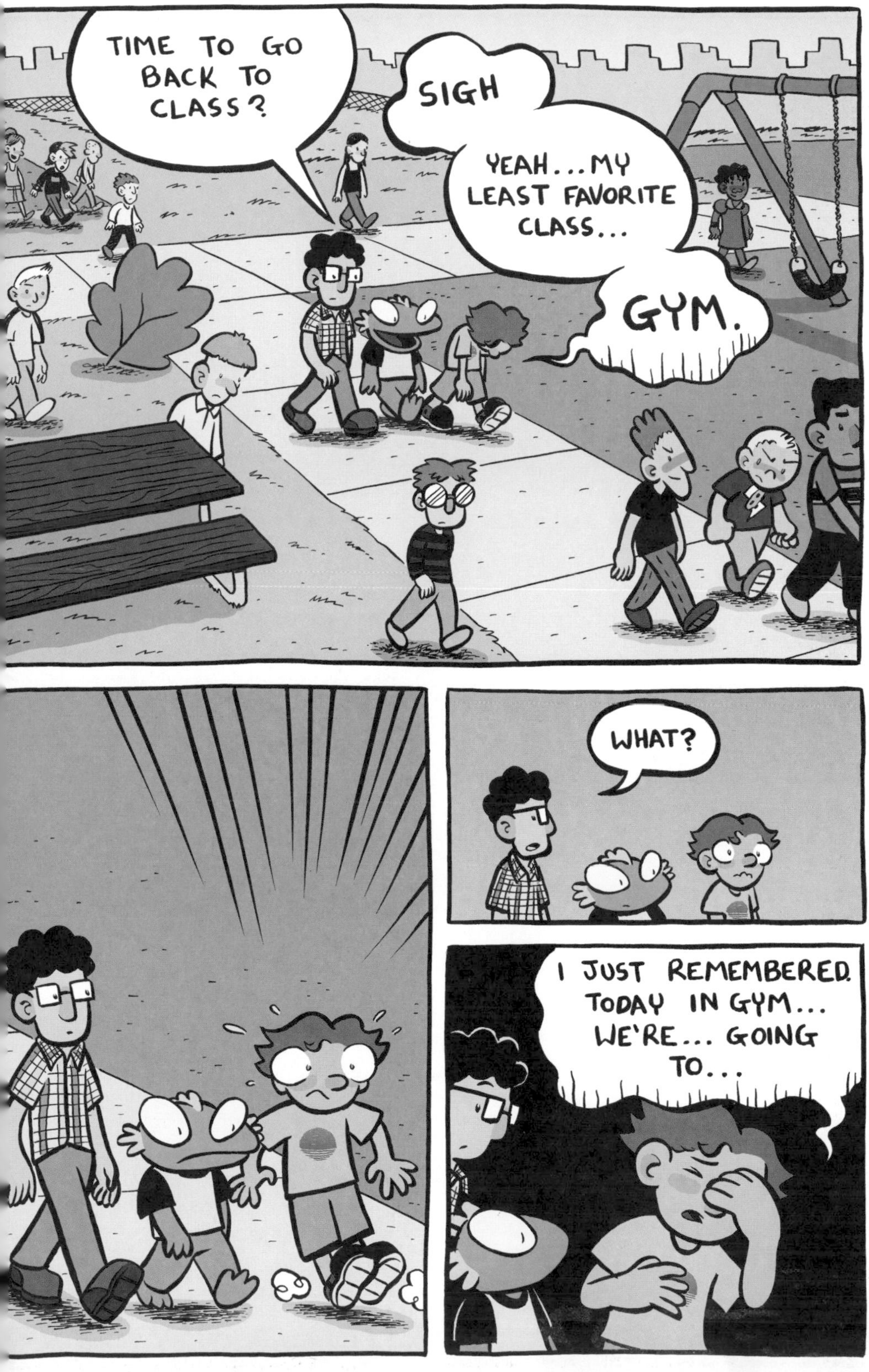
TIME TO GO BACK TO CLASS?
SIGH
YEAH...MY LEAST FAVORITE CLASS...
GYM.
WHAT?
I JUST REMEMBERED. TODAY IN GYM... WE'RE... GOING TO...

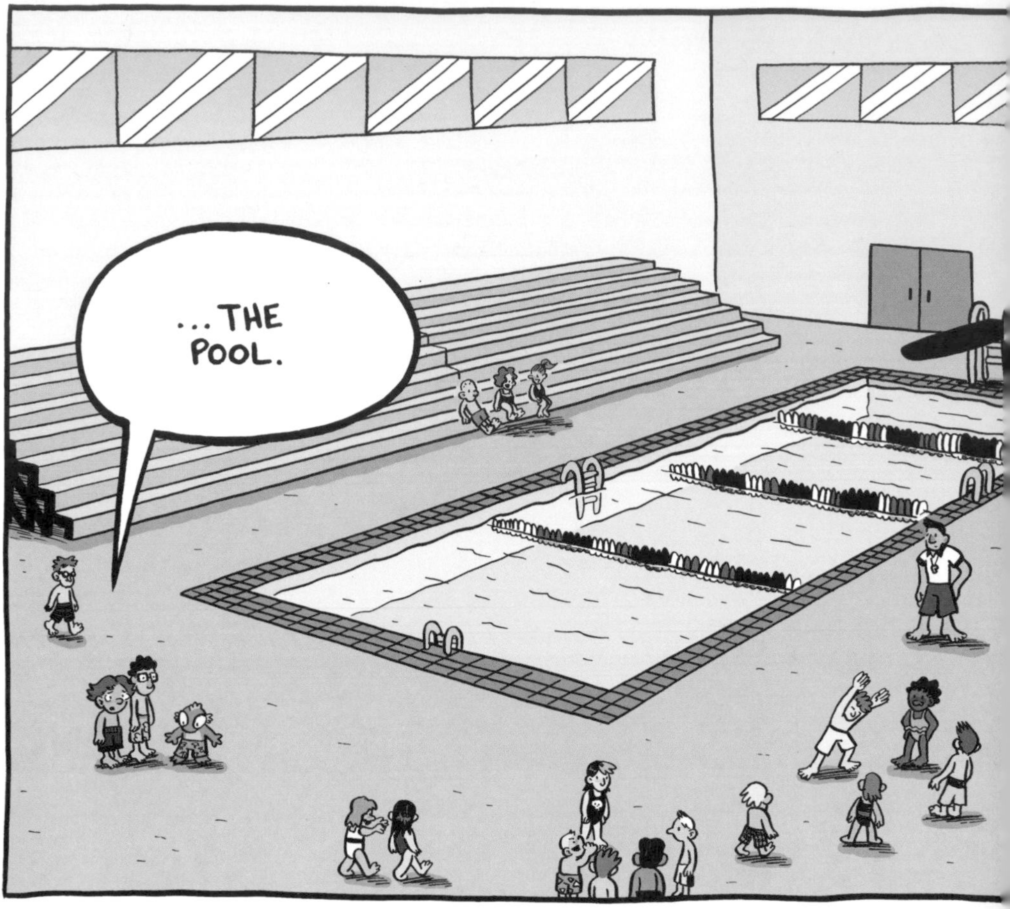
...THE POOL.

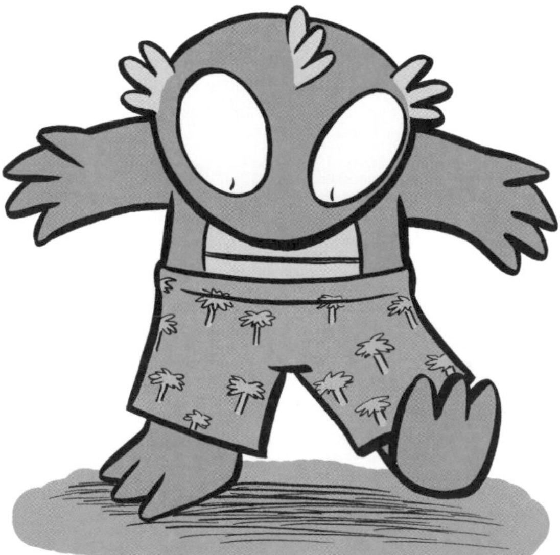

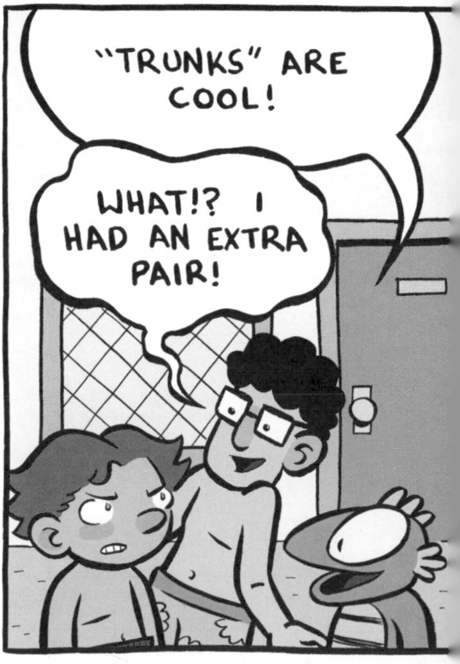
"TRUNKS" ARE COOL!
WHAT!? I HAD AN EXTRA PAIR!

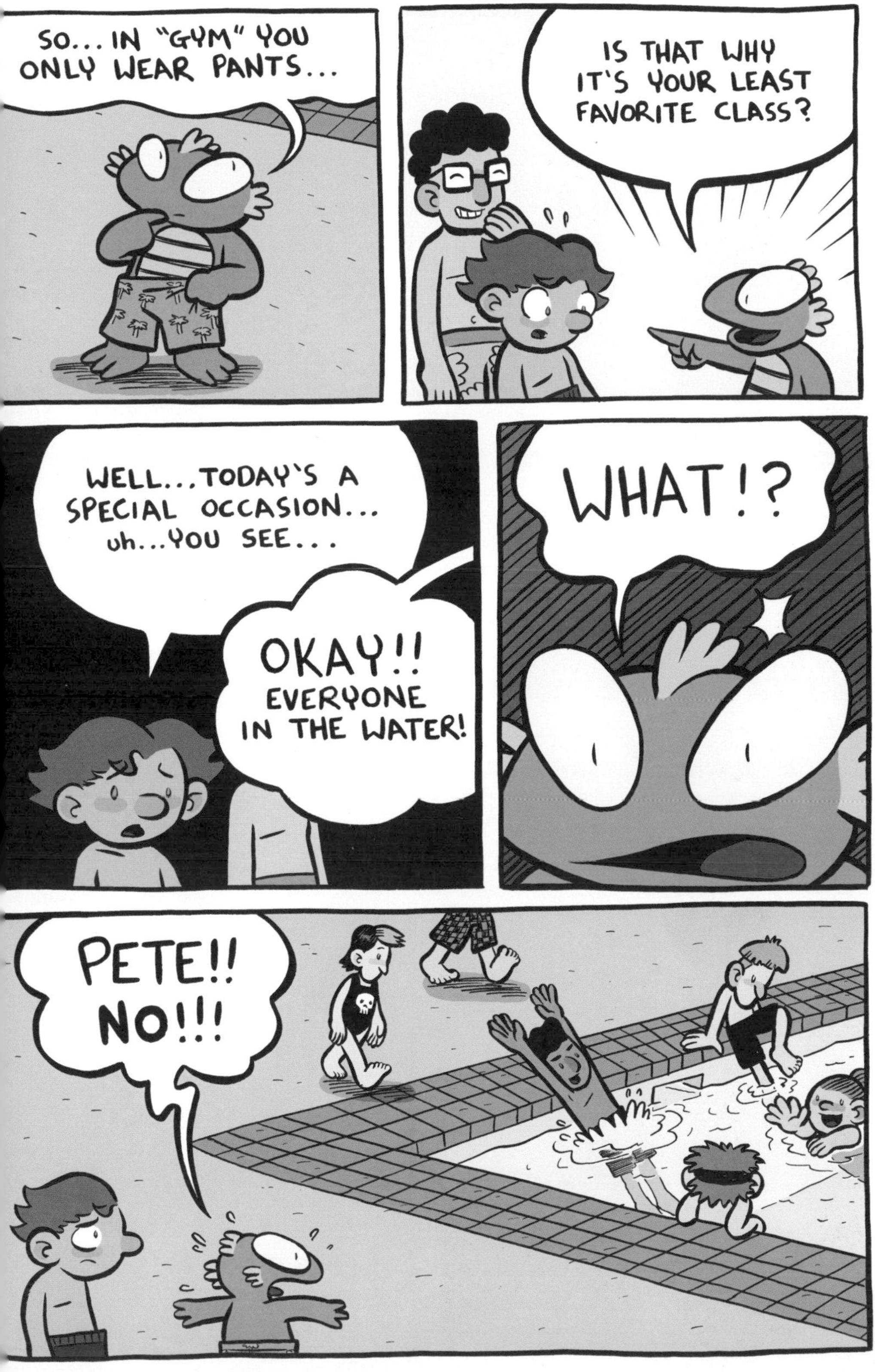
SO... IN "GYM" YOU ONLY WEAR PANTS...
IS THAT WHY IT'S YOUR LEAST FAVORITE CLASS?
WELL...TODAY'S A SPECIAL OCCASION... uh...YOU SEE...
OKAY!! EVERYONE IN THE WATER!
WHAT!?
PETE!! NO!!!

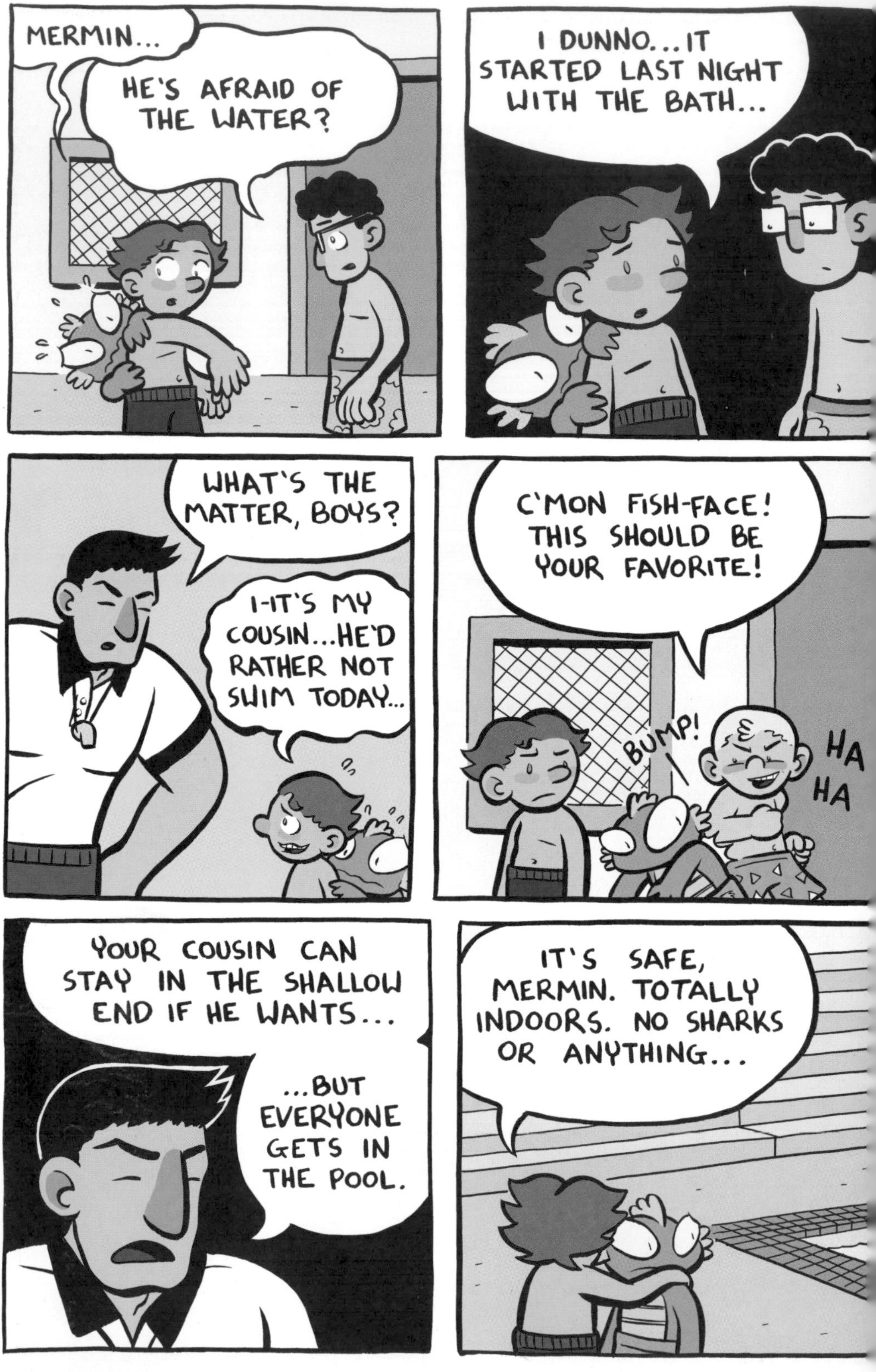
MERMIN...
HE'S AFRAID OF THE WATER?
I DUNNO...IT STARTED LAST NIGHT WITH THE BATH...
WHAT'S THE MATTER, BOYS?
I-IT'S MY COUSIN...HE'D RATHER NOT SWIM TODAY...
C'MON FISH-FACE! THIS SHOULD BE YOUR FAVORITE!
BUMP!
HA HA
YOUR COUSIN CAN STAY IN THE SHALLOW END IF HE WANTS...
...BUT EVERYONE GETS IN THE POOL.
IT'S SAFE, MERMIN. TOTALLY INDOORS. NO SHARKS OR ANYTHING...

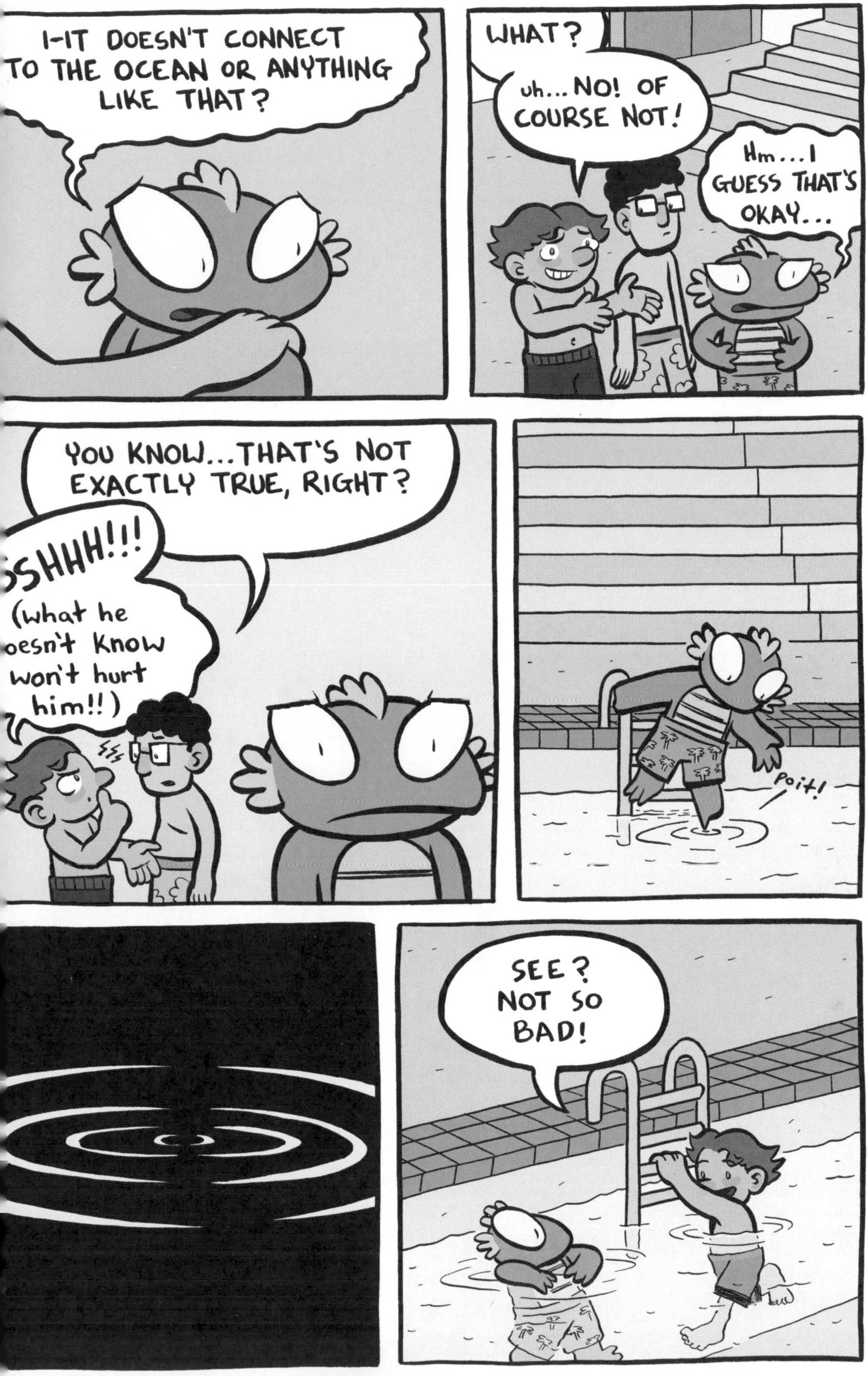

I-IT DOESN'T CONNECT TO THE OCEAN OR ANYTHING LIKE THAT?
WHAT?
uh... NO! OF COURSE NOT!
Hm...I GUESS THAT'S OKAY...
YOU KNOW...THAT'S NOT EXACTLY TRUE, RIGHT?
SHHH!!!
(what he oesn't know won't hurt him!!)
Poit!
SEE? NOT SO BAD!

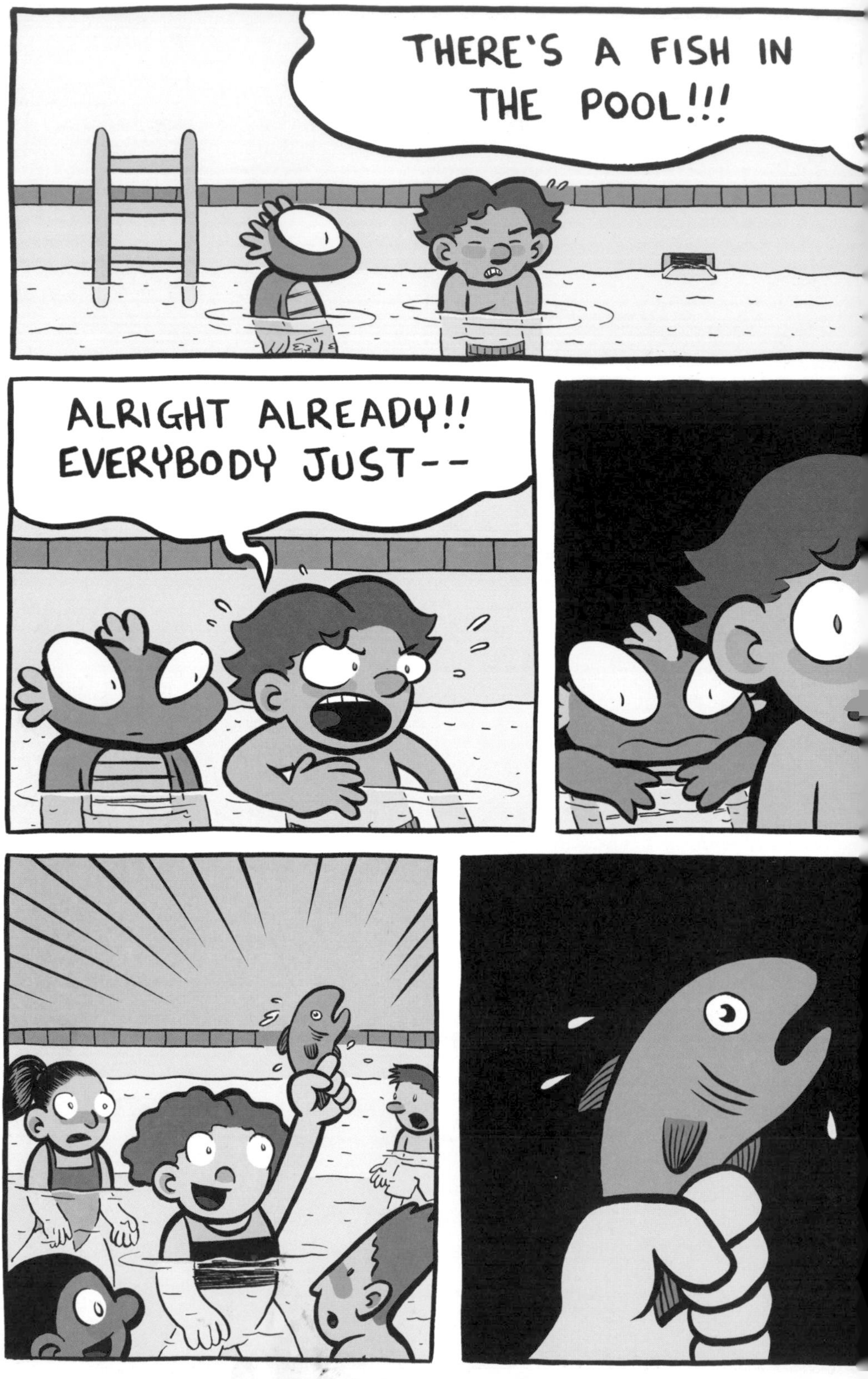
THERE'S A FISH IN THE POOL!!!
ALRIGHT ALREADY!! EVERYBODY JUST--

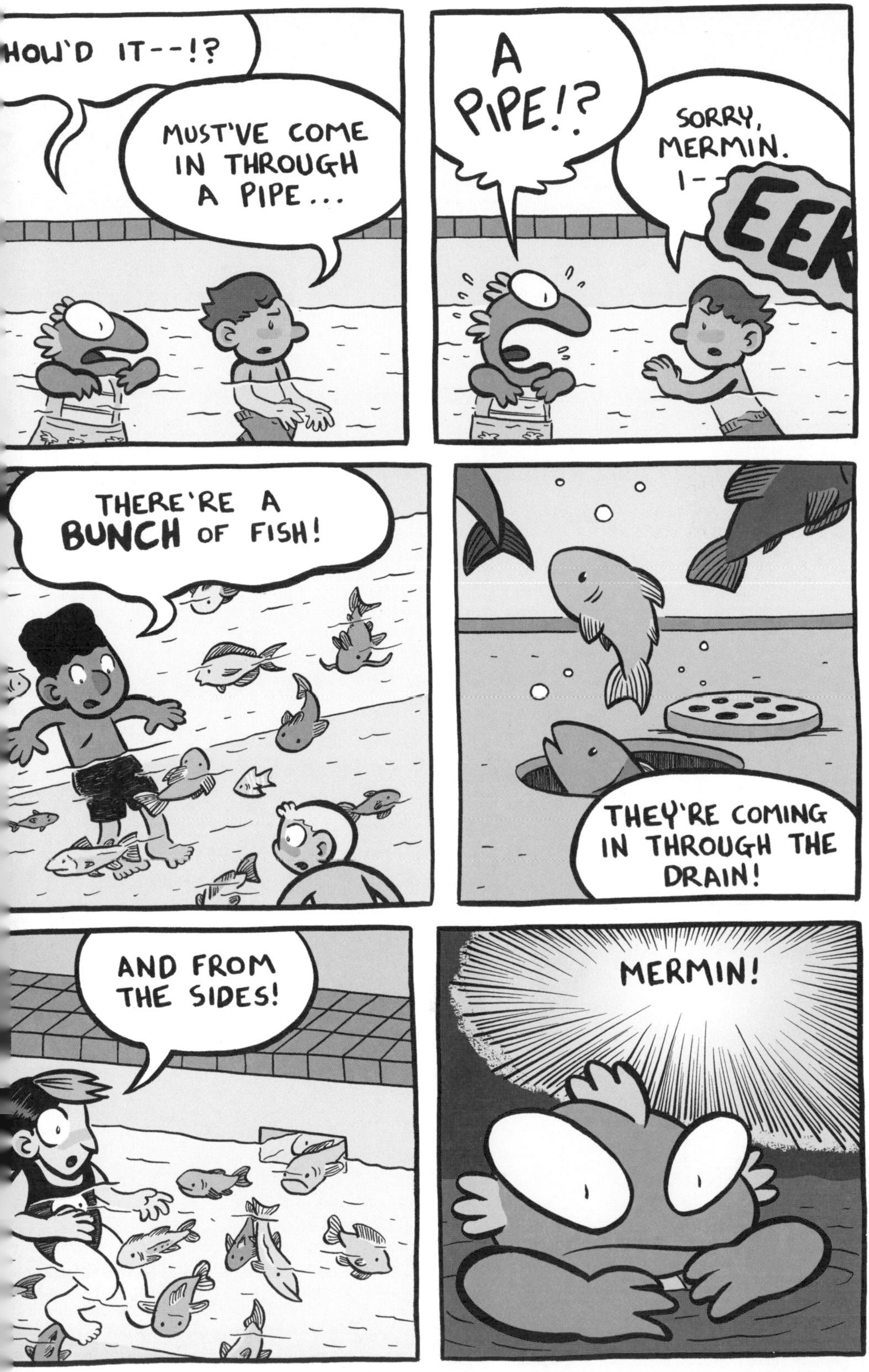
HOW'D IT--!?
MUST'VE COME IN THROUGH A PIPE...
A PIPE!?
SORRY, MERMIN. I--
EEK
THERE'RE A BUNCH OF FISH!
THEY'RE COMING IN THROUGH THE DRAIN!
AND FROM THE SIDES!
MERMIN!

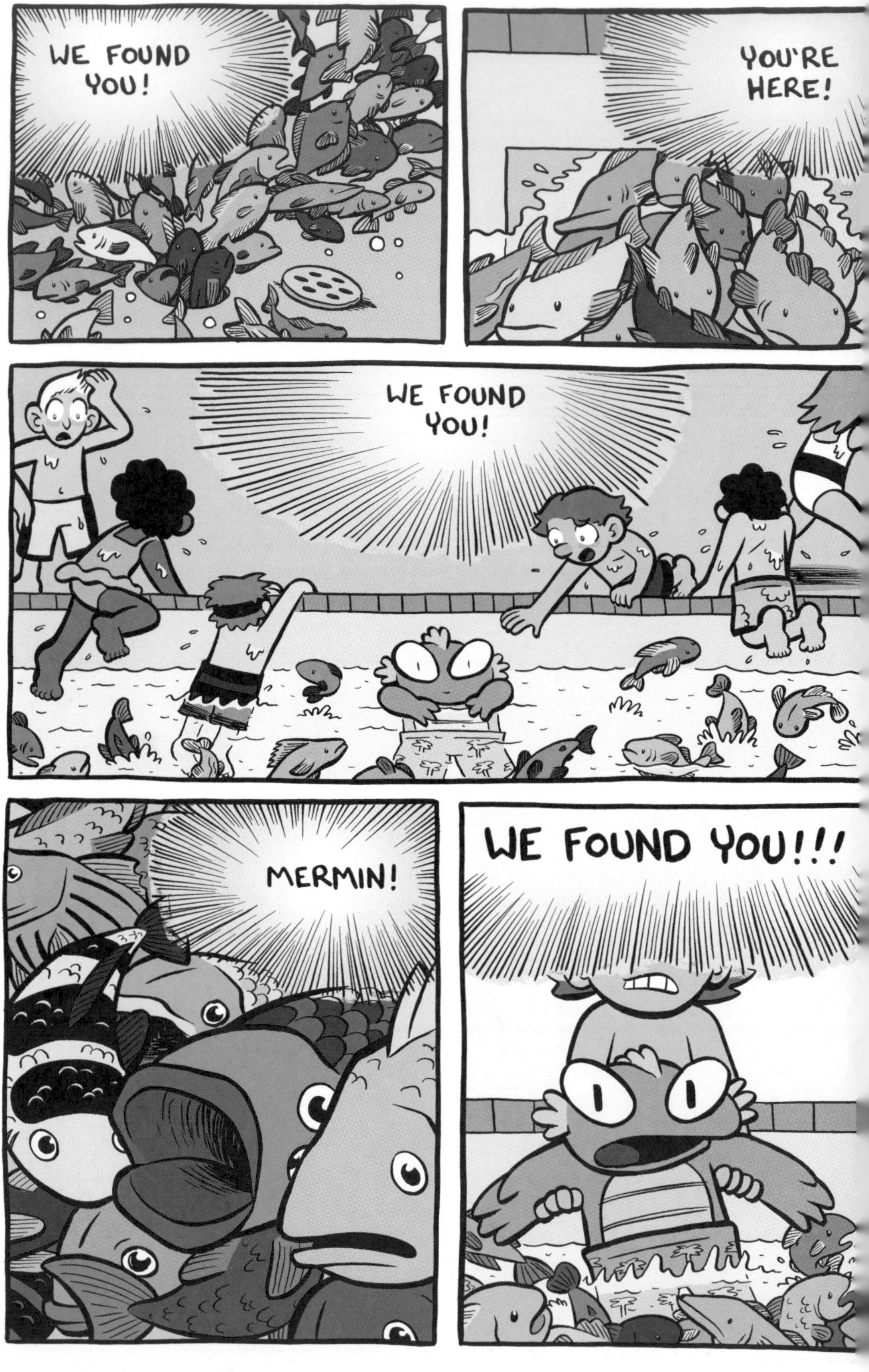
WE FOUND YOU!
YOU'RE HERE!
WE FOUND YOU!
MERMIN!
WE FOUND YOU!!!

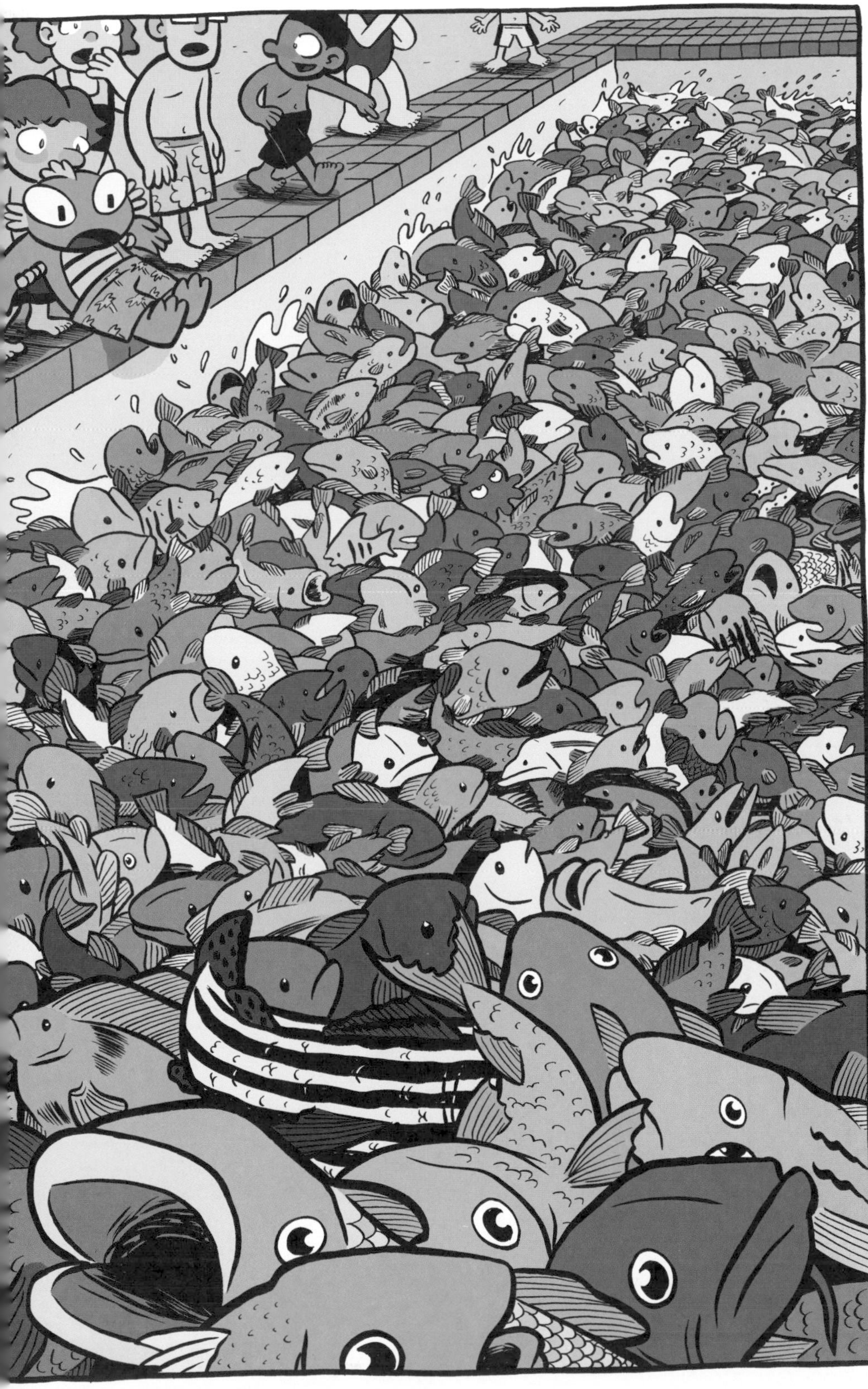

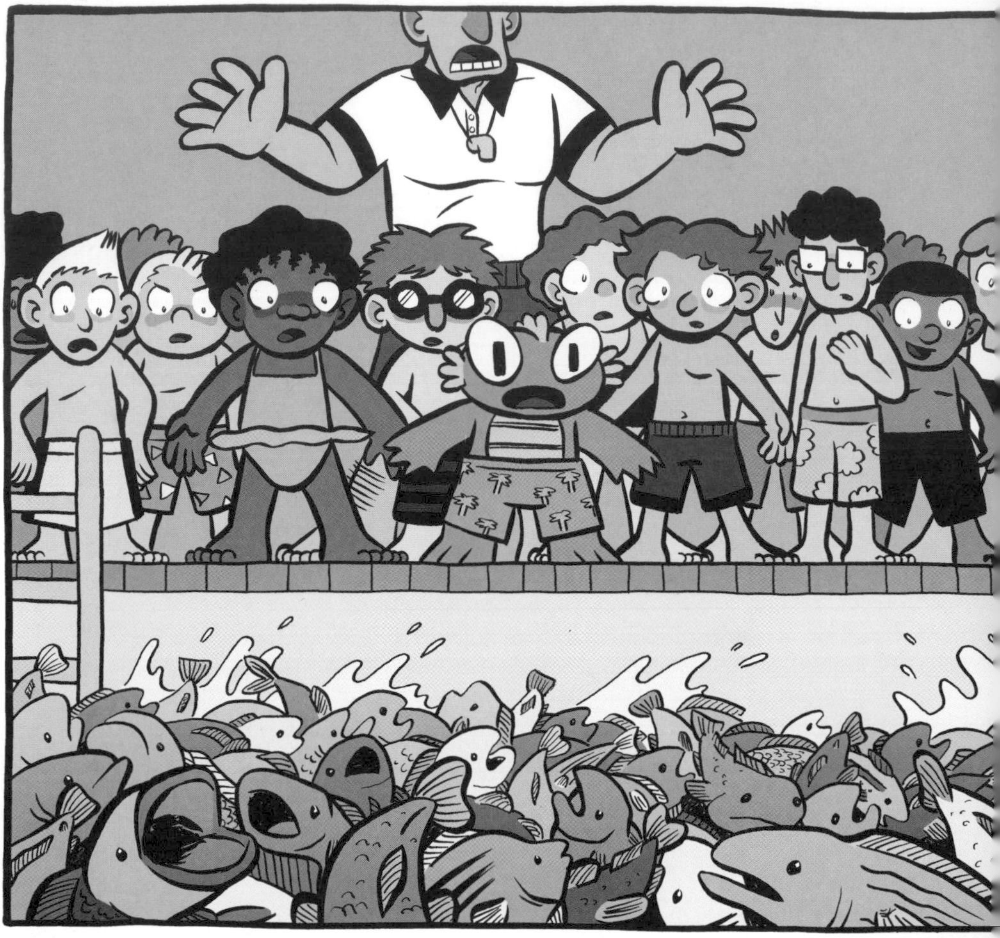

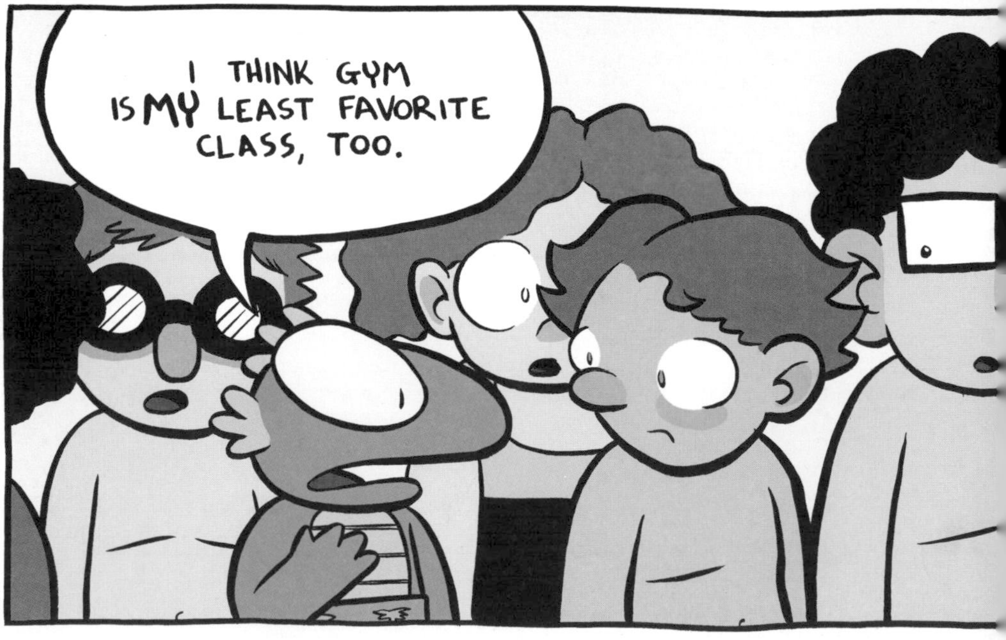
I THINK GYM IS MY LEAST FAVORITE CLASS, TOO.

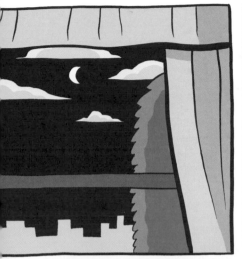

...AT LOCAL TEAWATER ELEMENTARY TODAY.

SPECIALISTS HAVE NOT YET DETERMINED THE CAUSE OF THIS **FISHY** PHENOMENON.

NEWS@10

Heh heh ... THANKFULLY WE SNUCK MERMIN OUT BEFORE THE REPORTERS ARRIVED...

PETER...WE REALLY SHOULD TAKE HIM TO THE AUTHORITIES...

NOD

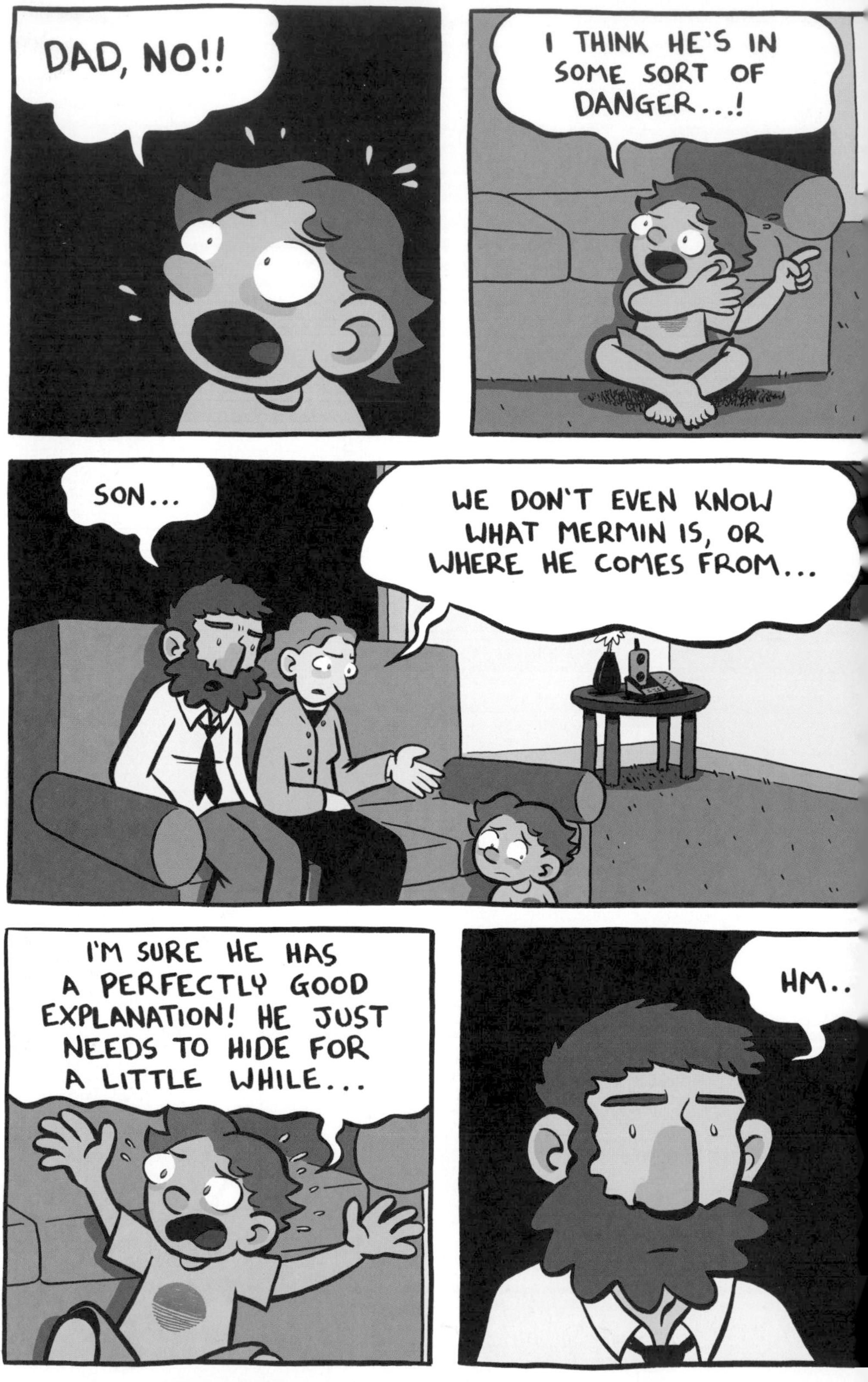
DAD, NO!!
I THINK HE'S IN SOME SORT OF DANGER...!
SON...
WE DON'T EVEN KNOW WHAT MERMIN IS, OR WHERE HE COMES FROM...
I'M SURE HE HAS A PERFECTLY GOOD EXPLANATION! HE JUST NEEDS TO HIDE FOR A LITTLE WHILE...
HM..

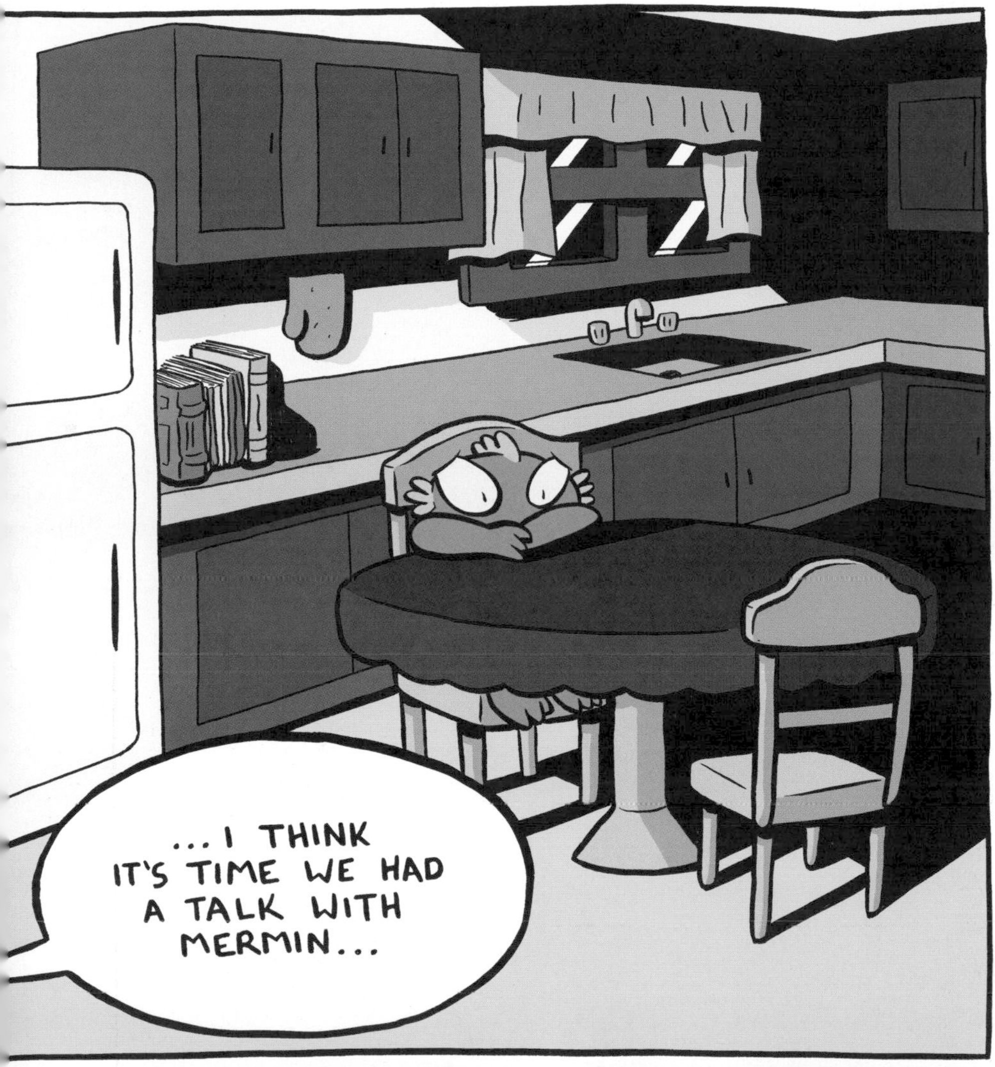
...I THINK IT'S TIME WE HAD A TALK WITH MERMIN...

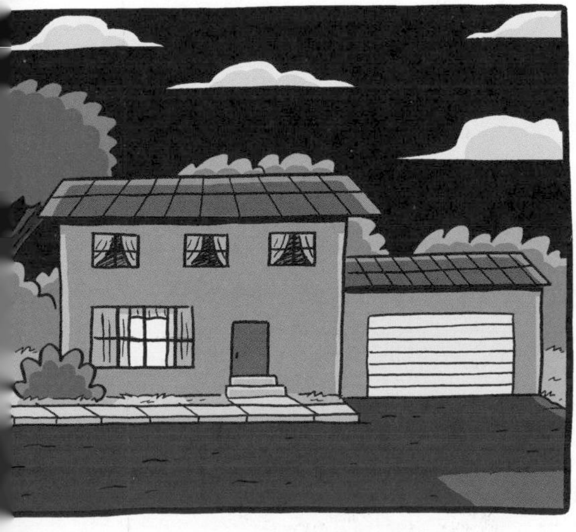

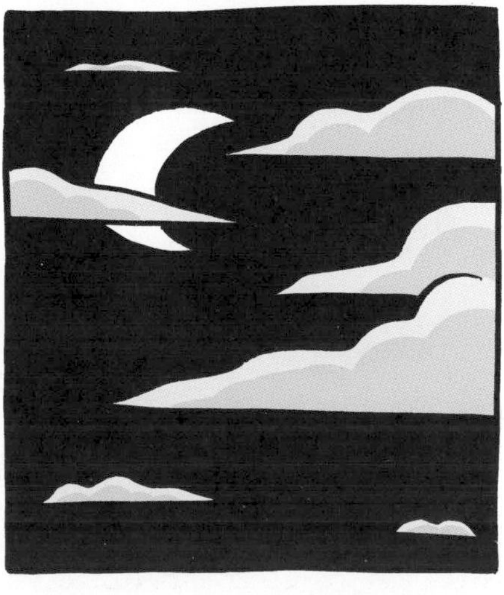

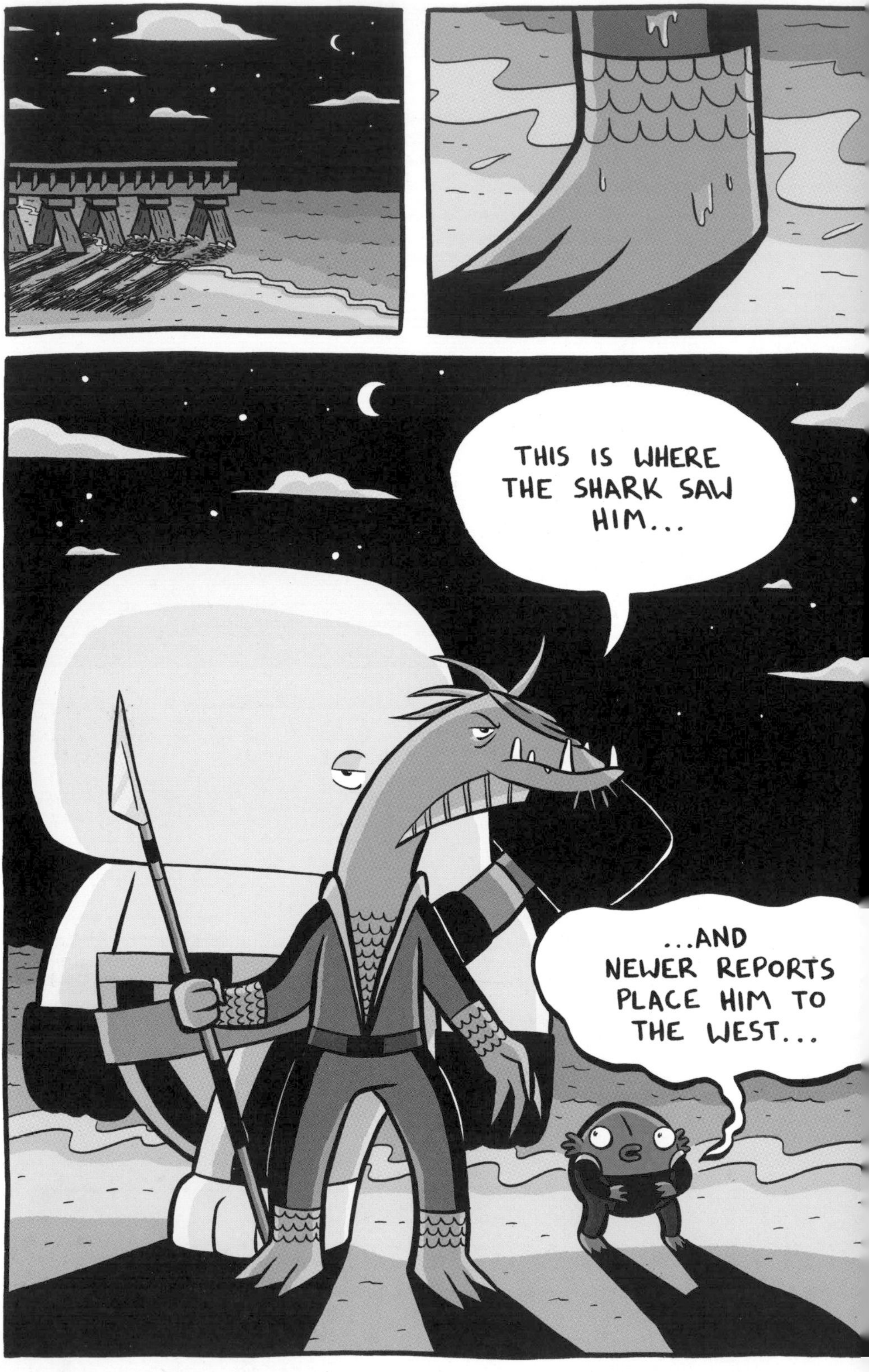
THIS IS WHERE THE SHARK SAW HIM...
...AND NEWER REPORTS PLACE HIM TO THE WEST...

CHAPTER TWO

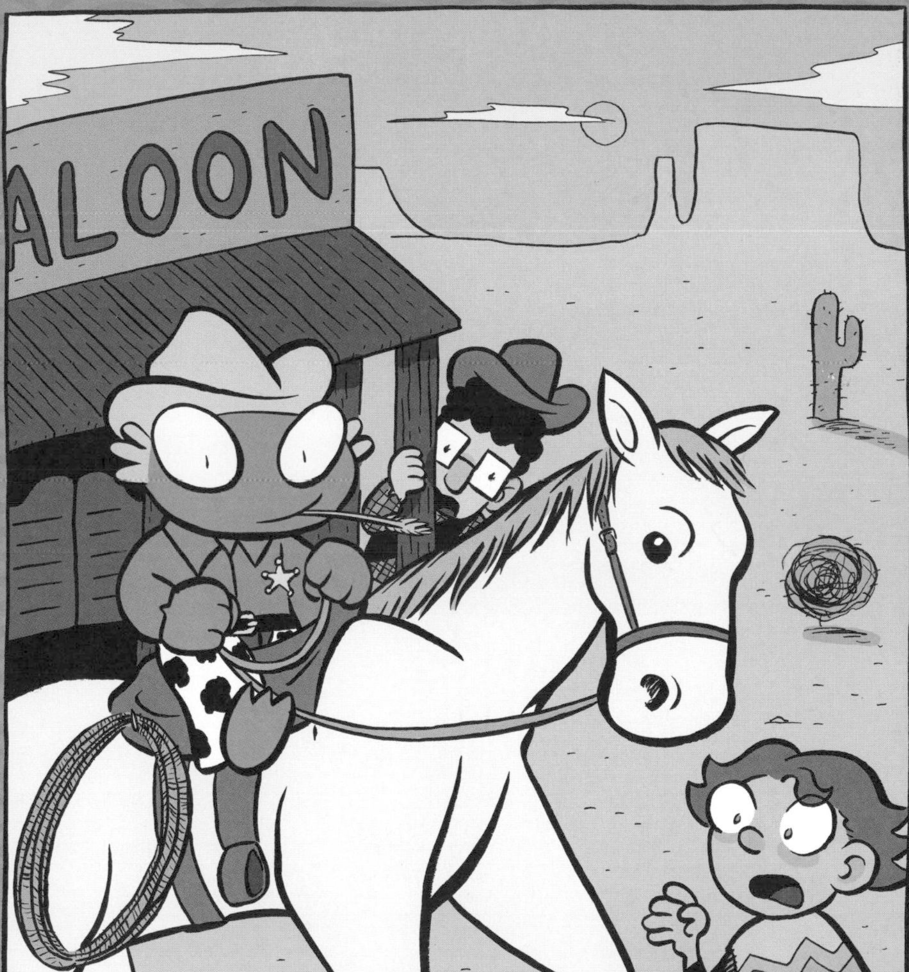
ALOON

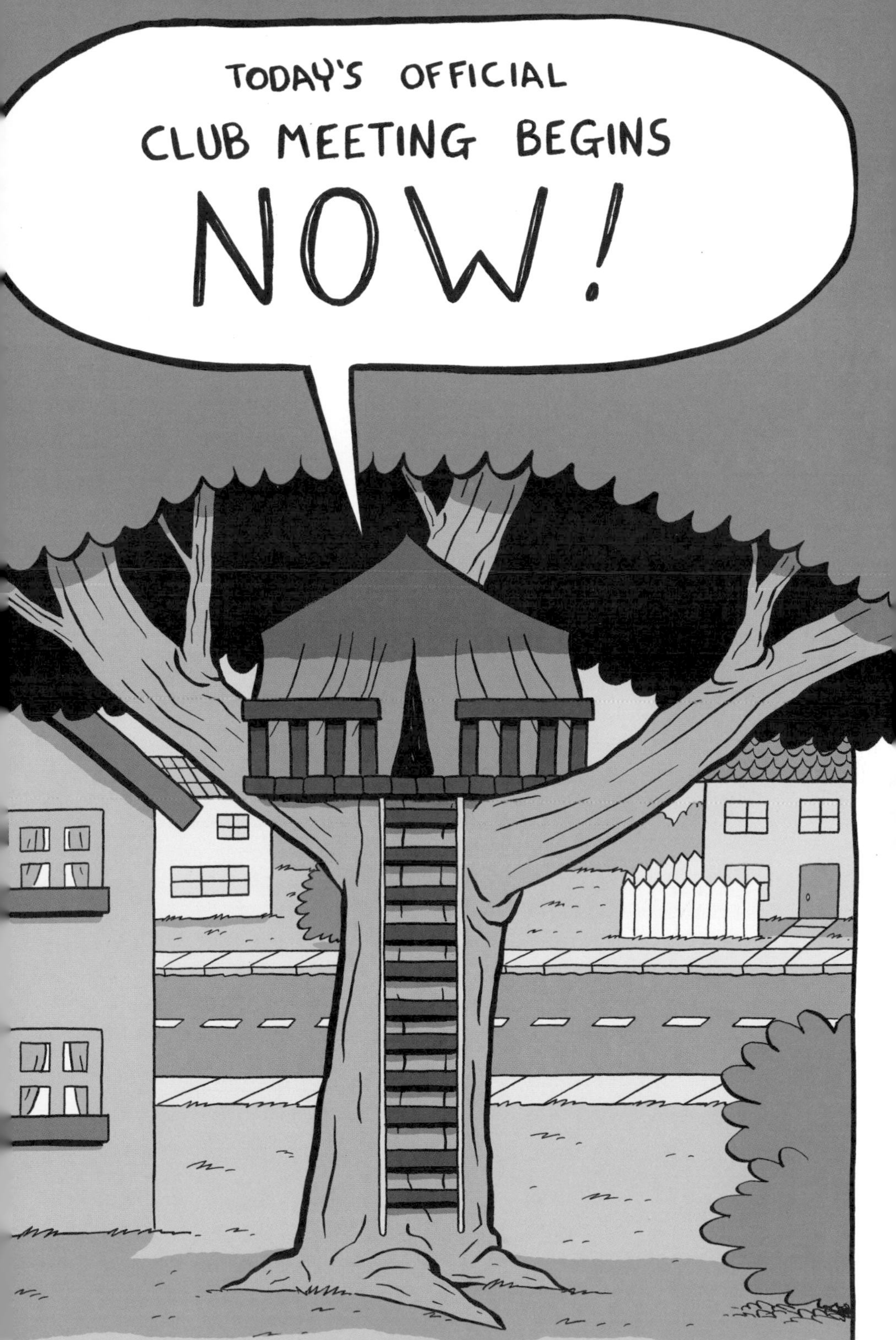
TODAY'S OFFICIAL CLUB MEETING BEGINS NOW!

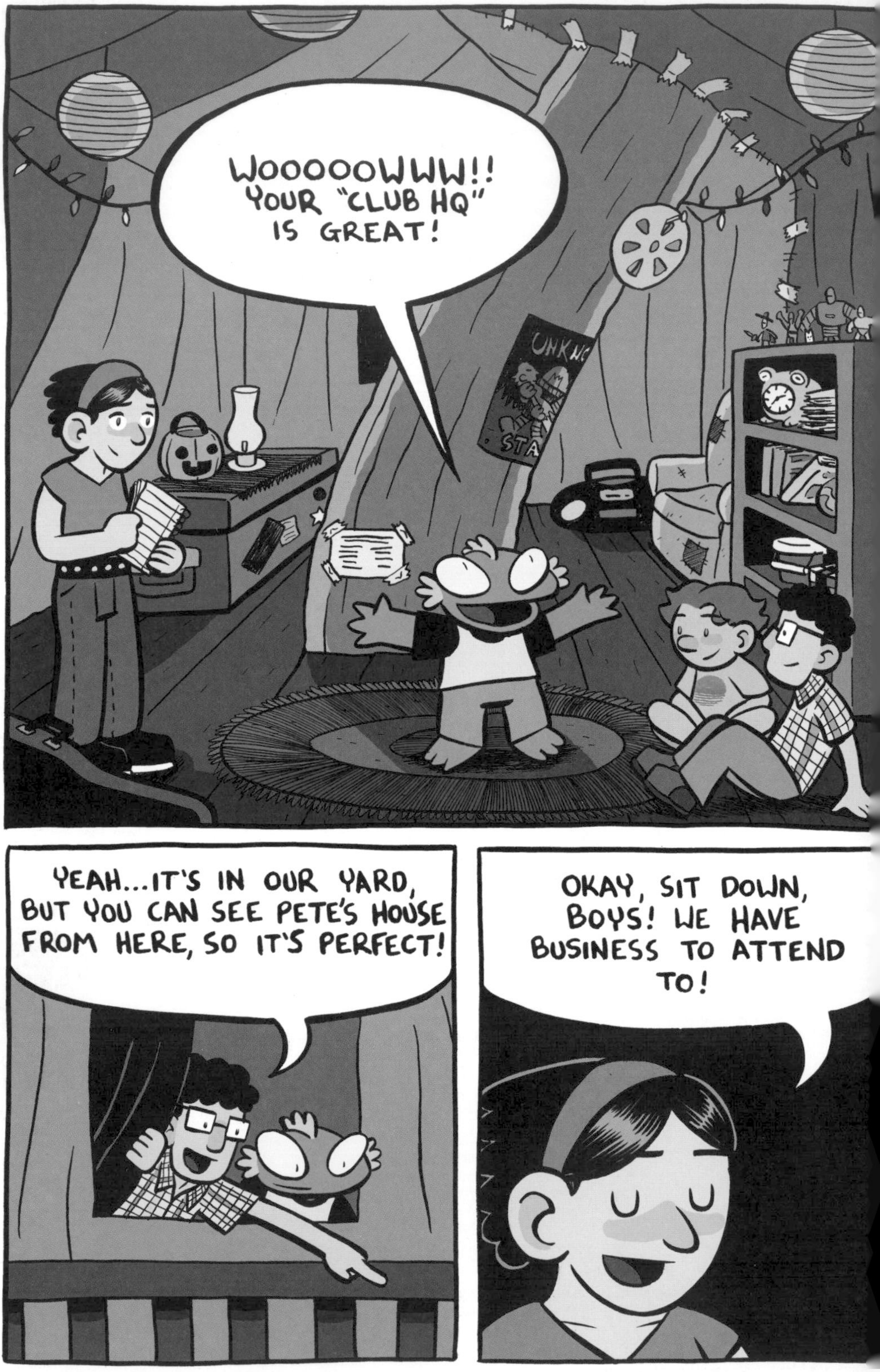
WOOOOOWWW!! YOUR "CLUB HQ" IS GREAT!
YEAH...IT'S IN OUR YARD, BUT YOU CAN SEE PETE'S HOUSE FROM HERE, SO IT'S PERFECT!
OKAY, SIT DOWN, BOYS! WE HAVE BUSINESS TO ATTEND TO!

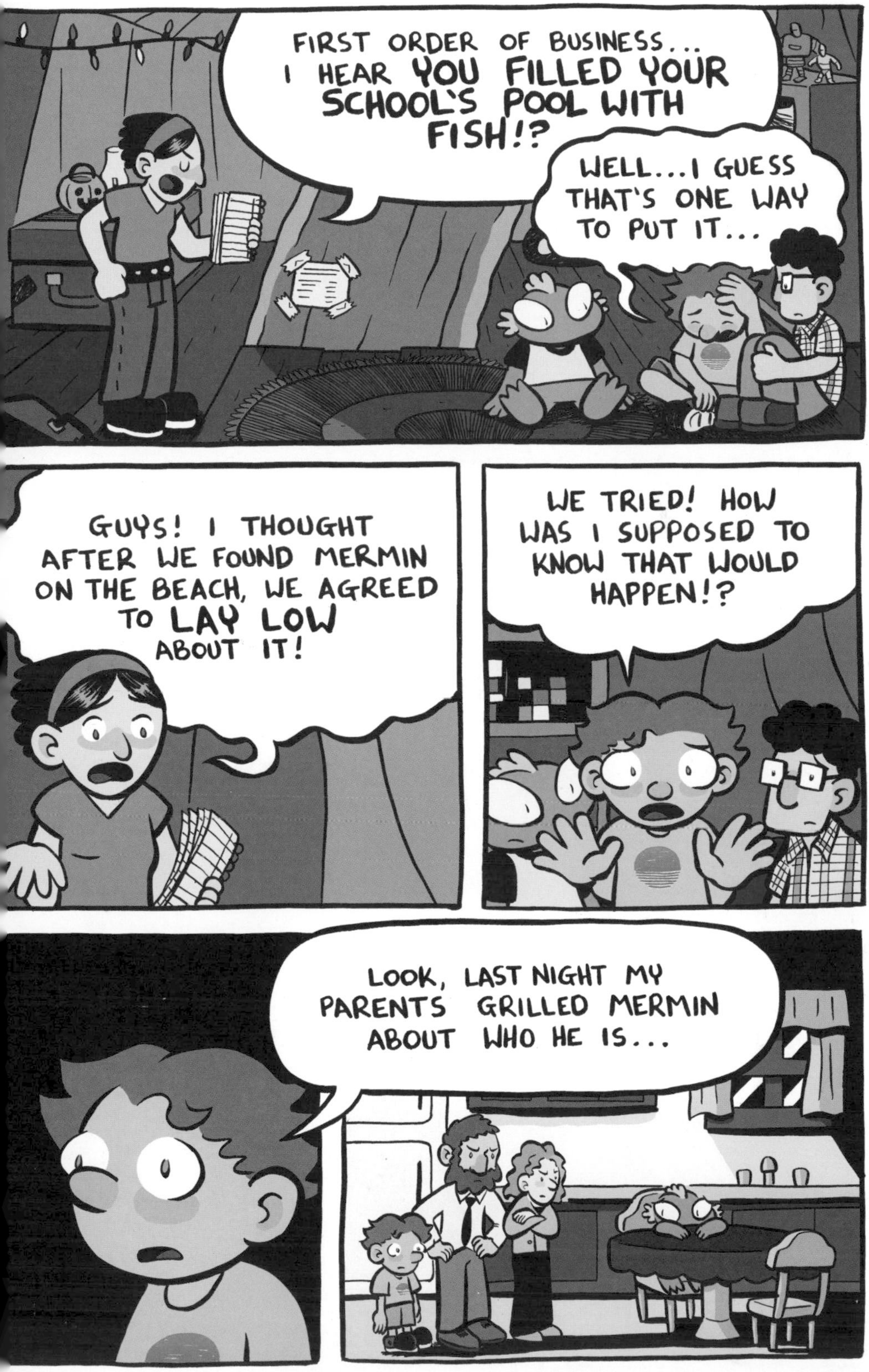
FIRST ORDER OF BUSINESS... I HEAR YOU FILLED YOUR SCHOOL'S POOL WITH FISH!?
WELL...I GUESS THAT'S ONE WAY TO PUT IT...
GUYS! I THOUGHT AFTER WE FOUND MERMIN ON THE BEACH, WE AGREED TO LAY LOW ABOUT IT!
WE TRIED! HOW WAS I SUPPOSED TO KNOW THAT WOULD HAPPEN!?
LOOK, LAST NIGHT MY PARENTS GRILLED MERMIN ABOUT WHO HE IS...

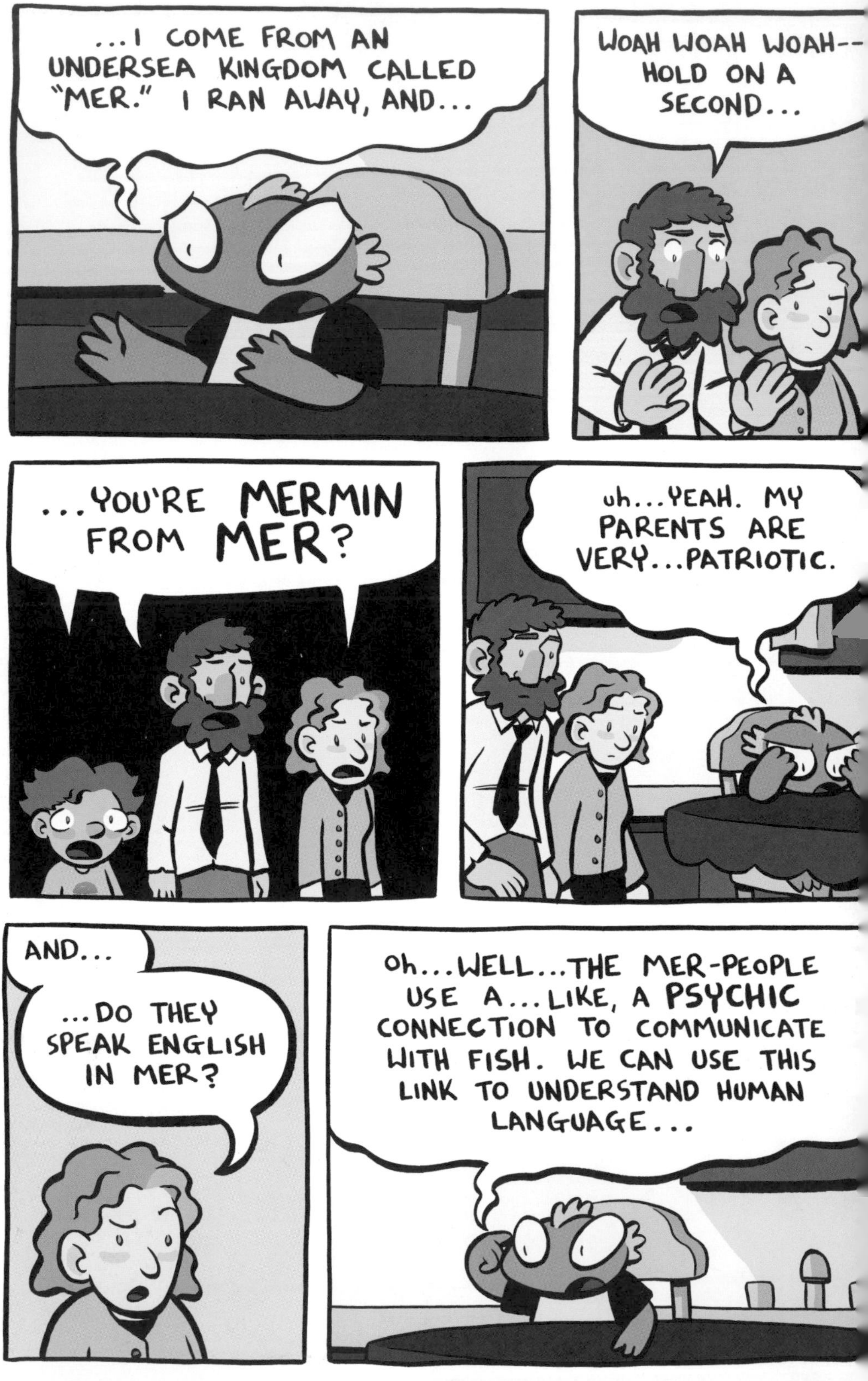
...I COME FROM AN UNDERSEA KINGDOM CALLED "MER." I RAN AWAY, AND...
WOAH WOAH WOAH-- HOLD ON A SECOND...
...YOU'RE MERMIN FROM MER?
Uh...YEAH. MY PARENTS ARE VERY...PATRIOTIC.
AND...
...DO THEY SPEAK ENGLISH IN MER?
Oh...WELL...THE MER-PEOPLE USE A...LIKE, A PSYCHIC CONNECTION TO COMMUNICATE WITH FISH. WE CAN USE THIS LINK TO UNDERSTAND HUMAN LANGUAGE...

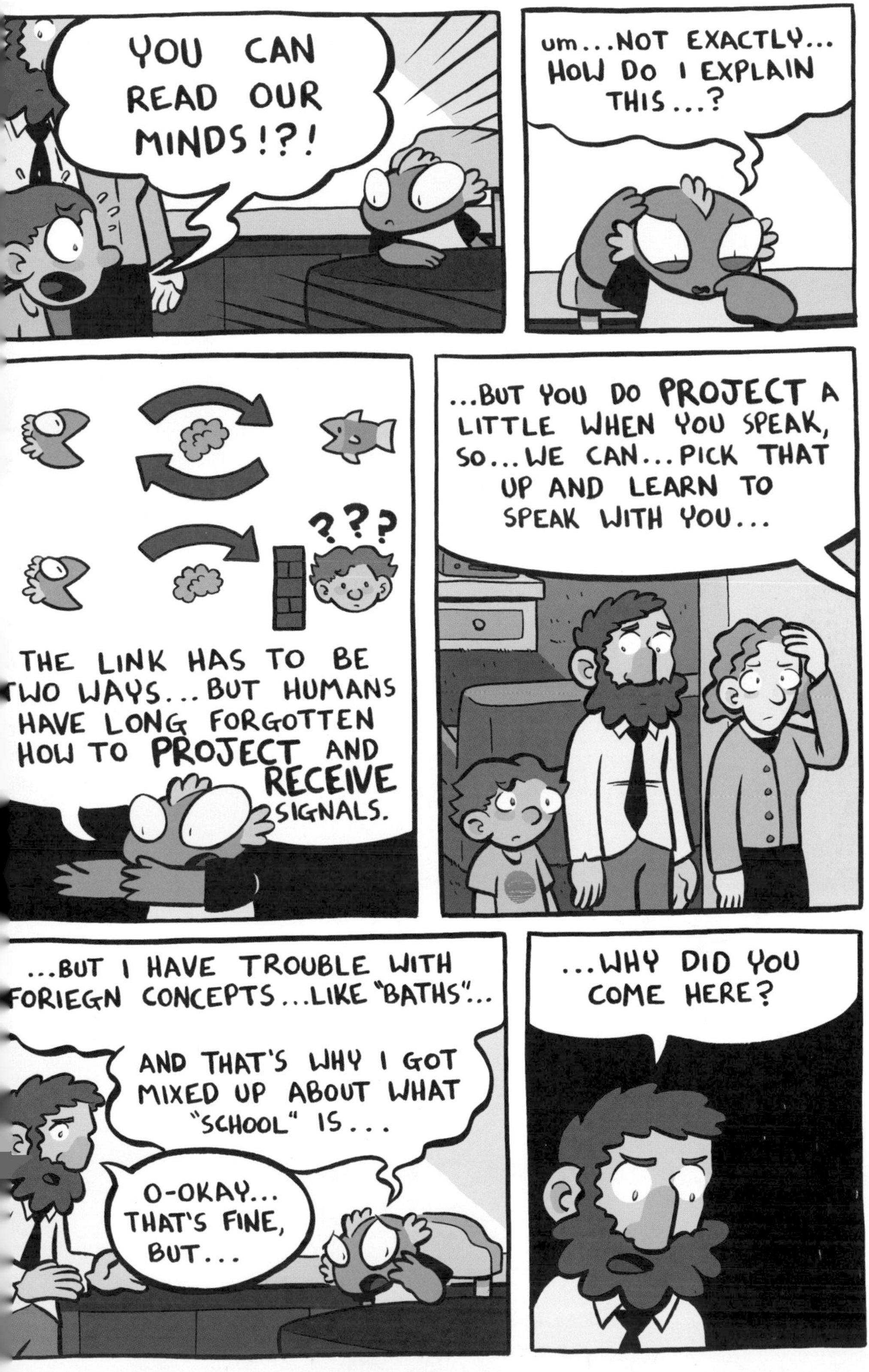
YOU CAN READ OUR MINDS!?!
um...NOT EXACTLY... HOW DO I EXPLAIN THIS...?
THE LINK HAS TO BE TWO WAYS... BUT HUMANS HAVE LONG FORGOTTEN HOW TO PROJECT AND RECEIVE SIGNALS.
???
...BUT YOU DO PROJECT A LITTLE WHEN YOU SPEAK, SO... WE CAN... PICK THAT UP AND LEARN TO SPEAK WITH YOU...
...BUT I HAVE TROUBLE WITH FORIEGN CONCEPTS...LIKE "BATHS"...
AND THAT'S WHY I GOT MIXED UP ABOUT WHAT "SCHOOL" IS...
O-OKAY... THAT'S FINE, BUT...
...WHY DID YOU COME HERE?

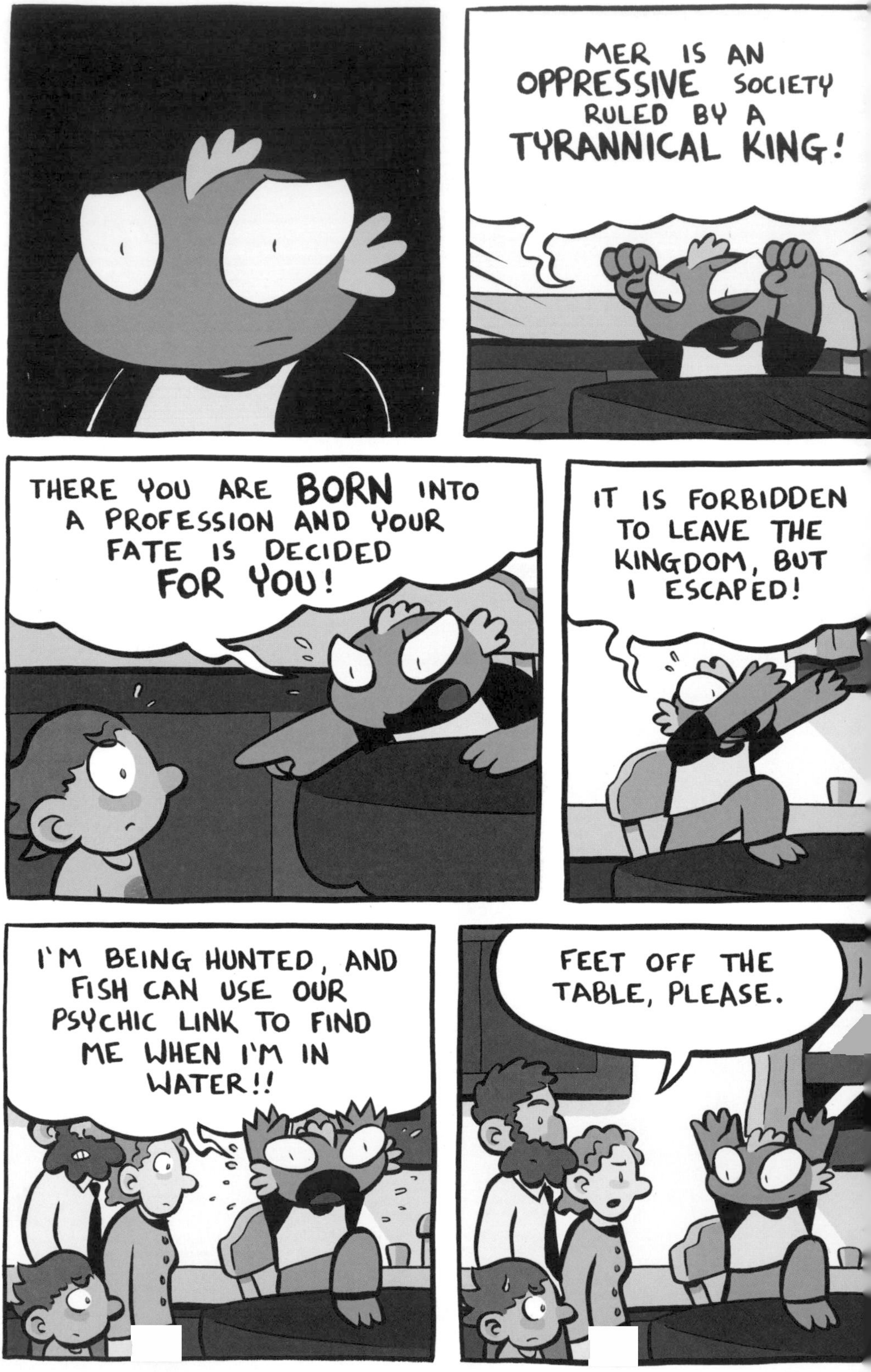
MER IS AN OPPRESSIVE SOCIETY RULED BY A TYRANNICAL KING!
THERE YOU ARE BORN INTO A PROFESSION AND YOUR FATE IS DECIDED FOR YOU!
IT IS FORBIDDEN TO LEAVE THE KINGDOM, BUT I ESCAPED!
I'M BEING HUNTED, AND FISH CAN USE OUR PSYCHIC LINK TO FIND ME WHEN I'M IN WATER!!
FEET OFF THE TABLE, PLEASE.

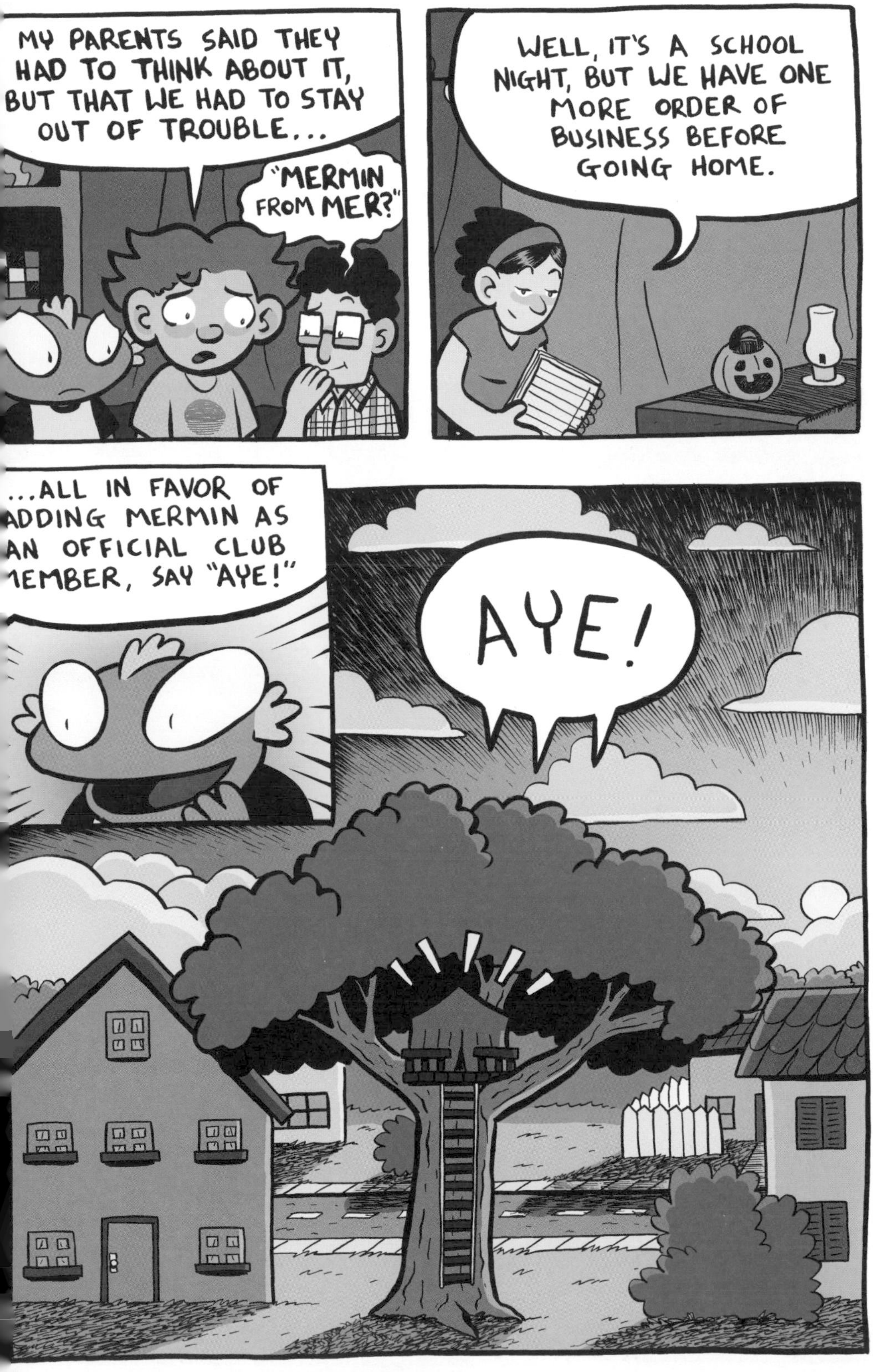
MY PARENTS SAID THEY HAD TO THINK ABOUT IT, BUT THAT WE HAD TO STAY OUT OF TROUBLE...
"MERMIN FROM MER?"
WELL, IT'S A SCHOOL NIGHT, BUT WE HAVE ONE MORE ORDER OF BUSINESS BEFORE GOING HOME.
...ALL IN FAVOR OF ADDING MERMIN AS AN OFFICIAL CLUB MEMBER, SAY "AYE!"
AYE!

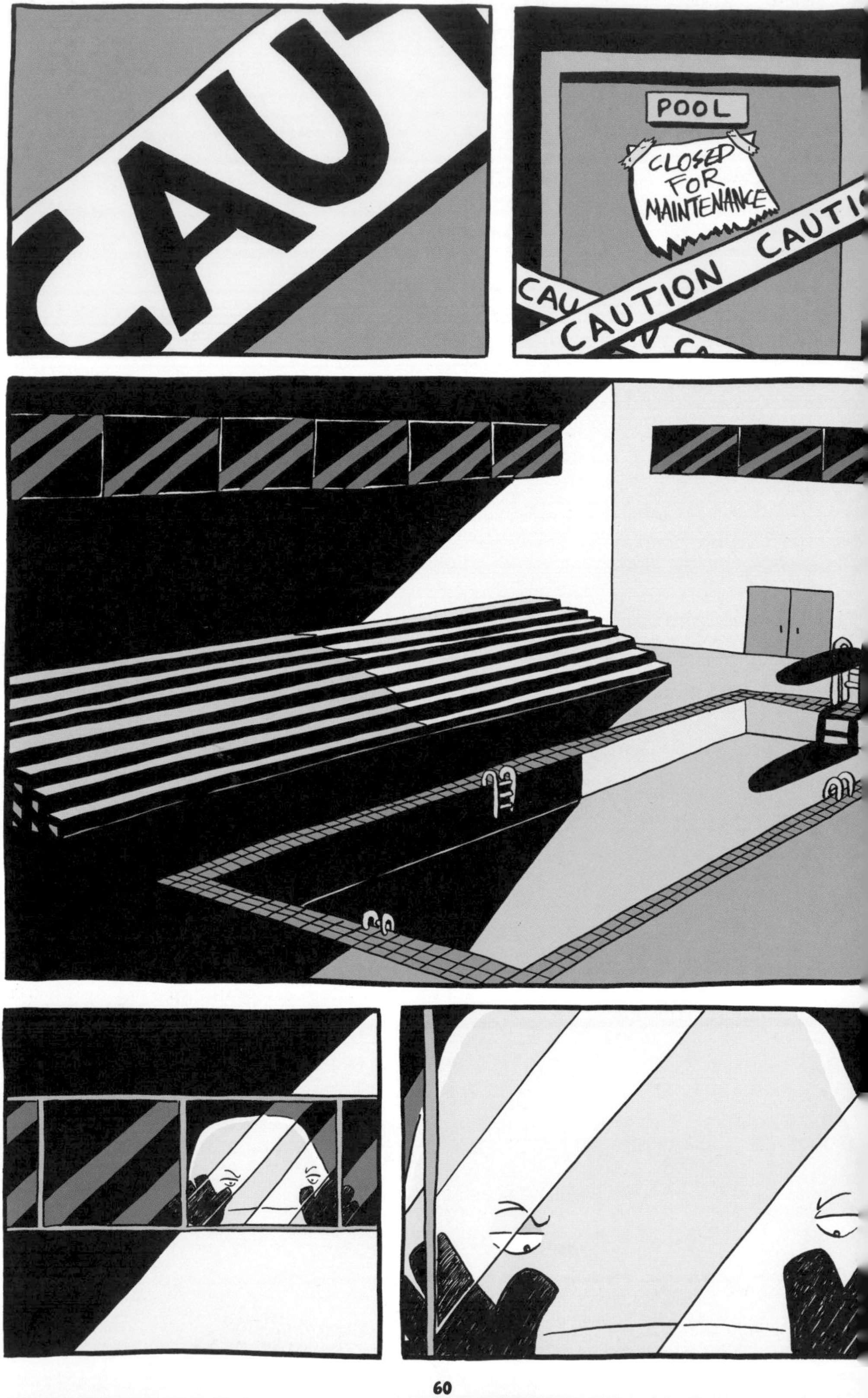
CAU
POOL
CLOSED FOR MAINTENANCE
CAUTION
CAUTI
CAU

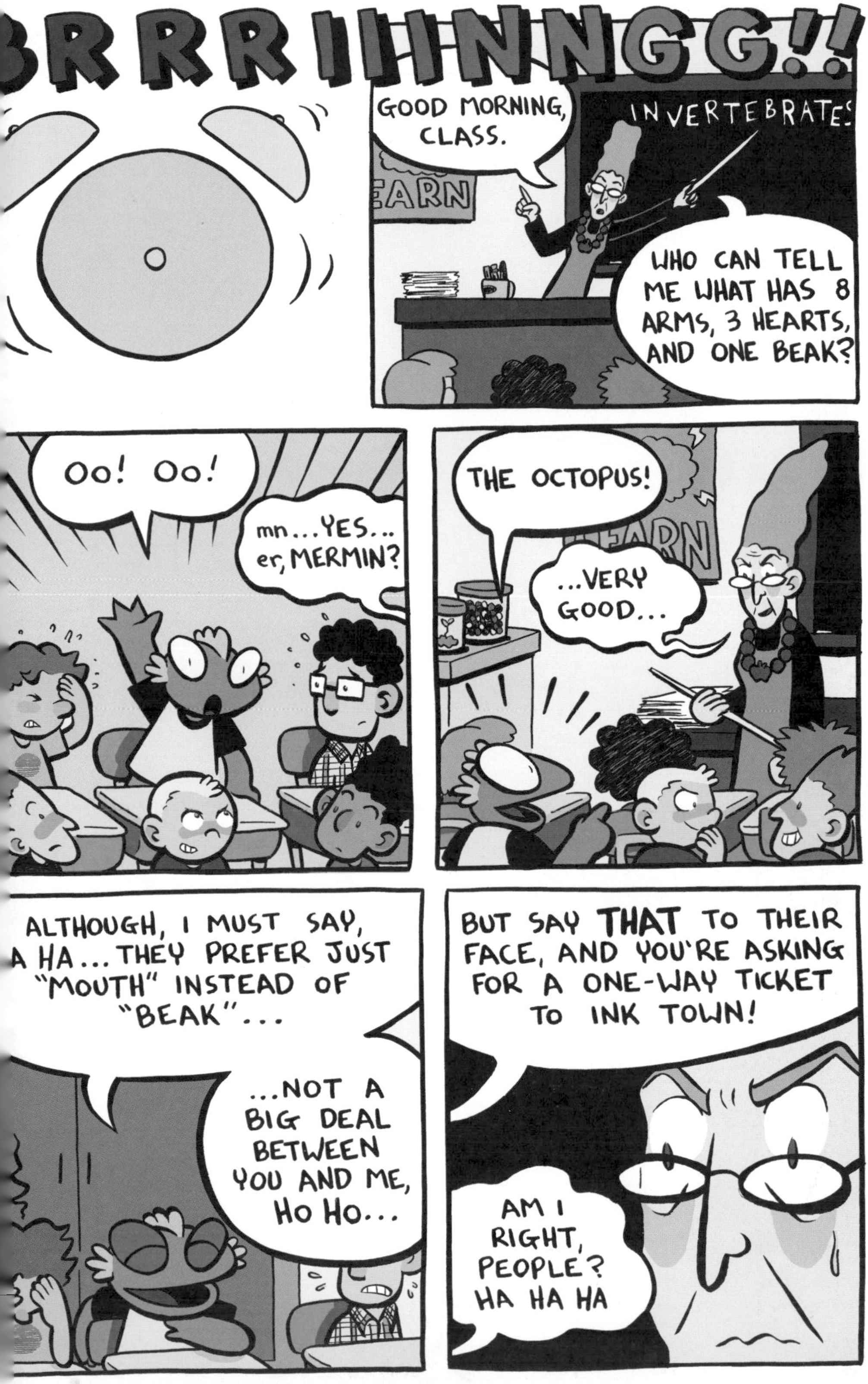
BRRRIIIINNGG!!
GOOD MORNING, CLASS.
INVERTEBRATES
EARN
WHO CAN TELL ME WHAT HAS 8 ARMS, 3 HEARTS, AND ONE BEAK?
Oo! Oo!
mn... YES... er, MERMIN?
THE OCTOPUS!
...VERY GOOD...
ALTHOUGH, I MUST SAY, A HA... THEY PREFER JUST "MOUTH" INSTEAD OF "BEAK"...
...NOT A BIG DEAL BETWEEN YOU AND ME, HO HO...
BUT SAY THAT TO THEIR FACE, AND YOU'RE ASKING FOR A ONE-WAY TICKET TO INK TOWN!
AM I RIGHT, PEOPLE? HA HA HA

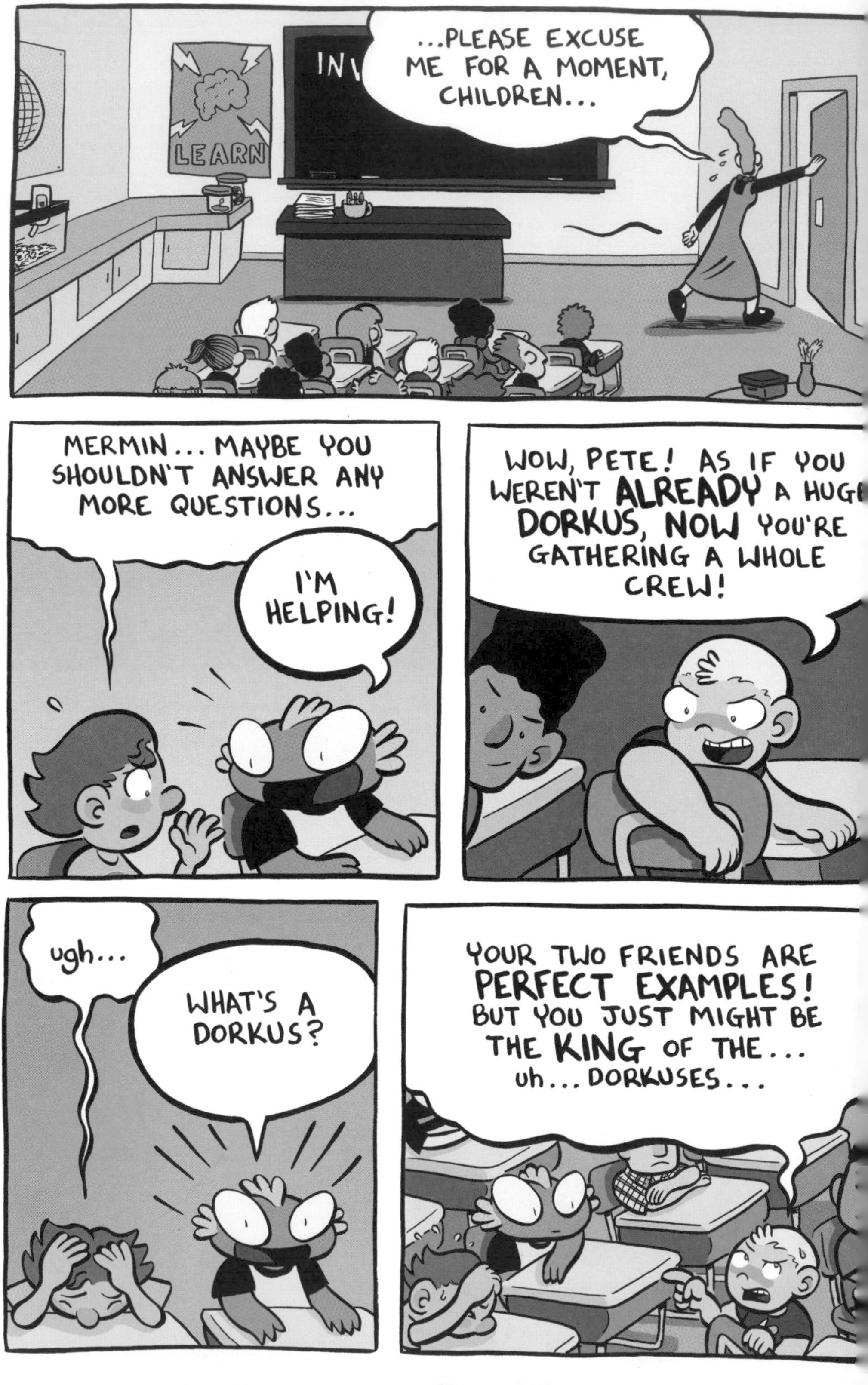
...PLEASE EXCUSE ME FOR A MOMENT, CHILDREN...
LEARN
MERMIN... MAYBE YOU SHOULDN'T ANSWER ANY MORE QUESTIONS...
I'M HELPING!
WOW, PETE! AS IF YOU WEREN'T ALREADY A HUGE DORKUS, NOW YOU'RE GATHERING A WHOLE CREW!
ugh...
WHAT'S A DORKUS?
YOUR TWO FRIENDS ARE PERFECT EXAMPLES! BUT YOU JUST MIGHT BE THE KING OF THE... uh... DORKUSES...

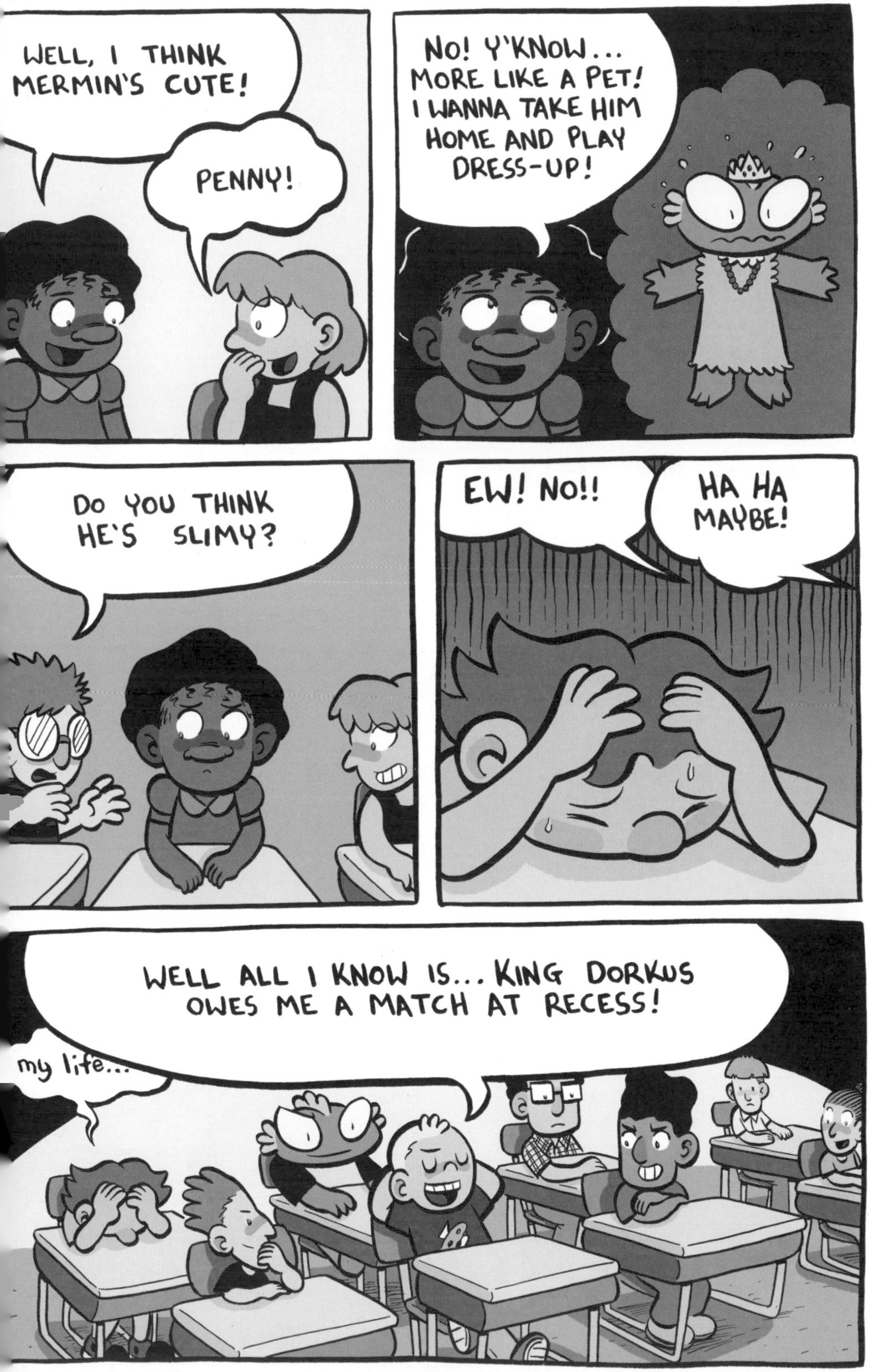
WELL, I THINK MERMIN'S CUTE!
PENNY!
NO! Y'KNOW... MORE LIKE A PET! I WANNA TAKE HIM HOME AND PLAY DRESS-UP!
DO YOU THINK HE'S SLIMY?
EW! NO!!
HA HA MAYBE!
WELL ALL I KNOW IS... KING DORKUS OWES ME A MATCH AT RECESS!
my life...

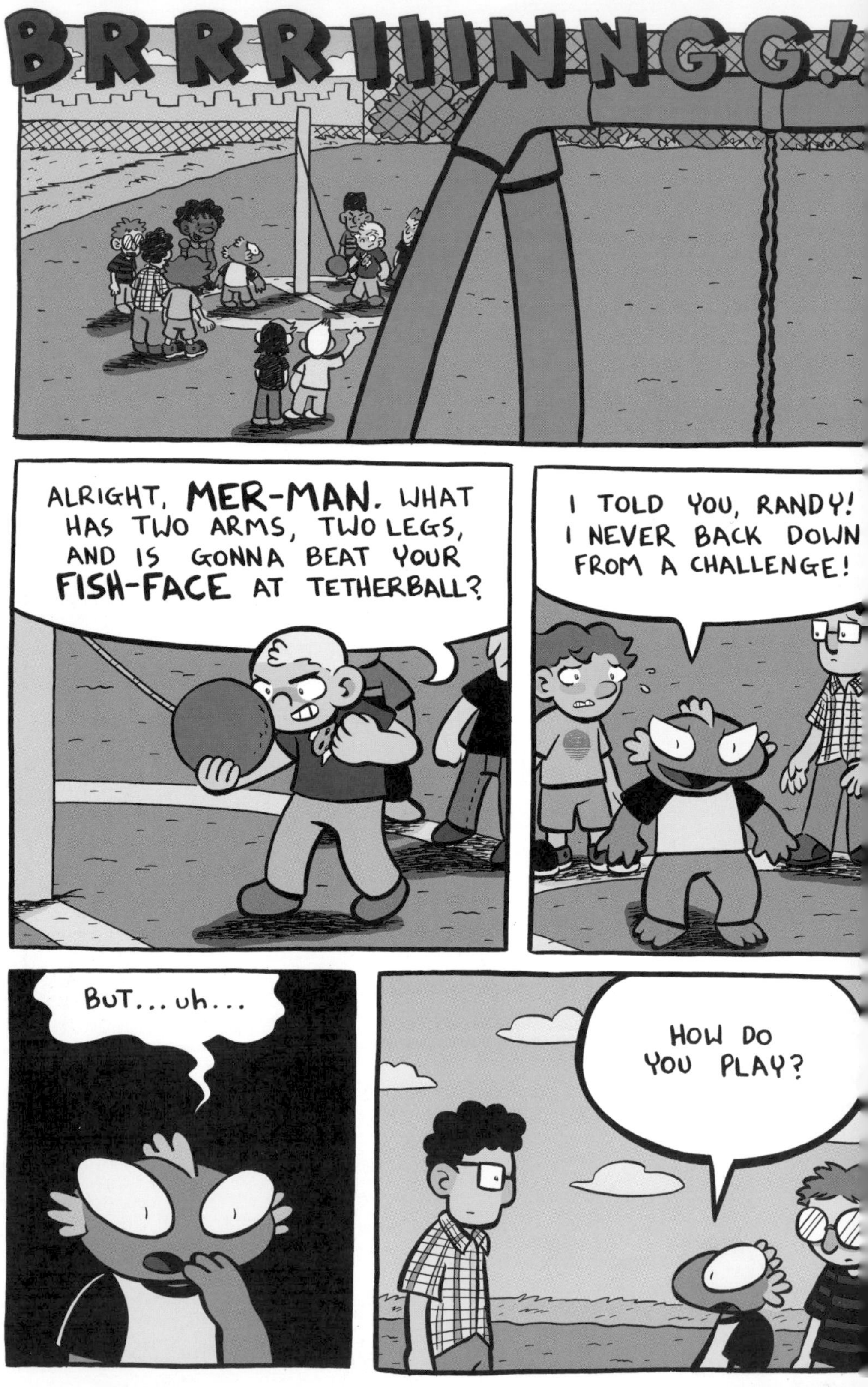
BRRRIIINNGG!
ALRIGHT, MER-MAN. WHAT HAS TWO ARMS, TWO LEGS, AND IS GONNA BEAT YOUR FISH-FACE AT TETHERBALL?
I TOLD YOU, RANDY! I NEVER BACK DOWN FROM A CHALLENGE!
BUT... uh...
HOW DO YOU PLAY?

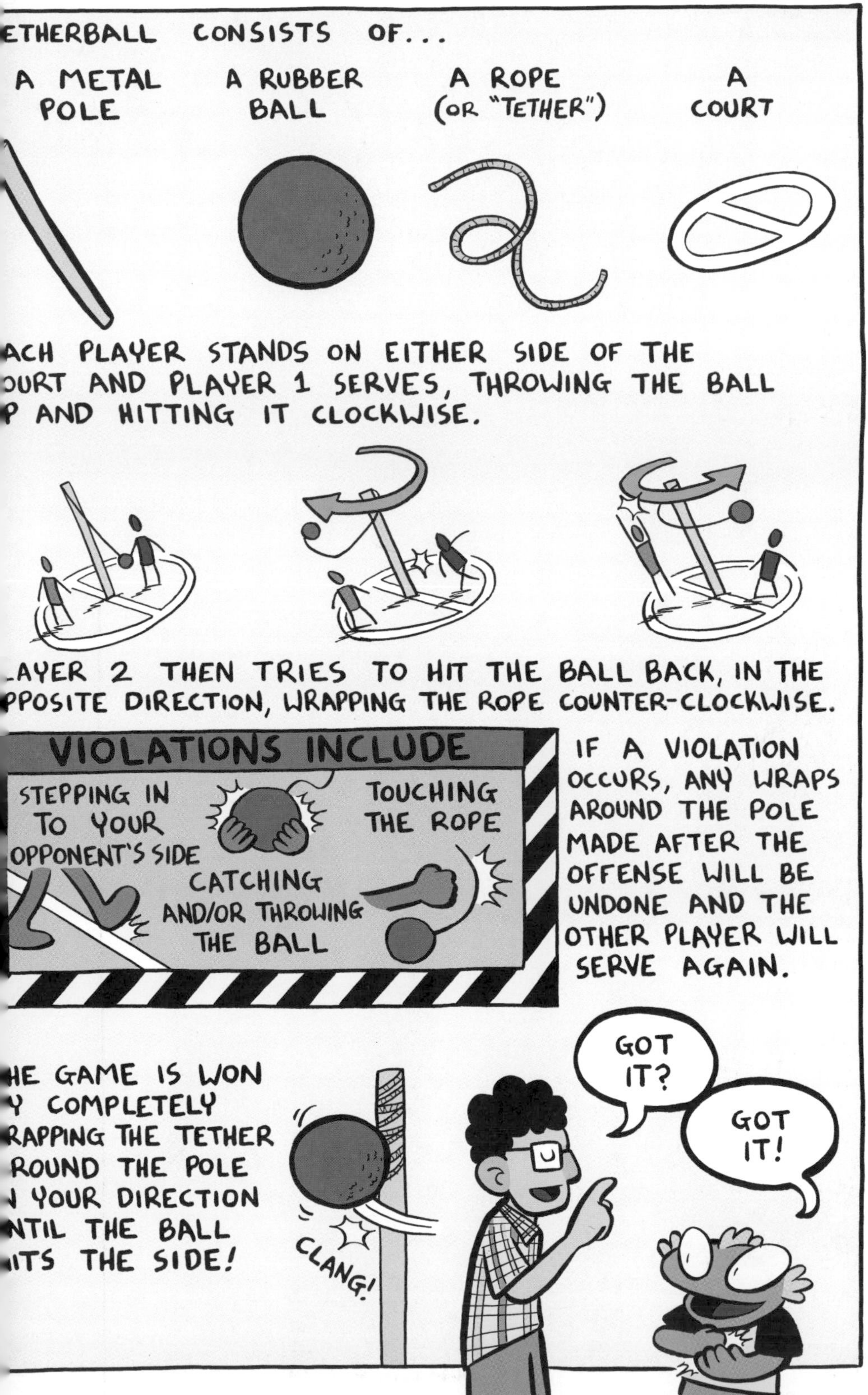
ETHERBALL CONSISTS OF...
A METAL POLE
A RUBBER BALL
A ROPE (OR "TETHER")
A COURT
ACH PLAYER STANDS ON EITHER SIDE OF THE
OURT AND PLAYER 1 SERVES, THROWING THE BALL
P AND HITTING IT CLOCKWISE.
LAYER 2 THEN TRIES TO HIT THE BALL BACK, IN THE
PPOSITE DIRECTION, WRAPPING THE ROPE COUNTER-CLOCKWISE.
VIOLATIONS INCLUDE
STEPPING IN TO YOUR OPPONENT'S SIDE
TOUCHING THE ROPE
CATCHING AND/OR THROWING THE BALL
IF A VIOLATION OCCURS, ANY WRAPS AROUND THE POLE MADE AFTER THE OFFENSE WILL BE UNDONE AND THE OTHER PLAYER WILL SERVE AGAIN.
HE GAME IS WON
Y COMPLETELY
RAPPING THE TETHER
ROUND THE POLE
N YOUR DIRECTION
NTIL THE BALL
ITS THE SIDE!
CLANG!
GOT IT?
GOT IT!

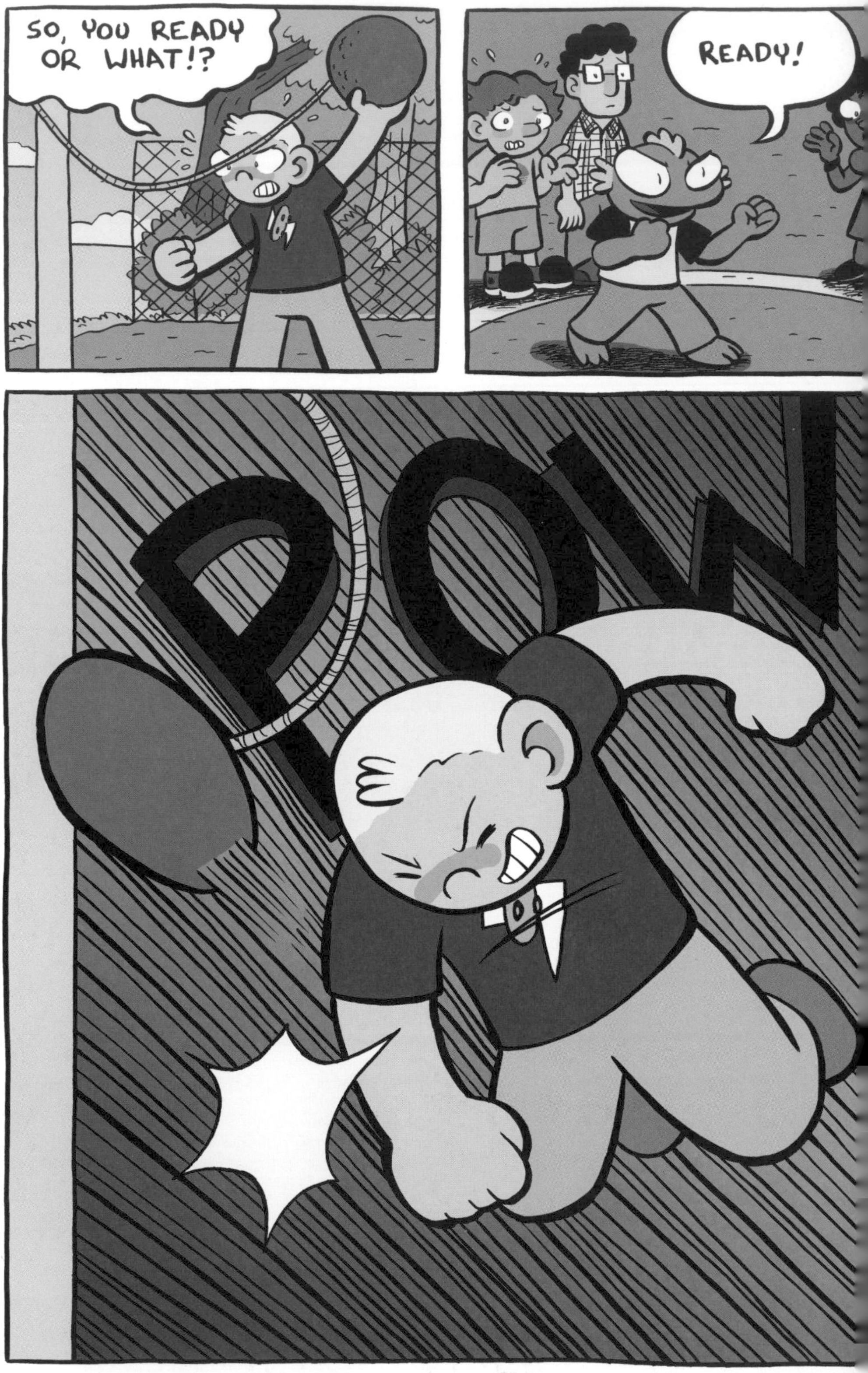
SO, YOU READY OR WHAT!?
READY!
POW

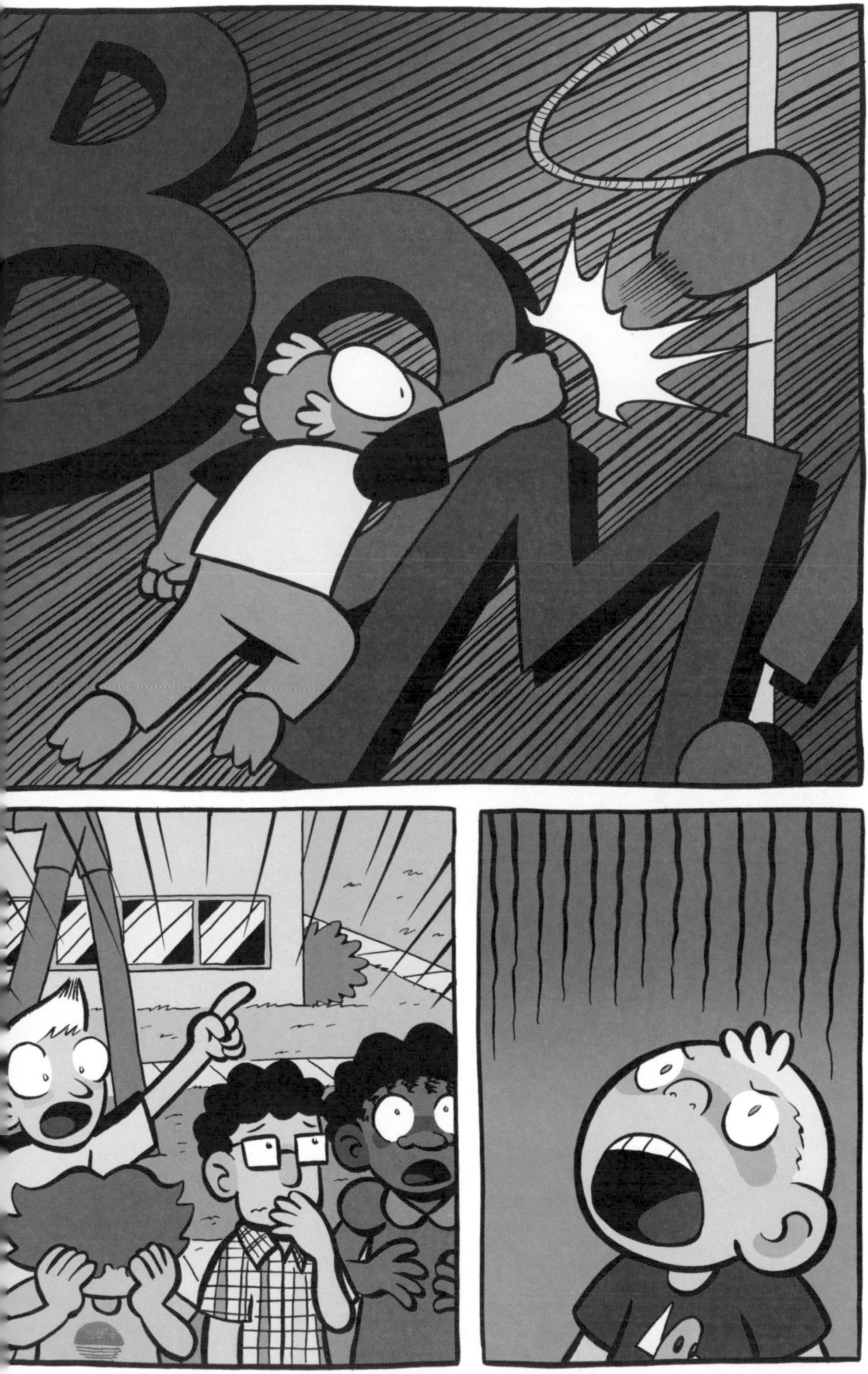

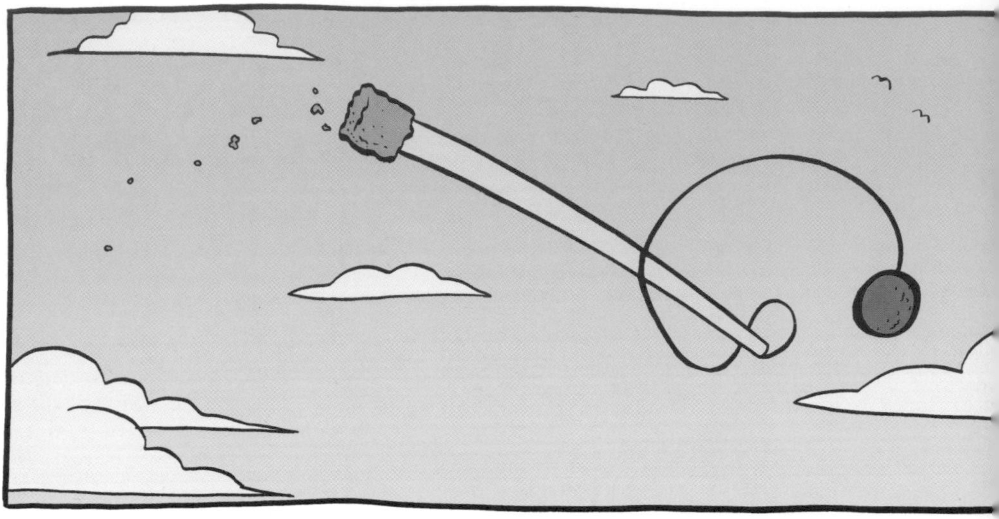

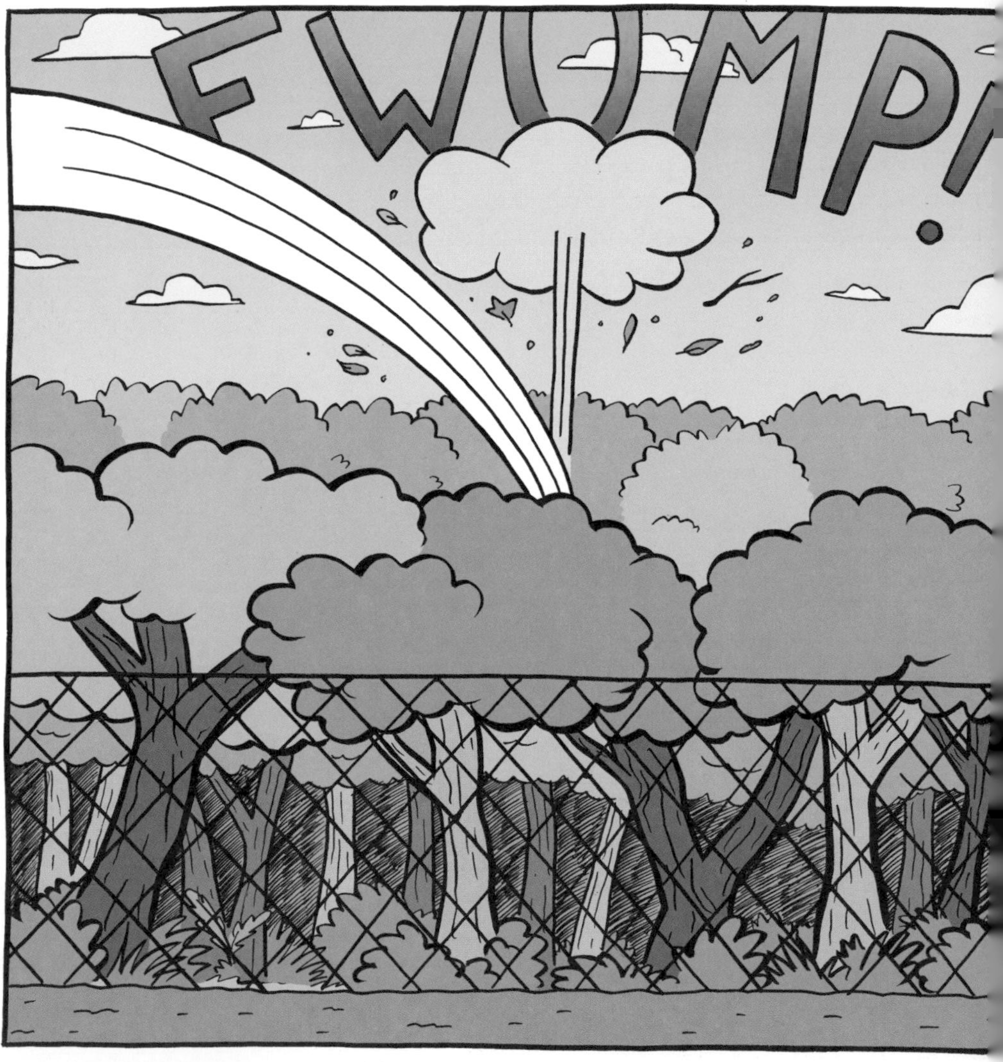
FWOMP!

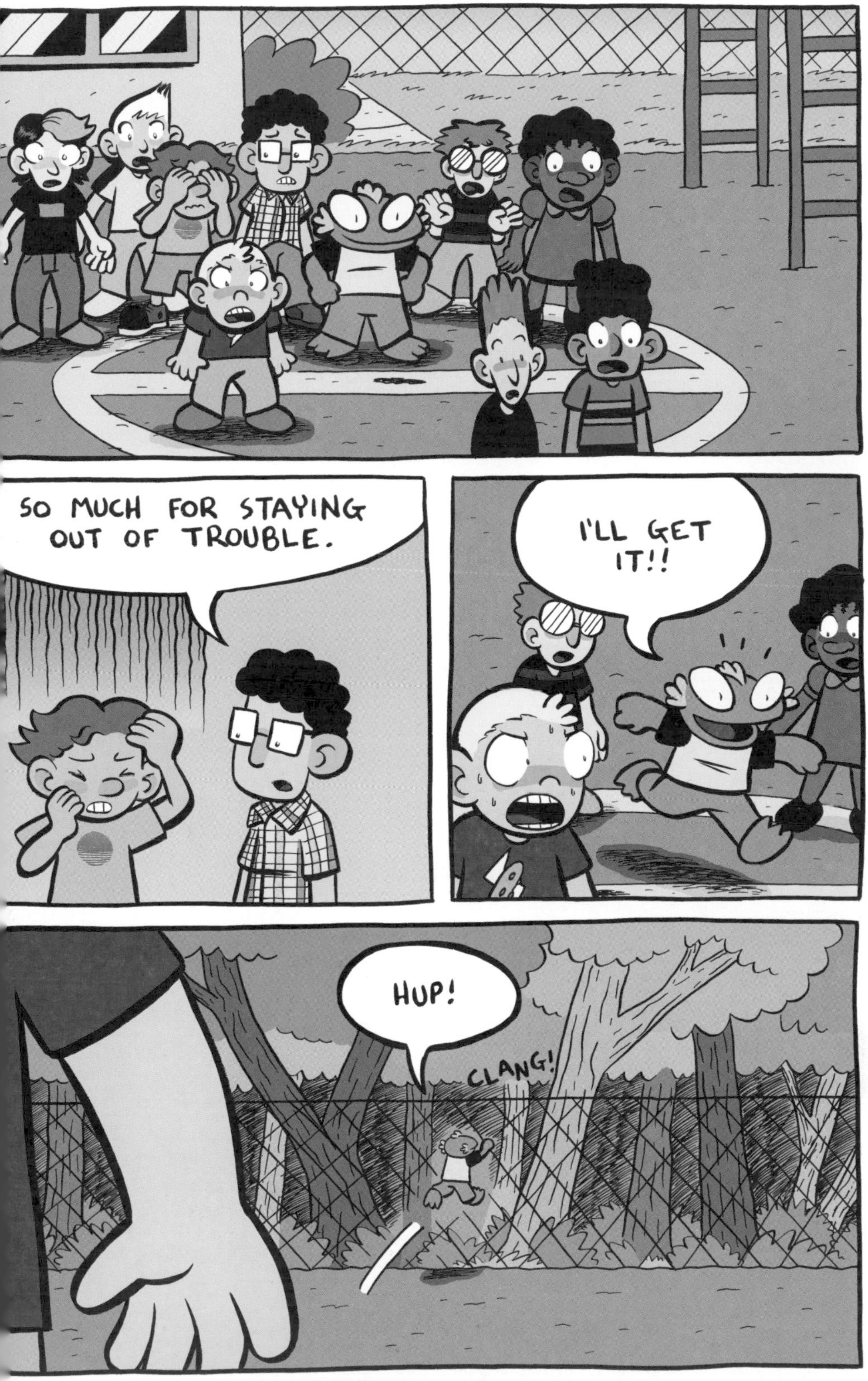
SO MUCH FOR STAYING OUT OF TROUBLE.
I'LL GET IT!!
HUP!
CLANG!

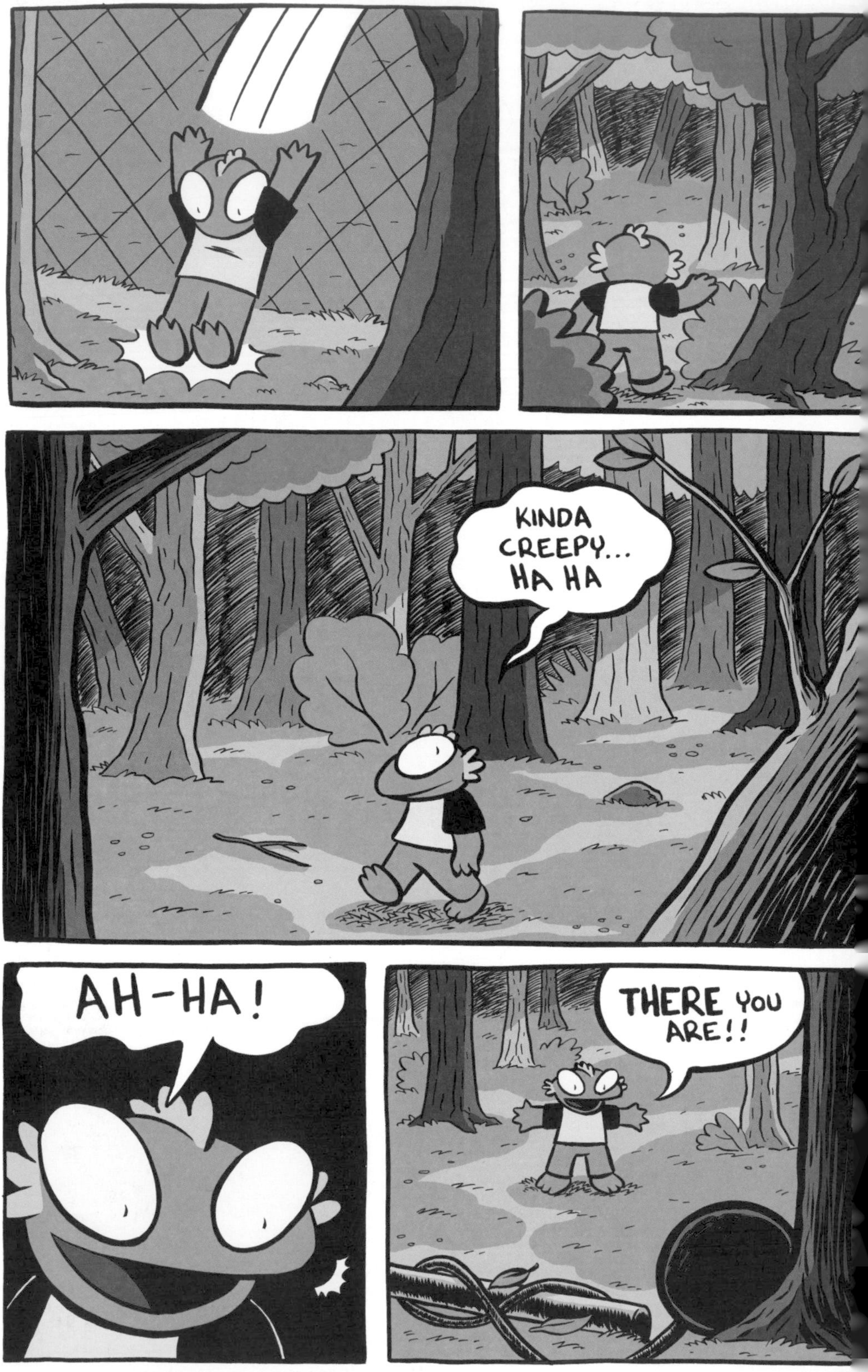
KINDA CREEPY... HA HA
AH-HA!
THERE YOU ARE!!

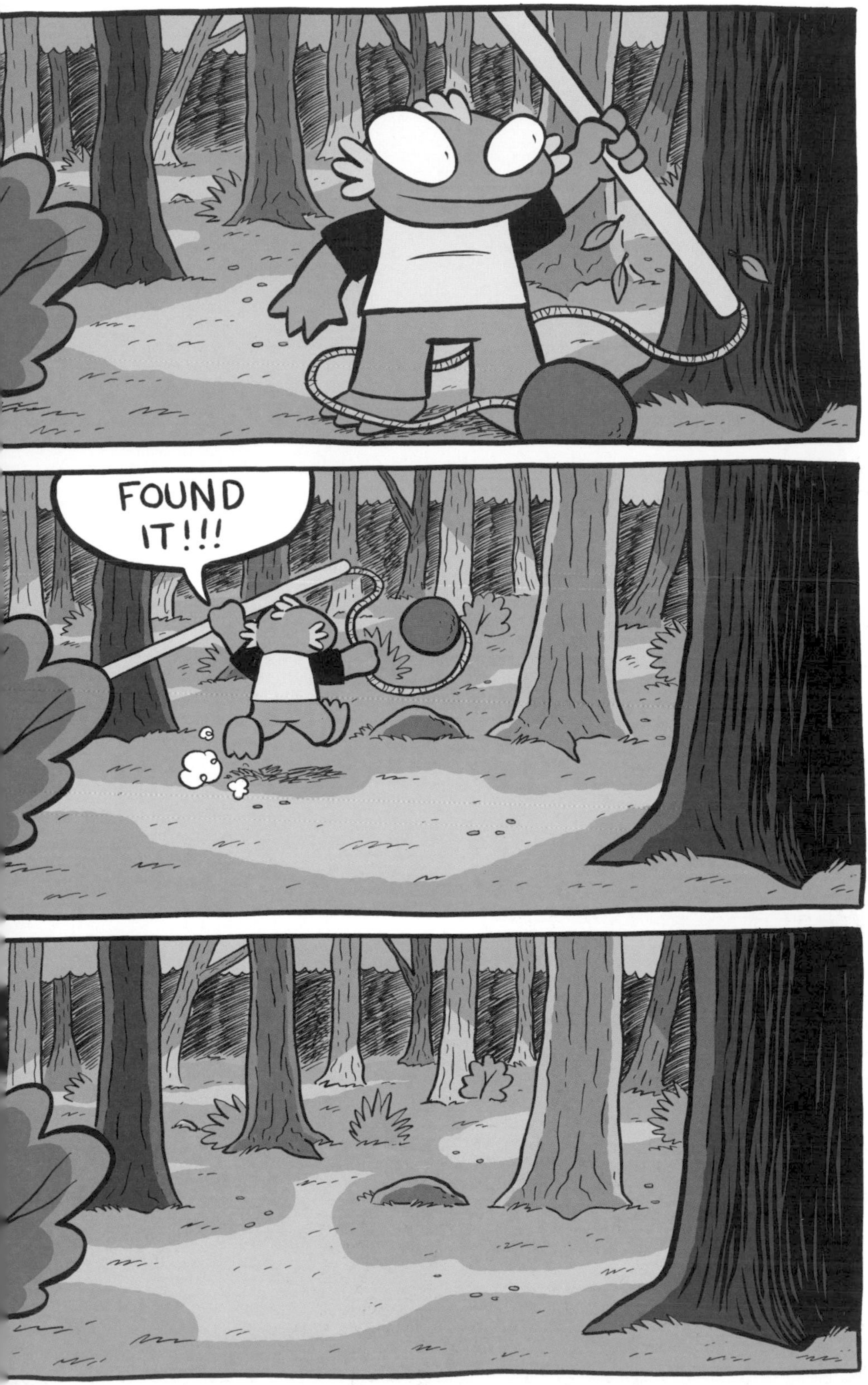
FOUND IT!!!

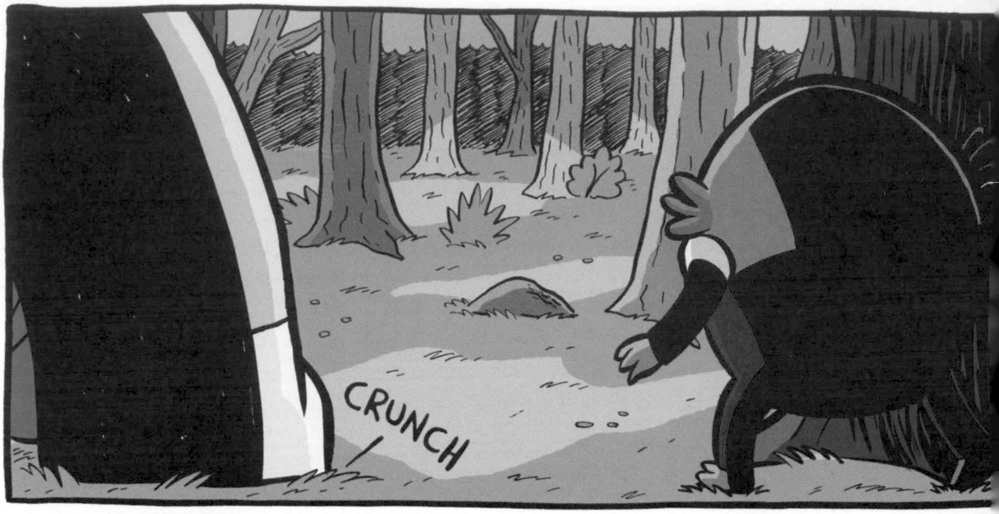
CRUNCH

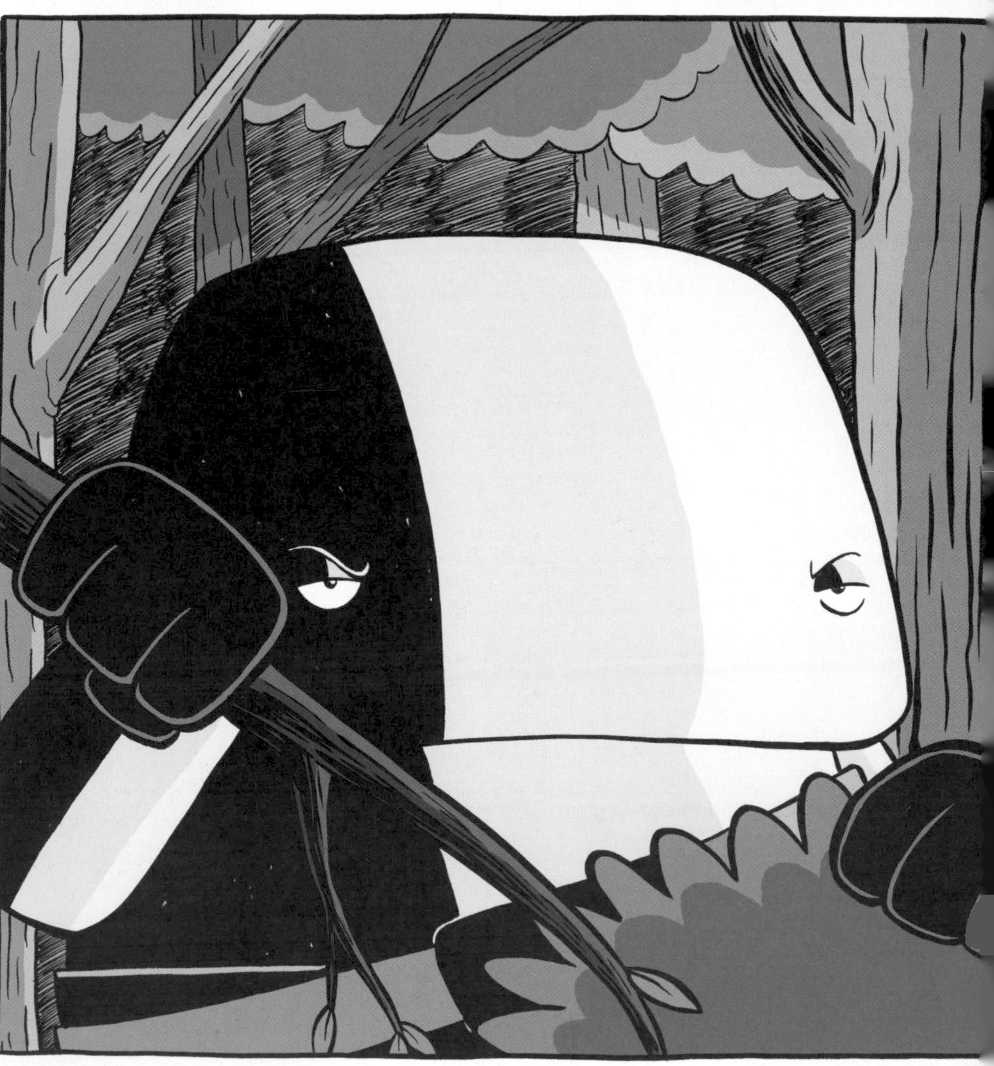

CHAPTER THREE

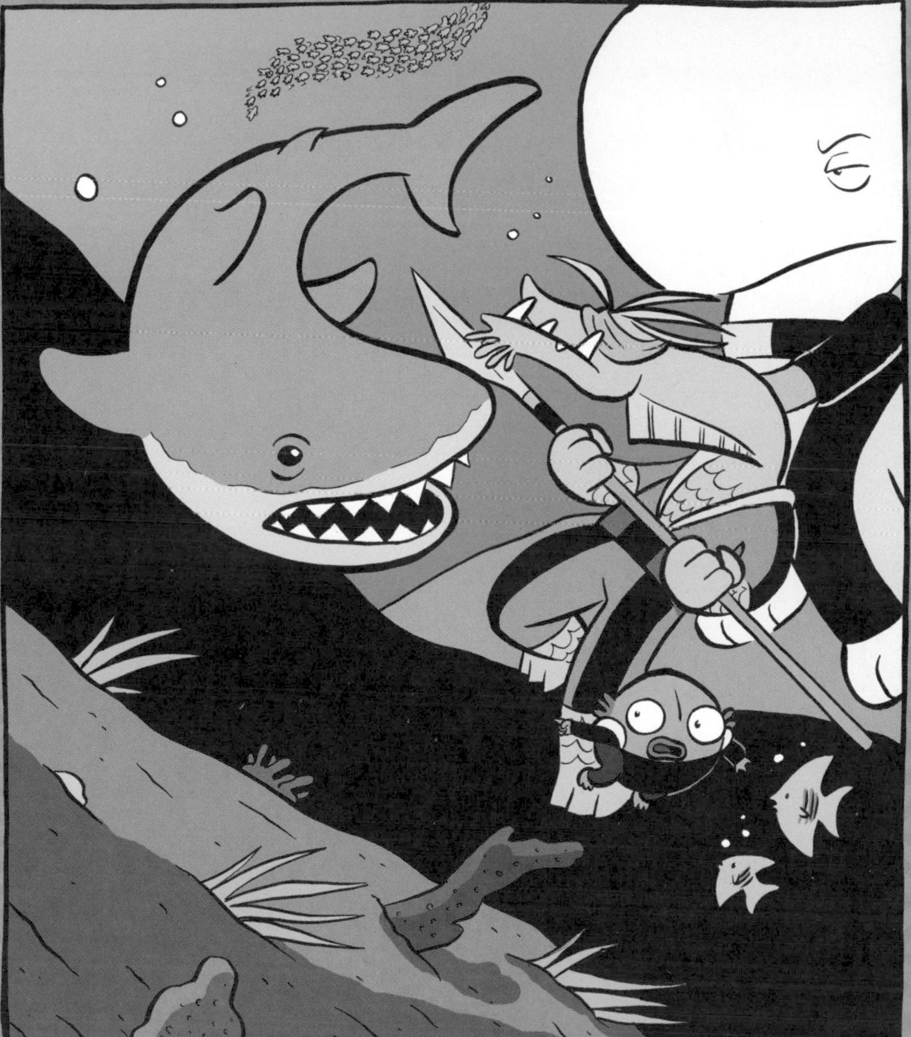

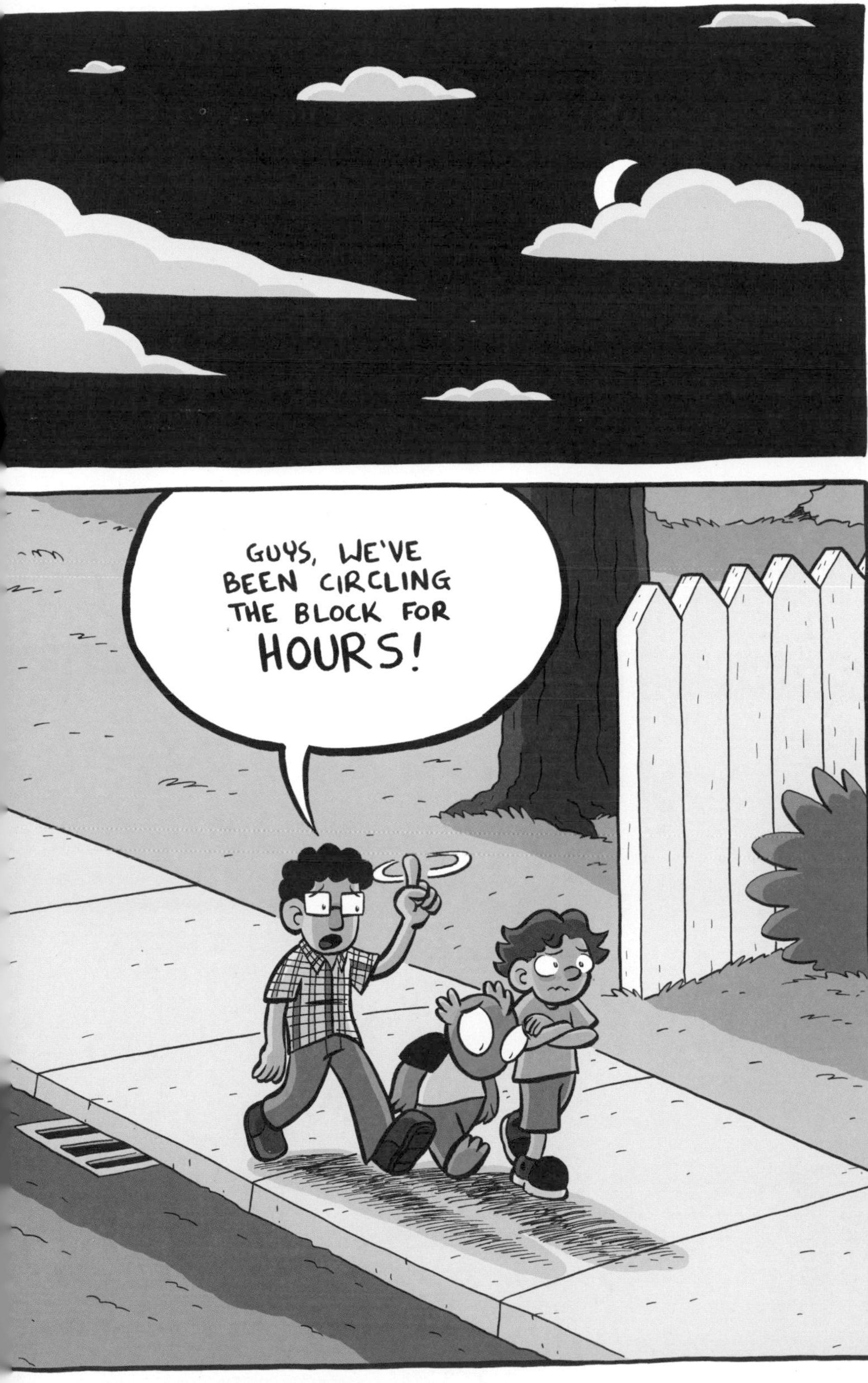
GUYS, WE'VE BEEN CIRCLING THE BLOCK FOR HOURS!

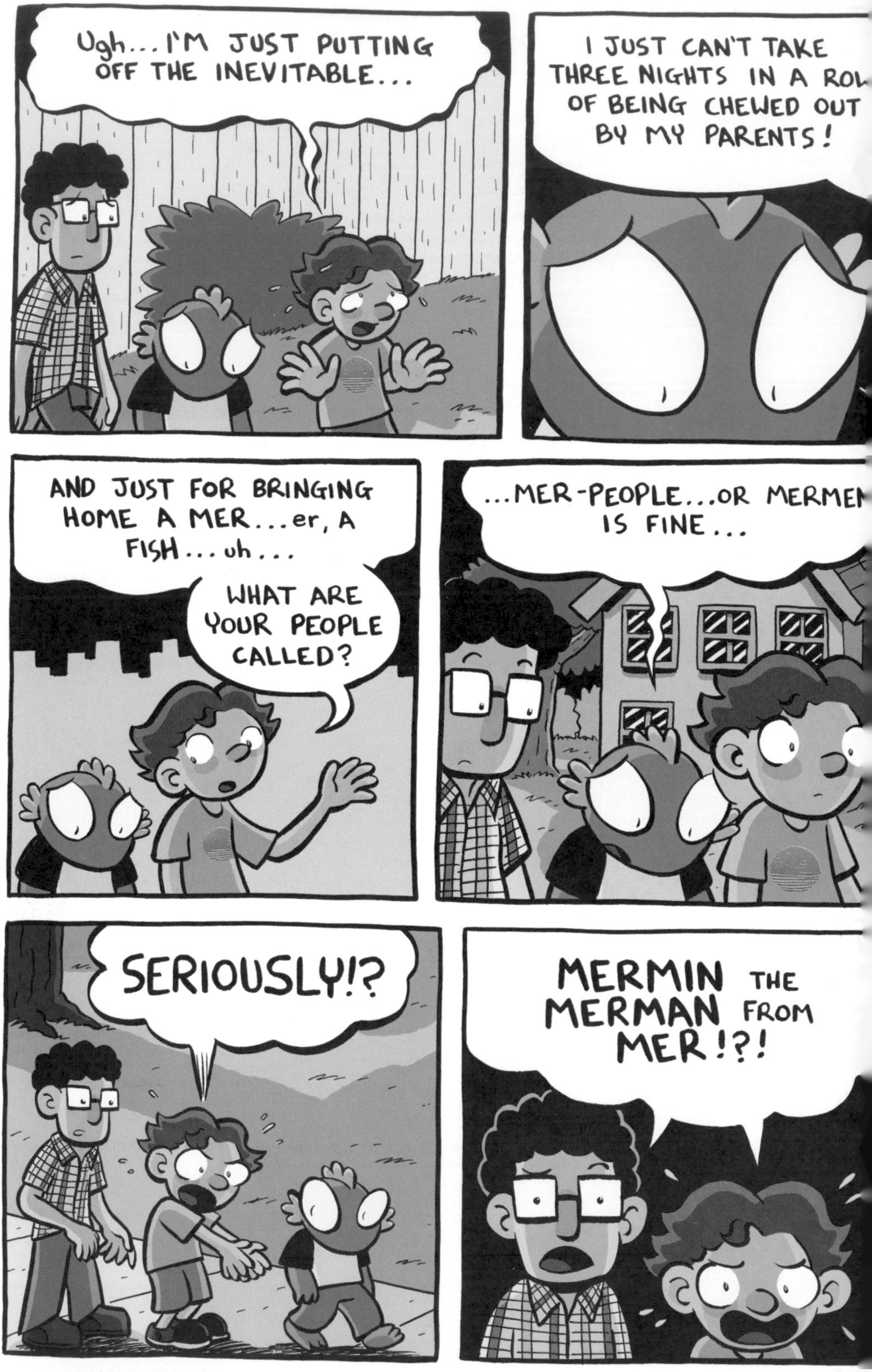
Ugh... I'M JUST PUTTING OFF THE INEVITABLE...
I JUST CAN'T TAKE THREE NIGHTS IN A ROW OF BEING CHEWED OUT BY MY PARENTS!
AND JUST FOR BRINGING HOME A MER...er, A FISH... uh...
WHAT ARE YOUR PEOPLE CALLED?
...MER-PEOPLE...OR MERMEN IS FINE...
SERIOUSLY!?
MERMIN THE MERMAN FROM MER!?!

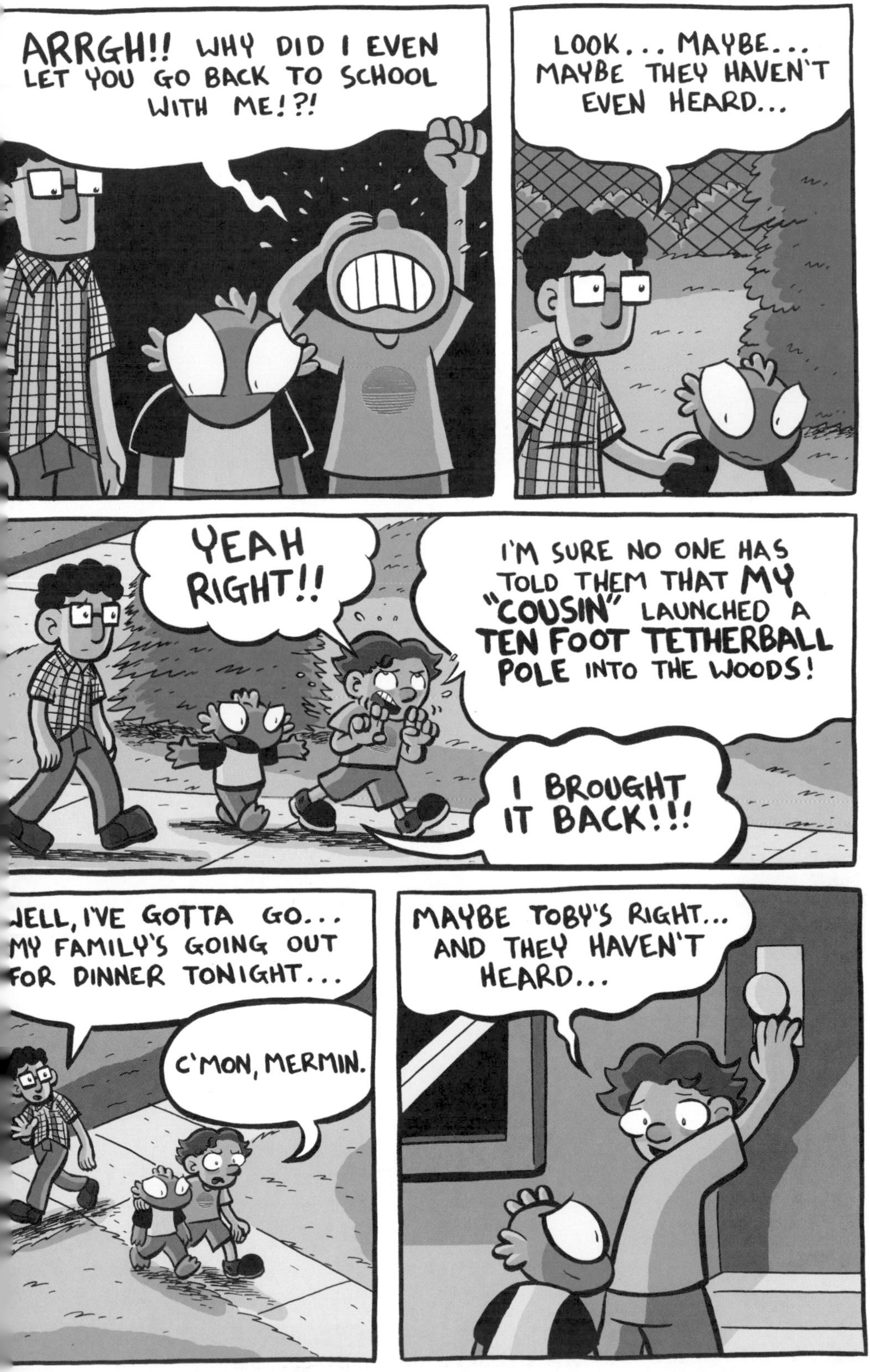
ARRGH!! WHY DID I EVEN LET YOU GO BACK TO SCHOOL WITH ME!?!
LOOK... MAYBE... MAYBE THEY HAVEN'T EVEN HEARD...
YEAH RIGHT!!
I'M SURE NO ONE HAS TOLD THEM THAT MY "COUSIN" LAUNCHED A TEN FOOT TETHERBALL POLE INTO THE WOODS!
I BROUGHT IT BACK!!!
WELL, I'VE GOTTA GO... MY FAMILY'S GOING OUT FOR DINNER TONIGHT...
C'MON, MERMIN.
MAYBE TOBY'S RIGHT... AND THEY HAVEN'T HEARD...

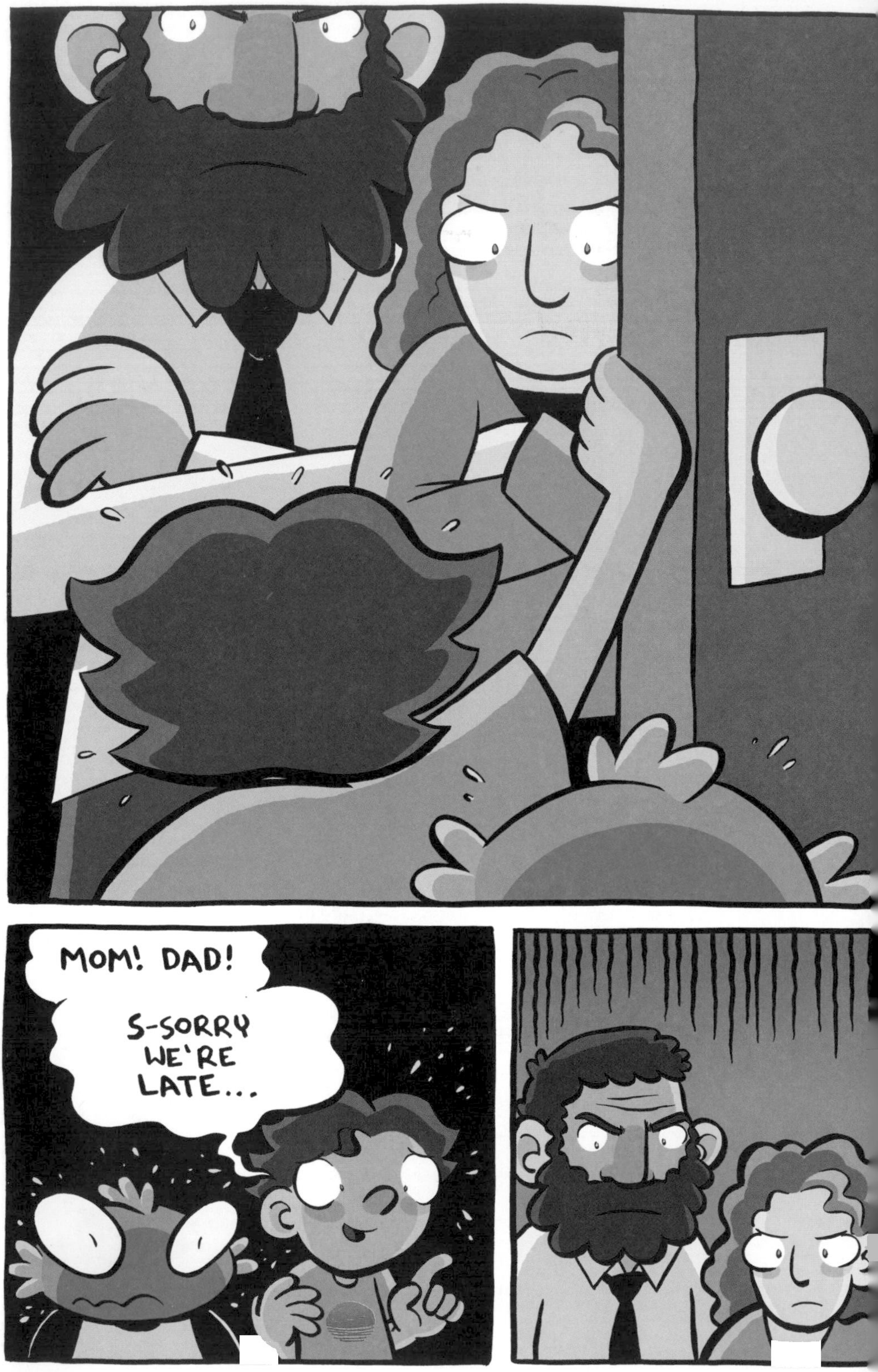
MOM! DAD!
S-SORRY WE'RE LATE...

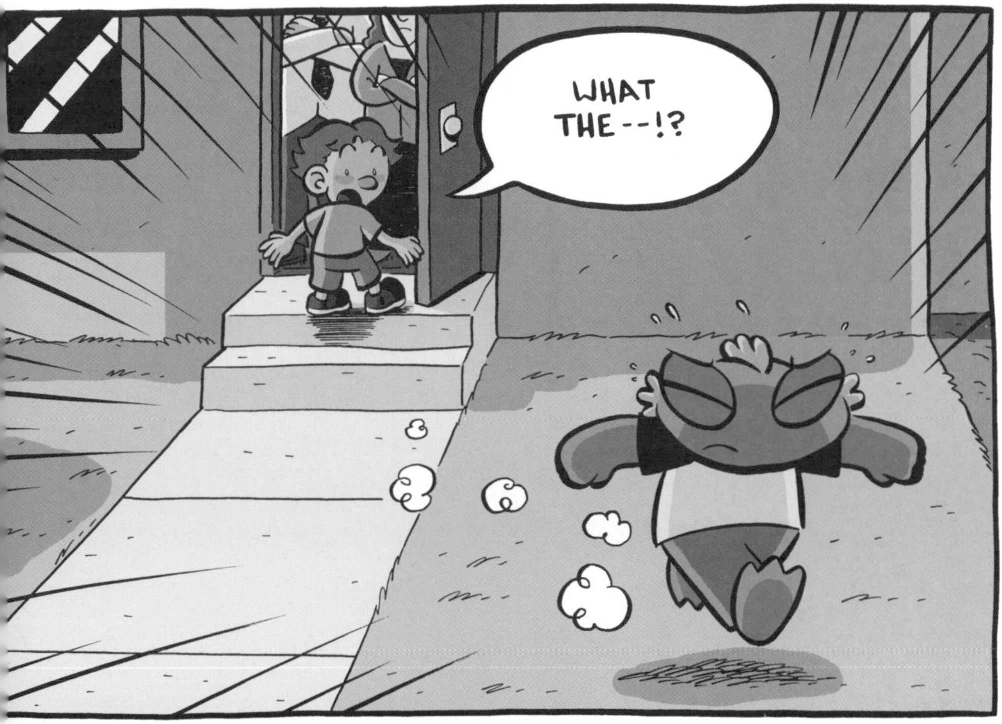
WHAT THE--!?

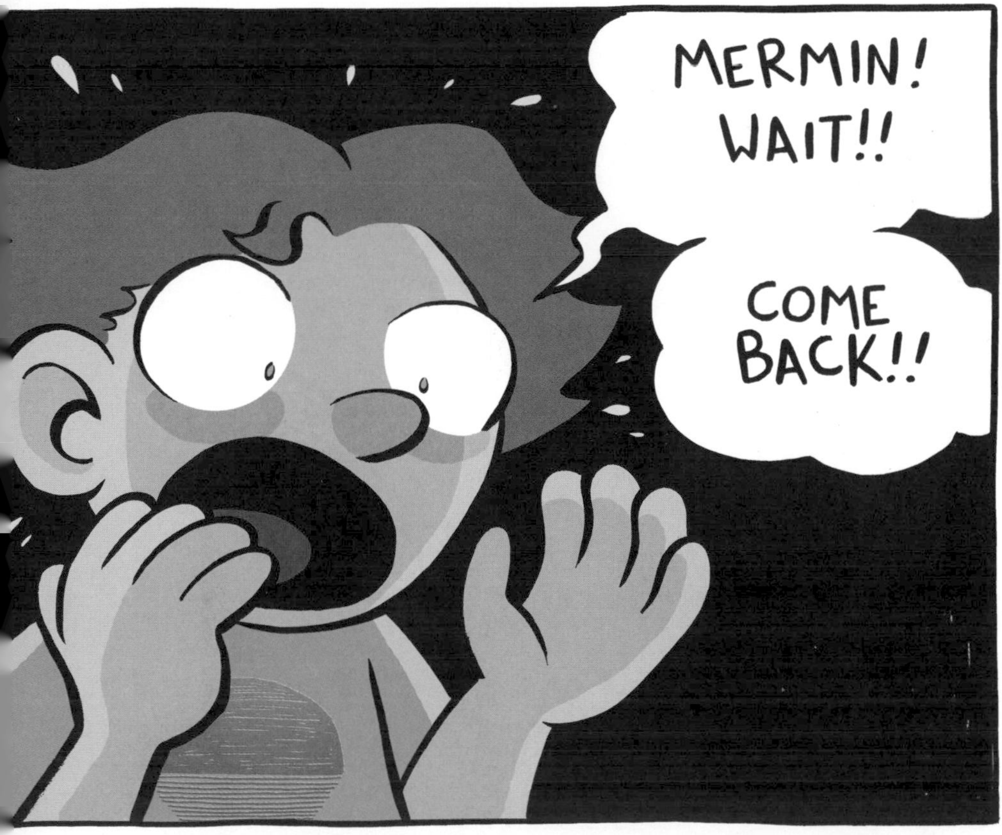
MERMIN! WAIT!!
COME BACK!!

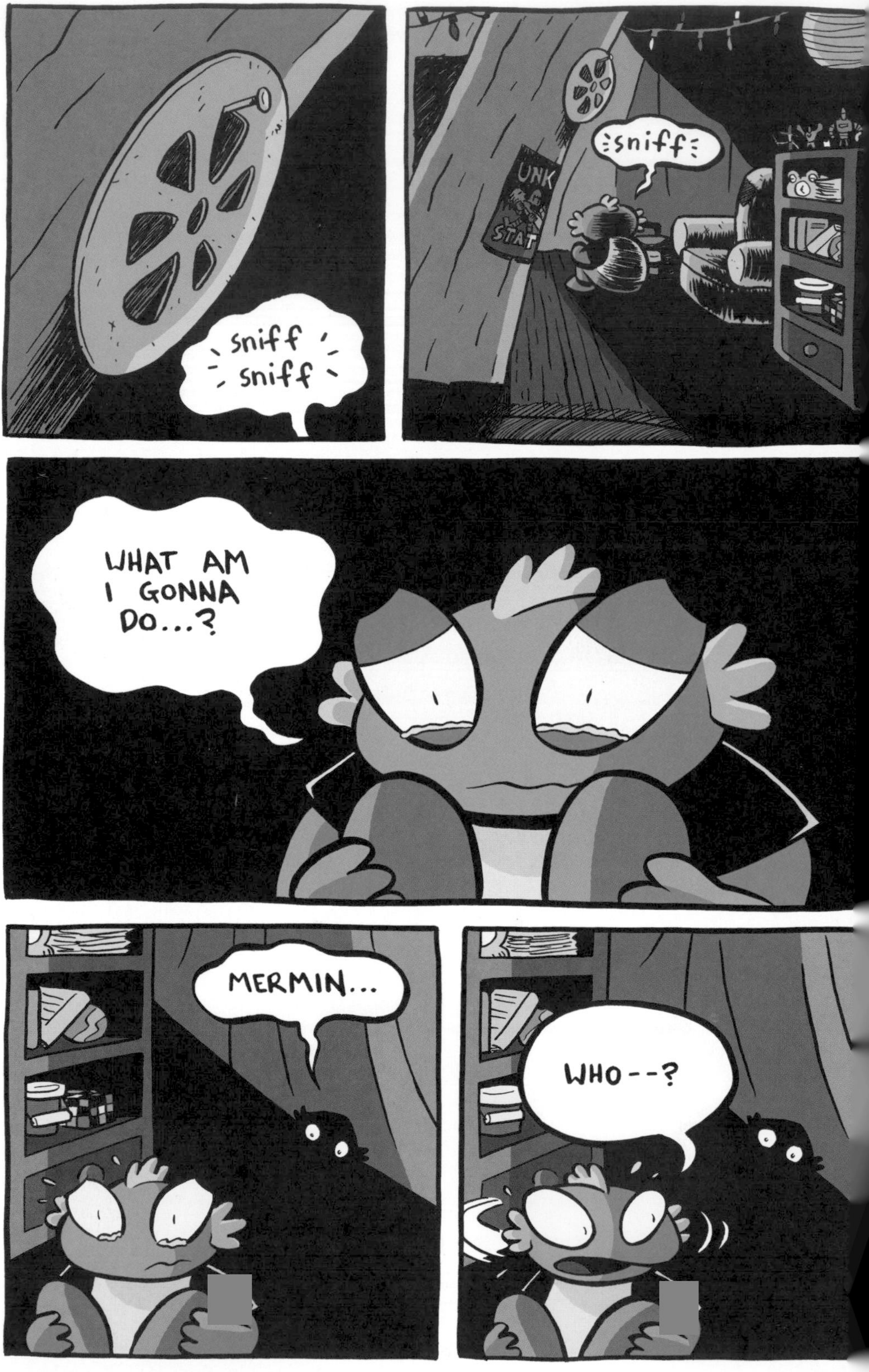
sniff sniff
UNK
STAT
sniff
WHAT AM I GONNA DO...?
MERMIN...
WHO--?

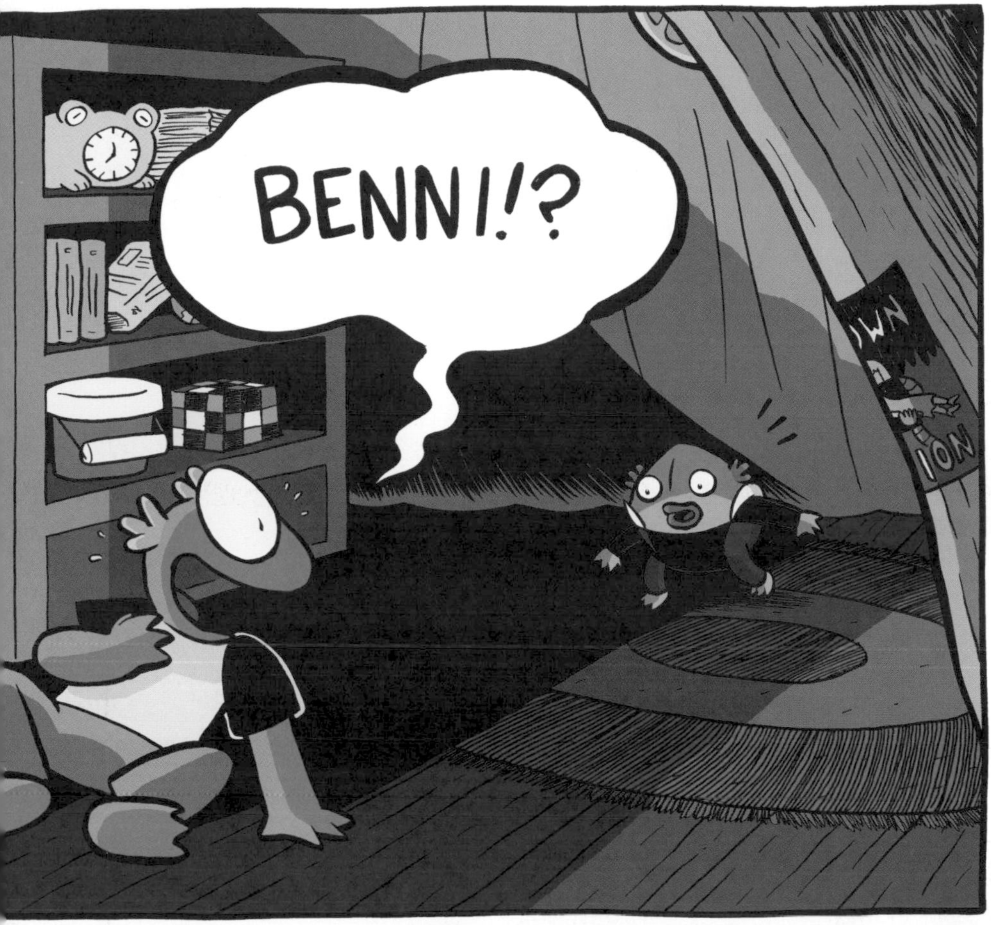
BENNI!?

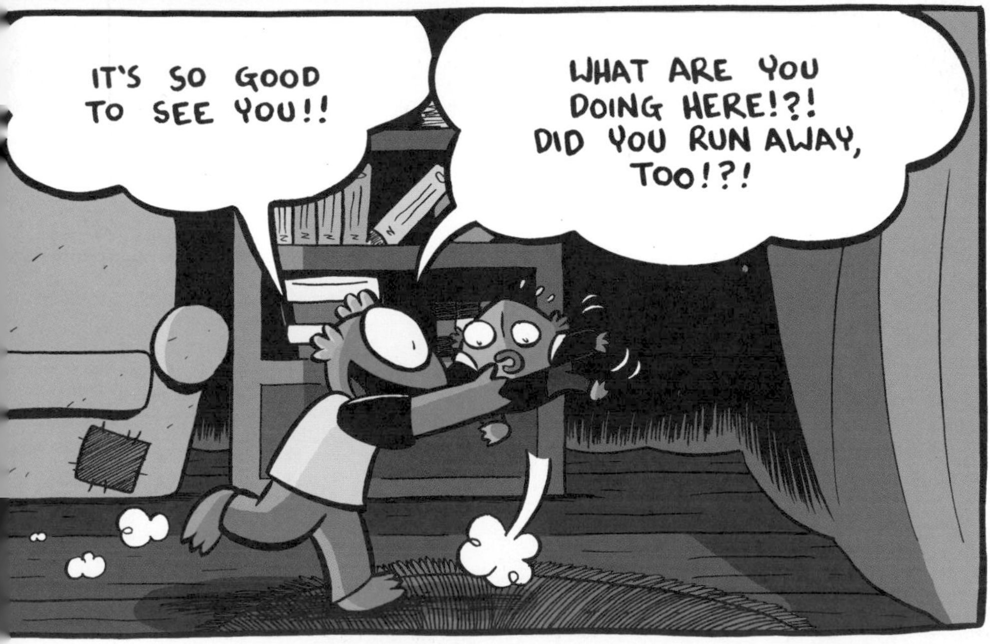
IT'S SO GOOD TO SEE YOU!!
WHAT ARE YOU DOING HERE!?! DID YOU RUN AWAY, TOO!?!

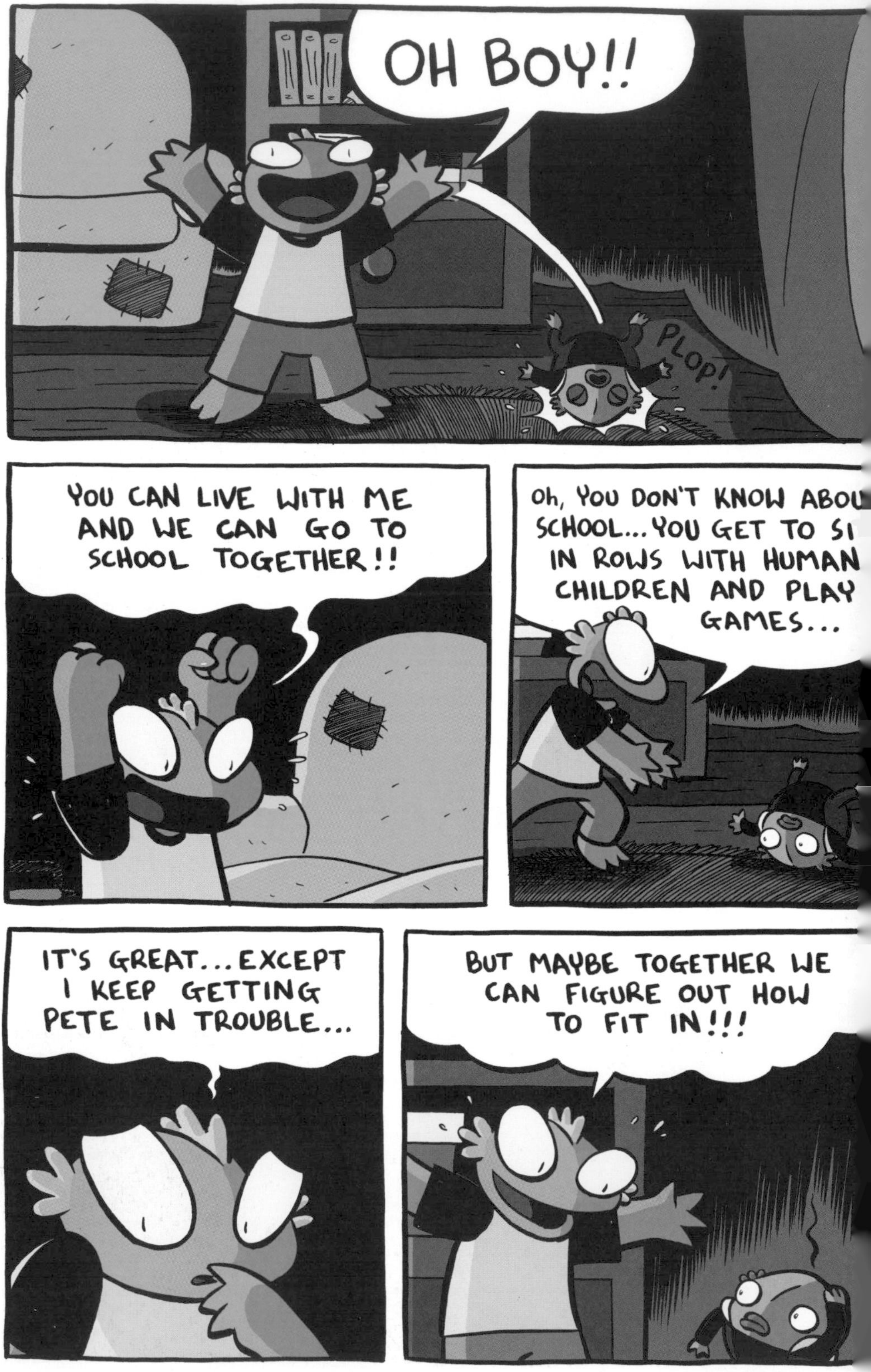
OH BOY!!
PLOP!
YOU CAN LIVE WITH ME AND WE CAN GO TO SCHOOL TOGETHER!!
Oh, YOU DON'T KNOW ABOU SCHOOL... YOU GET TO SI IN ROWS WITH HUMAN CHILDREN AND PLAY GAMES...
IT'S GREAT... EXCEPT I KEEP GETTING PETE IN TROUBLE...
BUT MAYBE TOGETHER WE CAN FIGURE OUT HOW TO FIT IN!!!

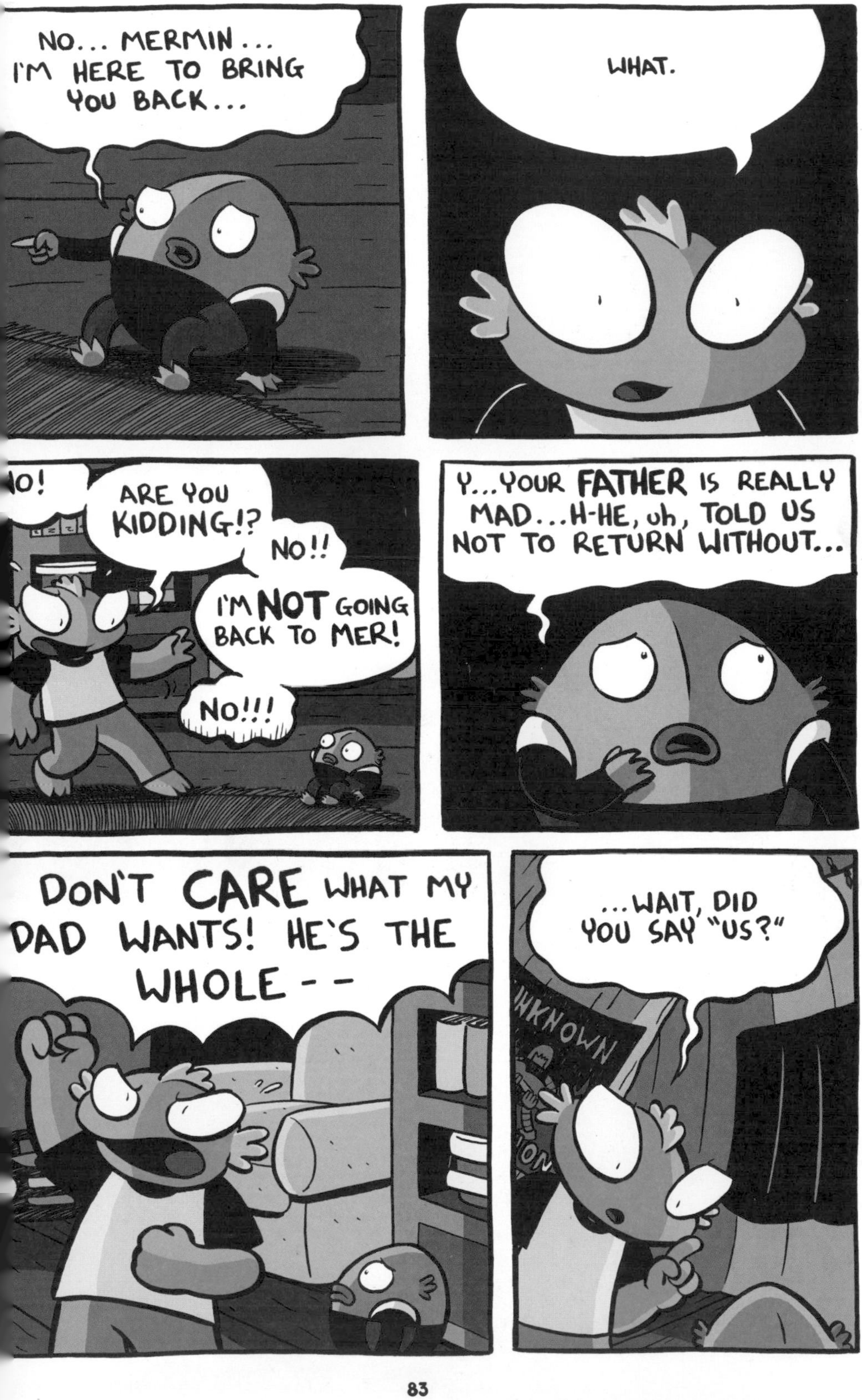
NO... MERMIN... I'M HERE TO BRING YOU BACK...
WHAT.
NO!
ARE YOU KIDDING!?
NO!!
I'M NOT GOING BACK TO MER!
NO!!!
Y...YOUR FATHER IS REALLY MAD...H-HE, uh, TOLD US NOT TO RETURN WITHOUT...
DON'T CARE WHAT MY DAD WANTS! HE'S THE WHOLE --
...WAIT, DID YOU SAY "US?"

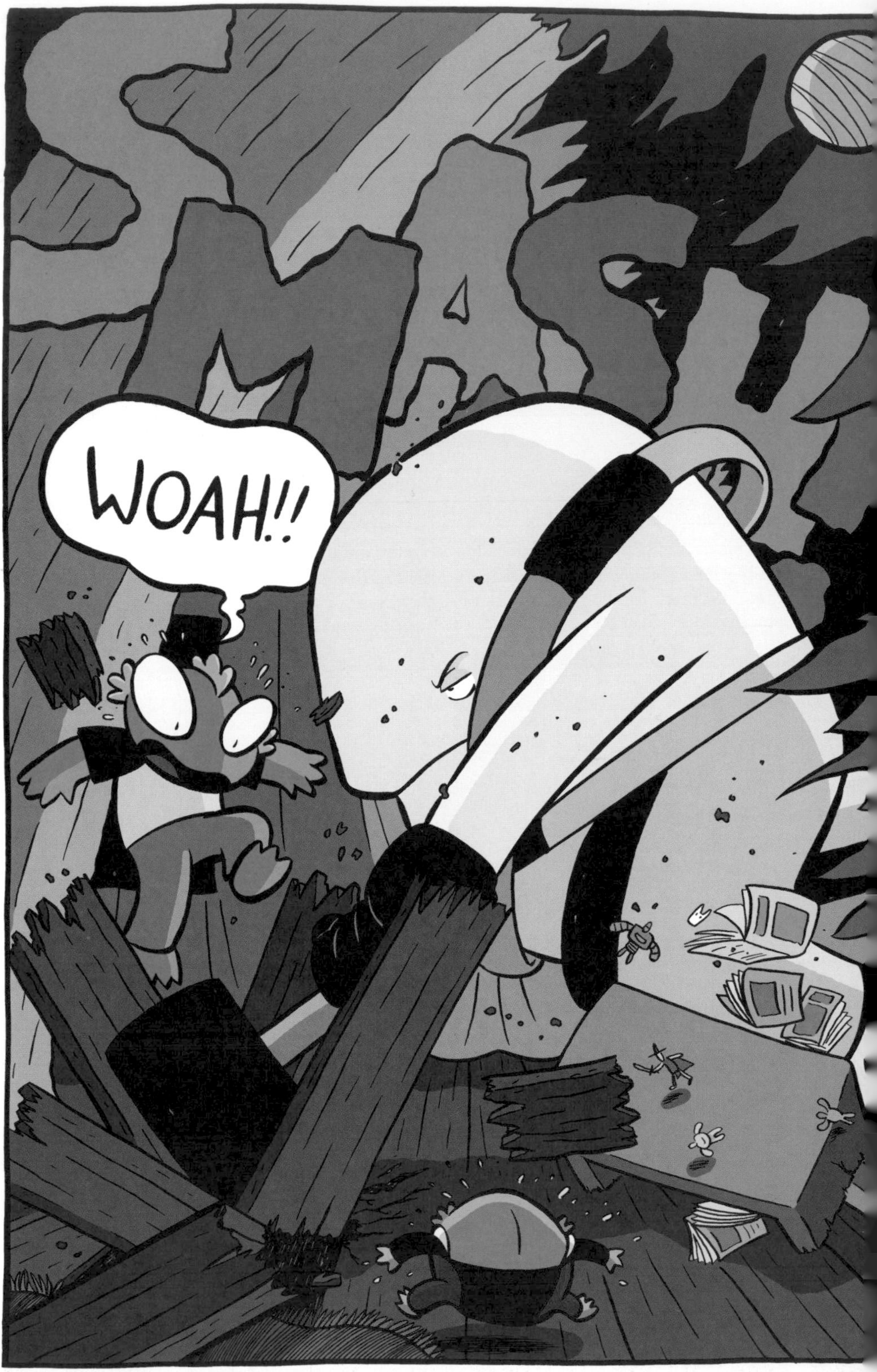
WOAH!!

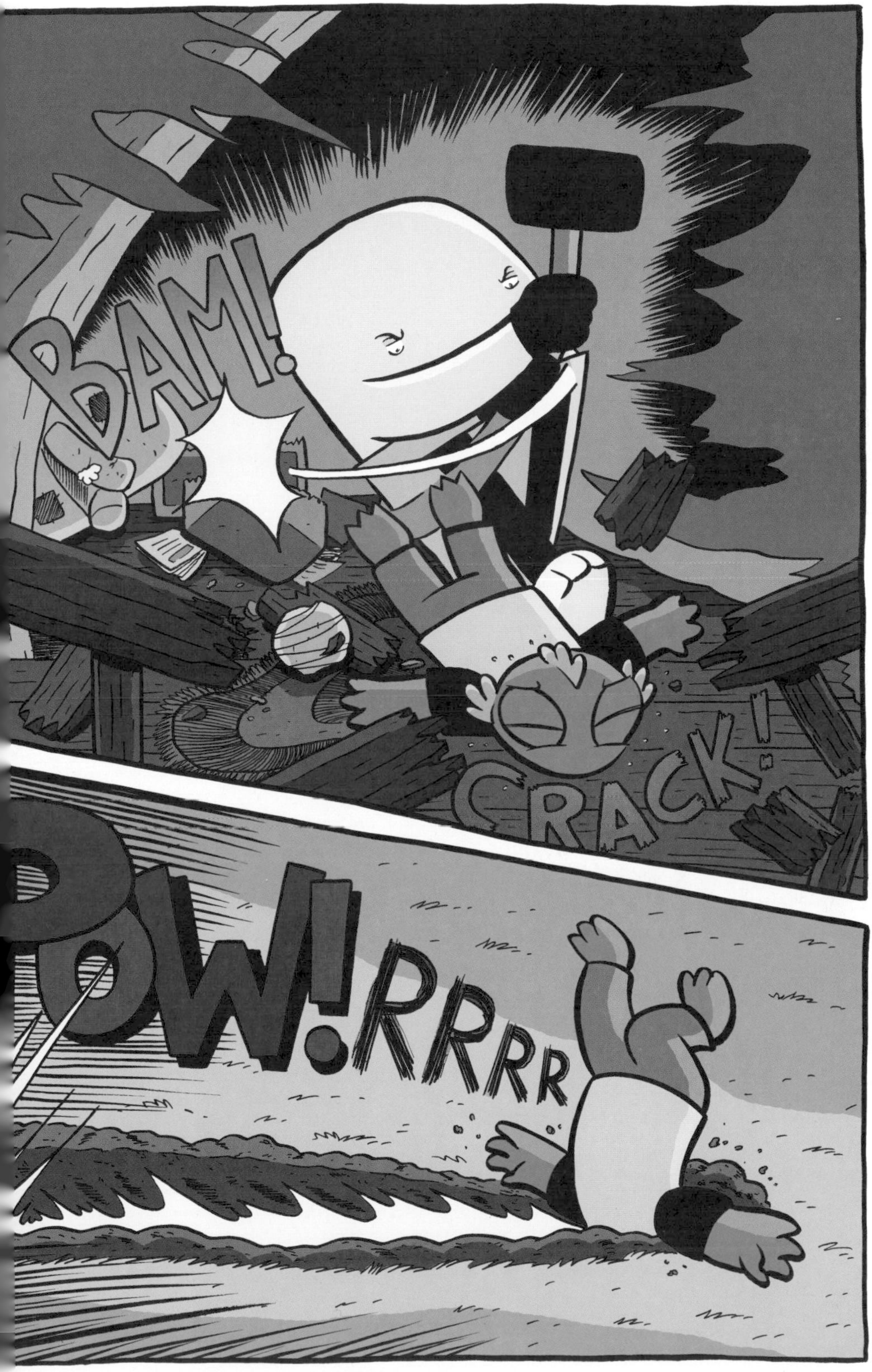

BAM!
CRACK!
POW!
RRRRR

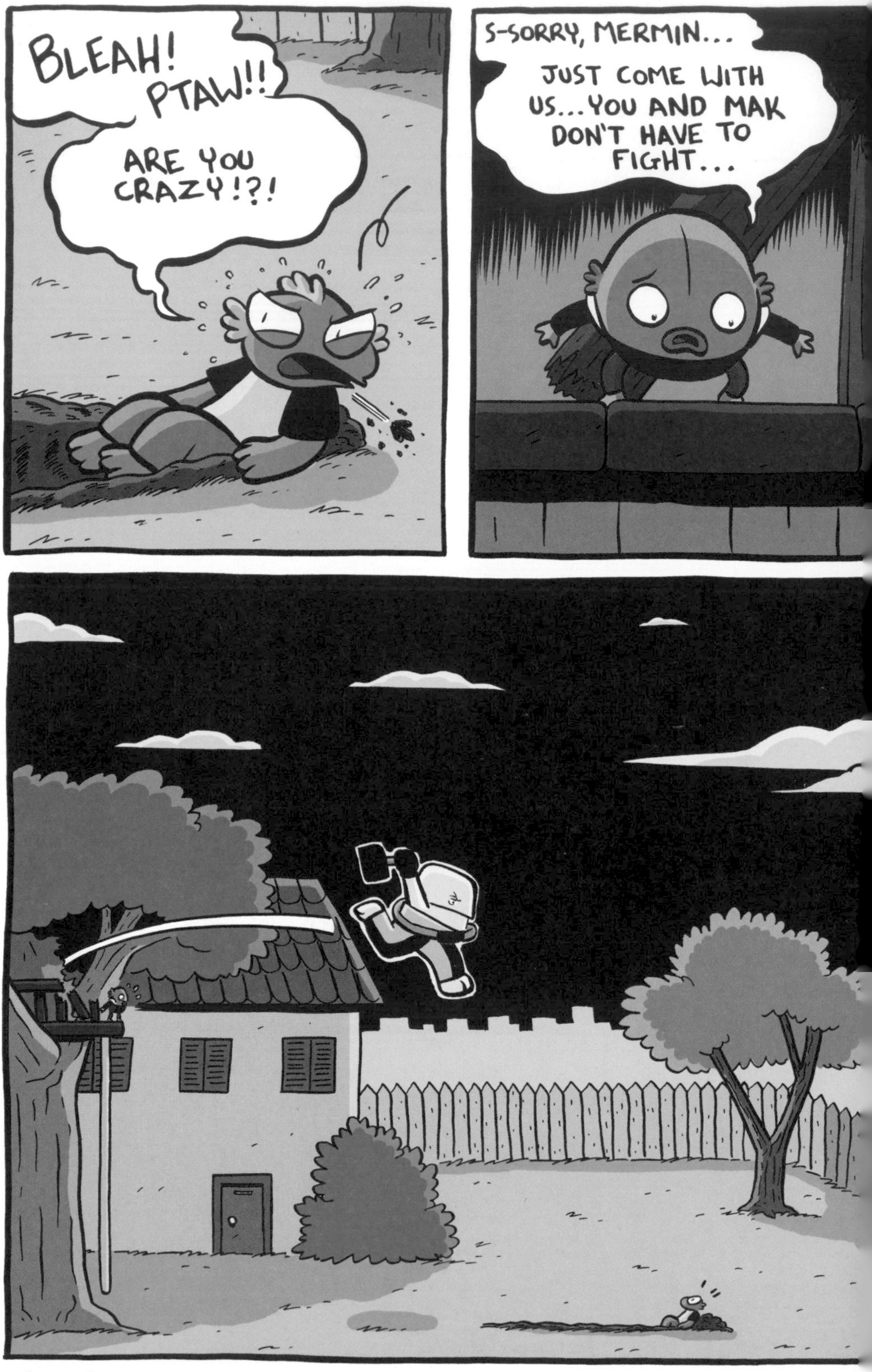
BLEAH! PTAW!!
ARE YOU CRAZY!?!
S-SORRY, MERMIN...
JUST COME WITH US...YOU AND MAK DON'T HAVE TO FIGHT...

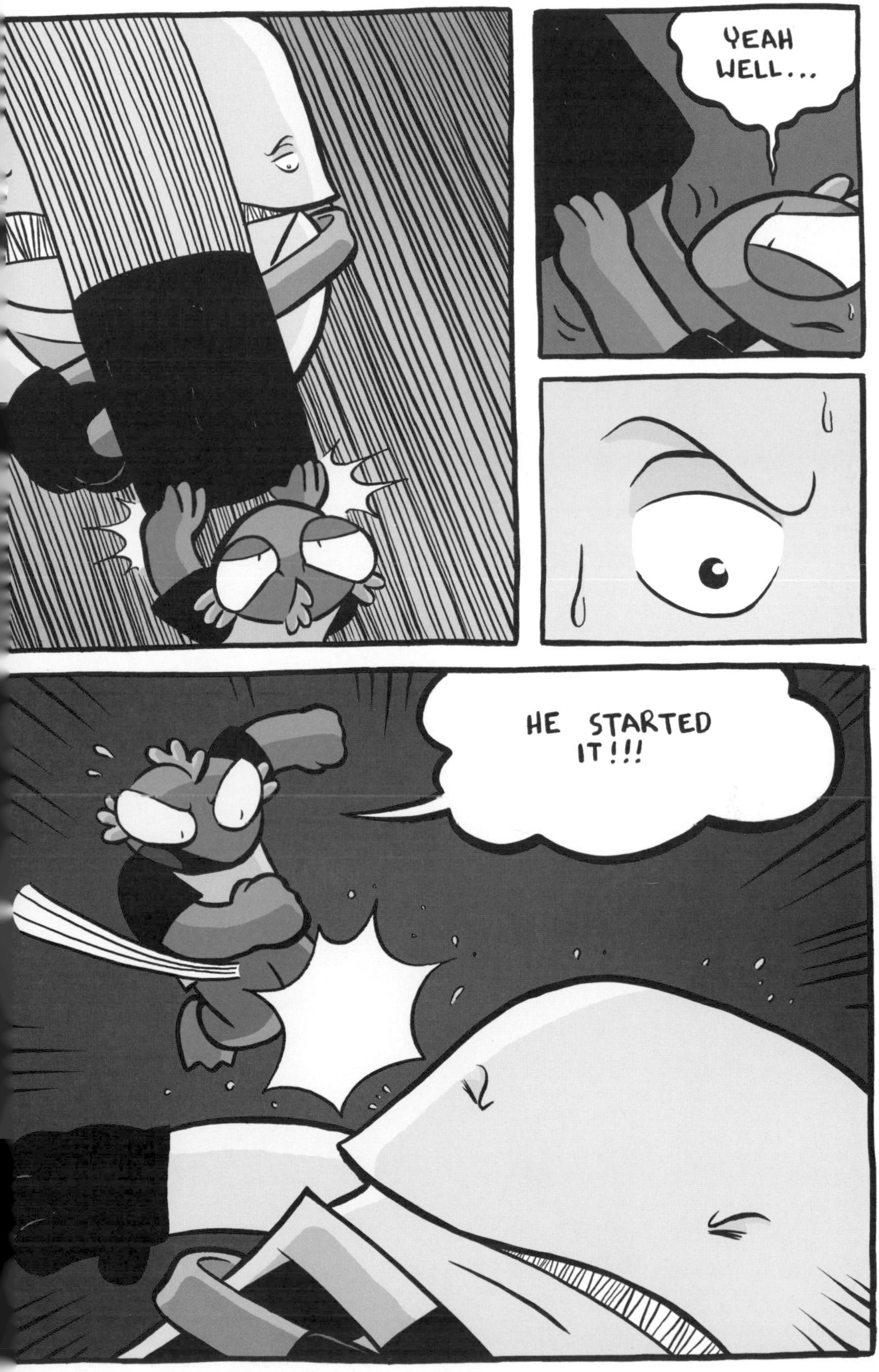
YEAH WELL...
HE STARTED IT!!!

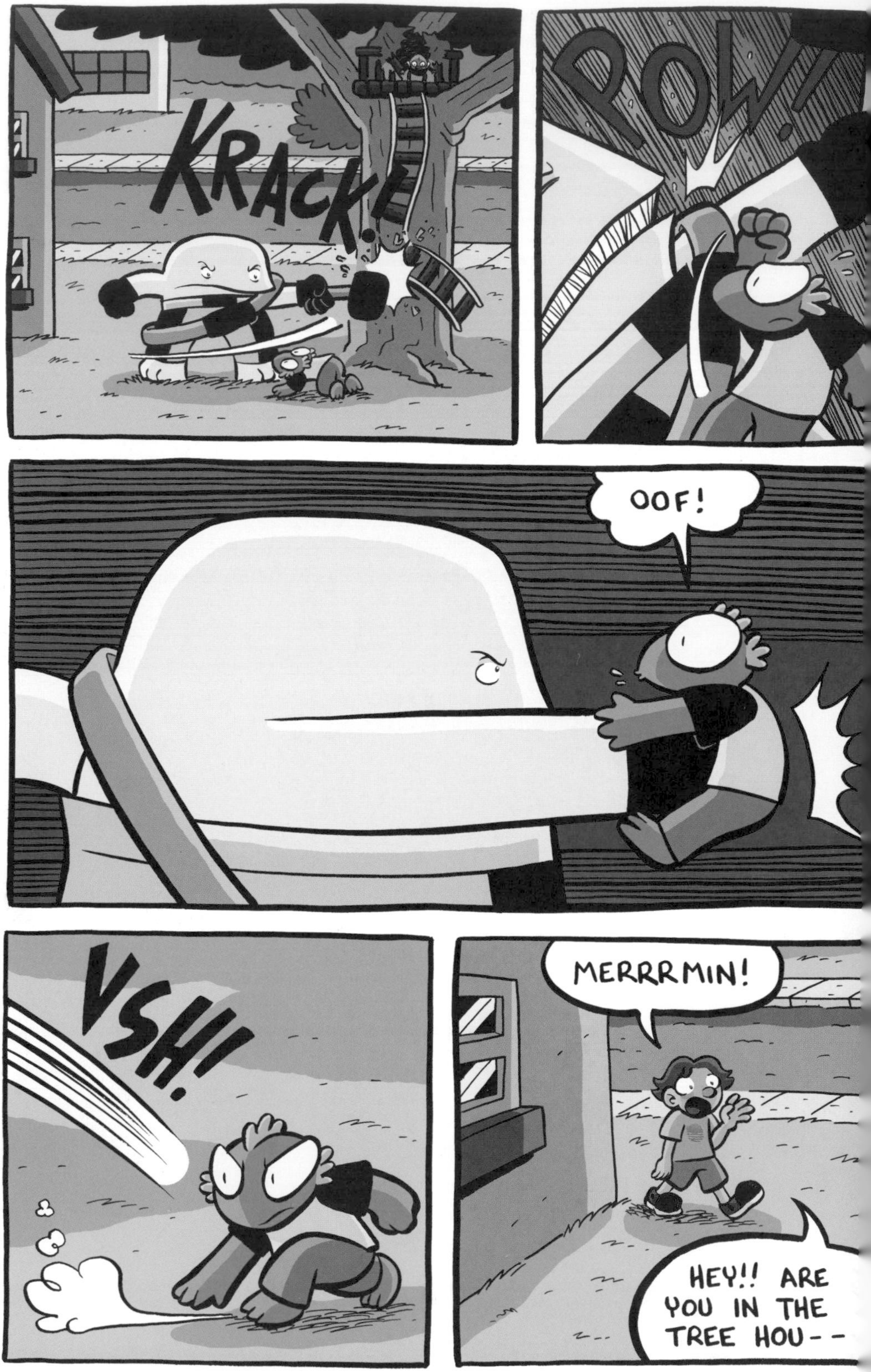
KRACK!
POW!!
OOF!
VSH!
MERRRMIN!
HEY!! ARE YOU IN THE TREE HOU--

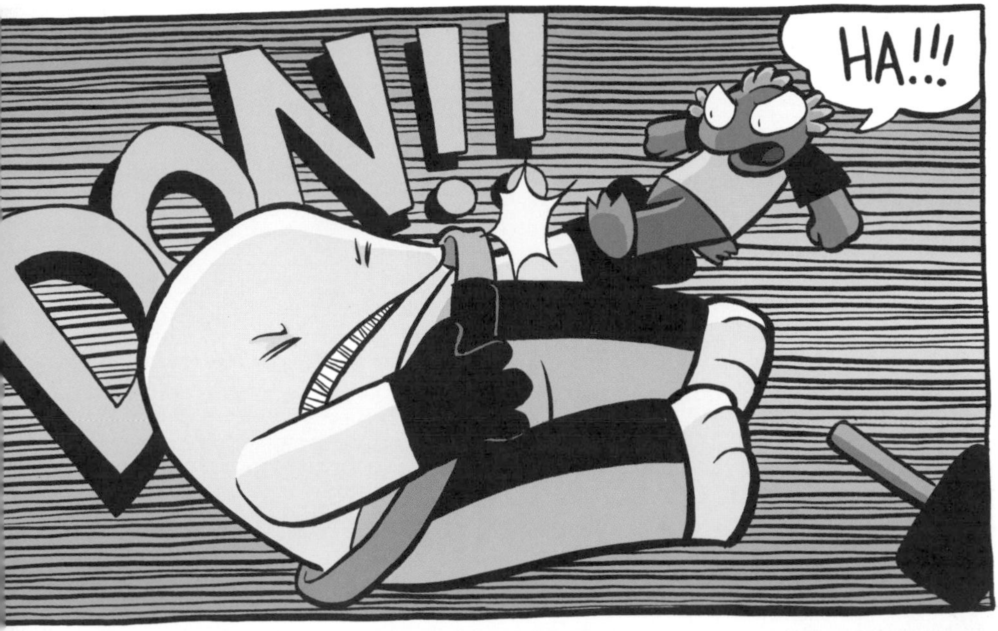
DON!!
HA!!!

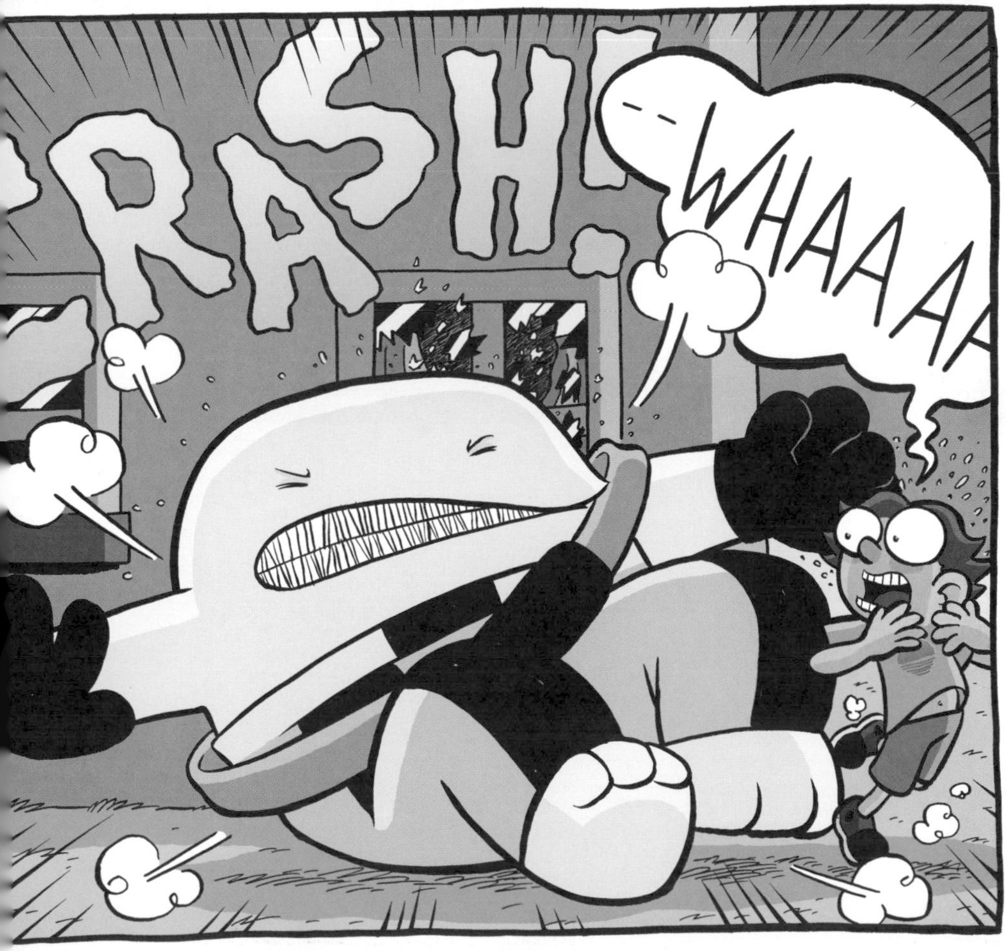
RASH!
--WHAAAA

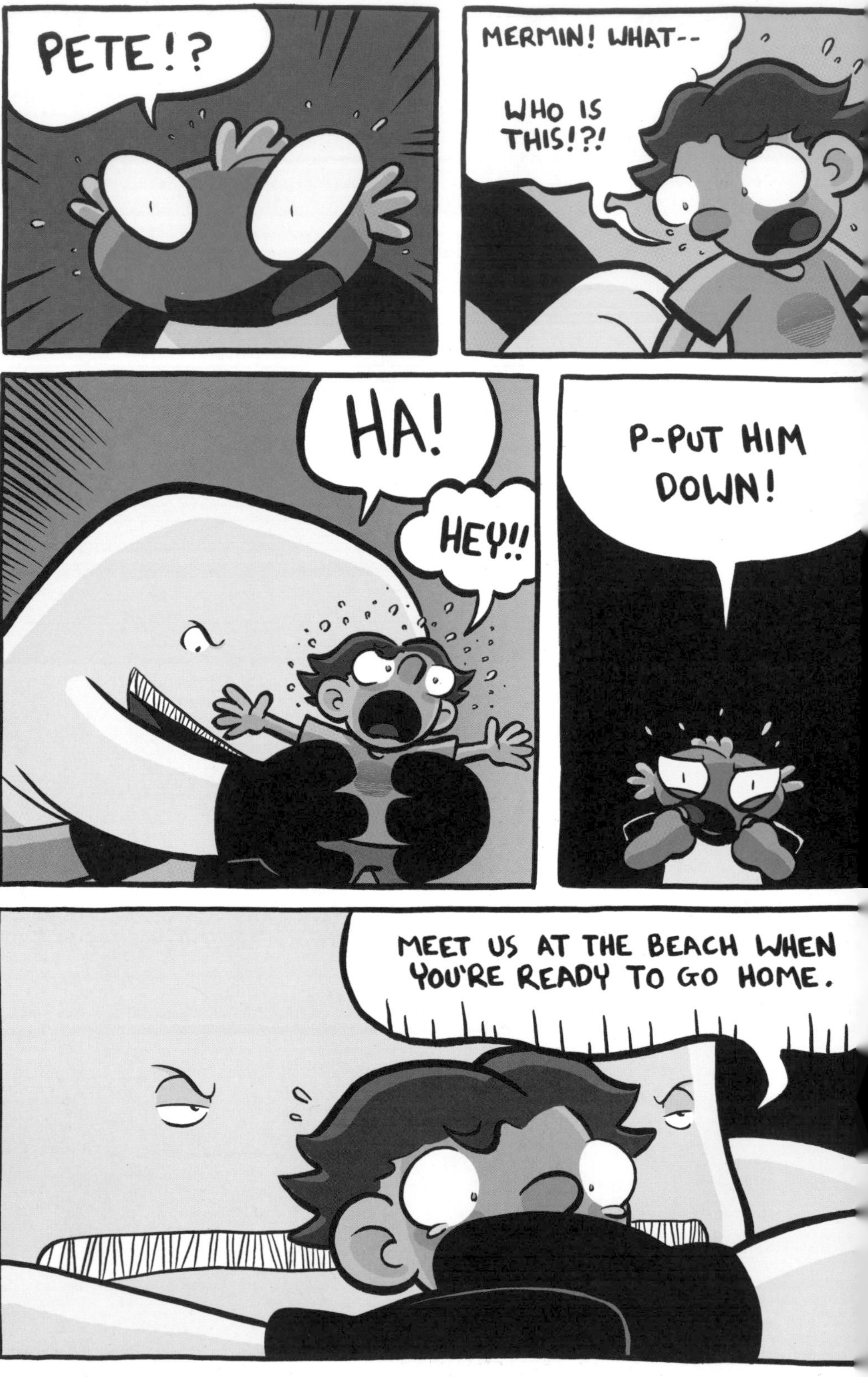
PETE!?
MERMIN! WHAT--
WHO IS THIS!?!
HA!
HEY!!
P-PUT HIM DOWN!
MEET US AT THE BEACH WHEN YOU'RE READY TO GO HOME.

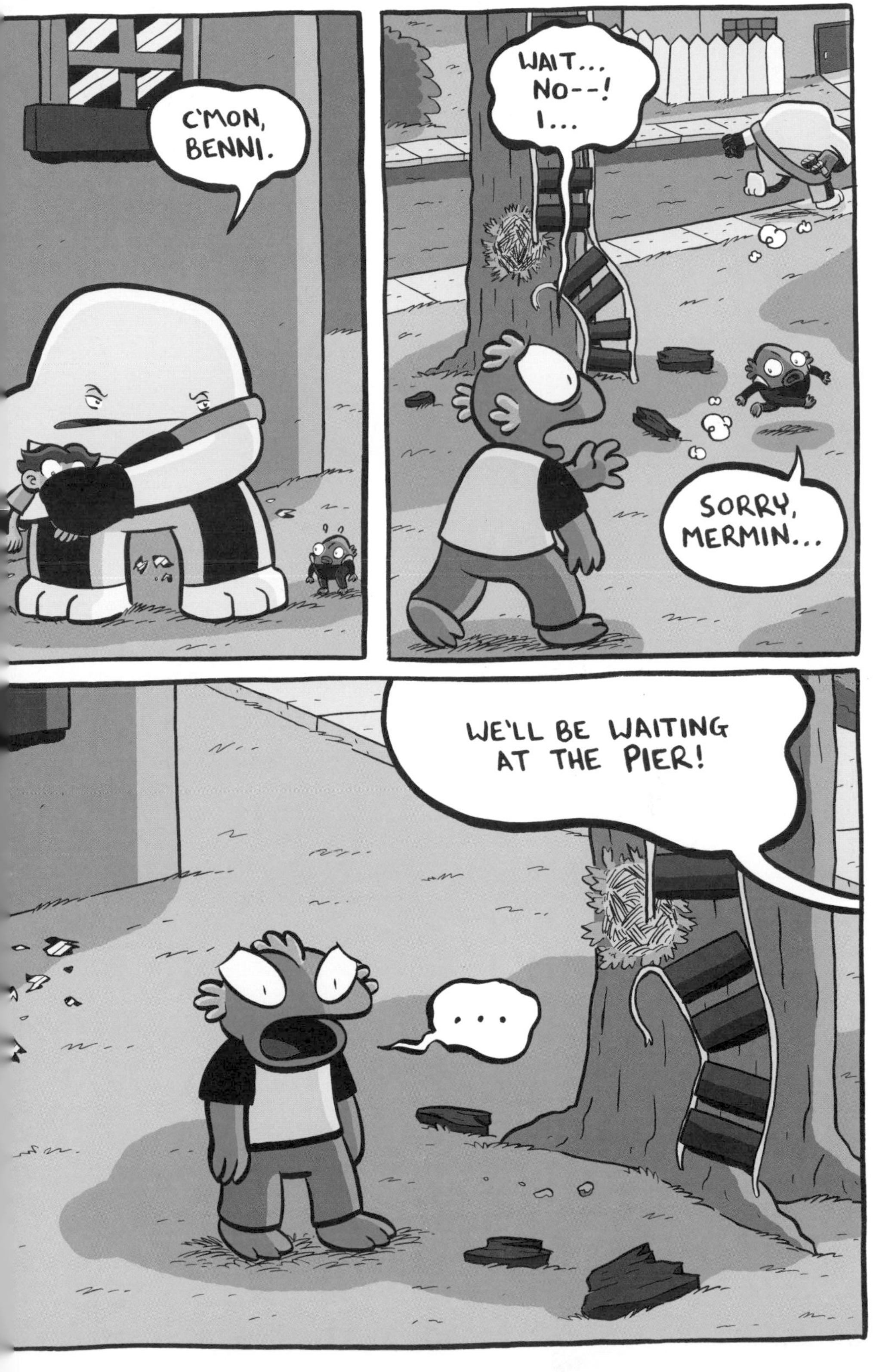
C'MON, BENNI.
WAIT..., NO--! I...
SORRY, MERMIN...
WE'LL BE WAITING AT THE PIER!
...

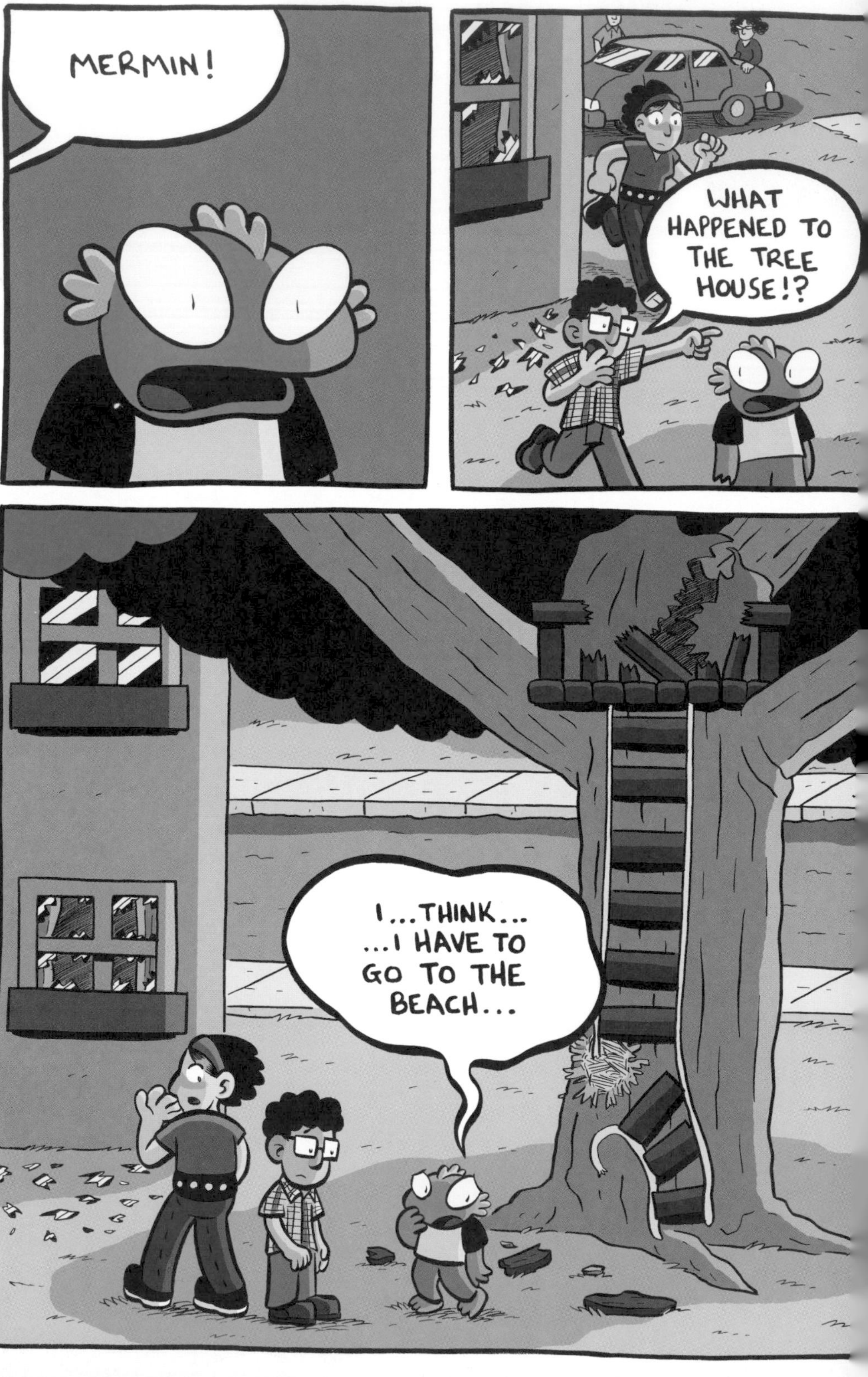
MERMIN!
WHAT HAPPENED TO THE TREE HOUSE!?
I...THINK...
...I HAVE TO GO TO THE BEACH...

CHAPTER FOUR

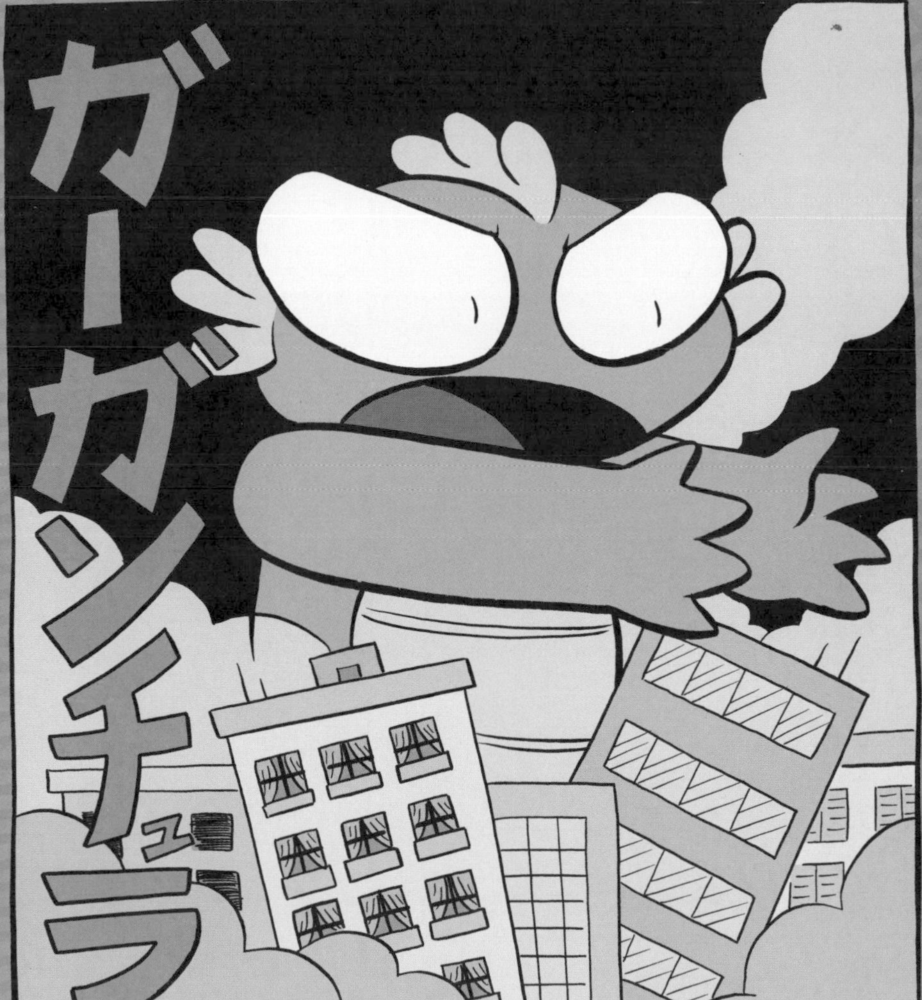
ガーガンチュラ

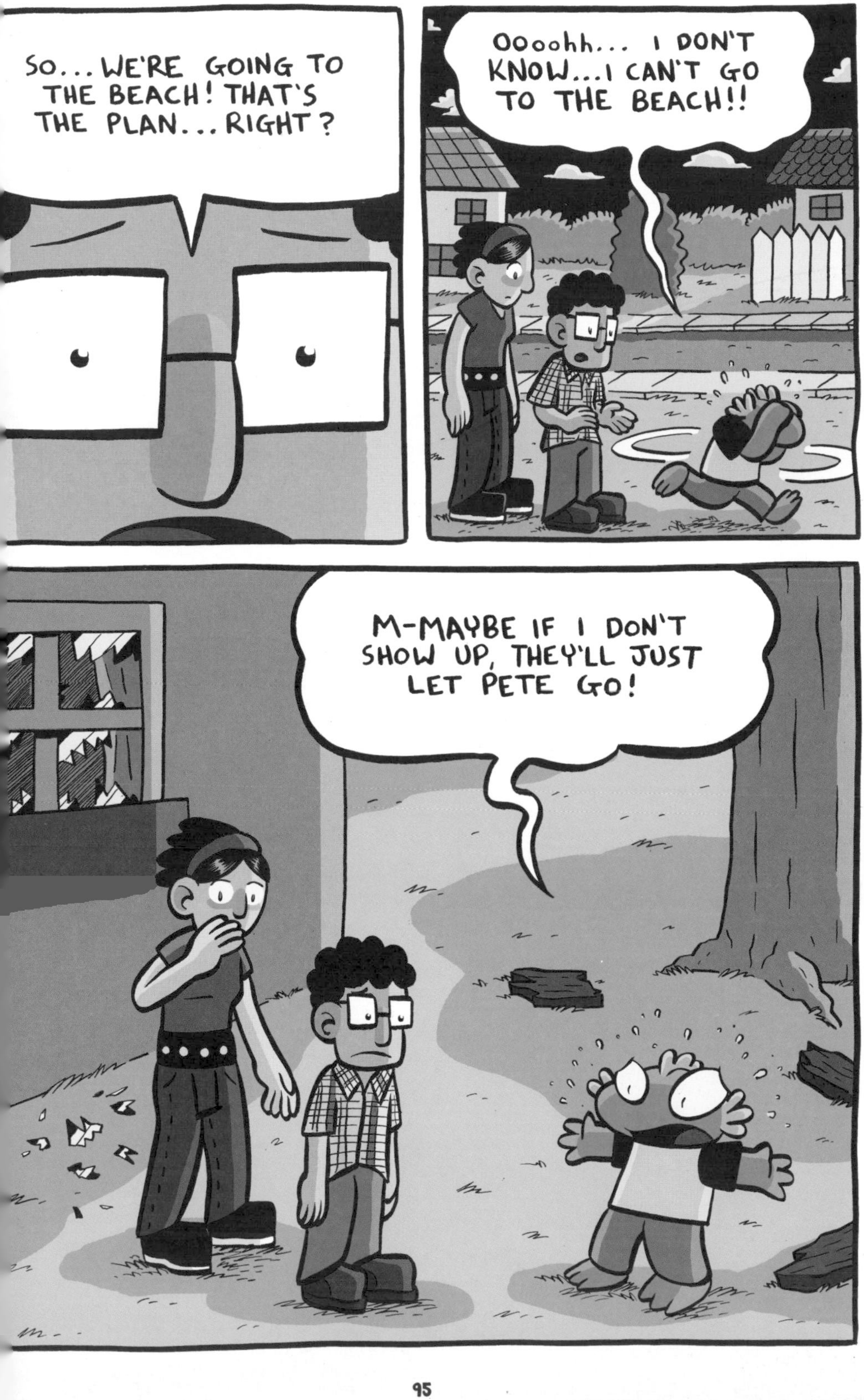
SO... WE'RE GOING TO THE BEACH! THAT'S THE PLAN... RIGHT?
OOoohh... I DON'T KNOW...I CAN'T GO TO THE BEACH!!
M-MAYBE IF I DON'T SHOW UP, THEY'LL JUST LET PETE GO!

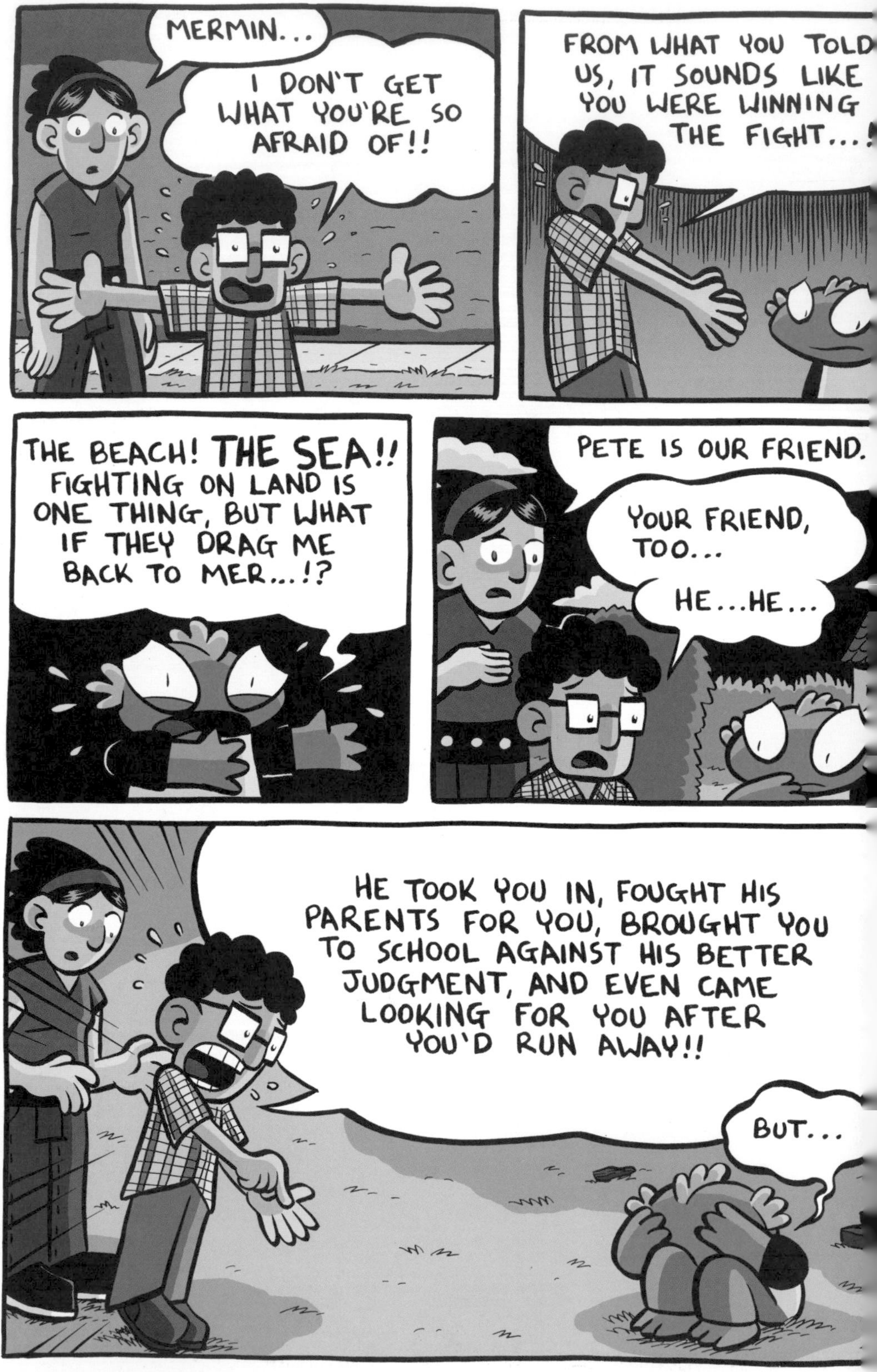
MERMIN...
I DON'T GET WHAT YOU'RE SO AFRAID OF!!
FROM WHAT YOU TOLD US, IT SOUNDS LIKE YOU WERE WINNING THE FIGHT...!
THE BEACH! THE SEA!! FIGHTING ON LAND IS ONE THING, BUT WHAT IF THEY DRAG ME BACK TO MER...!?
PETE IS OUR FRIEND.
YOUR FRIEND, TOO...
HE...HE...
HE TOOK YOU IN, FOUGHT HIS PARENTS FOR YOU, BROUGHT YOU TO SCHOOL AGAINST HIS BETTER JUDGMENT, AND EVEN CAME LOOKING FOR YOU AFTER YOU'D RUN AWAY!!
BUT...

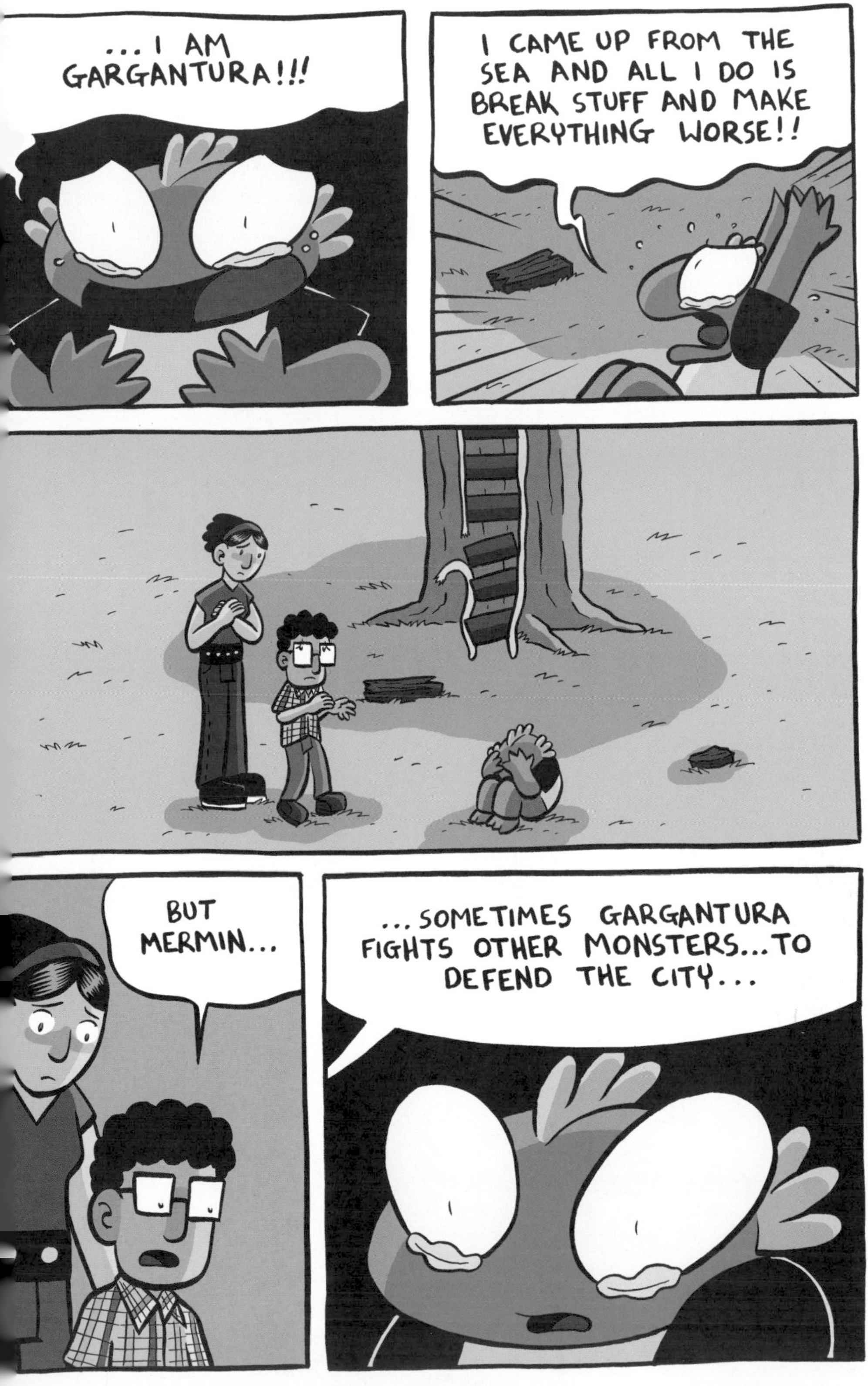

...I AM GARGANTURA!!!
I CAME UP FROM THE SEA AND ALL I DO IS BREAK STUFF AND MAKE EVERYTHING WORSE!!
BUT MERMIN...
...SOMETIMES GARGANTURA FIGHTS OTHER MONSTERS...TO DEFEND THE CITY...

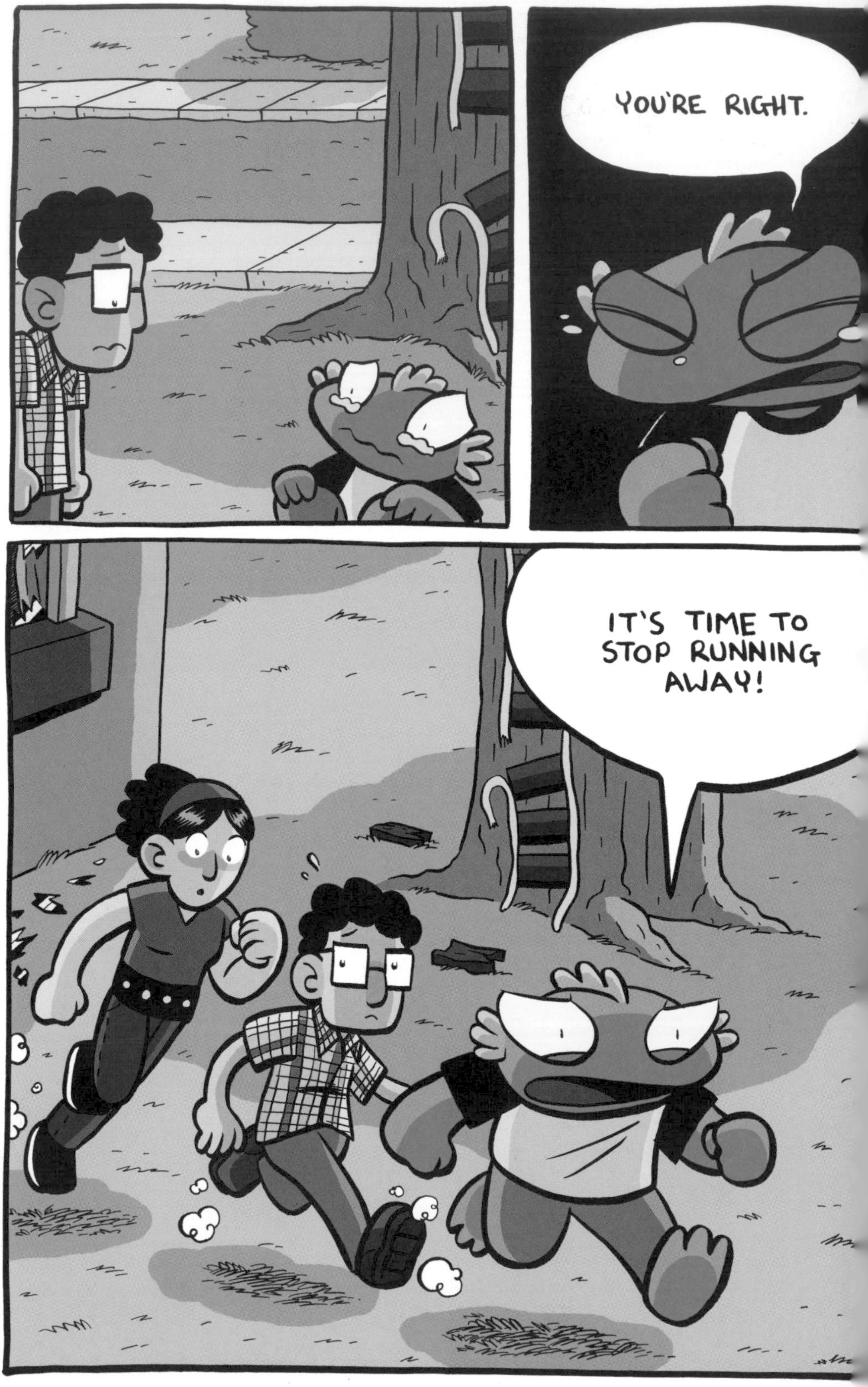
YOU'RE RIGHT.
IT'S TIME TO STOP RUNNING AWAY!

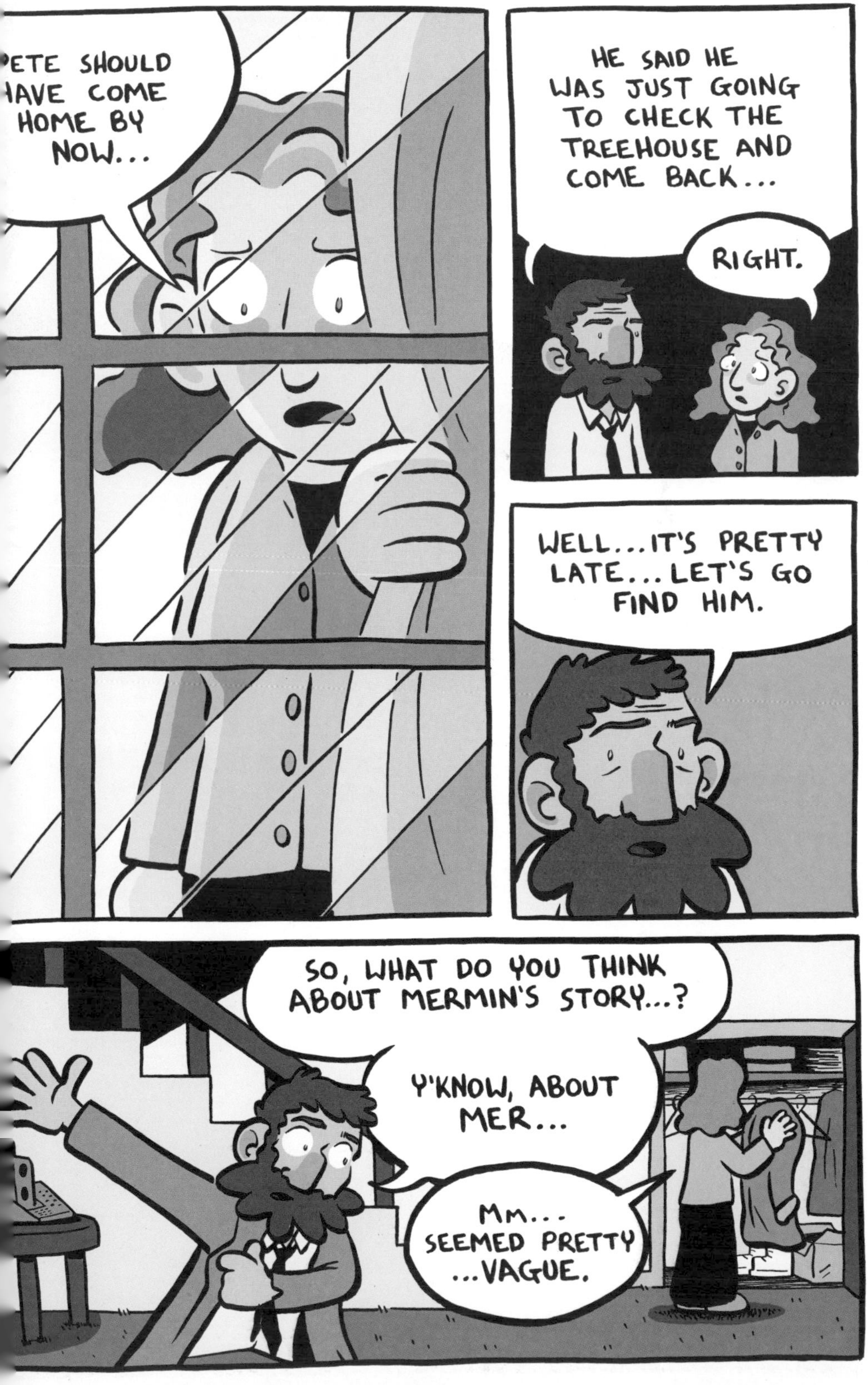
PETE SHOULD HAVE COME HOME BY NOW...
HE SAID HE WAS JUST GOING TO CHECK THE TREEHOUSE AND COME BACK...
RIGHT.
WELL... IT'S PRETTY LATE... LET'S GO FIND HIM.
SO, WHAT DO YOU THINK ABOUT MERMIN'S STORY...?
Y'KNOW, ABOUT MER...
Mm... SEEMED PRETTY ...VAGUE.

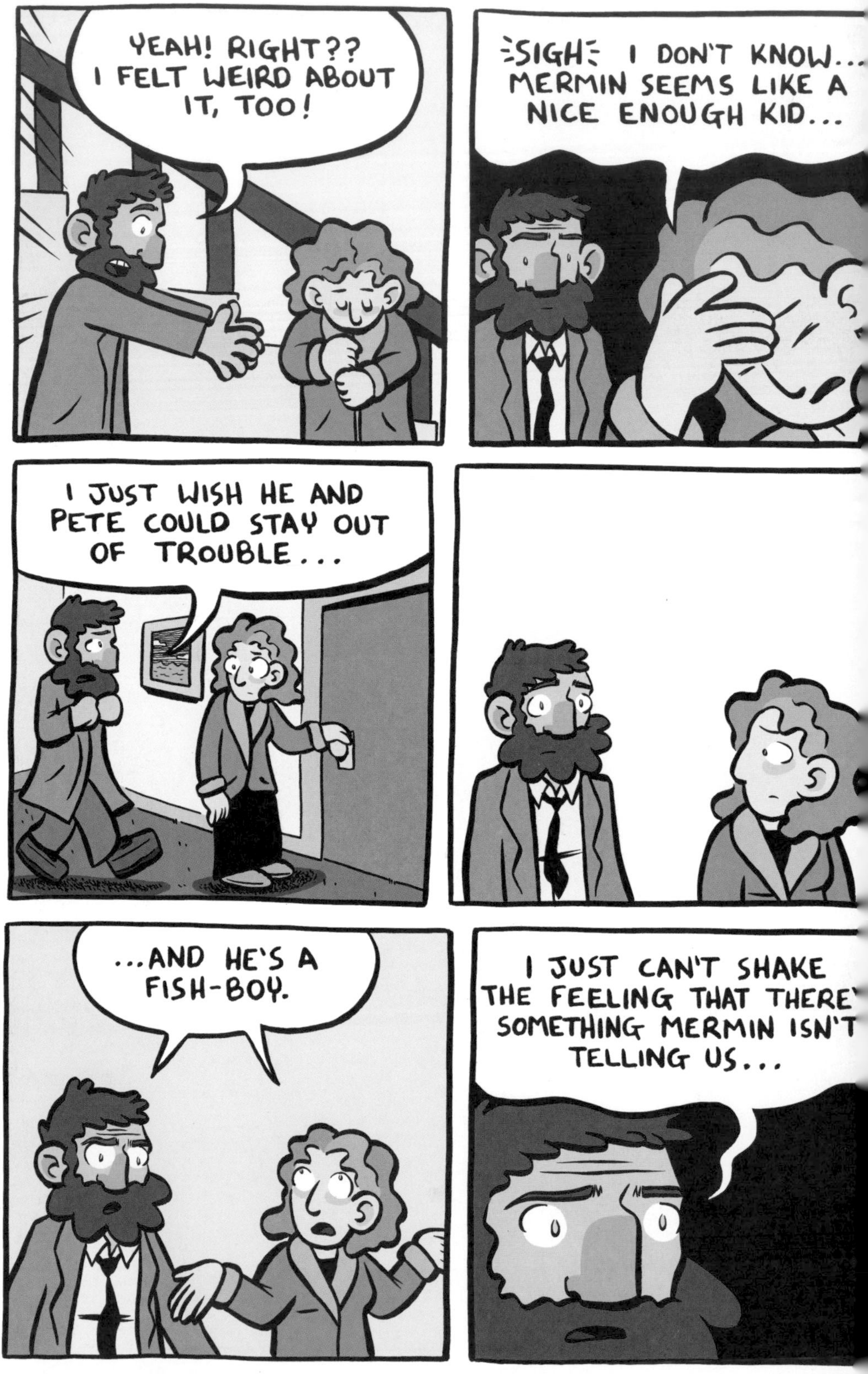
YEAH! RIGHT?? I FELT WEIRD ABOUT IT, TOO!
SIGH I DON'T KNOW... MERMIN SEEMS LIKE A NICE ENOUGH KID...
I JUST WISH HE AND PETE COULD STAY OUT OF TROUBLE...
...AND HE'S A FISH-BOY.
I JUST CAN'T SHAKE THE FEELING THAT THERE' SOMETHING MERMIN ISN'T TELLING US...

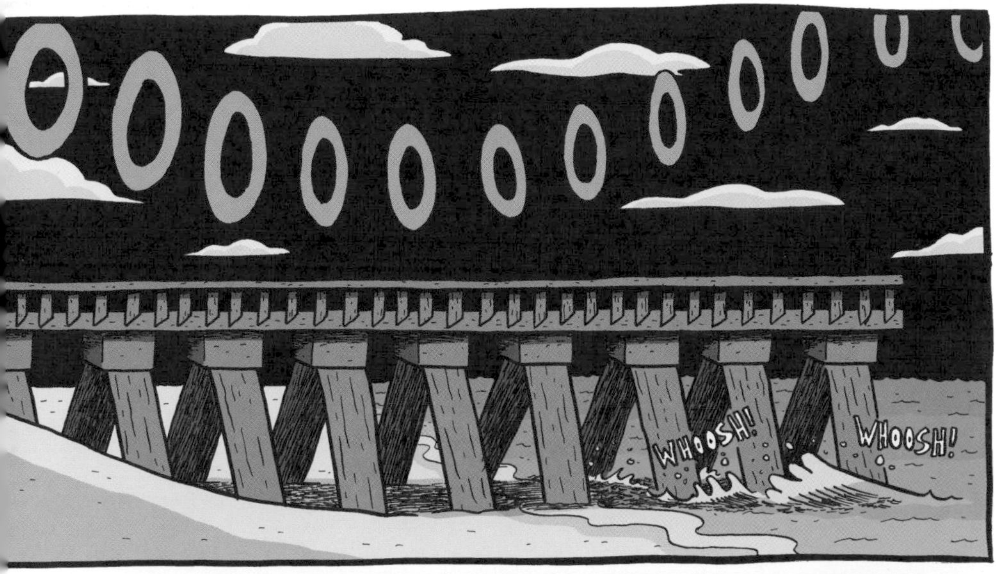
WHOOSH!
WHOOSH!
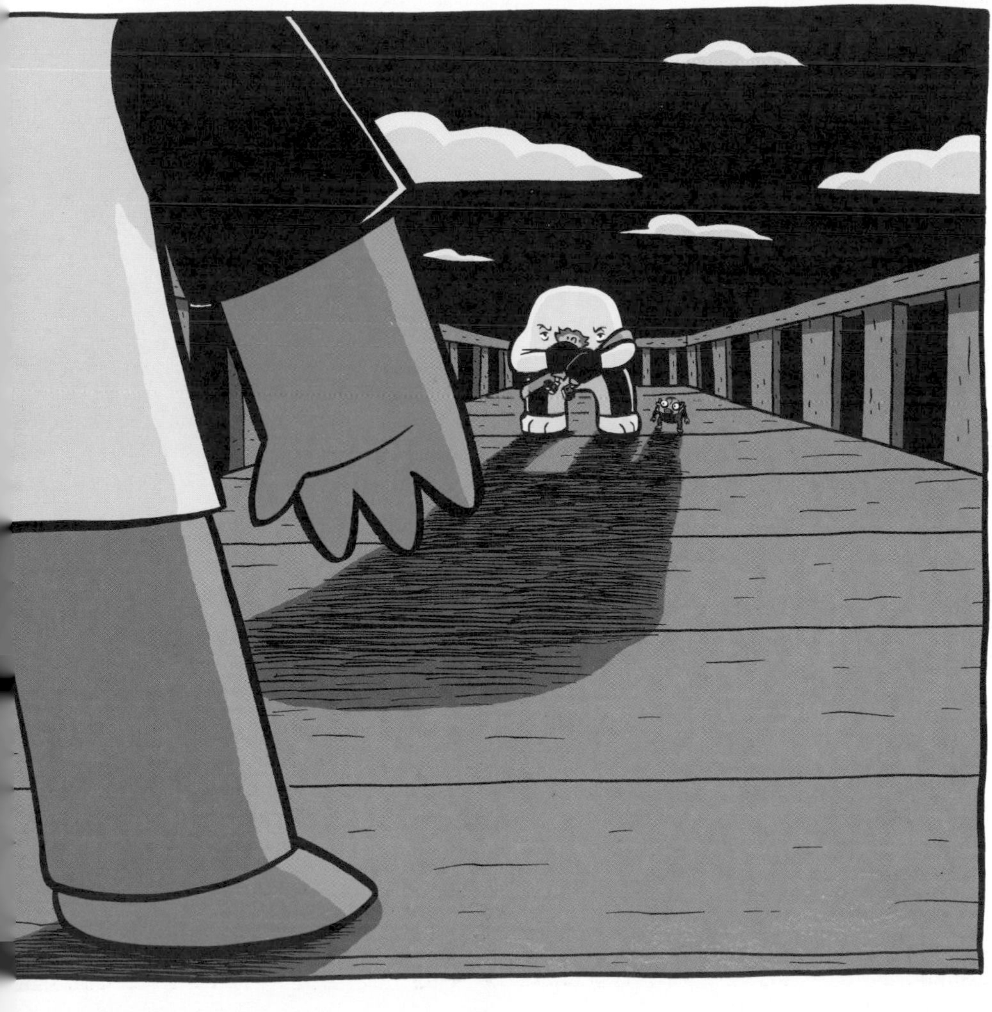

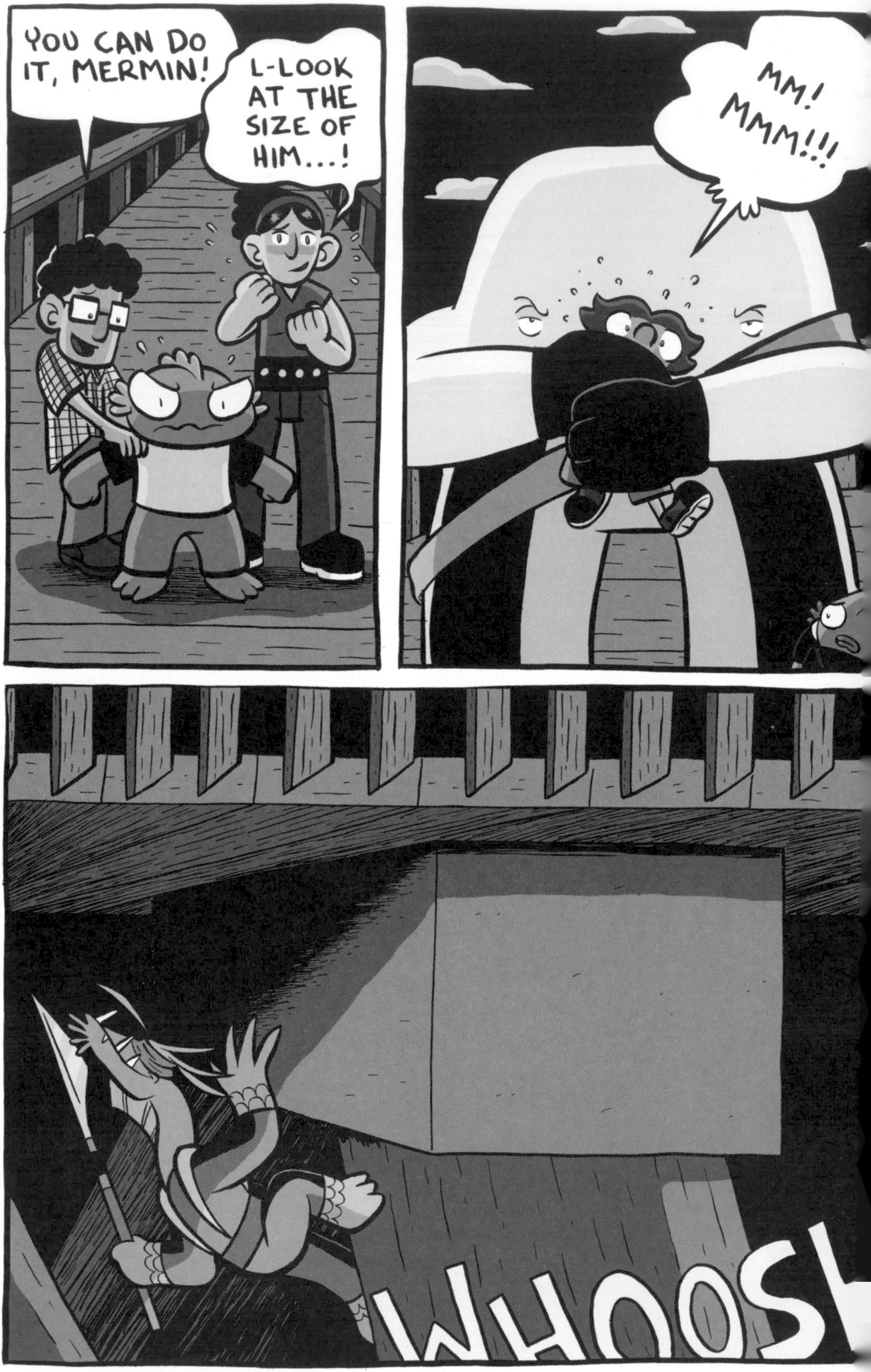
YOU CAN DO IT, MERMIN!
L-LOOK AT THE SIZE OF HIM...!
MM! MMM!!!
WHOOS

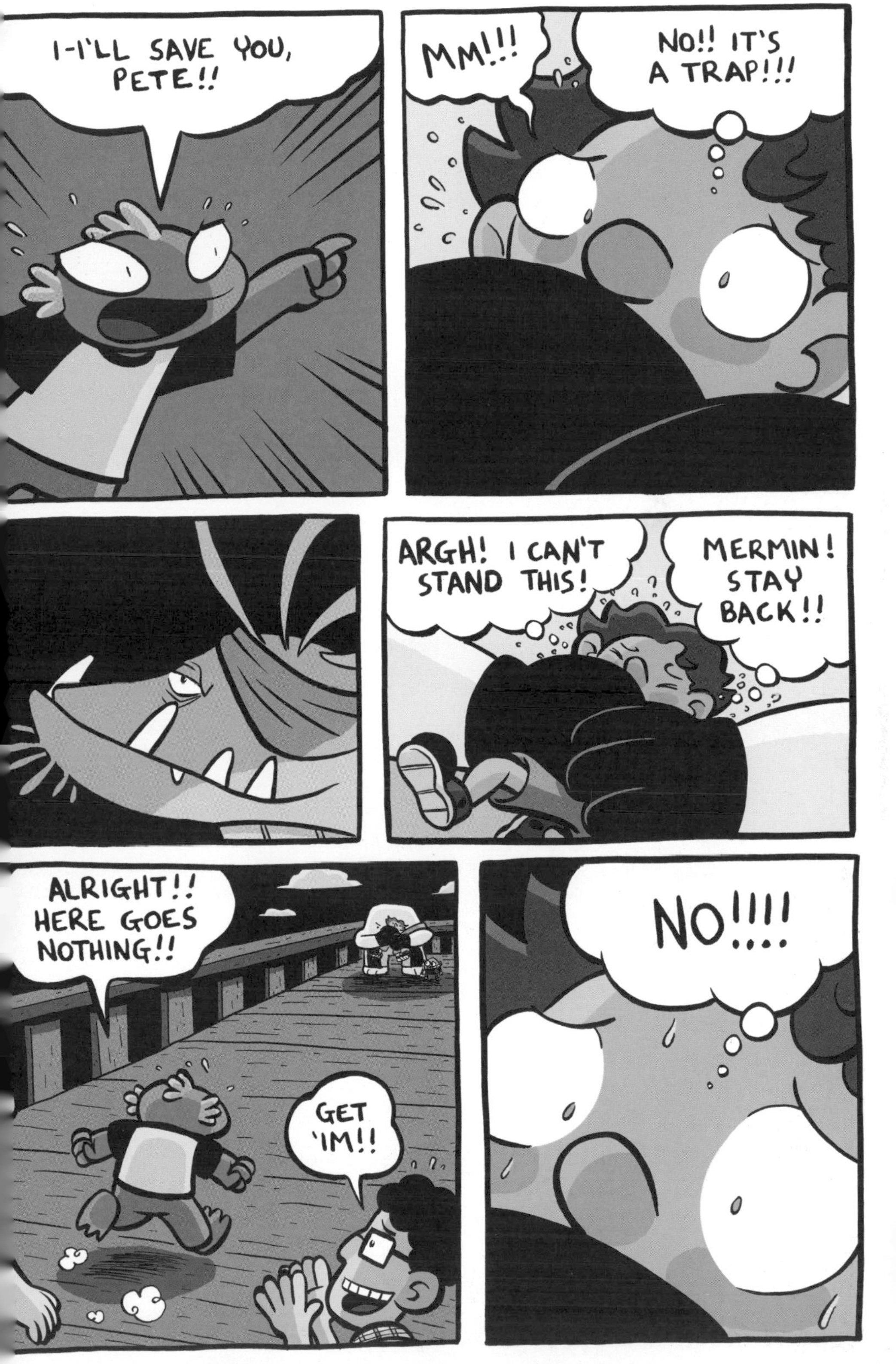
I-I'LL SAVE YOU, PETE!!
MM!!!
NO!! IT'S A TRAP!!!
ARGH! I CAN'T STAND THIS!
MERMIN! STAY BACK!!
ALRIGHT!! HERE GOES NOTHING!!
GET 'IM!!
NO!!!!

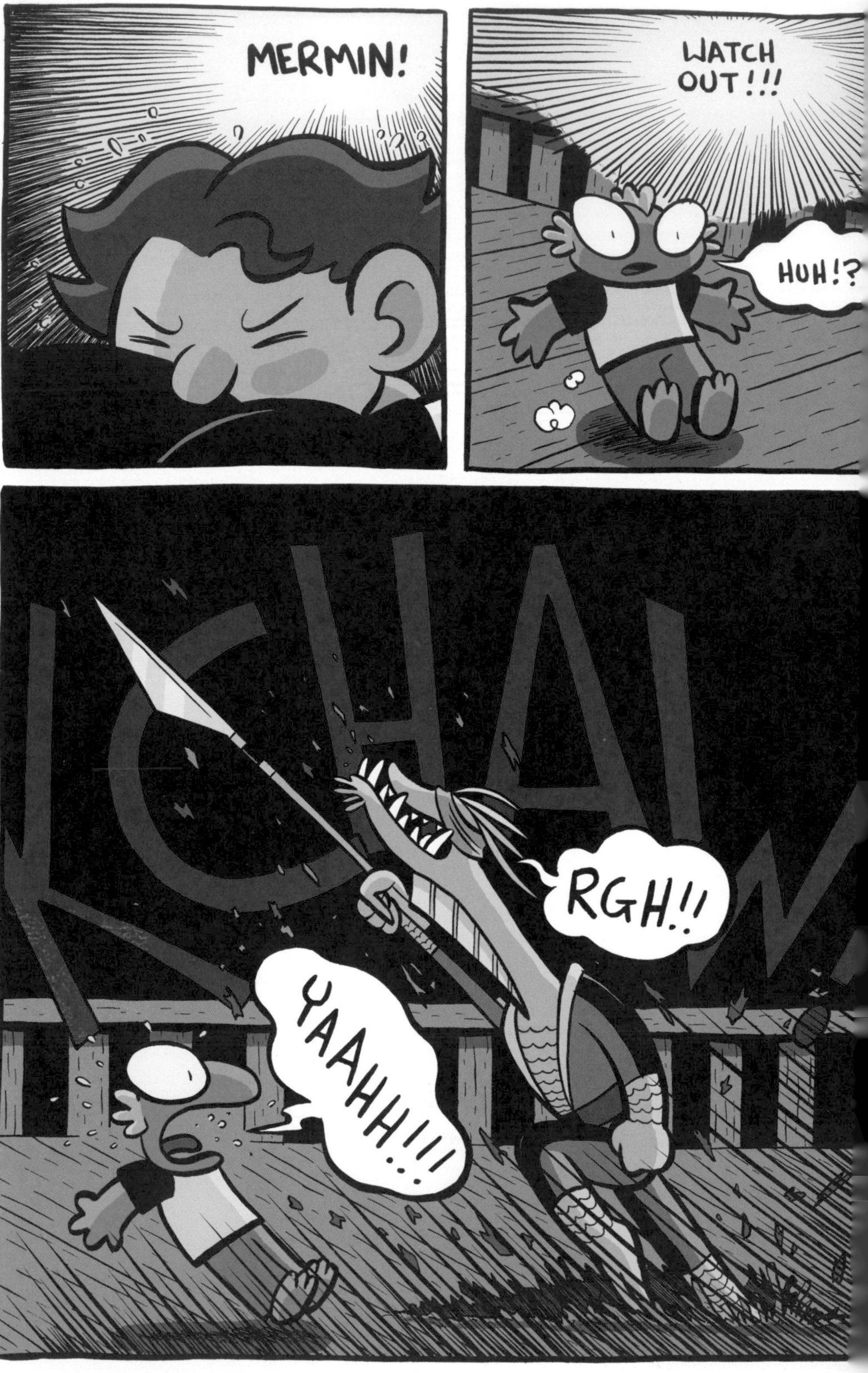
MERMIN!
WATCH OUT!!!
HUH!?
RGH!!
YAAHH!!!

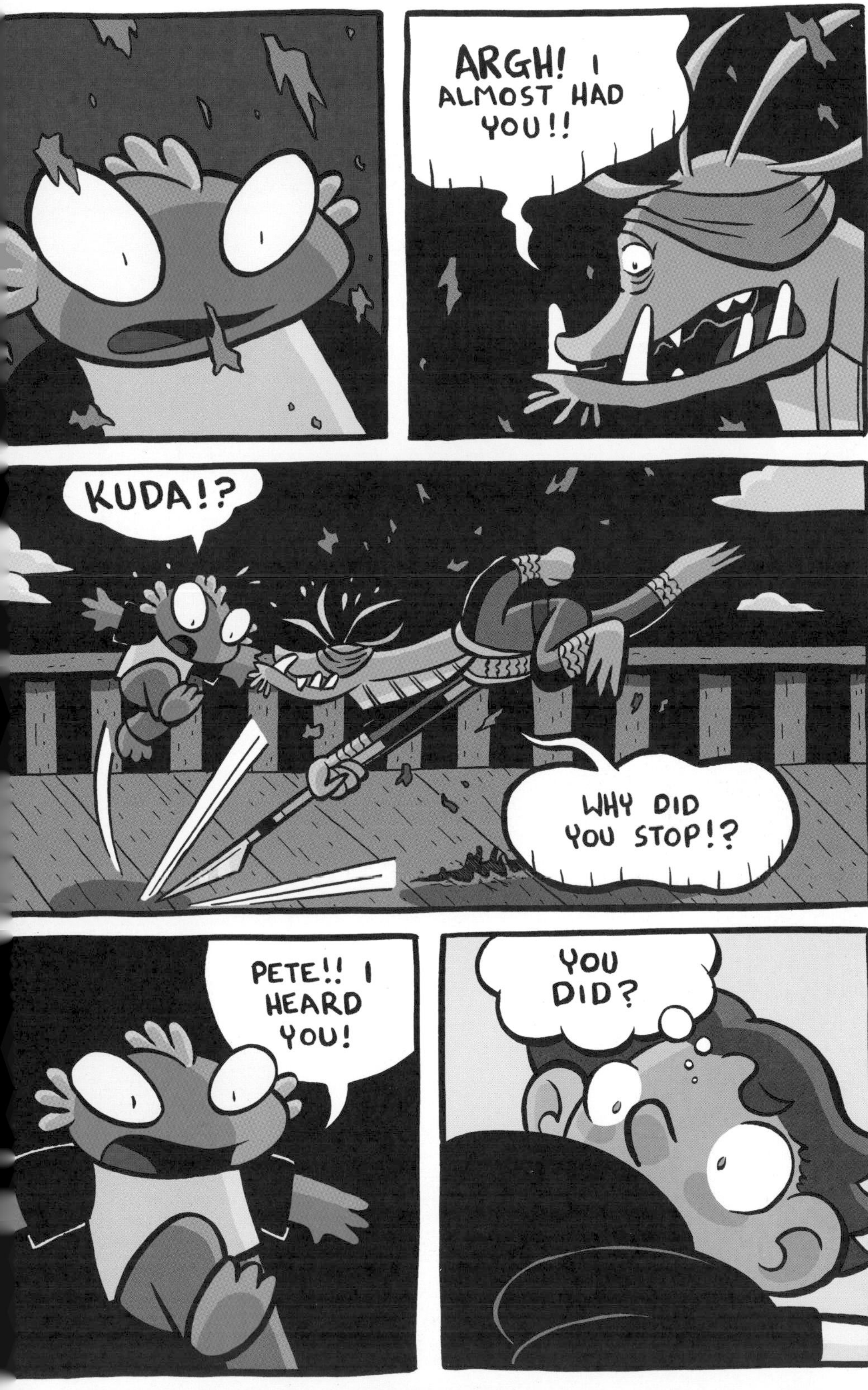
ARGH! I ALMOST HAD YOU!!
KUDA!?
WHY DID YOU STOP!?
PETE!! I HEARD YOU!
YOU DID?

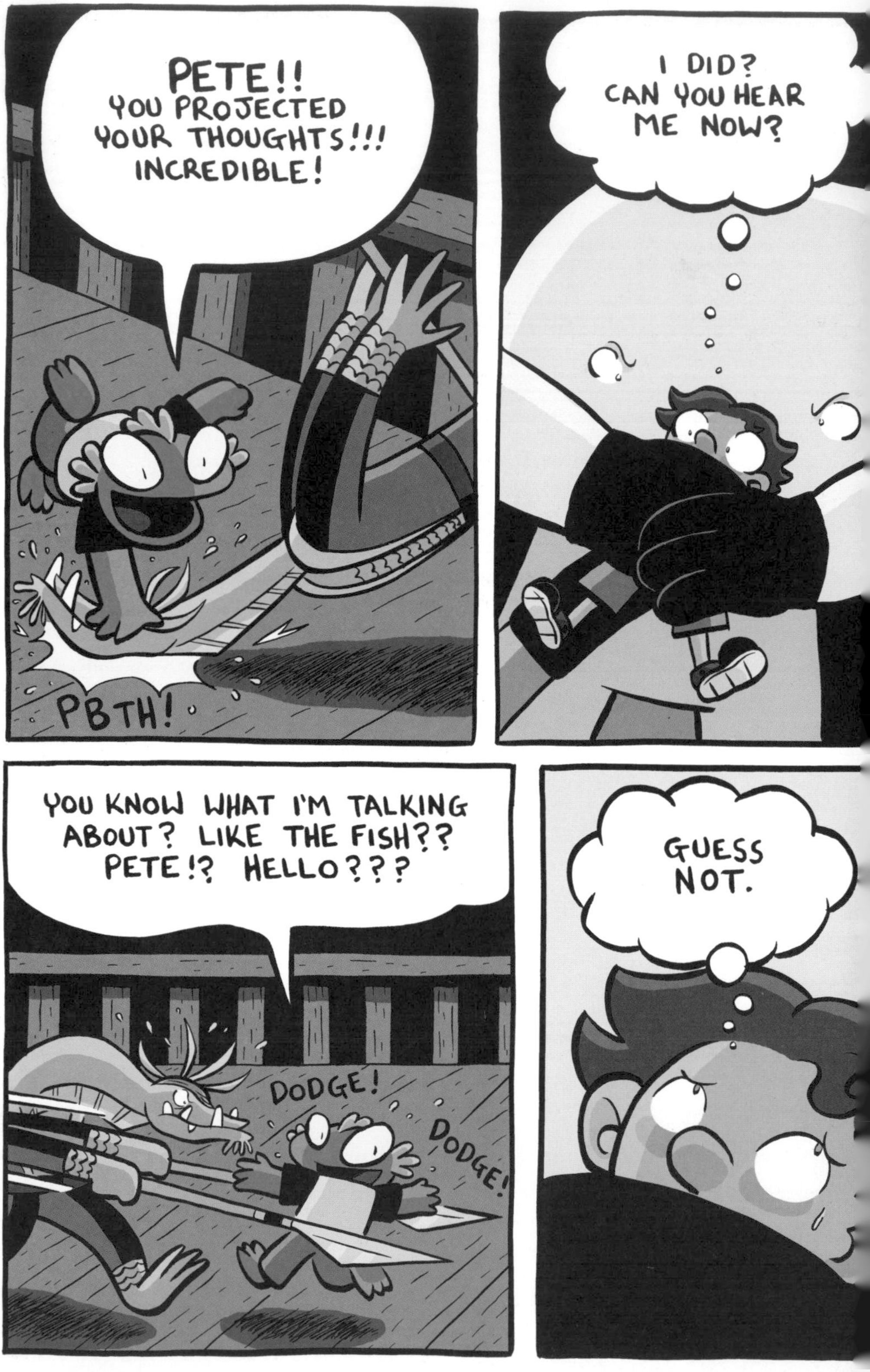
PETE!! YOU PROJECTED YOUR THOUGHTS!!! INCREDIBLE!
PBTH!
I DID? CAN YOU HEAR ME NOW?
YOU KNOW WHAT I'M TALKING ABOUT? LIKE THE FISH?? PETE!? HELLO???
DODGE!
DODGE!
GUESS NOT.

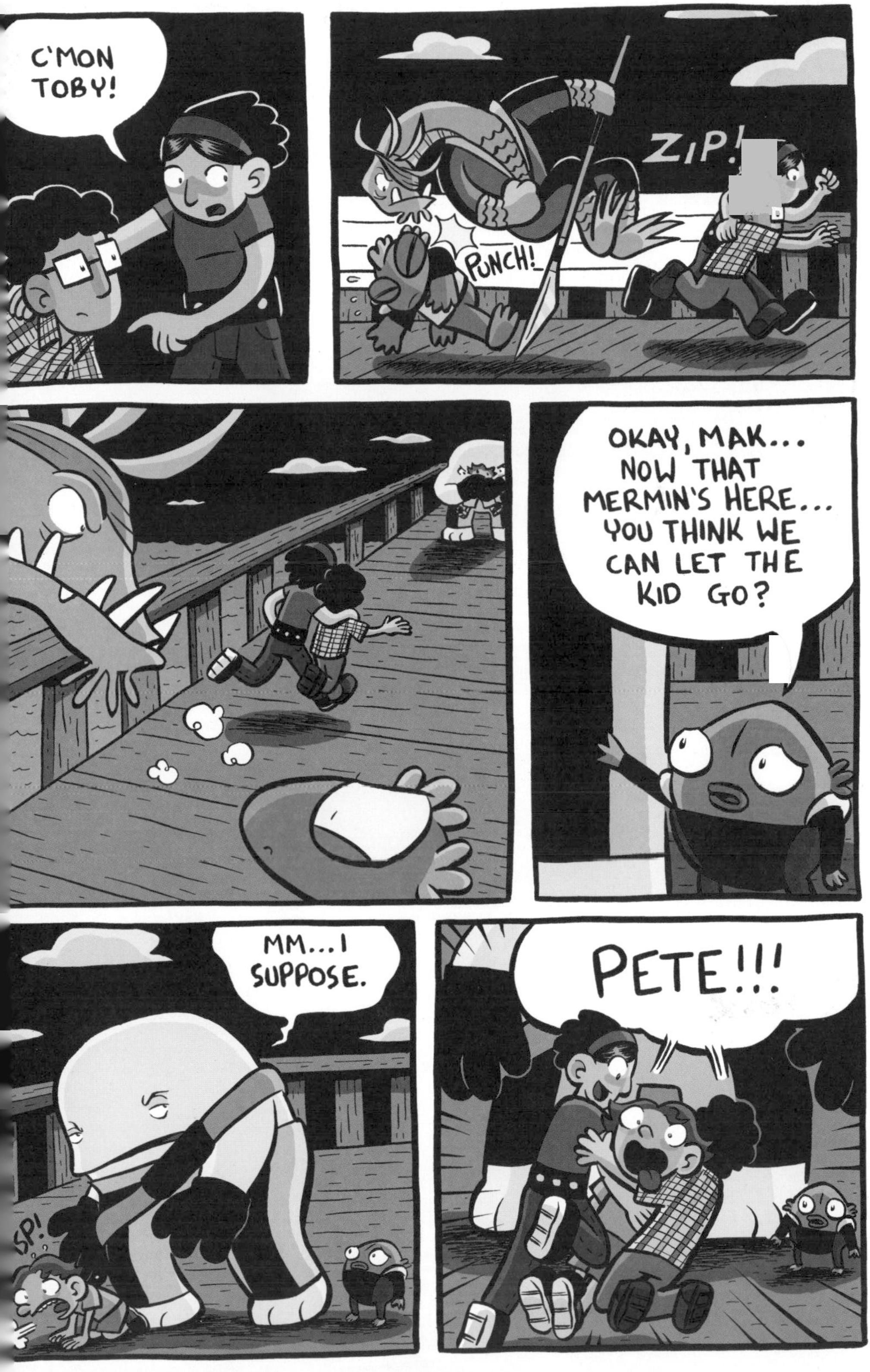
C'MON TOBY!
ZIP!
PUNCH!
OKAY, MAK... NOW THAT MERMIN'S HERE... YOU THINK WE CAN LET THE KID GO?
MM... I SUPPOSE.
PETE!!!

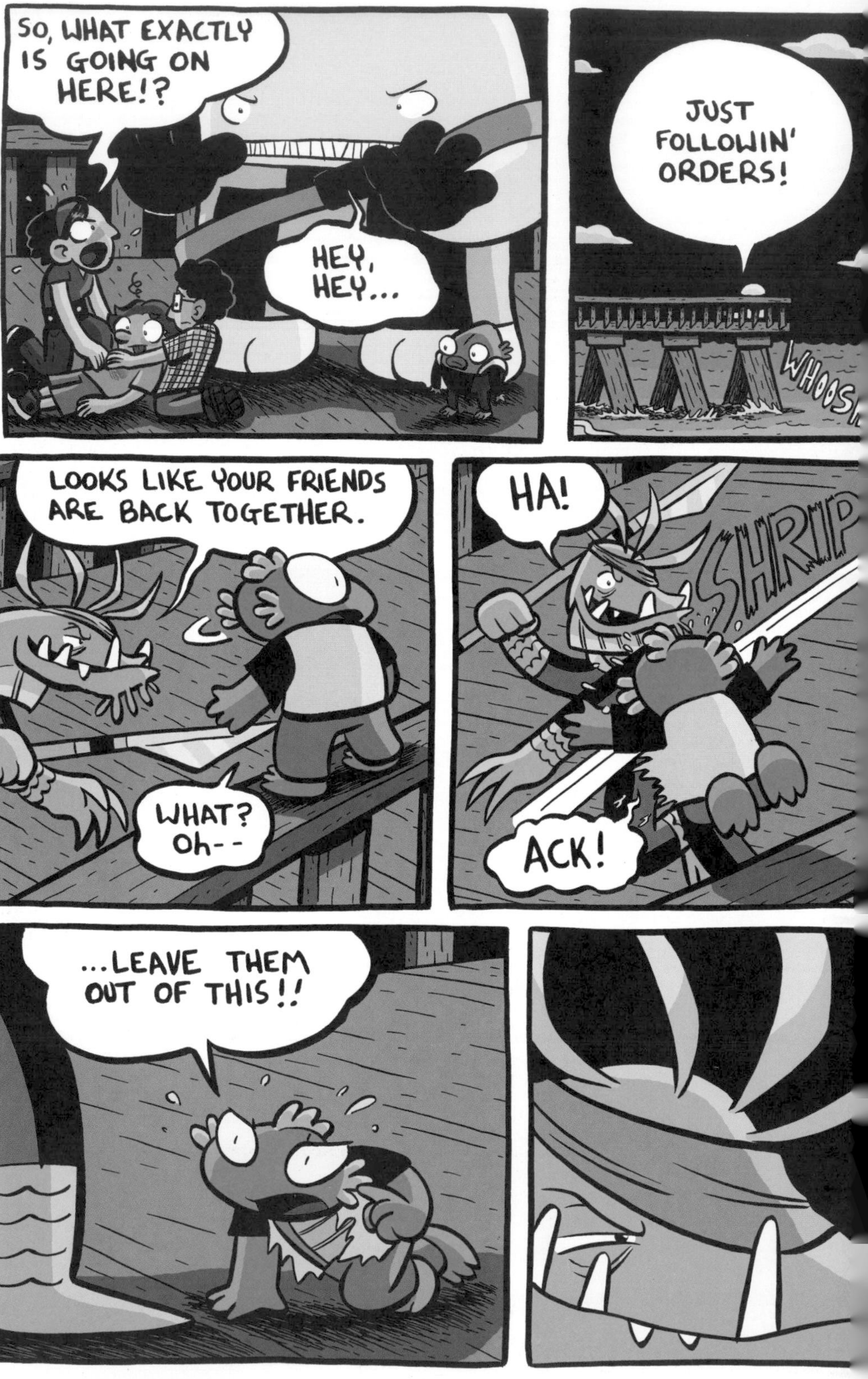
SO, WHAT EXACTLY IS GOING ON HERE!?
HEY, HEY...
JUST FOLLOWIN' ORDERS!
WHOOS
LOOKS LIKE YOUR FRIENDS ARE BACK TOGETHER.
WHAT? Oh--
HA!
SHRIP
ACK!
...LEAVE THEM OUT OF THIS!!

WHAT KIND OF **MANIAC** FATHER SENDS MERCENARIES AFTER HIS OWN SON!?!

uhhh...

IT'S COMPLICATED.

LOOK, KID...

MERMIN'S TOUGH...

SOCK!

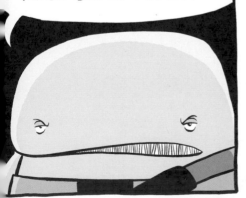

WE'RE **TRYING** TO JUST ROUGH HIM UP A BIT SO HE'LL COME HOME...

IT SOUNDS TO **ME** LIKE MER IS A TERRIBLE PLACE FILLED WITH **LUNATICS!**

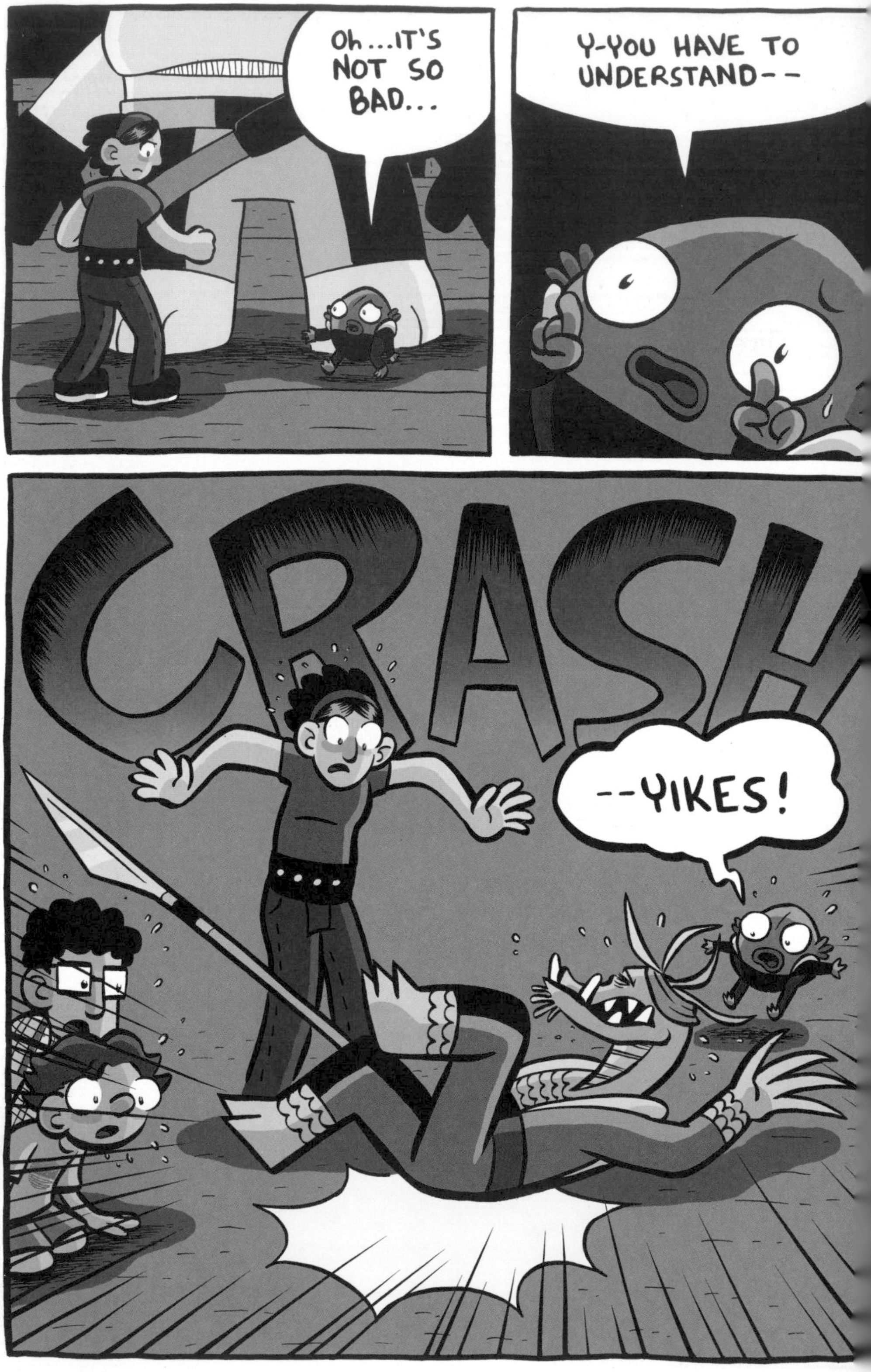
Oh...IT'S NOT SO BAD...
Y-YOU HAVE TO UNDERSTAND--
CRASH
--YIKES!

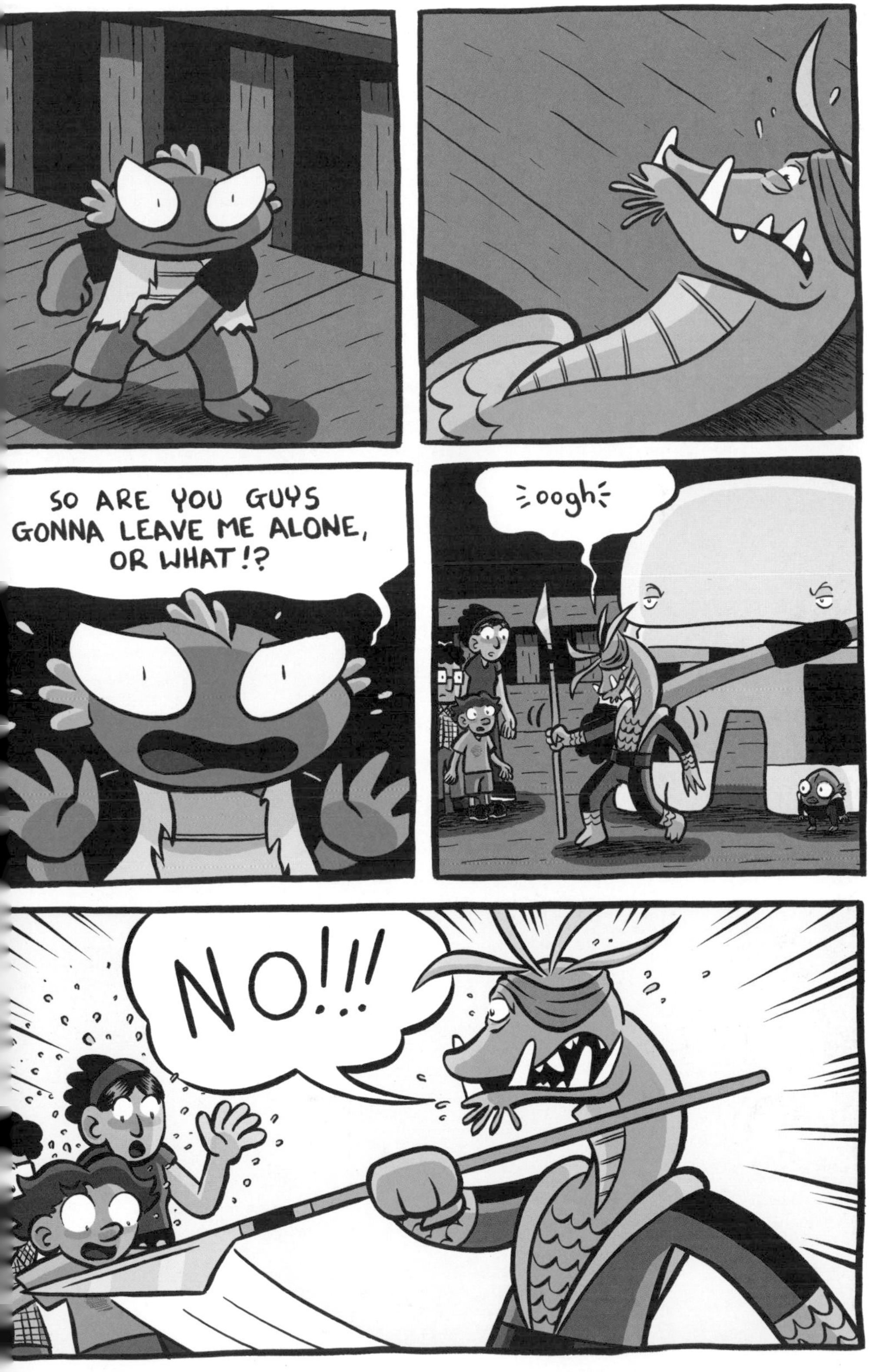
SO ARE YOU GUYS GONNA LEAVE ME ALONE, OR WHAT!?
oogh
NO!!!

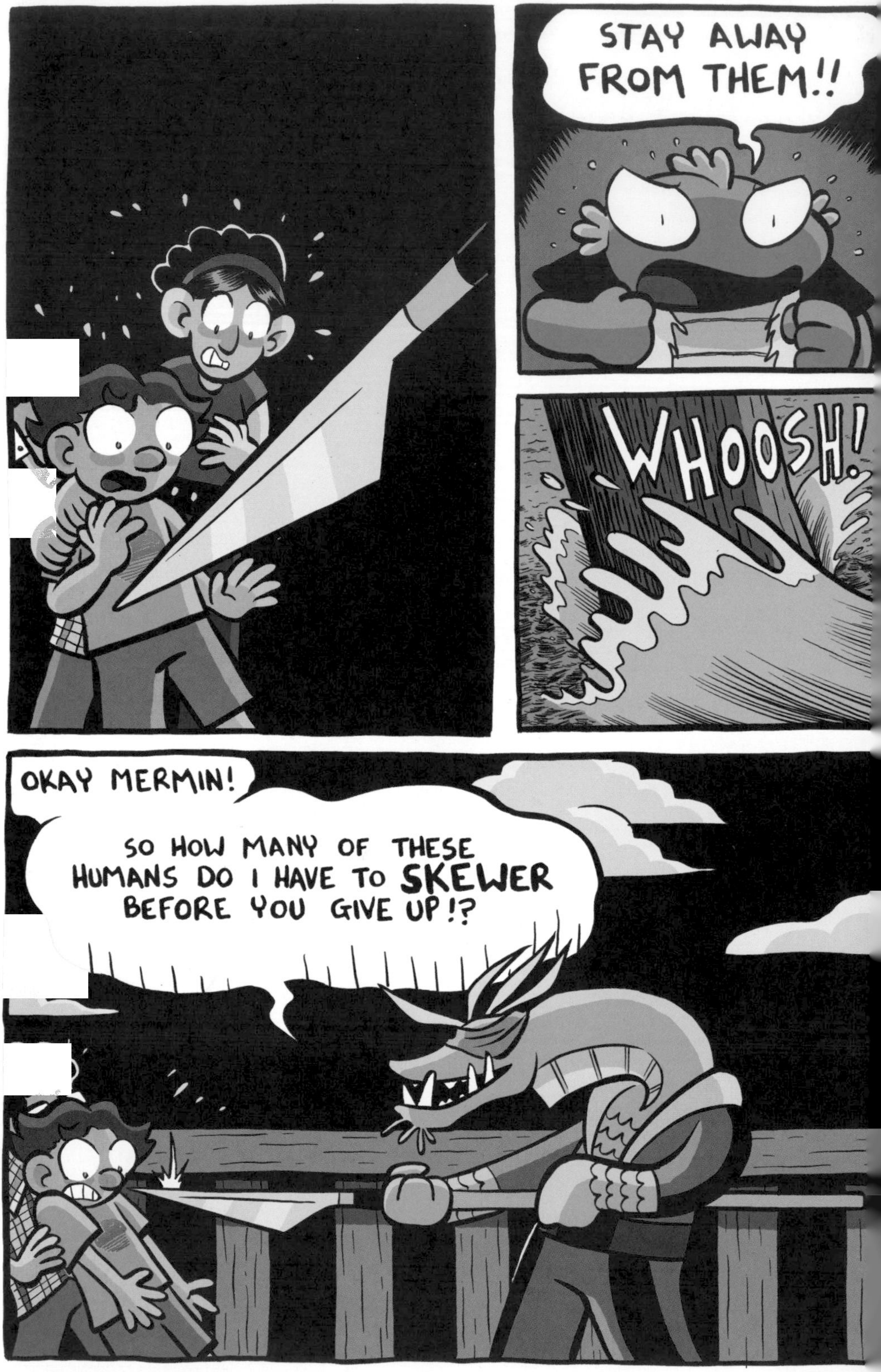
STAY AWAY FROM THEM!!
WHOOSH!
OKAY MERMIN!
SO HOW MANY OF THESE HUMANS DO I HAVE TO SKEWER BEFORE YOU GIVE UP!?

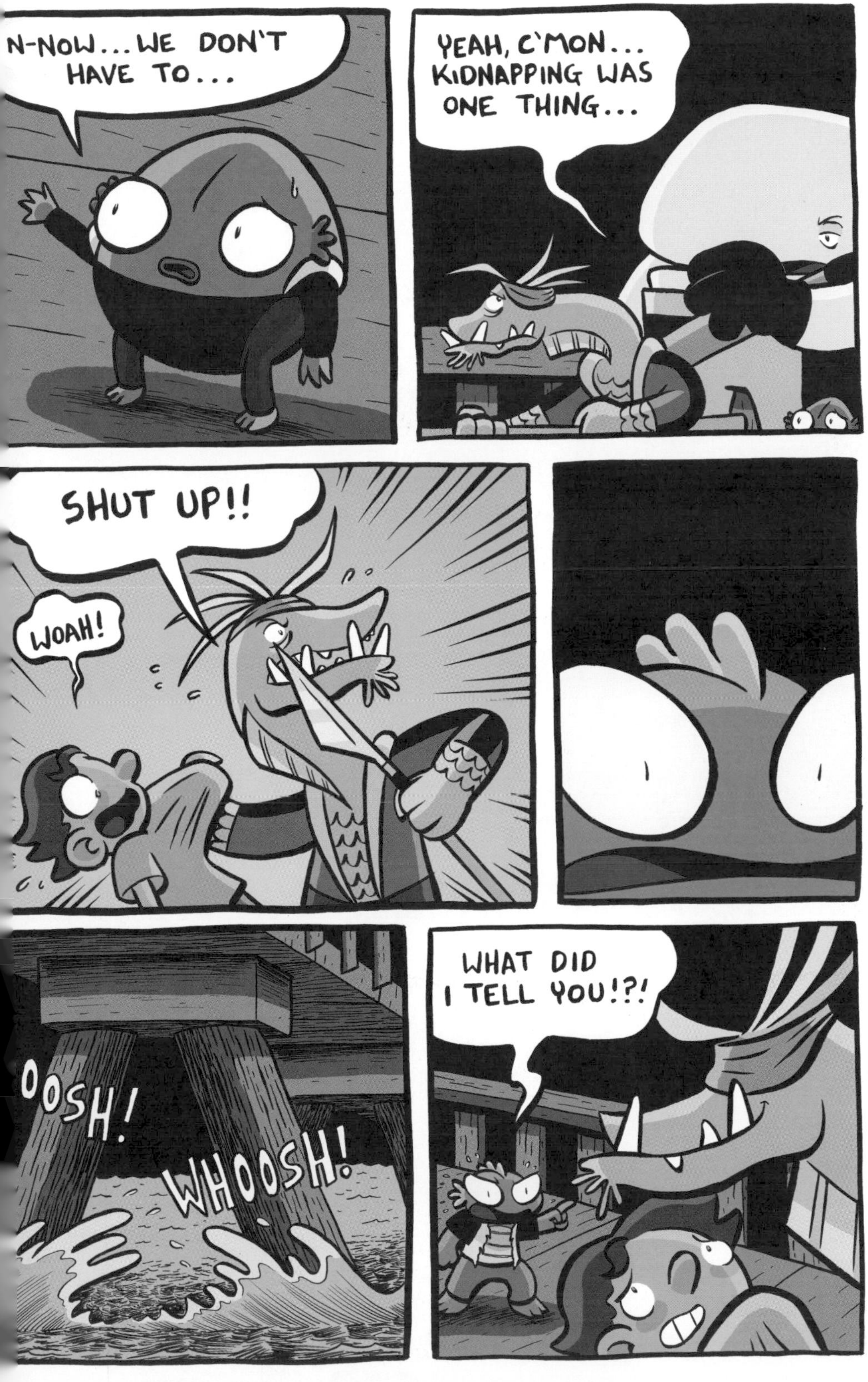
N-NOW... WE DON'T HAVE TO...
YEAH, C'MON... KIDNAPPING WAS ONE THING...
SHUT UP!!
WOAH!
OOSH!
WHOOSH!
WHAT DID I TELL YOU!?!

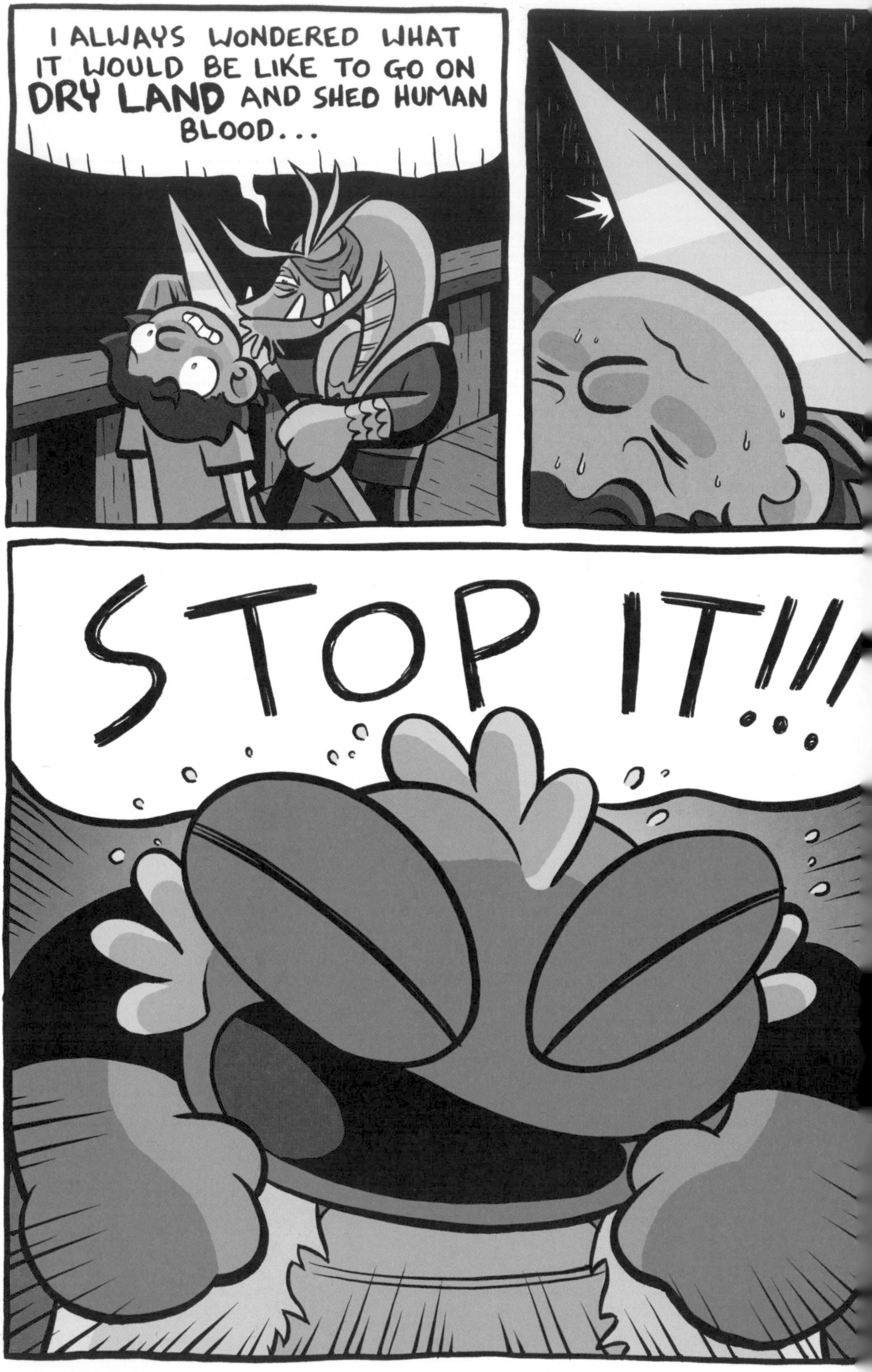
I ALWAYS WONDERED WHAT IT WOULD BE LIKE TO GO ON DRY LAND AND SHED HUMAN BLOOD...
STOP IT!!!

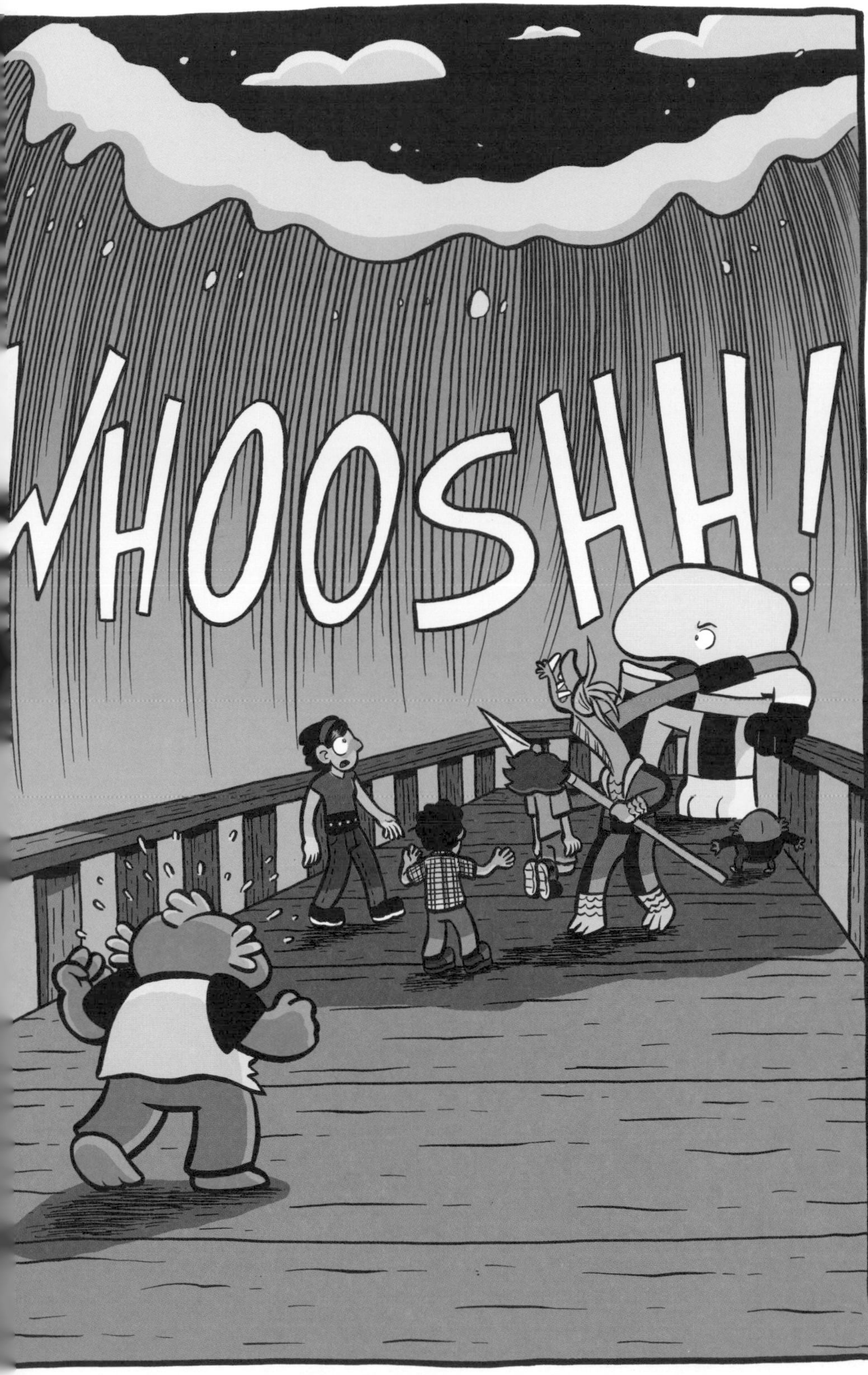
WHOOSHH!

CHAPTER FIVE

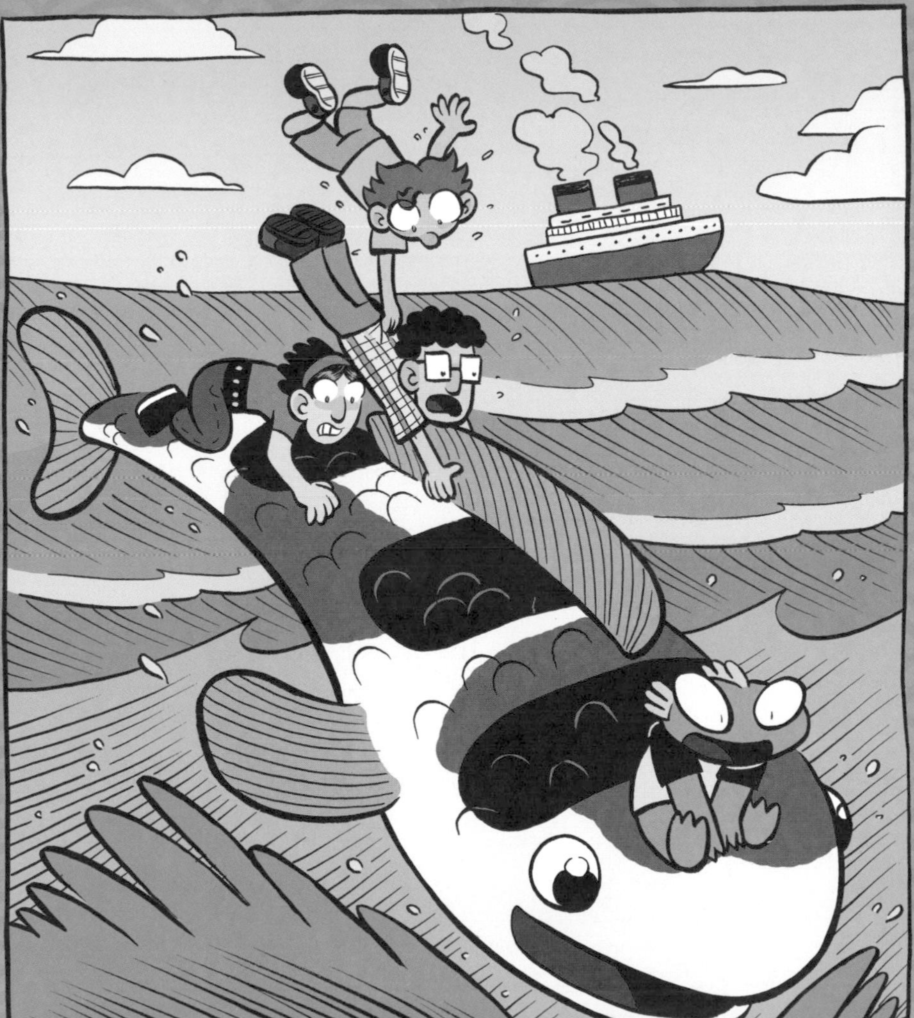

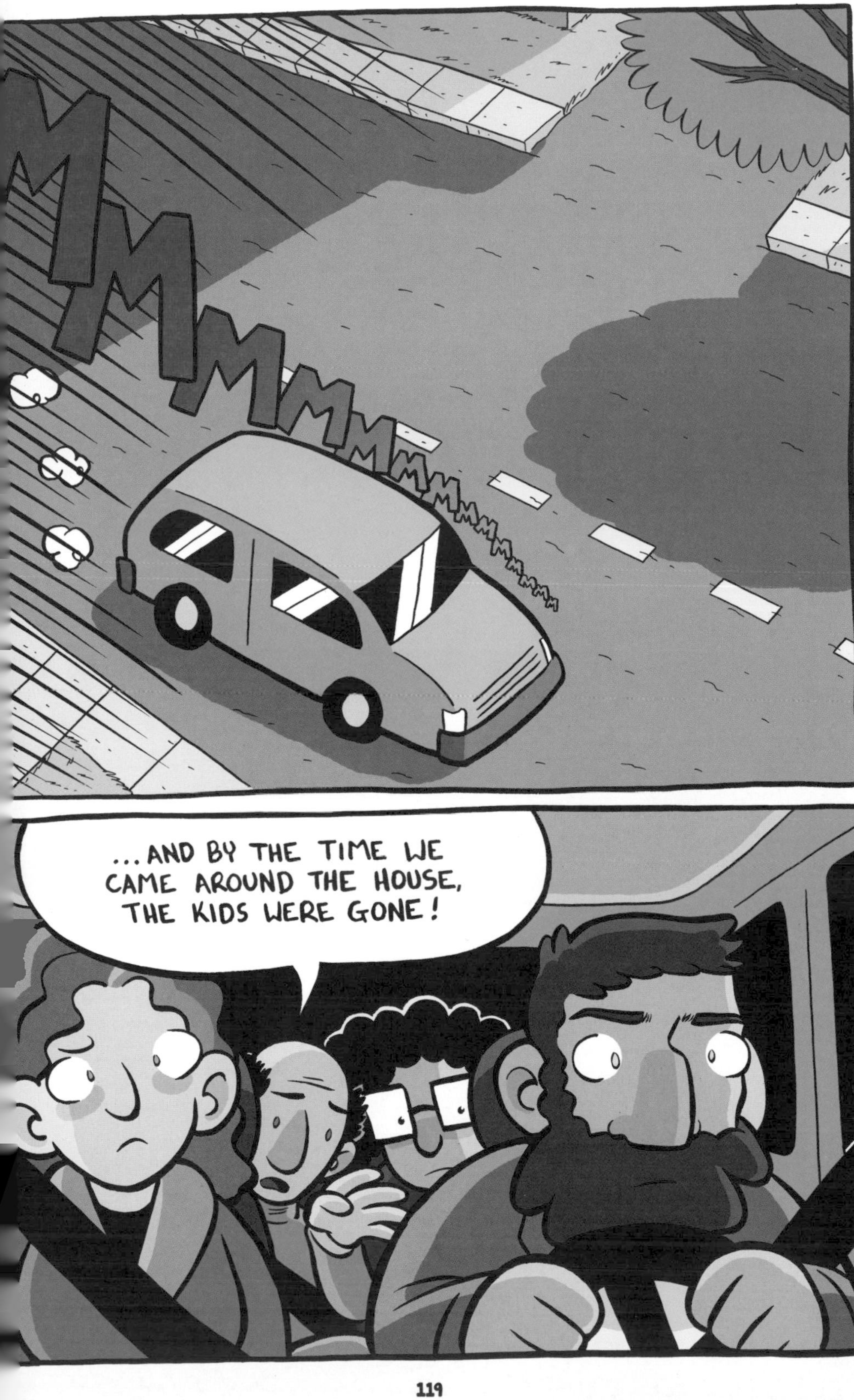
MMMMMMMMMMMMMMMM
...AND BY THE TIME WE CAME AROUND THE HOUSE, THE KIDS WERE GONE!

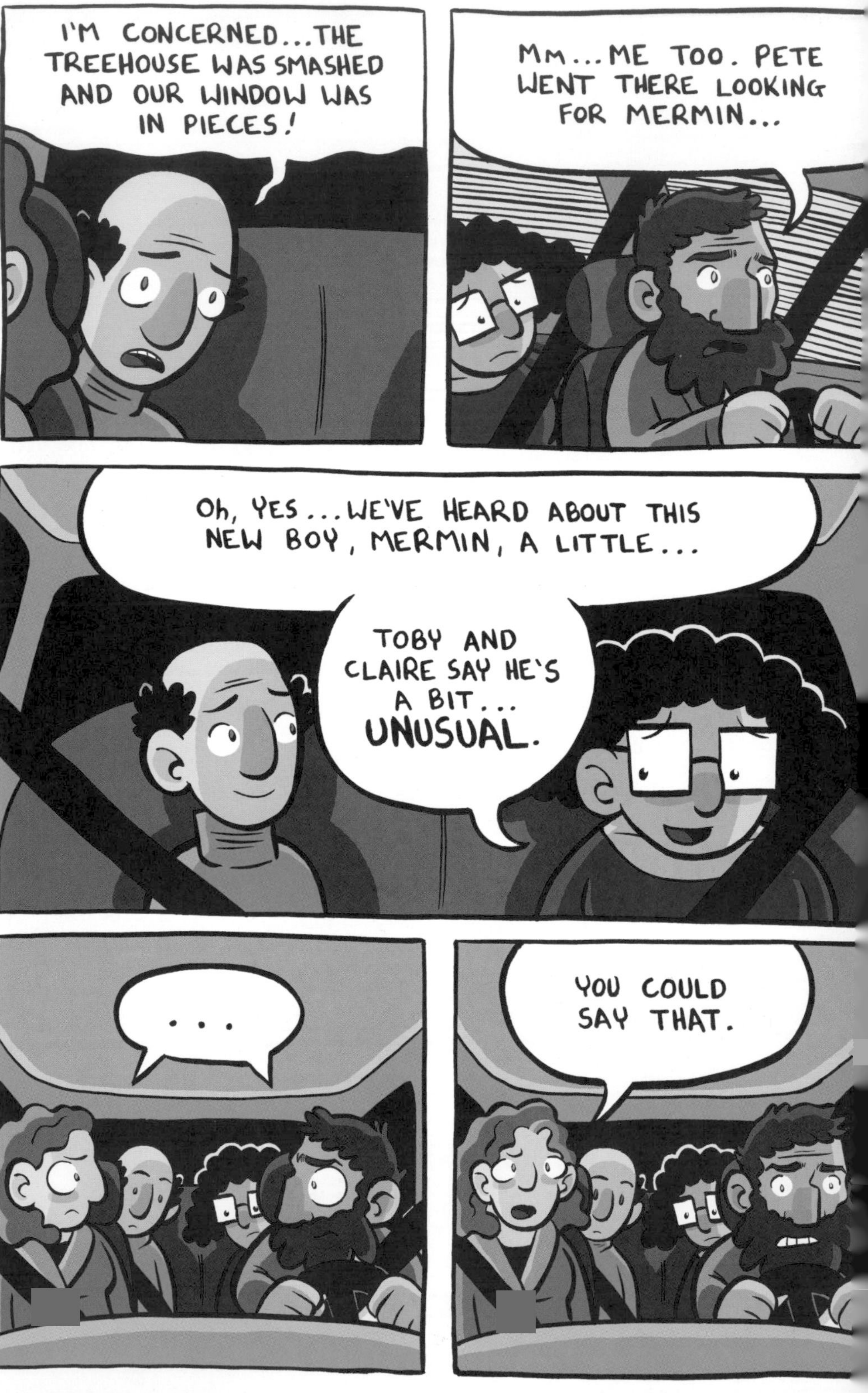
I'M CONCERNED...THE TREEHOUSE WAS SMASHED AND OUR WINDOW WAS IN PIECES!
Mm...ME TOO. PETE WENT THERE LOOKING FOR MERMIN...
Oh, YES...WE'VE HEARD ABOUT THIS NEW BOY, MERMIN, A LITTLE...
TOBY AND CLAIRE SAY HE'S A BIT... UNUSUAL.
...
YOU COULD SAY THAT.

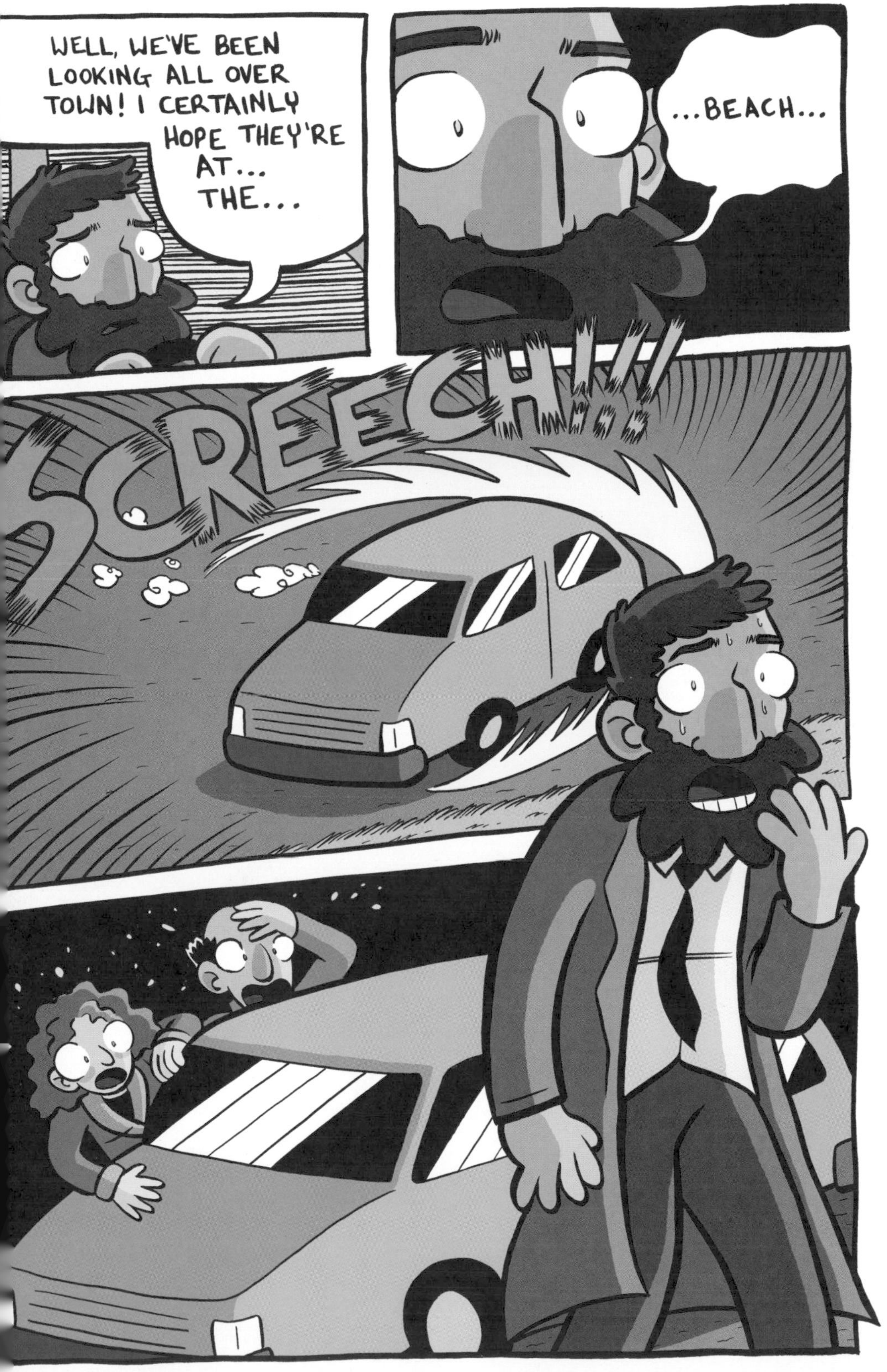
WELL, WE'VE BEEN LOOKING ALL OVER TOWN! I CERTAINLY HOPE THEY'RE AT... THE...
...BEACH...
SCREECH!!!

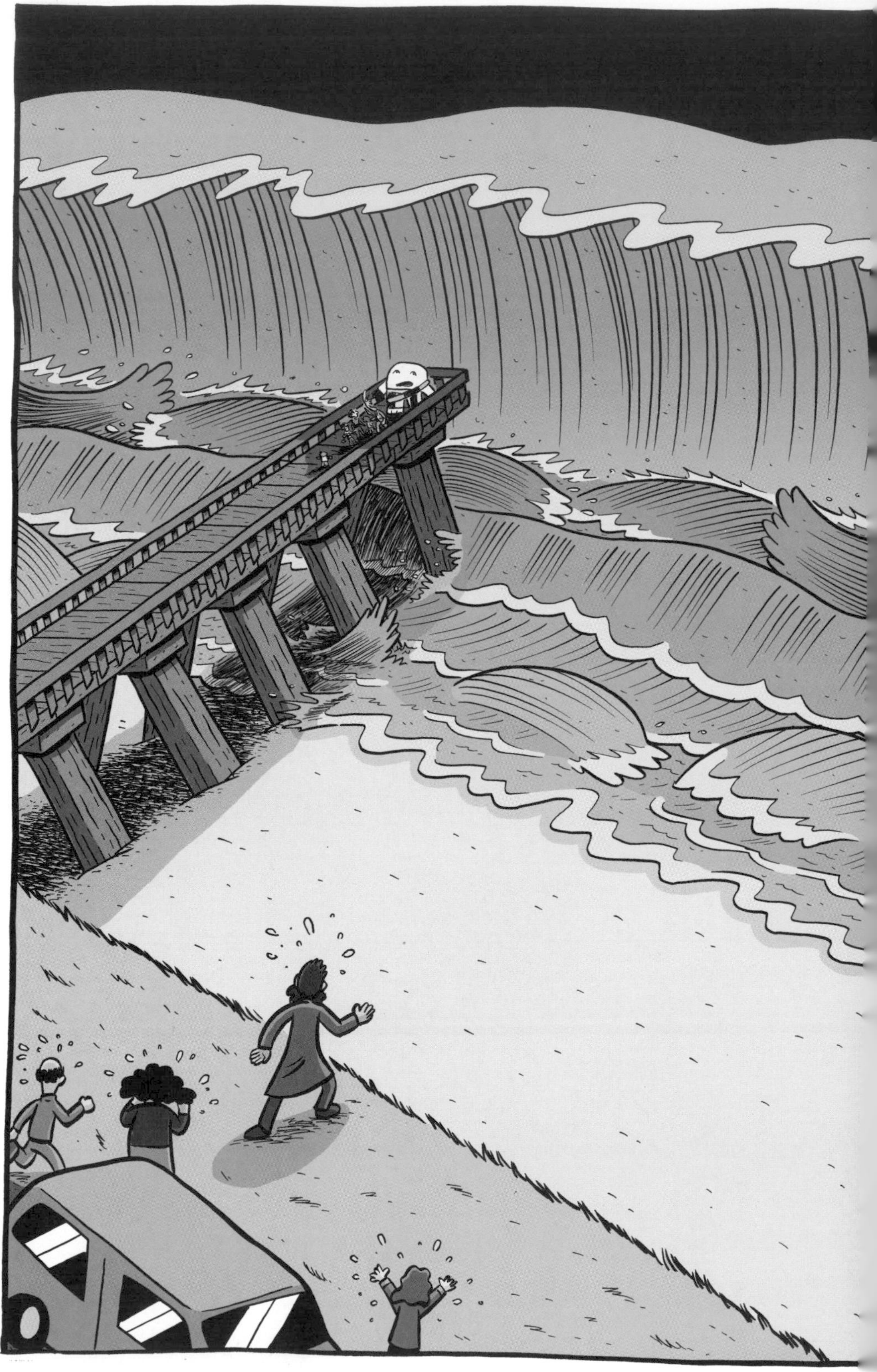

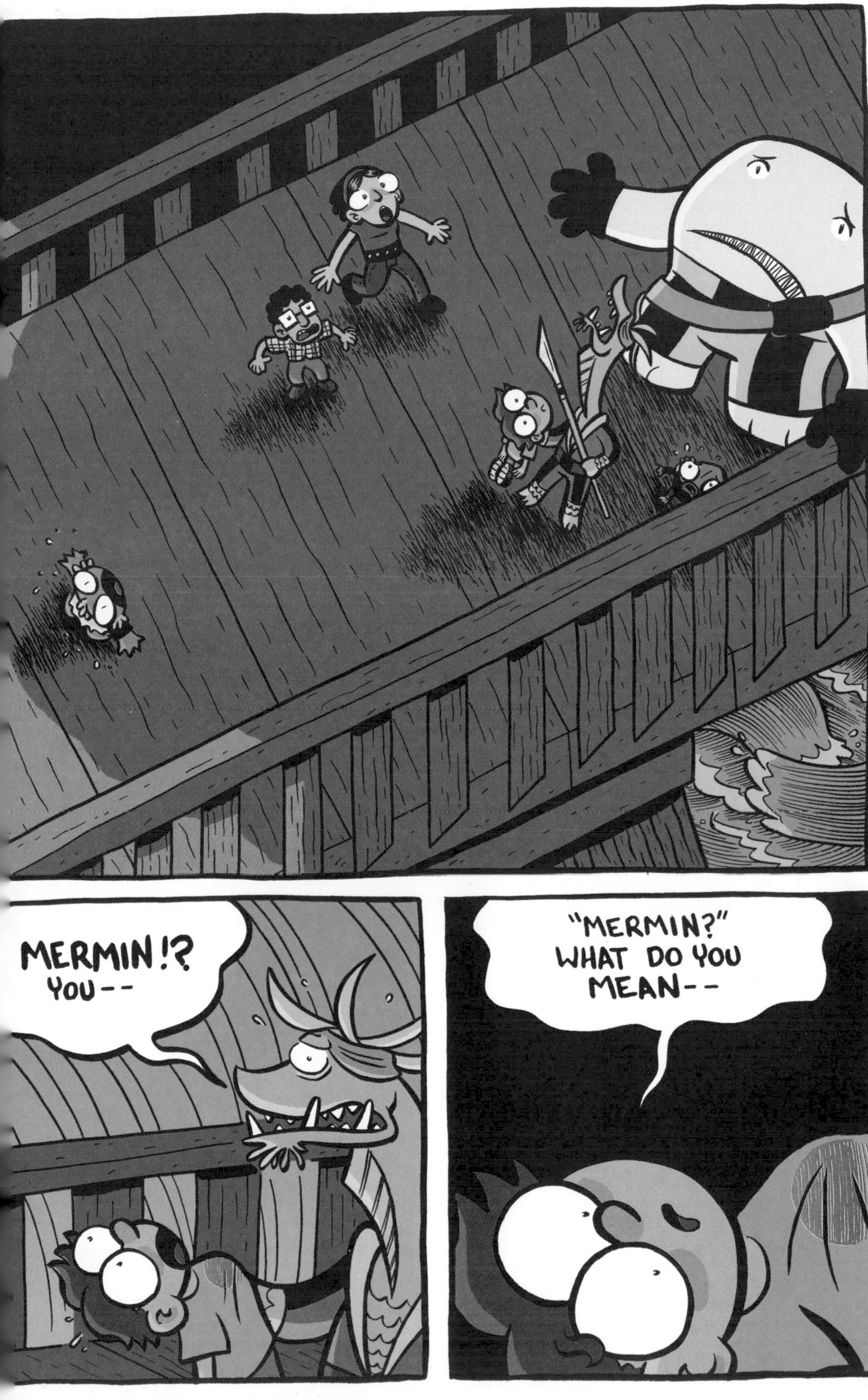
MERMIN!? YOU--
"MERMIN?" WHAT DO YOU MEAN--

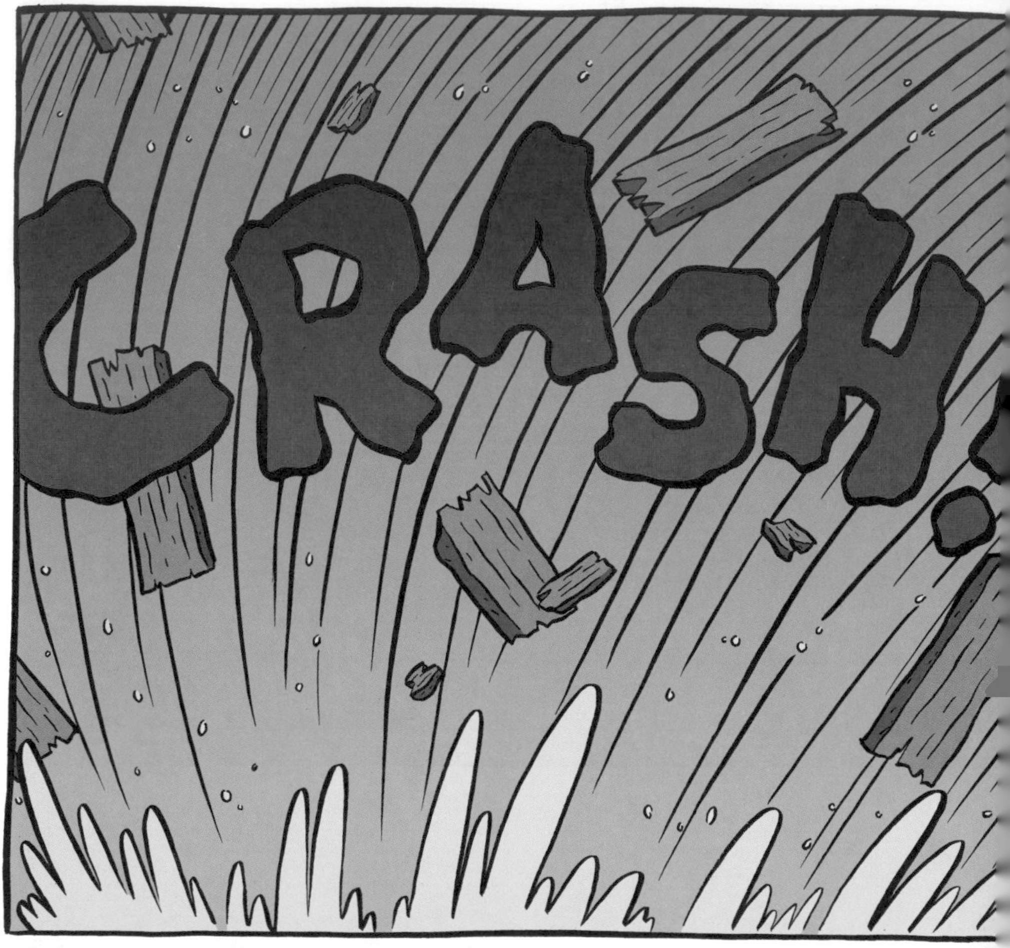
CRASH!

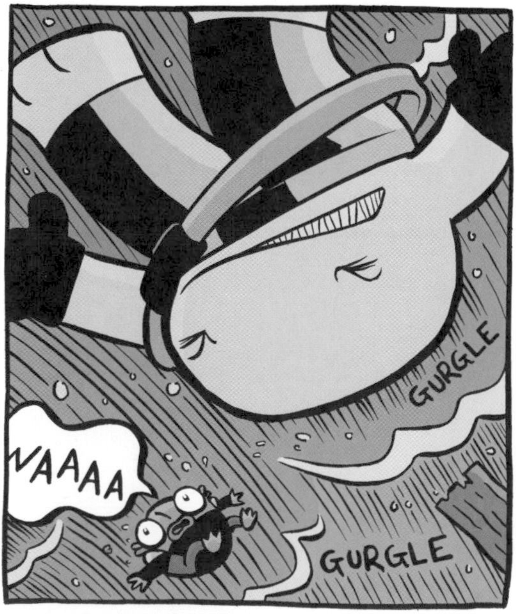
GURGLE
NAAAA
GURGLE

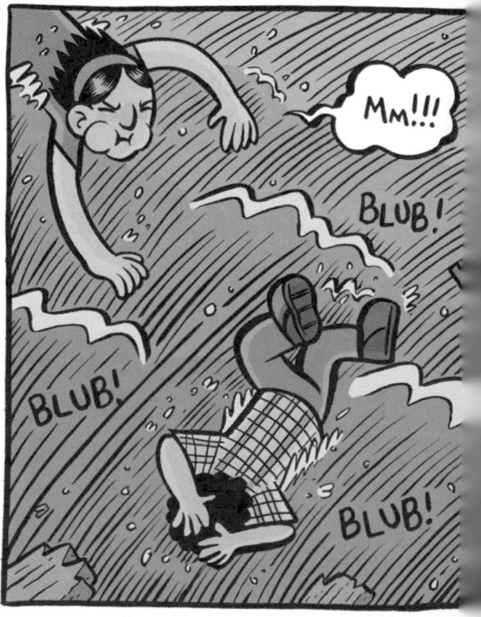
MM!!!
BLUB!
BLUB!
BLUB!

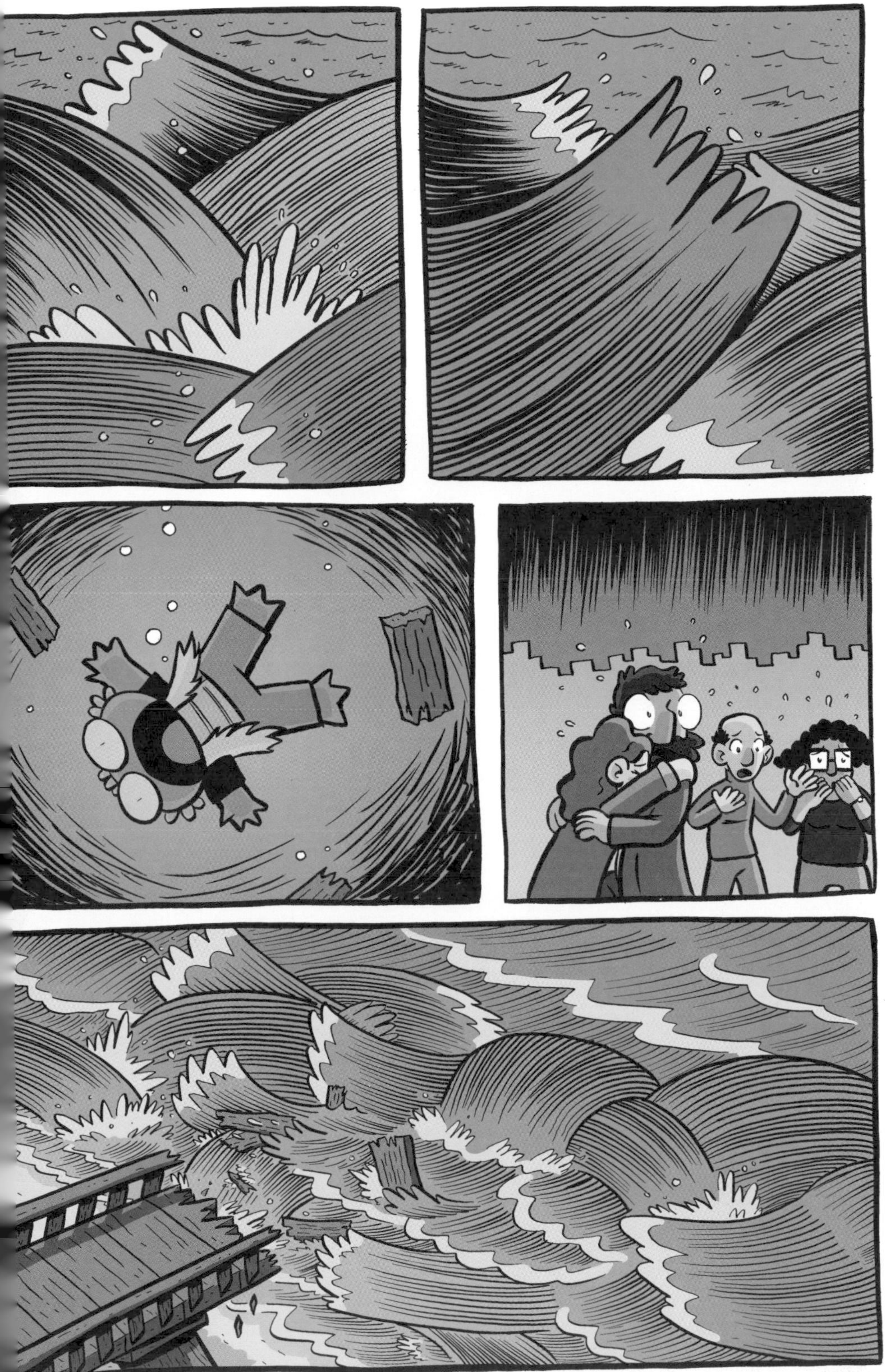

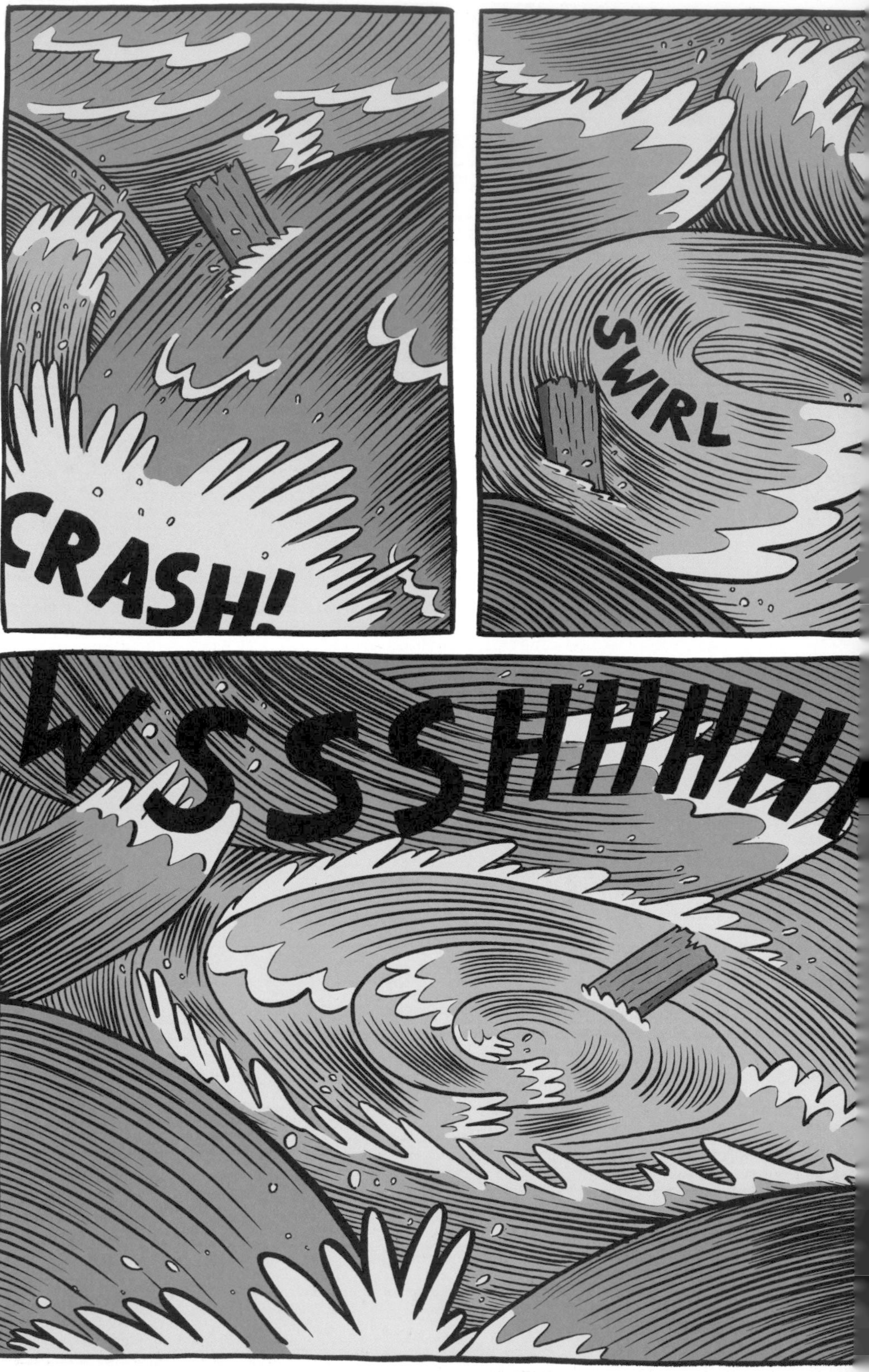
CRASH!
SWIRL
WSSSHHHH

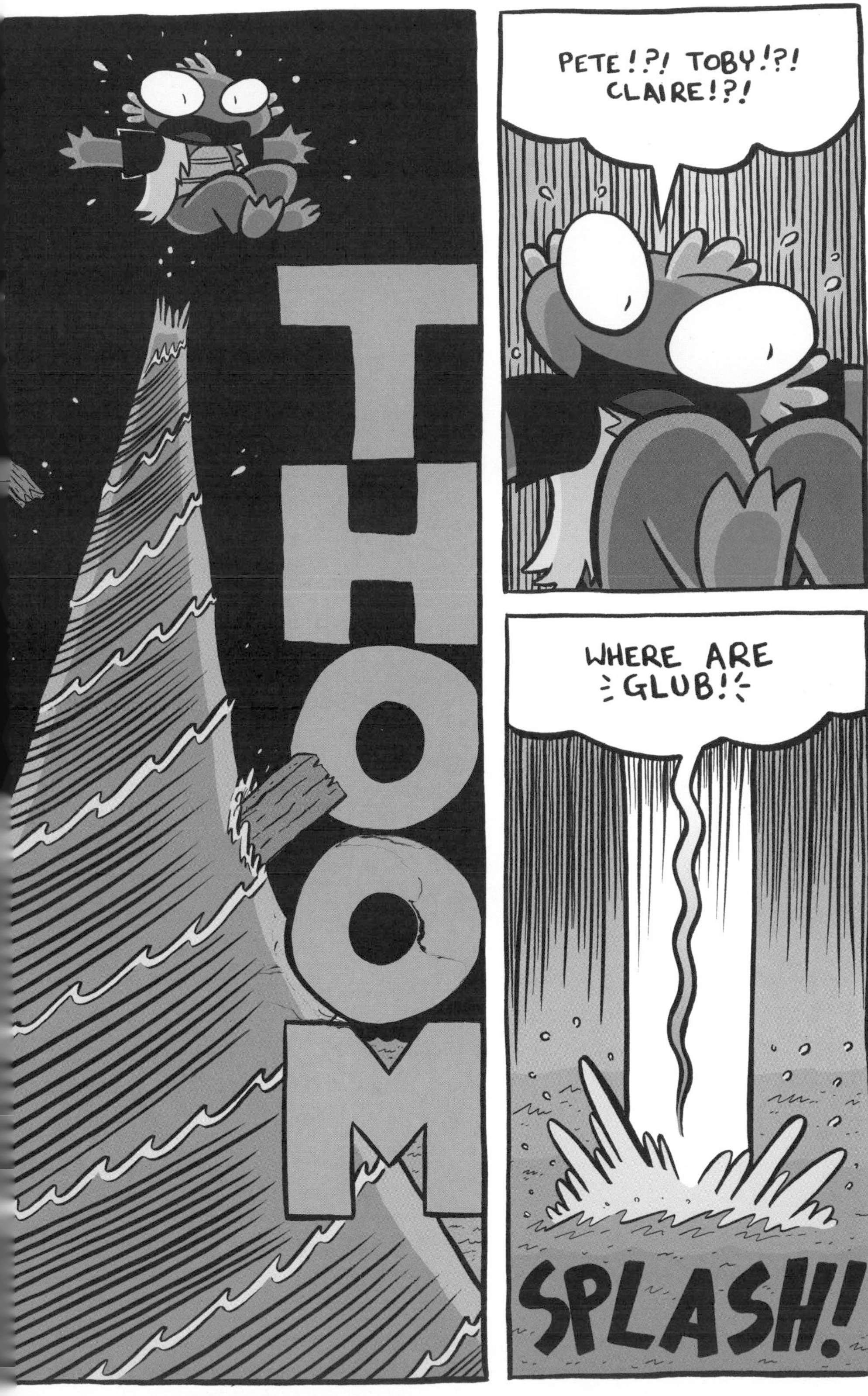
THOOM
PETE!?! TOBY!?! CLAIRE!?!
WHERE ARE GLUB!
SPLASH!

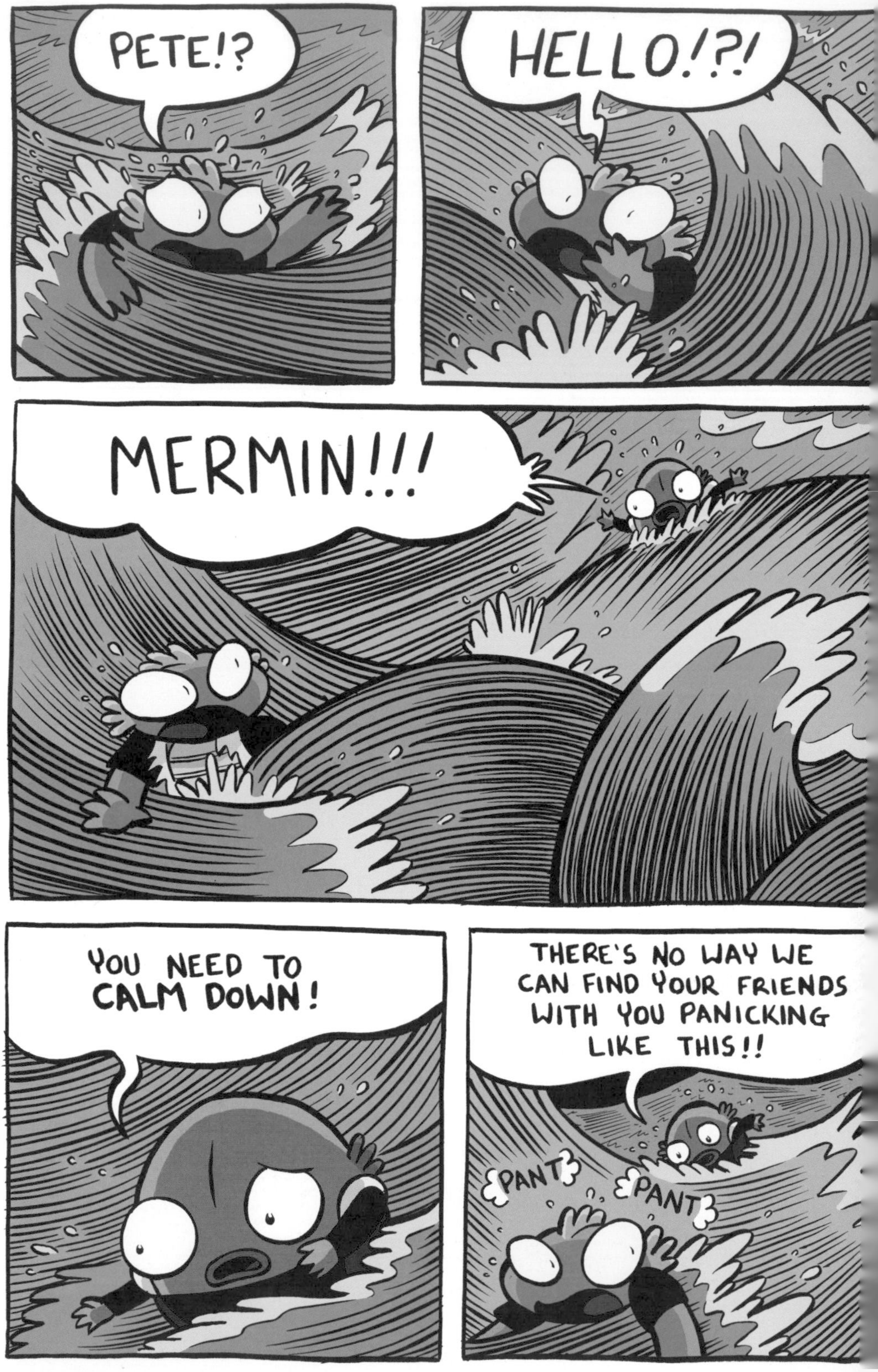
PETE!?
HELLO!?!
MERMIN!!!
YOU NEED TO CALM DOWN!
THERE'S NO WAY WE CAN FIND YOUR FRIENDS WITH YOU PANICKING LIKE THIS!!
PANT
PANT

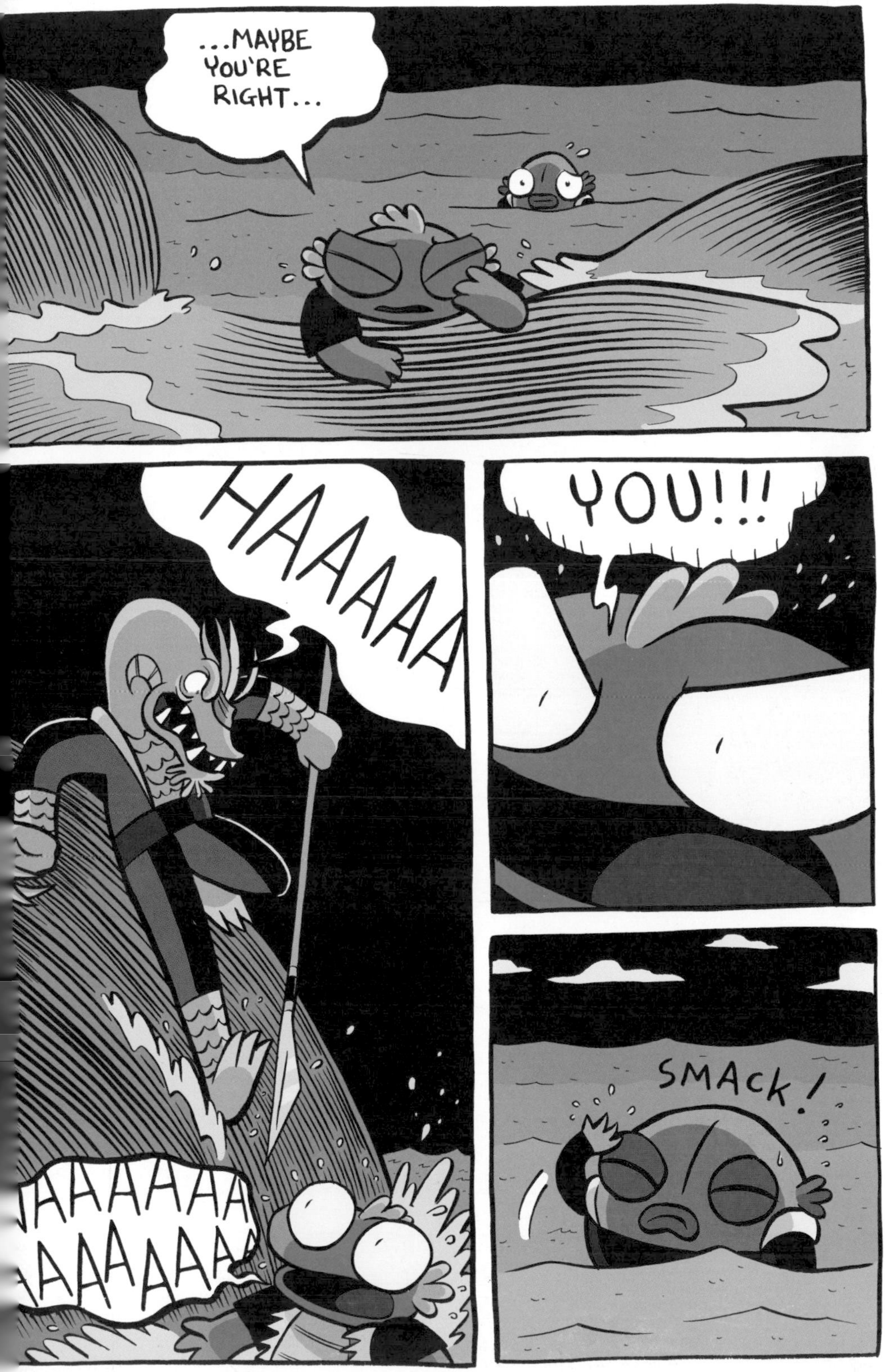
...MAYBE YOU'RE RIGHT...
HAAAAAA
AAAAAAAA AAAAAAAA
YOU!!!
SMACK!

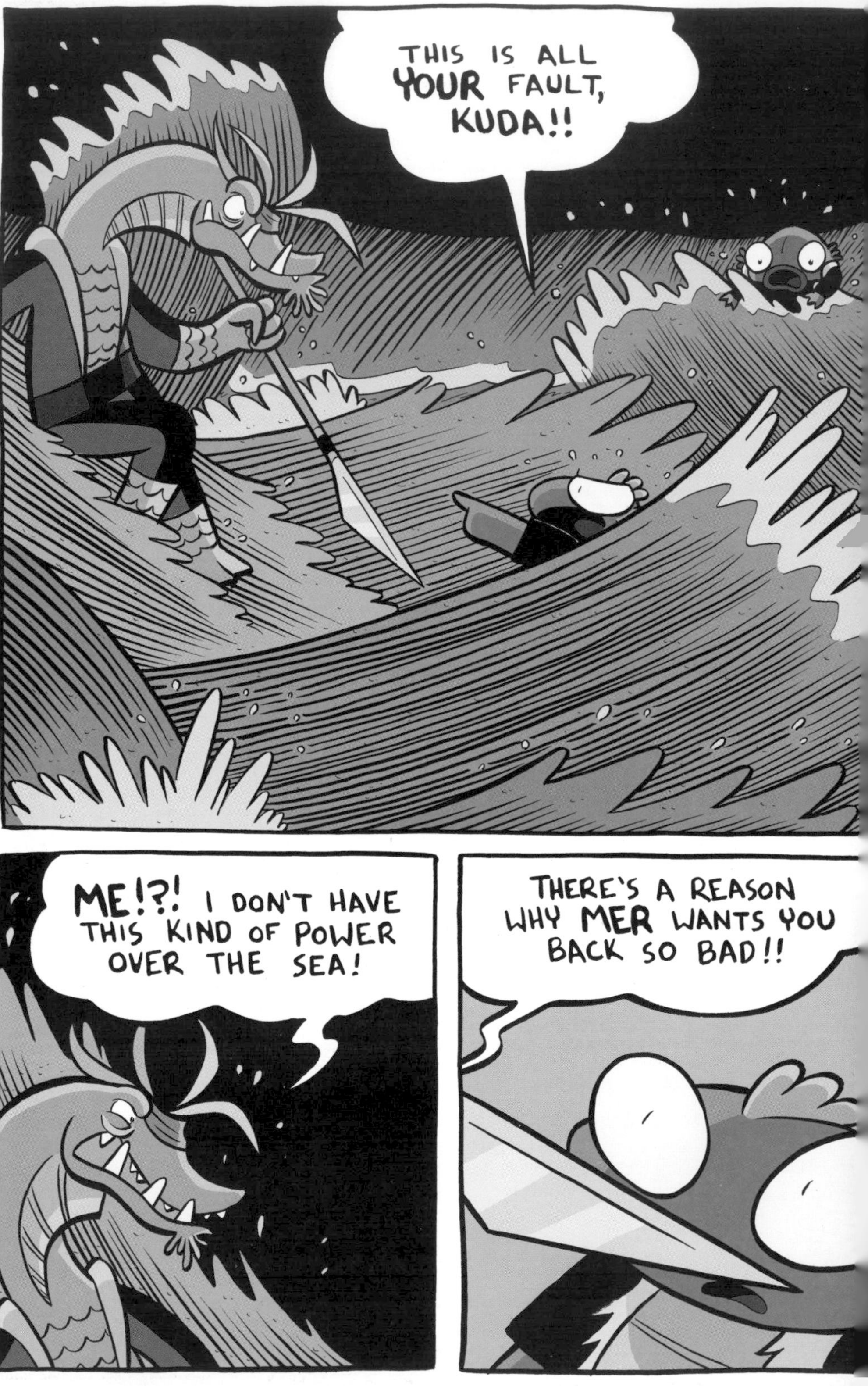
THIS IS ALL YOUR FAULT, KUDA!!
ME!?! I DON'T HAVE THIS KIND OF POWER OVER THE SEA!
THERE'S A REASON WHY MER WANTS YOU BACK SO BAD!!

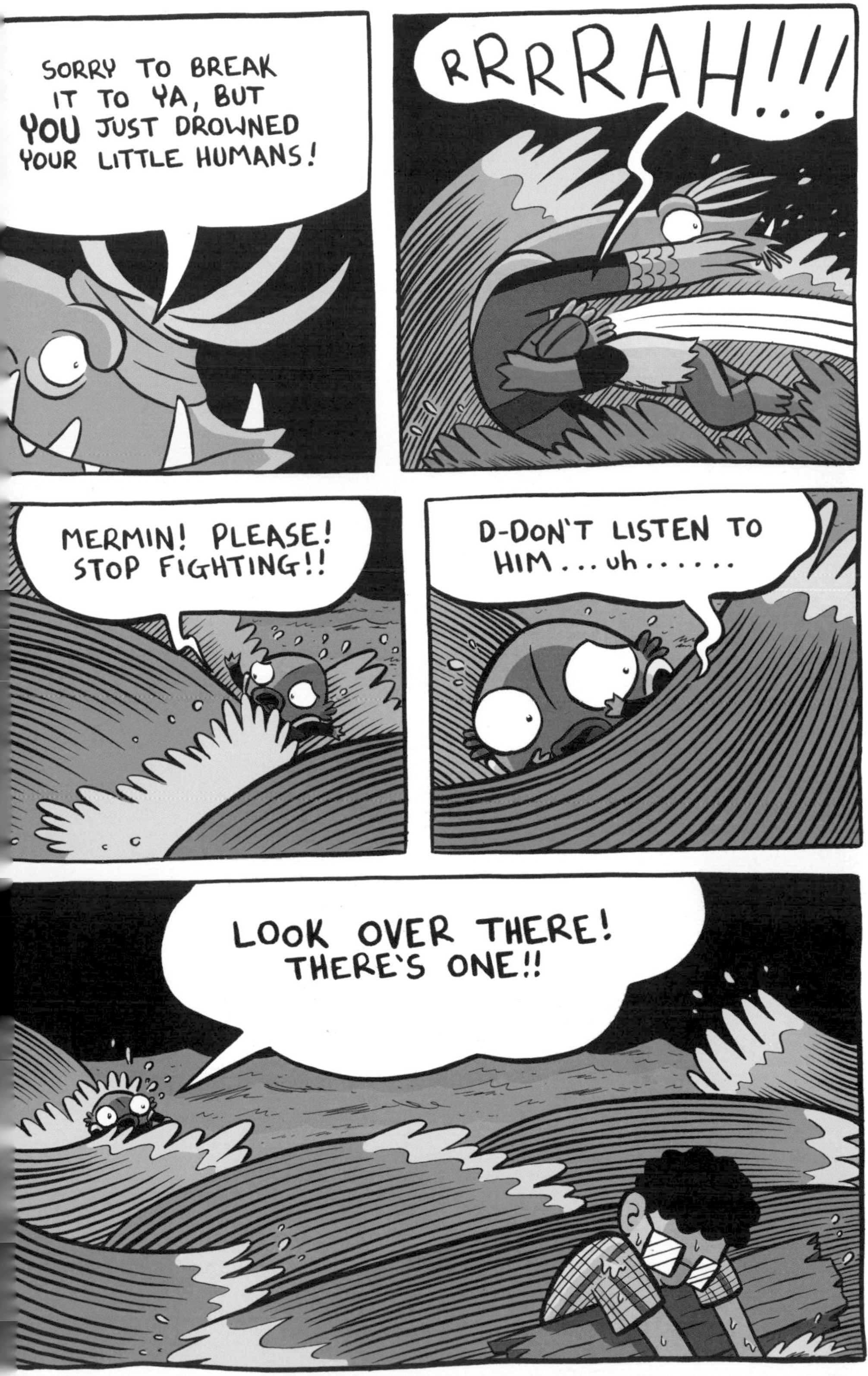
SORRY TO BREAK IT TO YA, BUT YOU JUST DROWNED YOUR LITTLE HUMANS!
RRRRAH!!!
MERMIN! PLEASE! STOP FIGHTING!!
D-DON'T LISTEN TO HIM...uh......
LOOK OVER THERE! THERE'S ONE!!

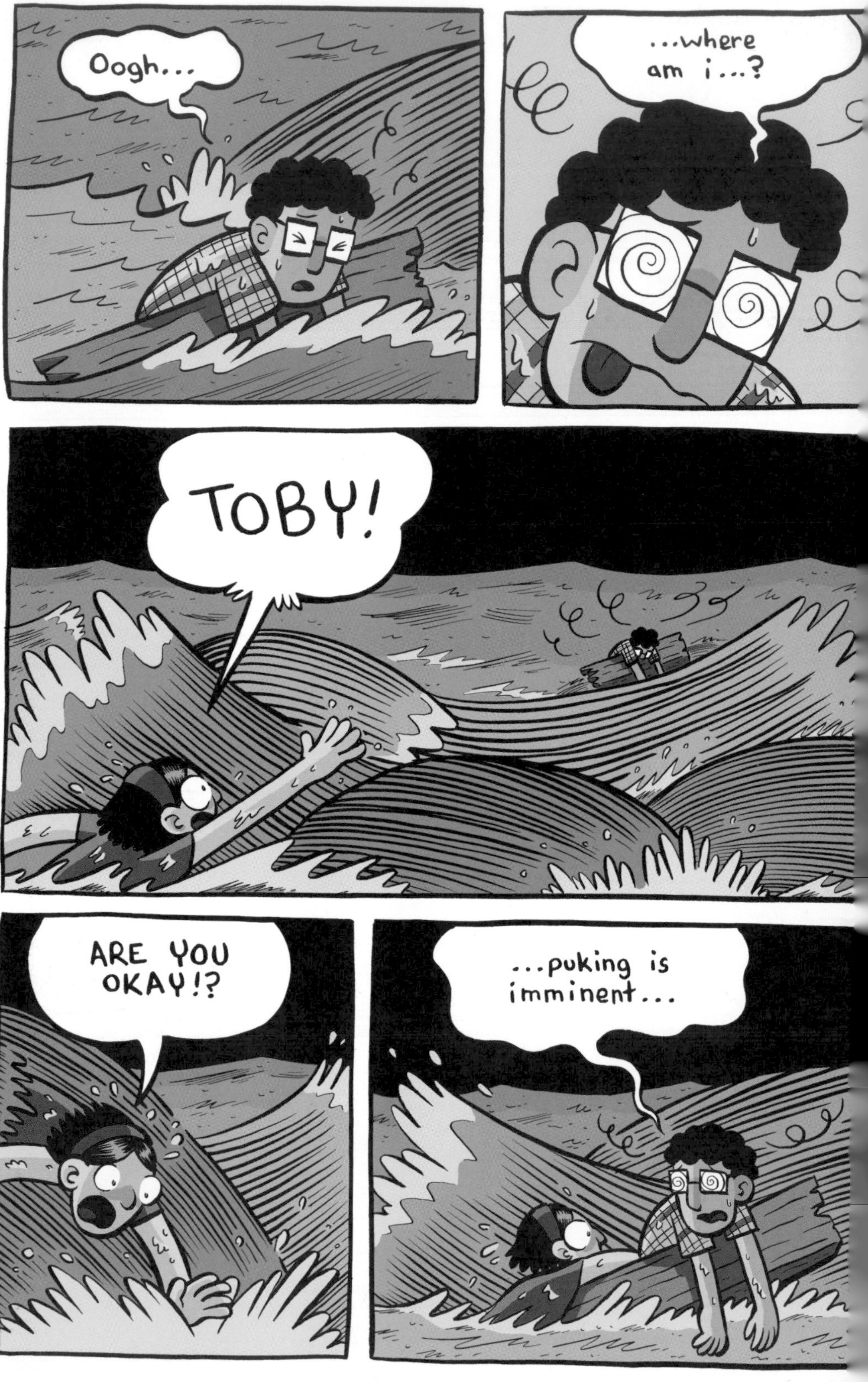
Oogh...
...where am i...?
TOBY!
ARE YOU OKAY!?
...puking is imminent...

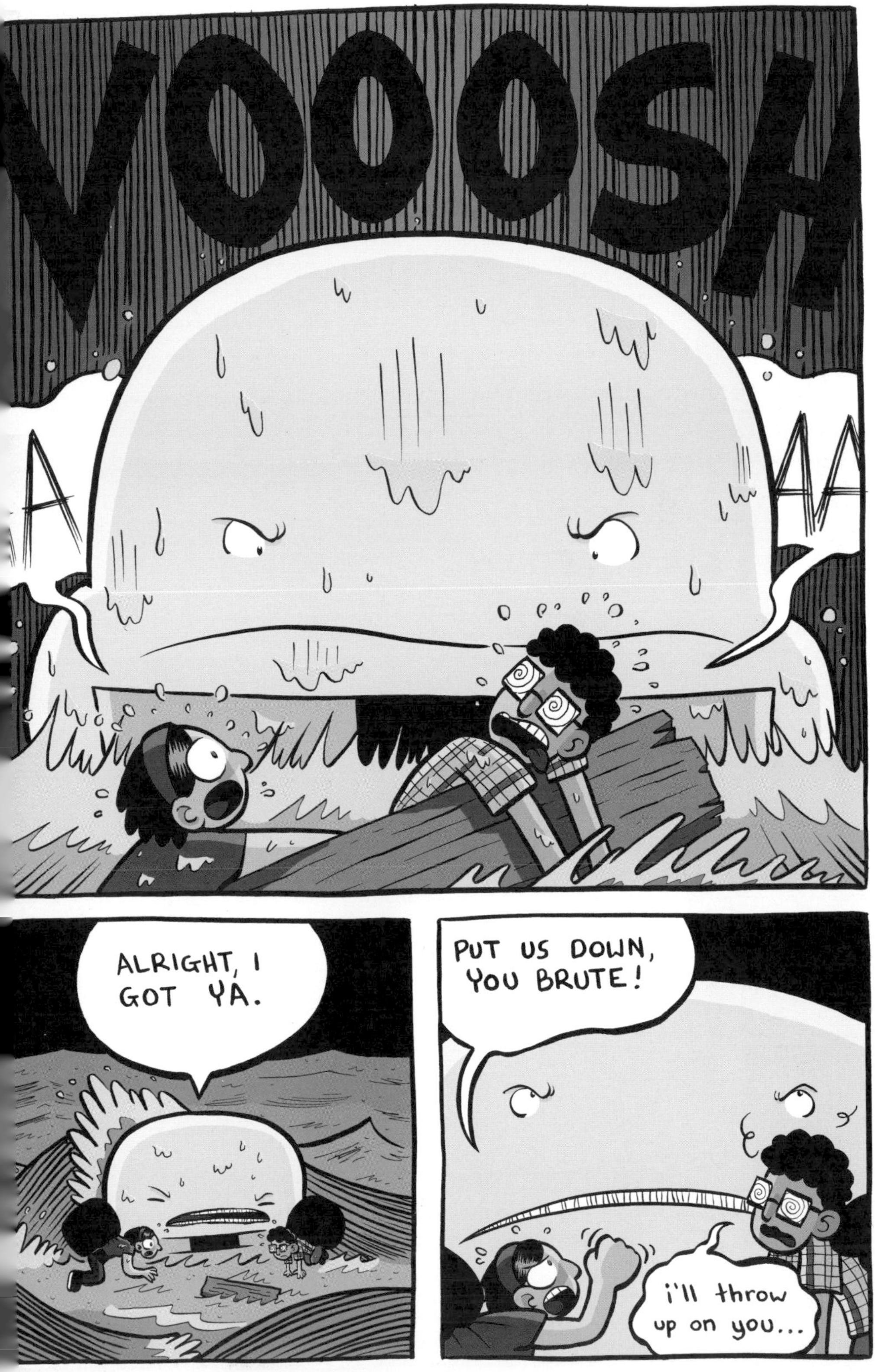
ALRIGHT, I GOT YA.
PUT US DOWN, YOU BRUTE!
i'll throw up on you...

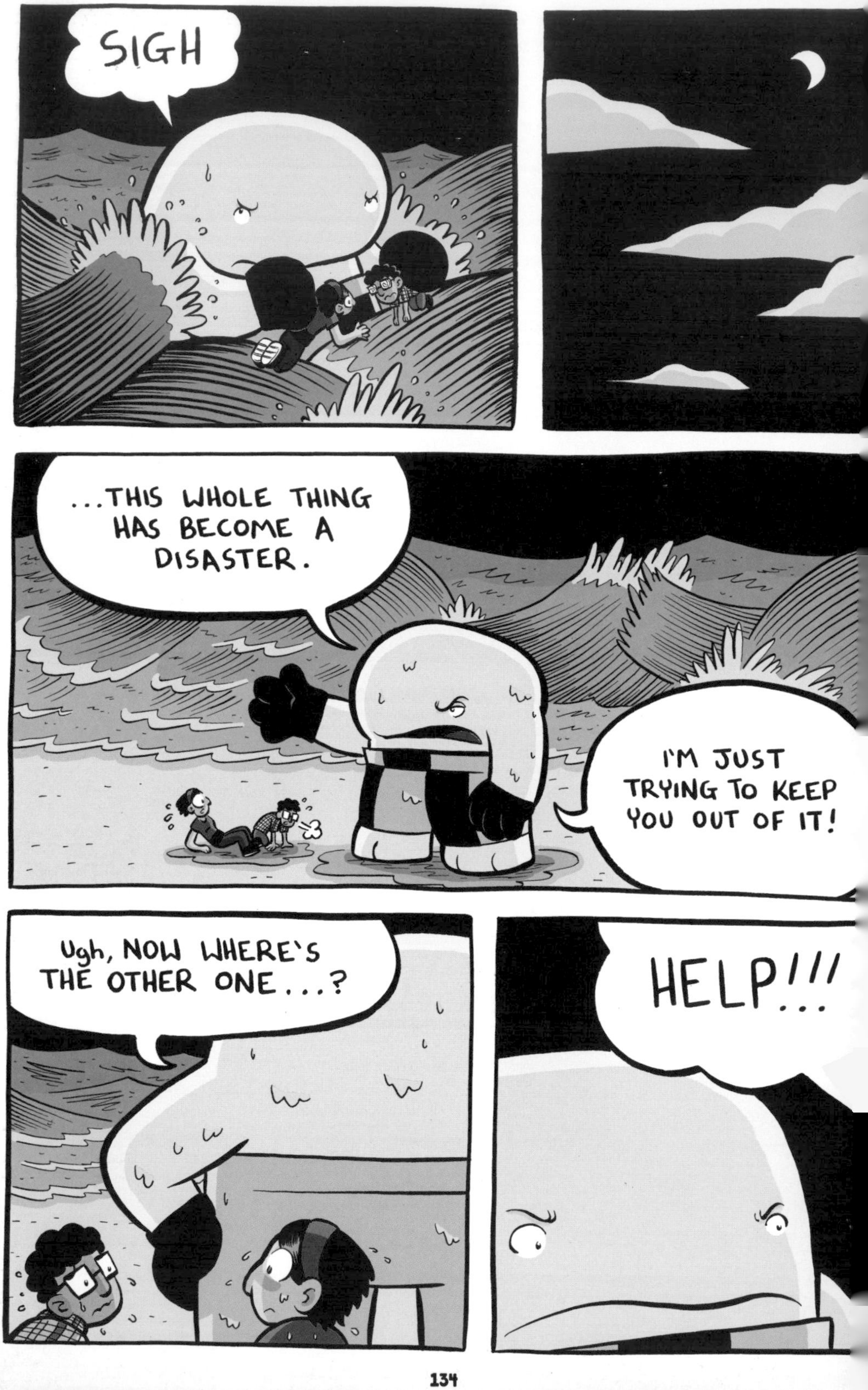
SIGH
...THIS WHOLE THING HAS BECOME A DISASTER.
I'M JUST TRYING TO KEEP YOU OUT OF IT!
Ugh, NOW WHERE'S THE OTHER ONE...?
HELP!!!...

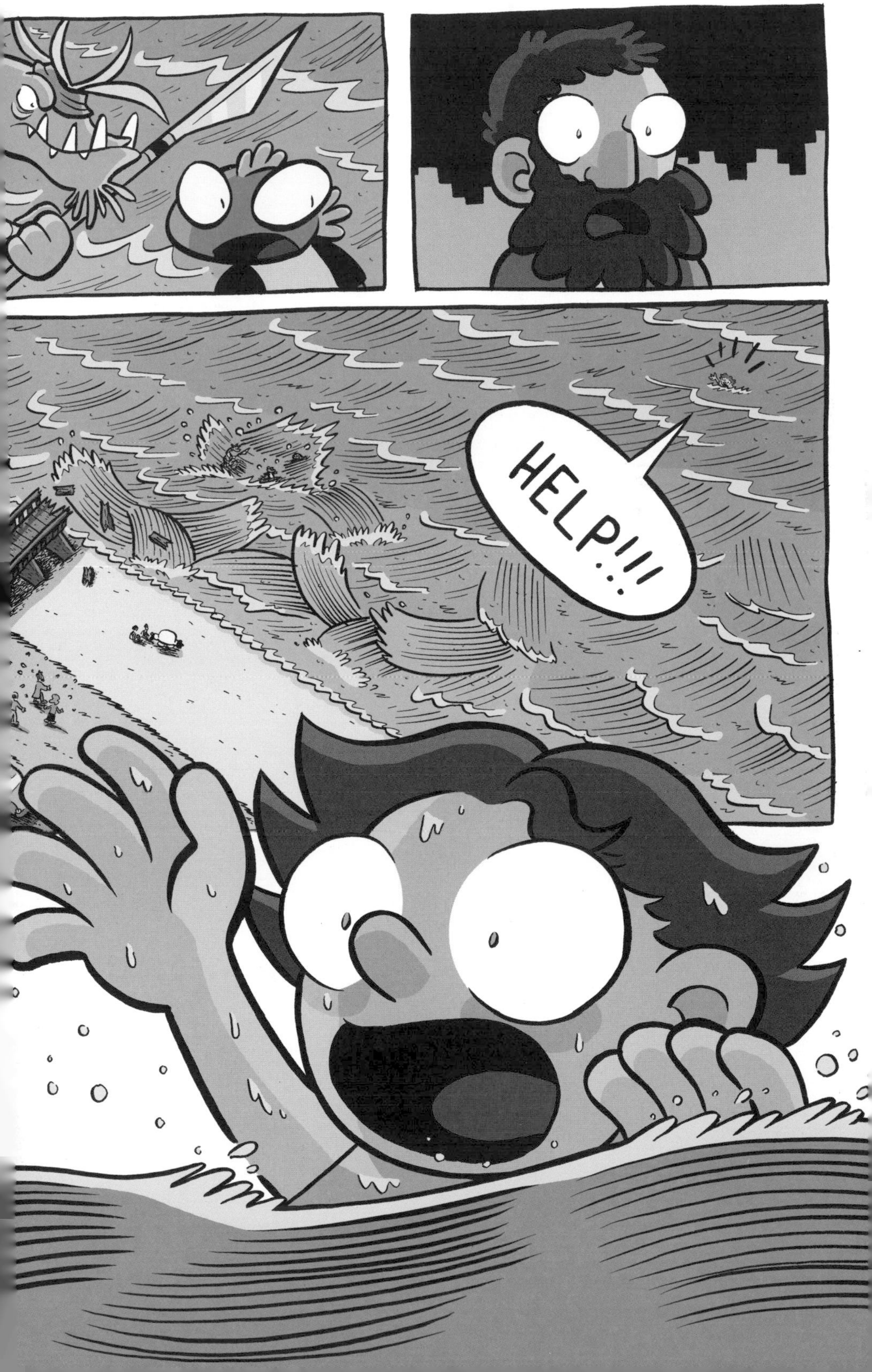
HELP!!!

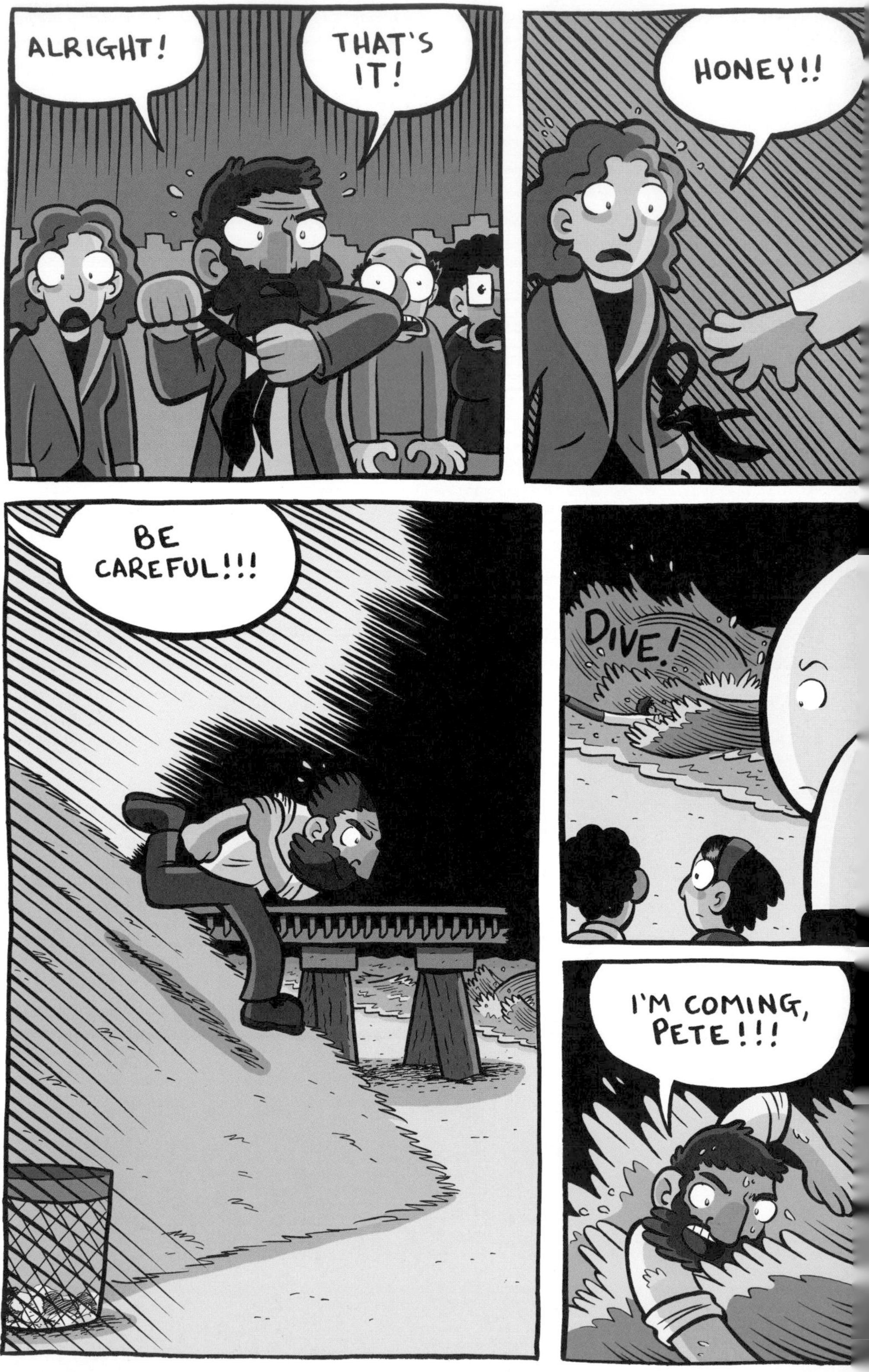
ALRIGHT!
THAT'S IT!
HONEY!!
BE CAREFUL!!!
DIVE!
I'M COMING, PETE!!!

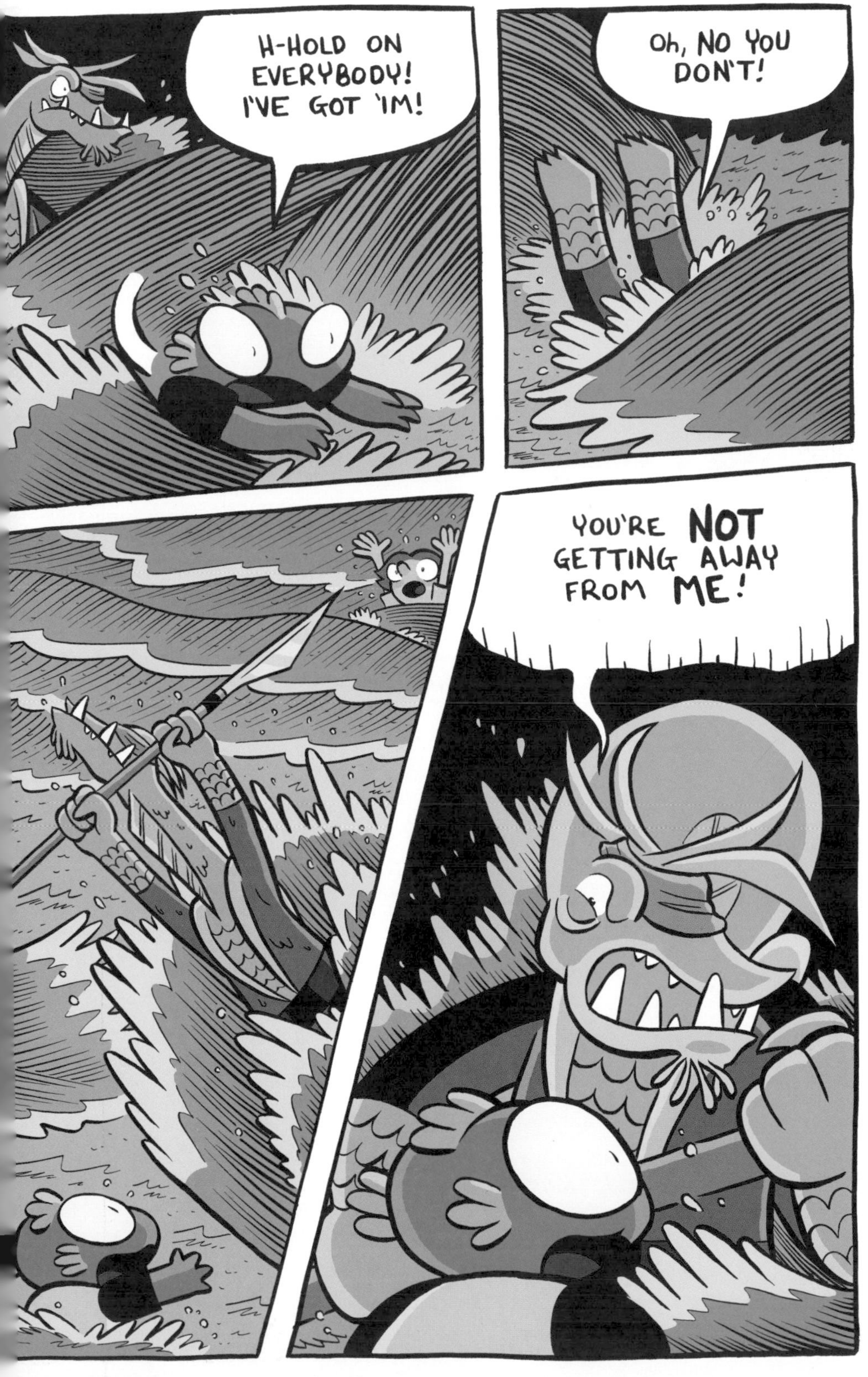
H-HOLD ON EVERYBODY! I'VE GOT 'IM!
Oh, NO YOU DON'T!
YOU'RE NOT GETTING AWAY FROM ME!

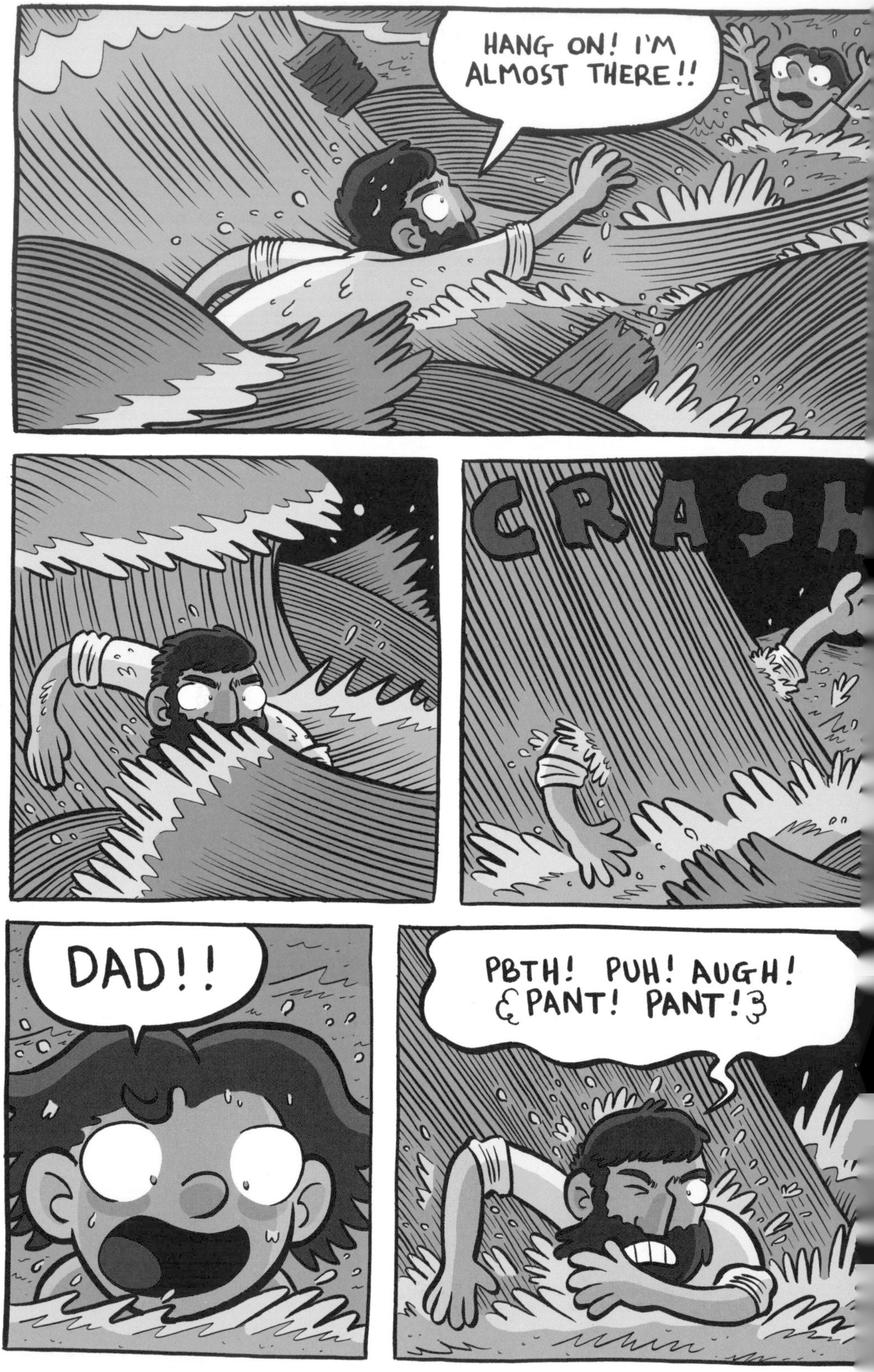
HANG ON! I'M ALMOST THERE!!
CRASH
DAD!!
PBTH! PUH! AUGH! {PANT! PANT!}

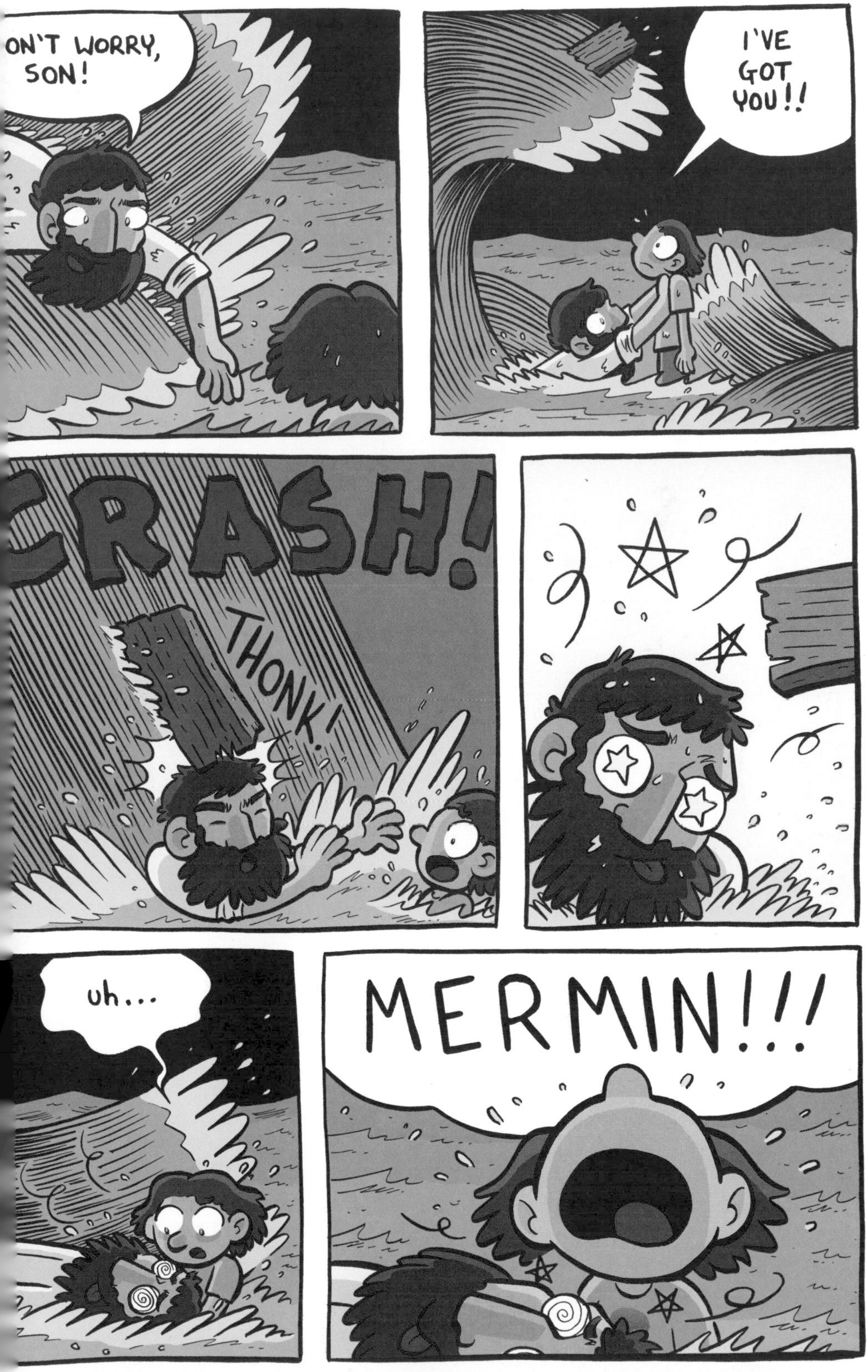
ON'T WORRY, SON!
I'VE GOT YOU!!
CRASH!
THONK!
uh...
MERMIN!!!

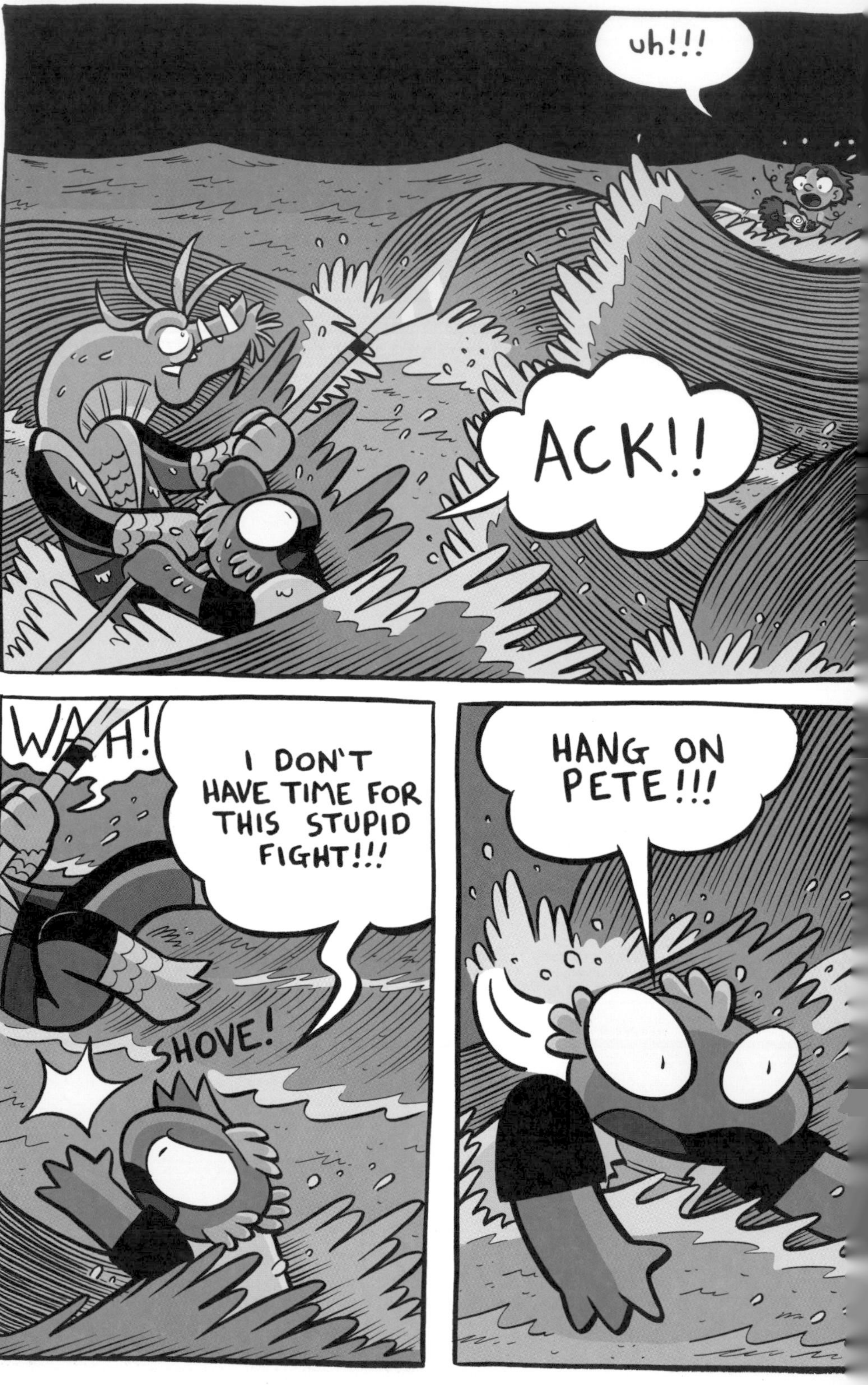
uh!!!
ACK!!
WAH!
I DON'T HAVE TIME FOR THIS STUPID FIGHT!!!
SHOVE!
HANG ON PETE!!!

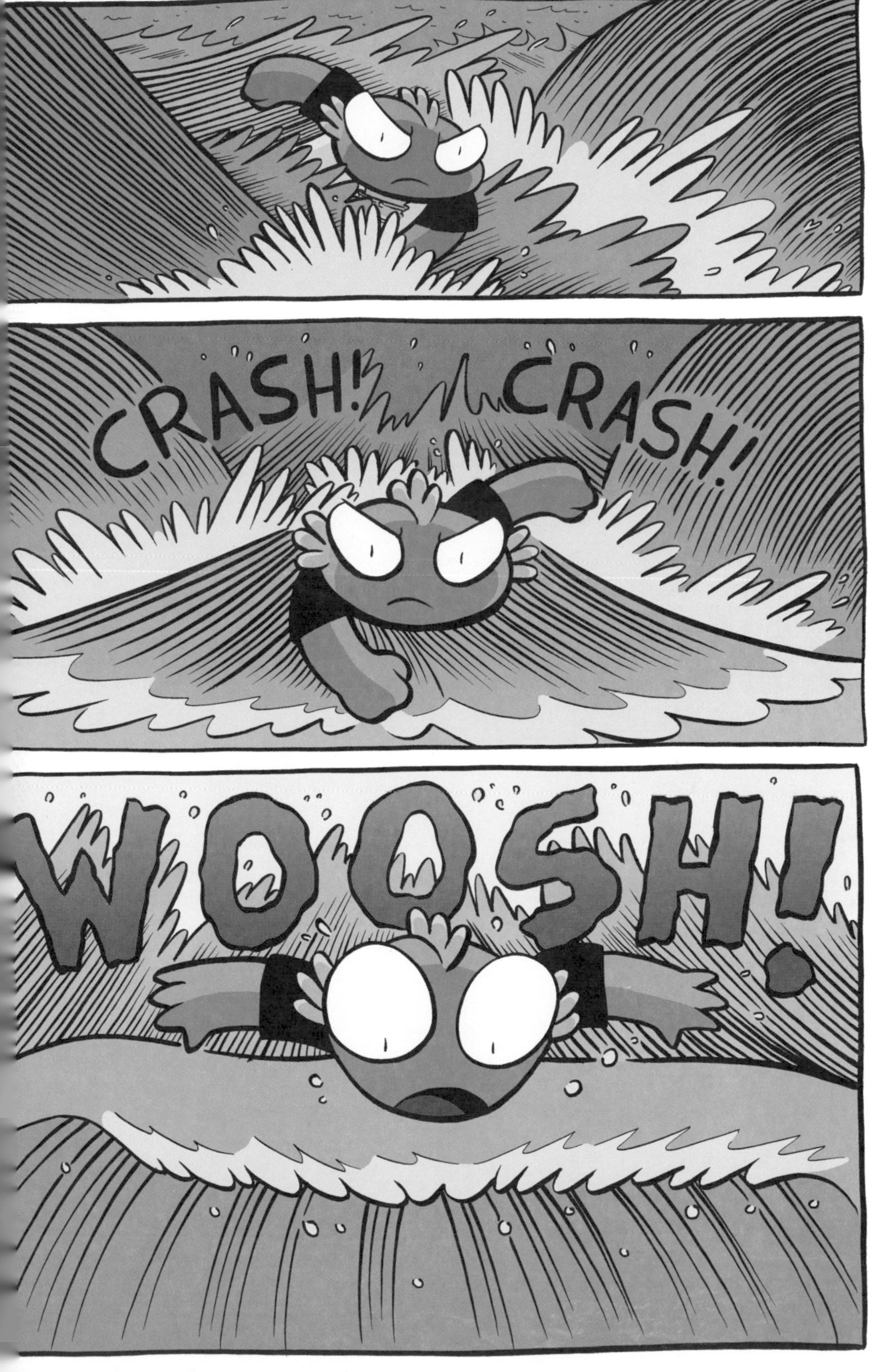
CRASH! CRASH!
WOOSH!

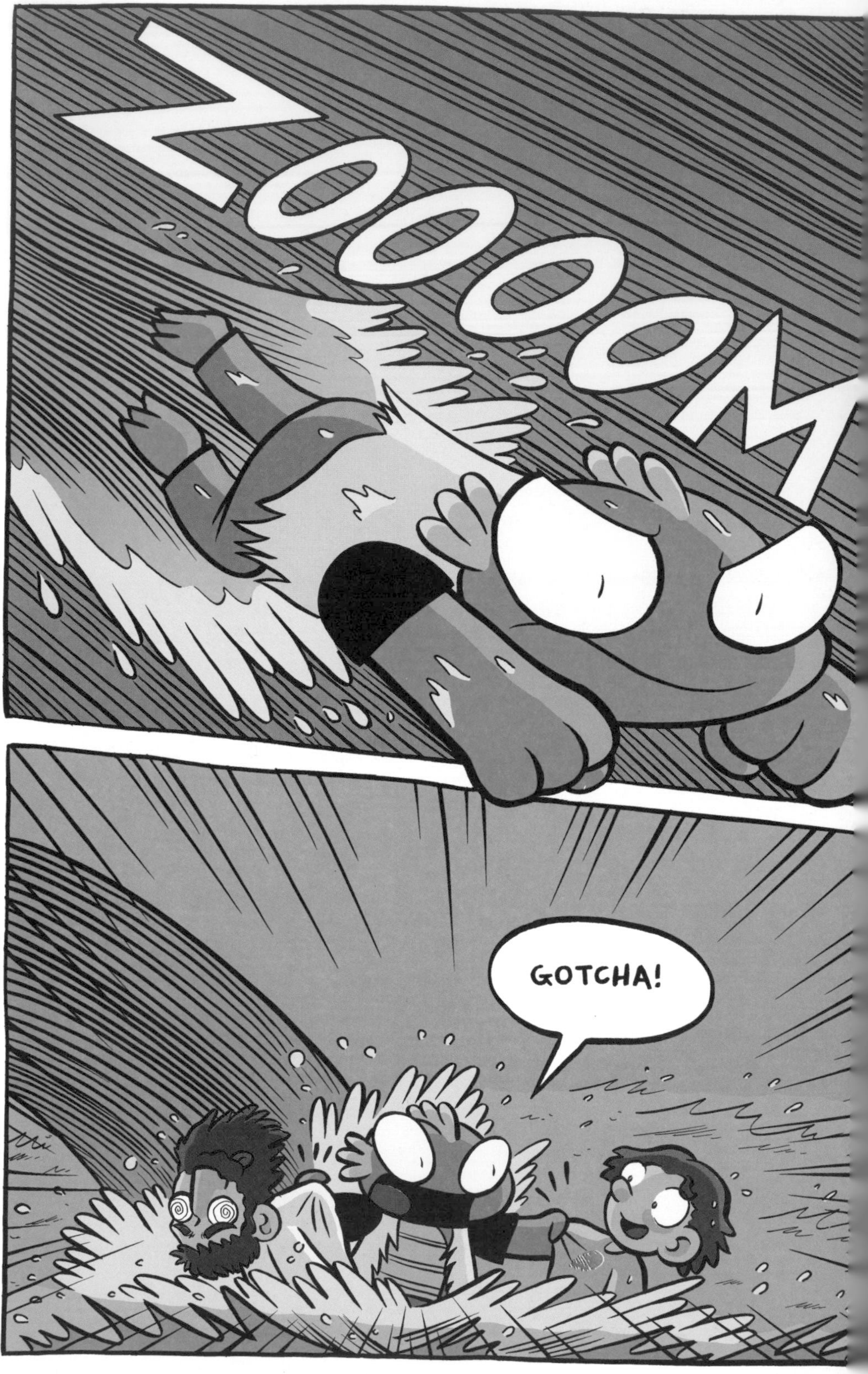
ZOOOOM
GOTCHA!

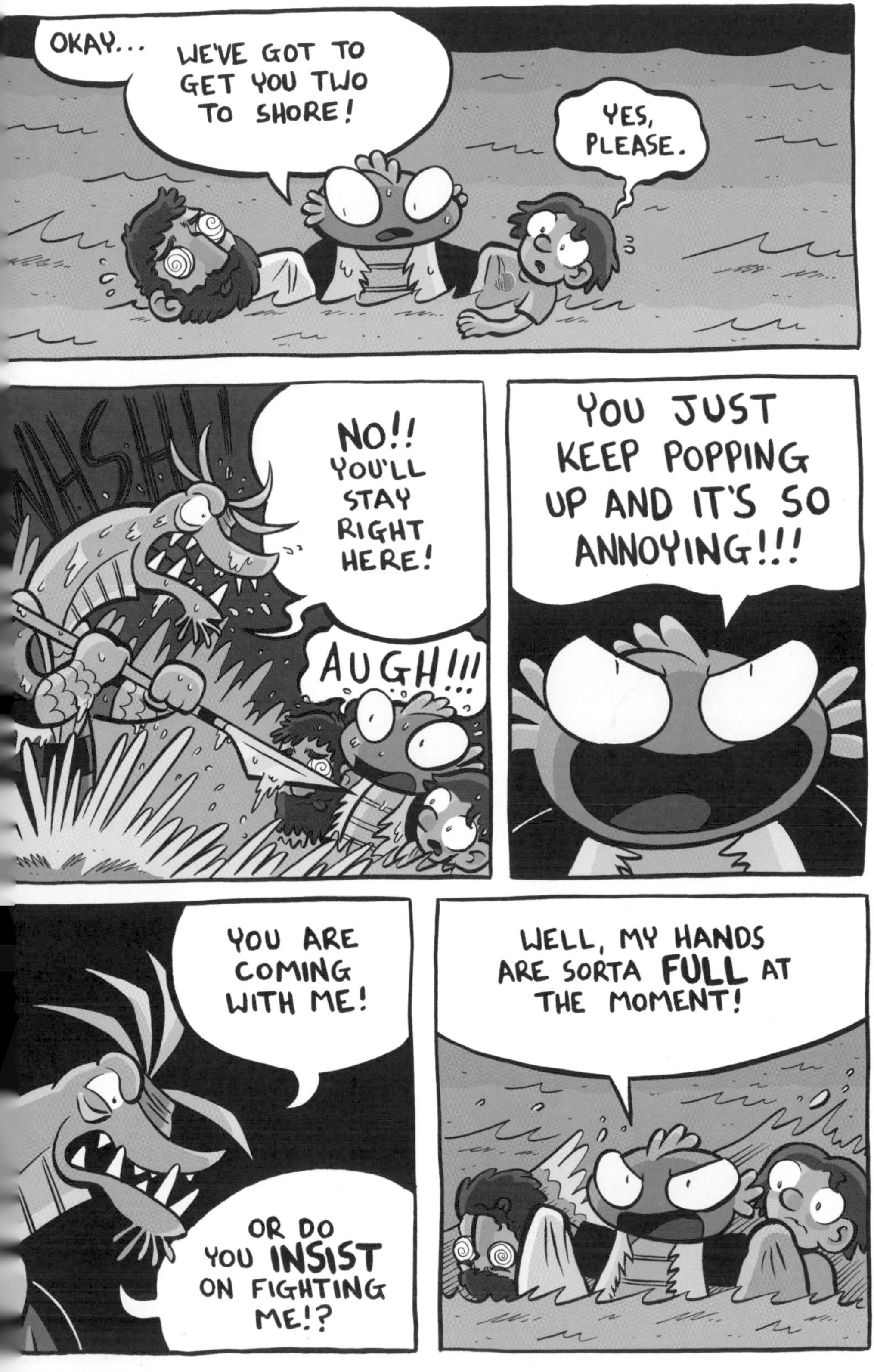
OKAY...
WE'VE GOT TO GET YOU TWO TO SHORE!
YES, PLEASE.
NO!! YOU'LL STAY RIGHT HERE!
AUGH!!!
YOU JUST KEEP POPPING UP AND IT'S SO ANNOYING!!!
YOU ARE COMING WITH ME!
OR DO YOU INSIST ON FIGHTING ME!?
WELL, MY HANDS ARE SORTA FULL AT THE MOMENT!

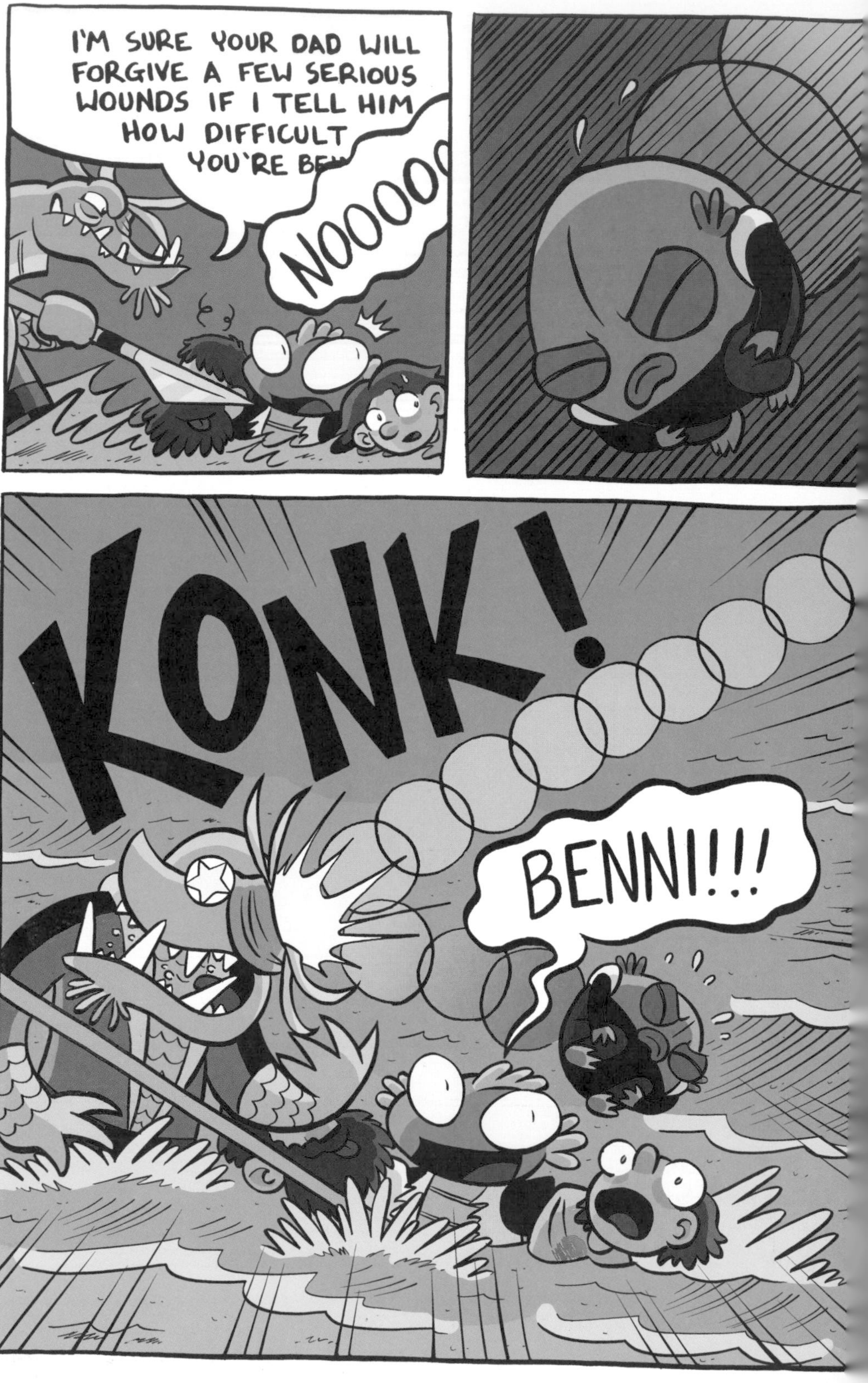

I'M SURE YOUR DAD WILL FORGIVE A FEW SERIOUS WOUNDS IF I TELL HIM HOW DIFFICULT YOU'RE BE
NOOOOO
KONK!
BENNI!!!

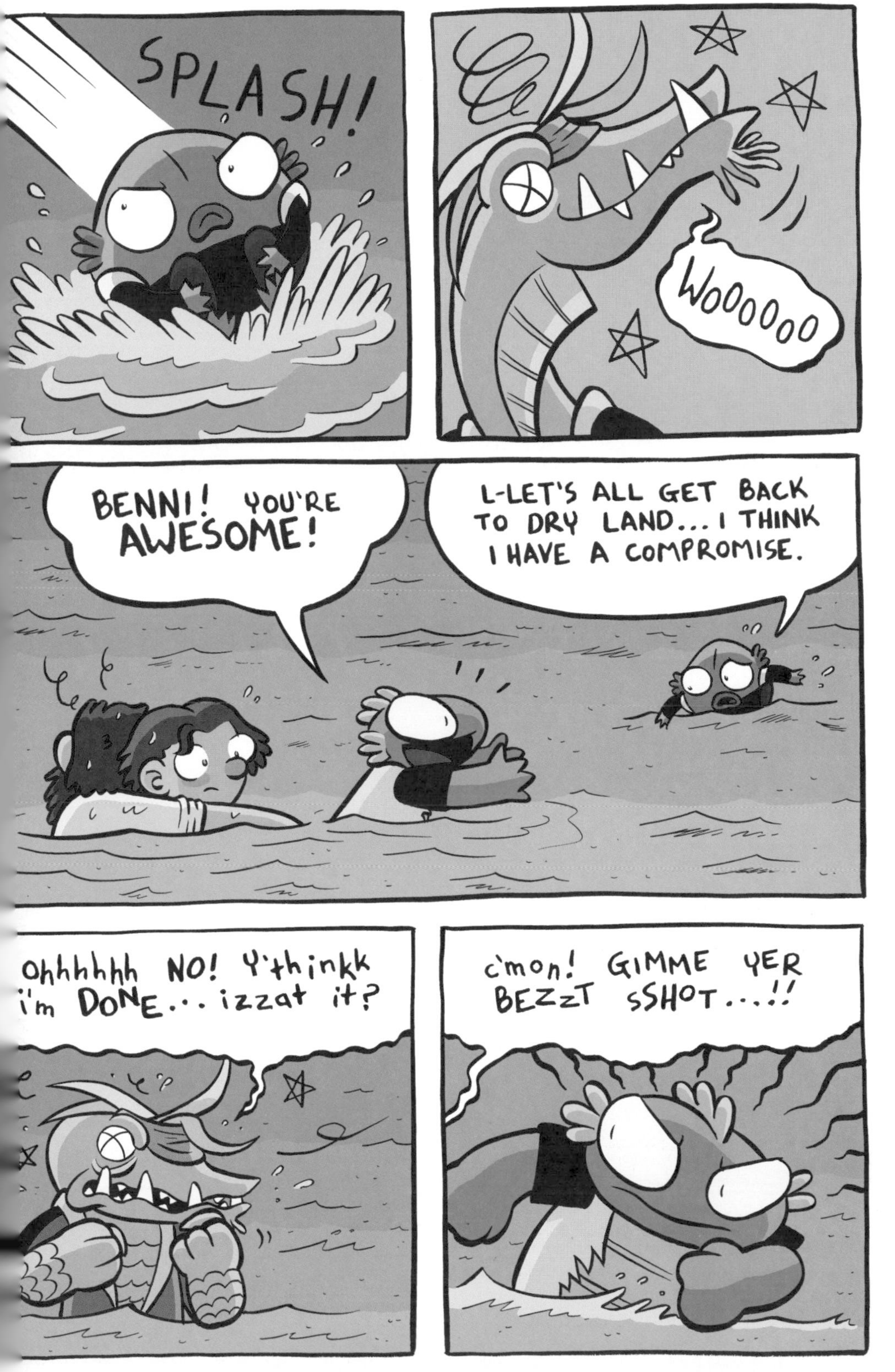
SPLASH!
WoOOOOO
BENNI! YOU'RE AWESOME!
L-LET'S ALL GET BACK TO DRY LAND... I THINK I HAVE A COMPROMISE.
ohhhhhh NO! Y'thinkk i'm DONE... izzat it?
c'mon! GIMME YER BEZzT sSHOT...!!

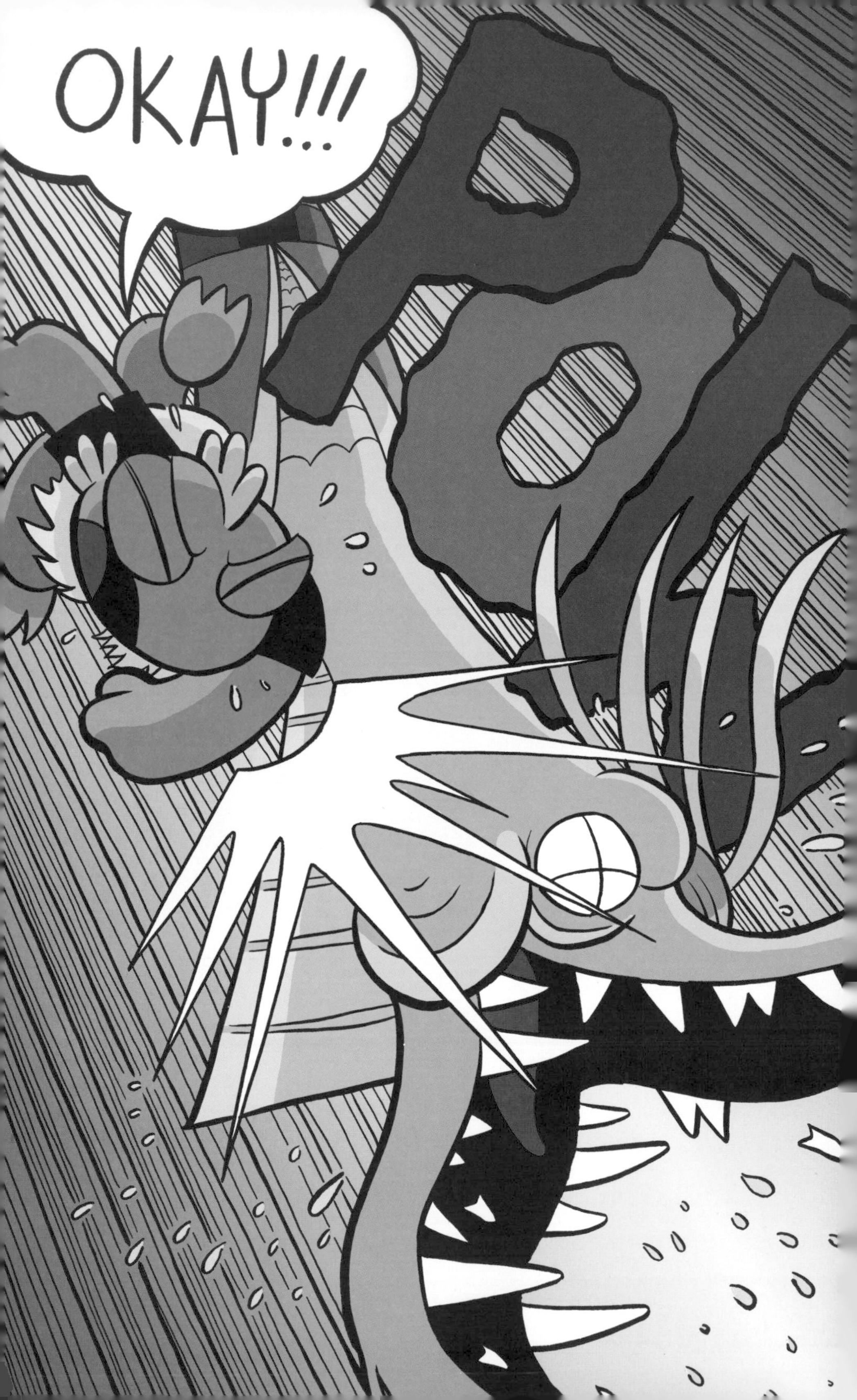
OKAY!!!...

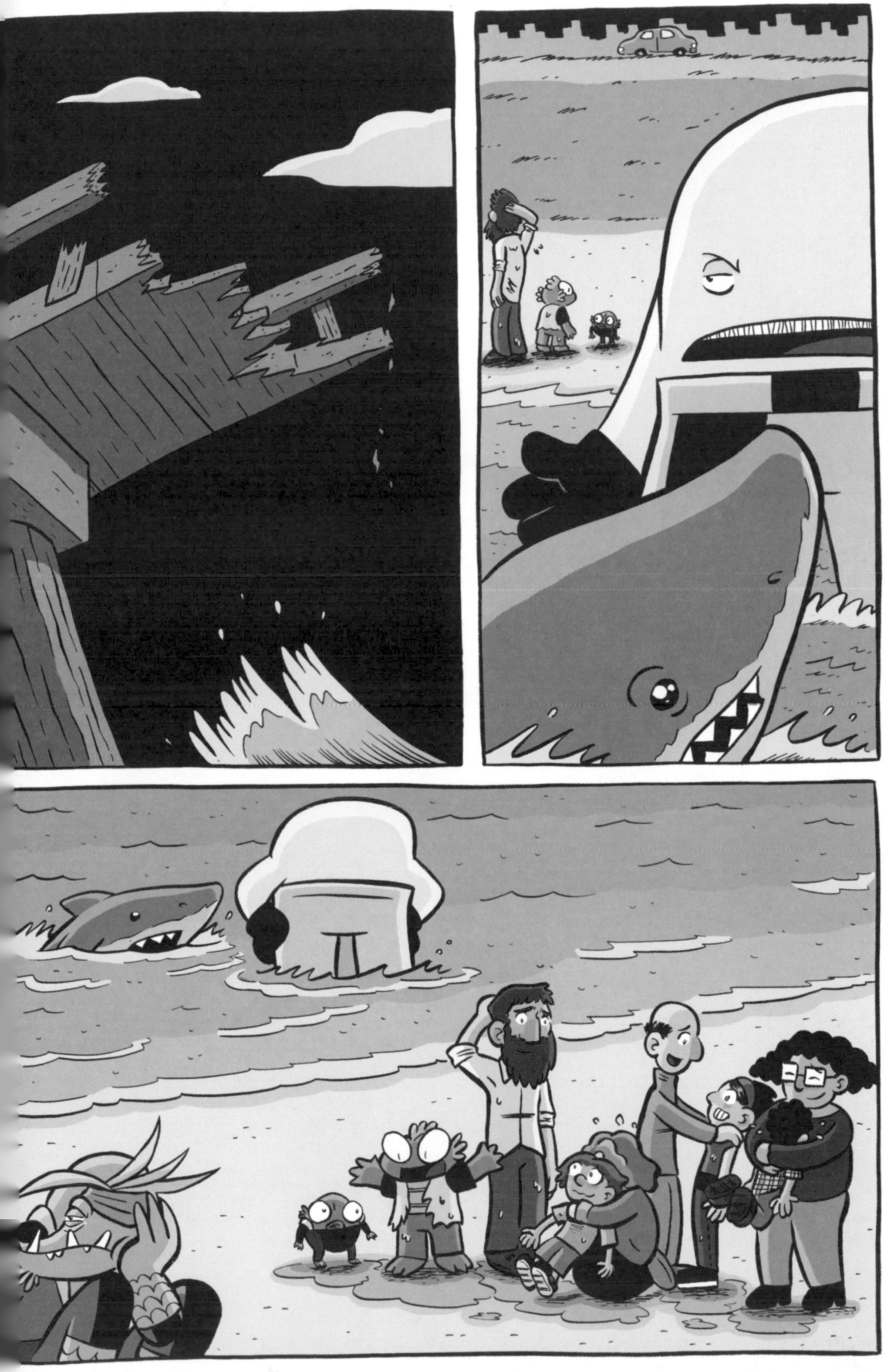

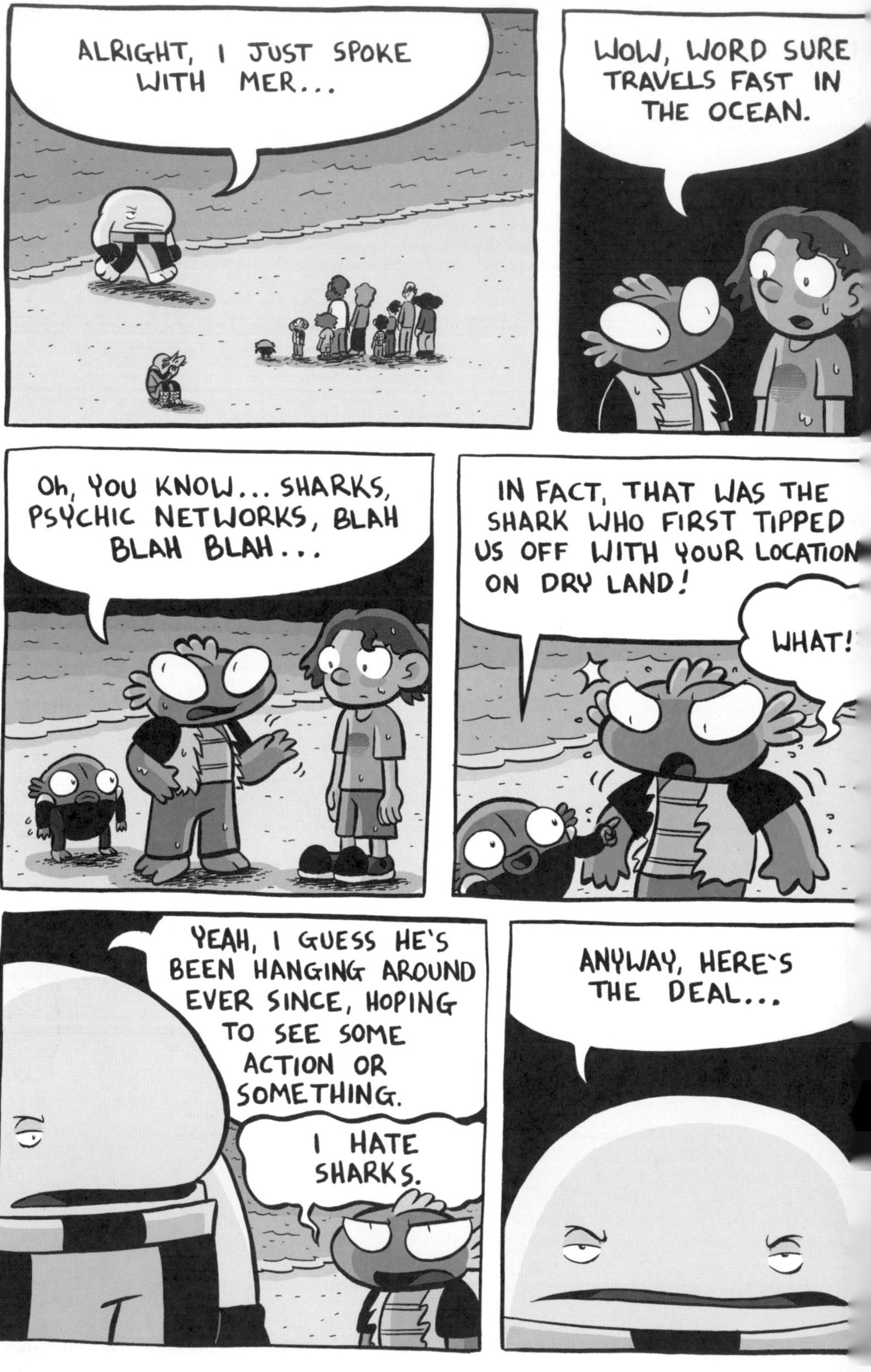
ALRIGHT, I JUST SPOKE WITH MER...
WOW, WORD SURE TRAVELS FAST IN THE OCEAN.
Oh, YOU KNOW... SHARKS, PSYCHIC NETWORKS, BLAH BLAH BLAH...
IN FACT, THAT WAS THE SHARK WHO FIRST TIPPED US OFF WITH YOUR LOCATION ON DRY LAND!
WHAT!
YEAH, I GUESS HE'S BEEN HANGING AROUND EVER SINCE, HOPING TO SEE SOME ACTION OR SOMETHING.
I HATE SHARKS.
ANYWAY, HERE'S THE DEAL...

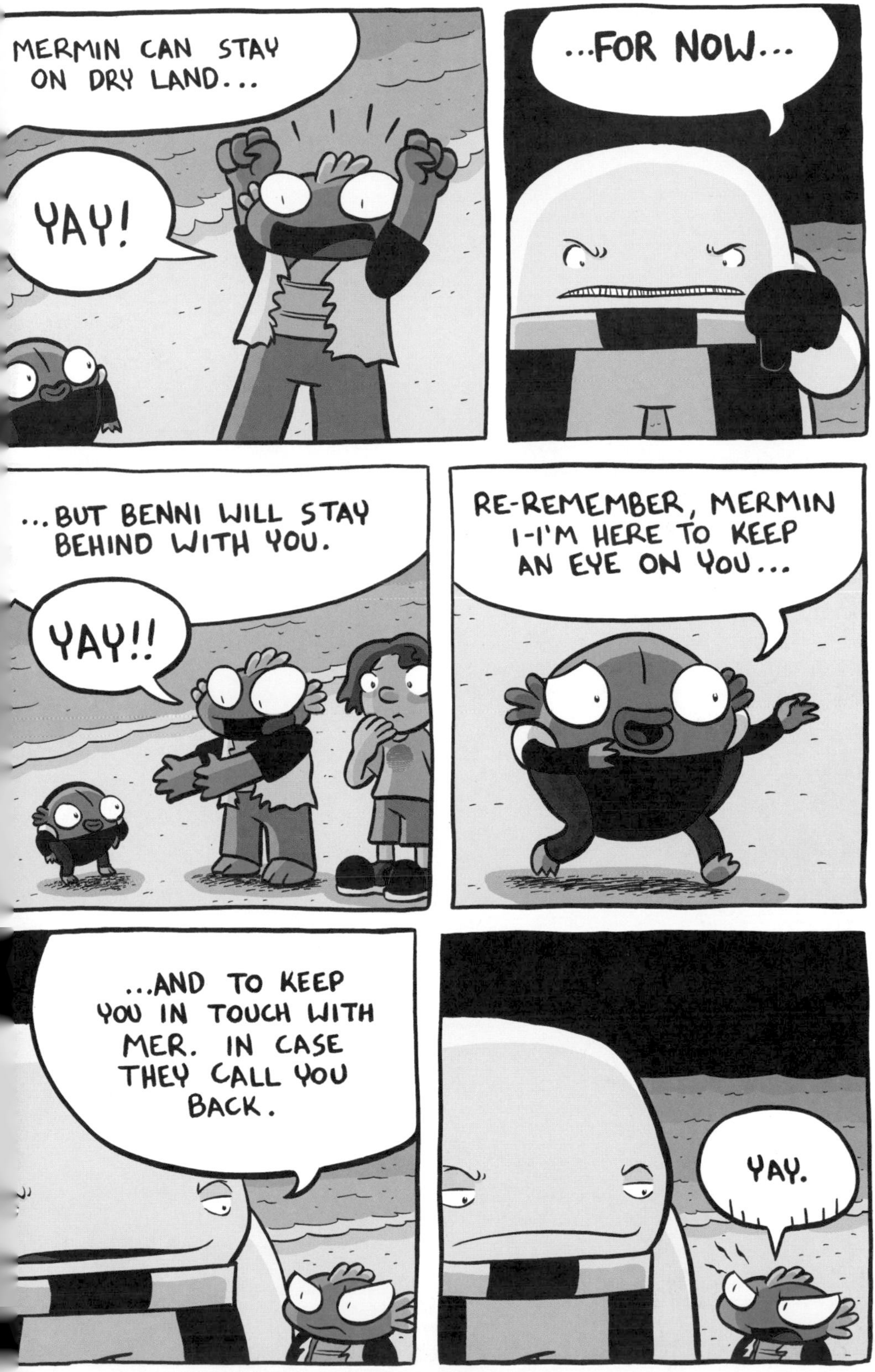
MERMIN CAN STAY ON DRY LAND...
YAY!
...FOR NOW...
...BUT BENNI WILL STAY BEHIND WITH YOU.
YAY!!
RE-REMEMBER, MERMIN I-I'M HERE TO KEEP AN EYE ON YOU...
...AND TO KEEP YOU IN TOUCH WITH MER. IN CASE THEY CALL YOU BACK.
YAY.

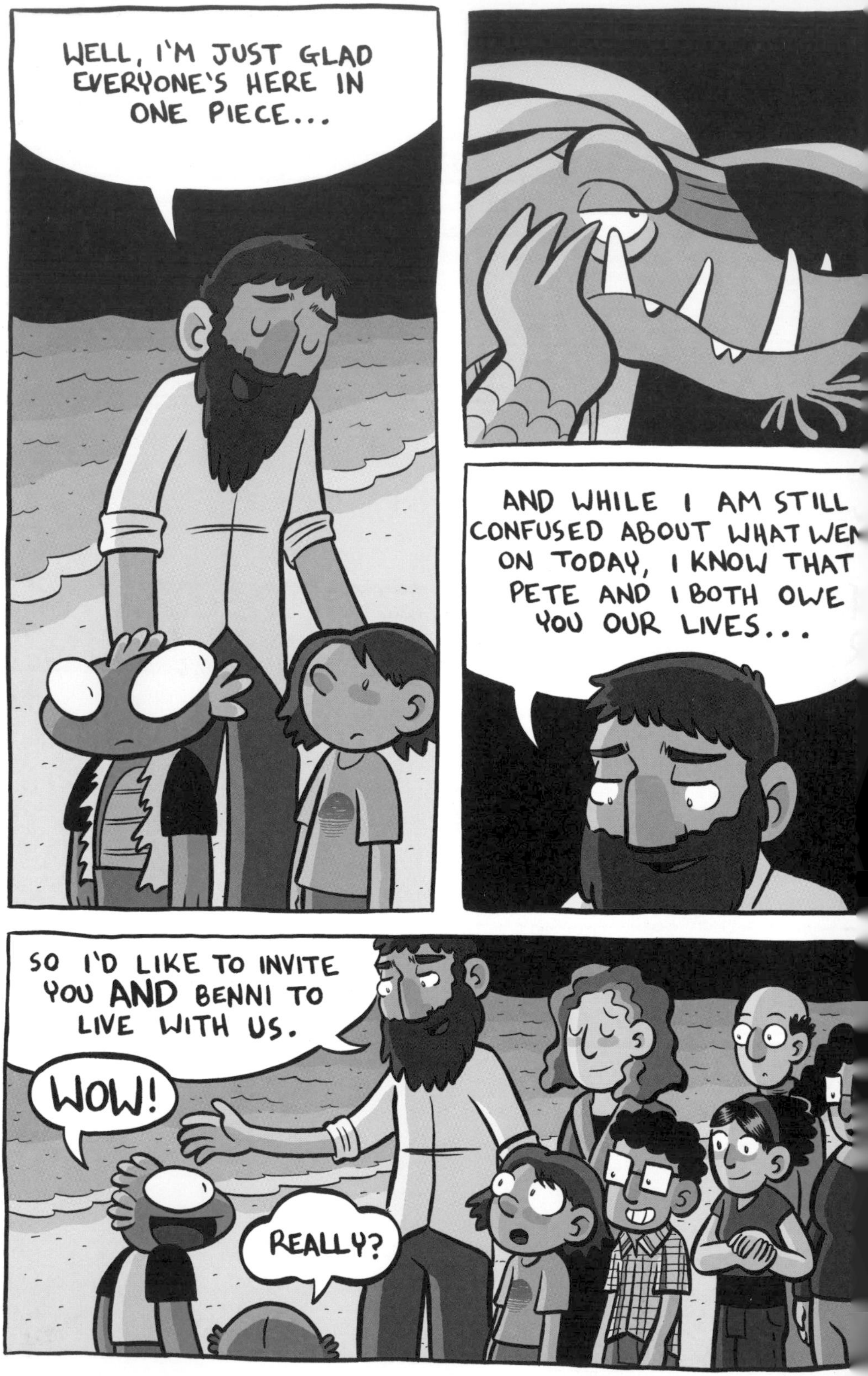
WELL, I'M JUST GLAD EVERYONE'S HERE IN ONE PIECE...
AND WHILE I AM STILL CONFUSED ABOUT WHAT WEN ON TODAY, I KNOW THAT PETE AND I BOTH OWE YOU OUR LIVES...
SO I'D LIKE TO INVITE YOU AND BENNI TO LIVE WITH US.
WOW!
REALLY?

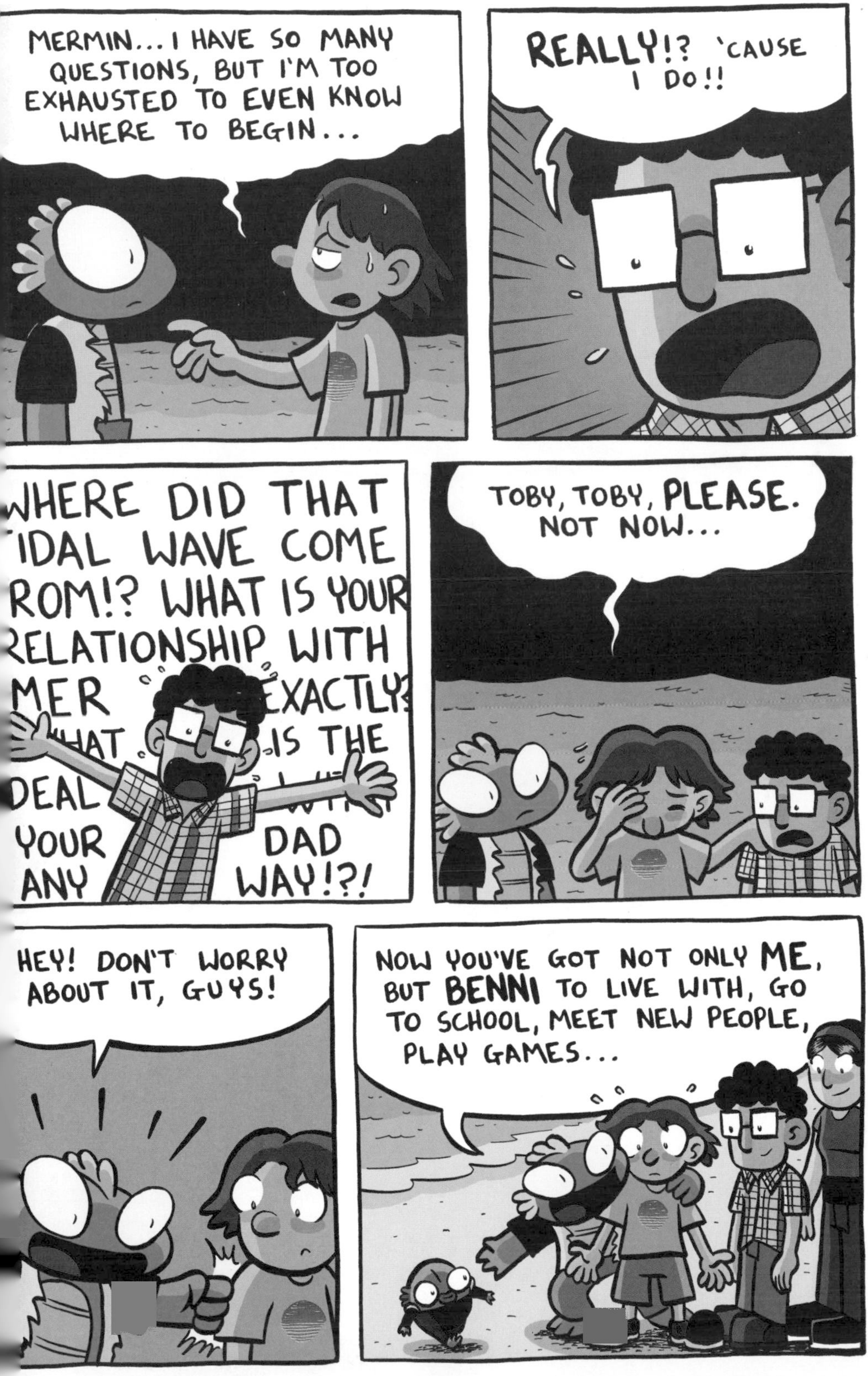
MERMIN... I HAVE SO MANY QUESTIONS, BUT I'M TOO EXHAUSTED TO EVEN KNOW WHERE TO BEGIN...
REALLY!? 'CAUSE I DO!!
WHERE DID THAT IDAL WAVE COME ROM!? WHAT IS YOUR RELATIONSHIP WITH MER EXACTLY? IS THE DEAL YOUR DAD ANY WAY!?!
TOBY, TOBY, PLEASE. NOT NOW...
HEY! DON'T WORRY ABOUT IT, GUYS!
NOW YOU'VE GOT NOT ONLY ME, BUT BENNI TO LIVE WITH, GO TO SCHOOL, MEET NEW PEOPLE, PLAY GAMES...

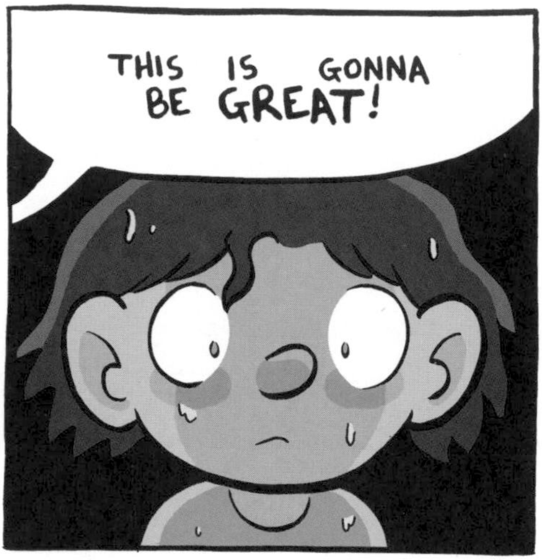
THIS IS GONNA BE GREAT!